About t

K.J. Backer was born in Corbett, OR in 1986. She grew up on a Christmas Tree farm enjoying the fragrant scents of Blue Spruce and Douglas Fir, surrounded by friendly animals, before moving to the Big Sky State in 1996. She credits her close family bonds, wild imagination, and love for books to her humble, country upbringing. She worked as a U.S. Capitol Intern in 2004, graduated from Montana State University- Billings with a degree in History Education in 2009, and taught History at a local high school for five years whilst "secretly" writing her first novel, Nav'Aria: The Marked Heir (published in 2019).

K.J. Backer has a huge love and appreciation for other cultures, adoption, travel, history, fantasy, and the written word. She lives in Billings, MT with her amazing husband, wonderful daughter, two adorable Pomeranians, and handsome new tortoise.

Nav'Aria: The Pyre of Tarsin is the second book of the Nav'Aria series. Follow Backer on social media and at kjbacker.com to learn more!

Cover design by SelfPubBookCovers.com/Terry Emilia
Maps by K.J. Backer (Inkarnate Pro)
Edited and Proofread by Heather Peers

K.J. Backer
Visit author website at **kjbacker.com**

Printed in the United States of America

First Edition: October 2019

ISBN-13: 978-1-7329206-3-7

NAV'ARIA⁺
THE PYRE OF
TARSIN

K.J. Backer

For Keil.

My forever love.

Nav'Alodon Mountains

Land of the Trolls

The Kingdom

Lure River

Castle Dintarran

Lake Thread

PROLOGUE

Many Cycles Ago

"You will never find me!"

Dew glistened upon the green blades of grass spilling forth across the lush meadow. The sun's rays warmed Tarsin's face as he smiled, listening to L'Asha's lilting voice intermittently calling to him as the breeze carried the sound to and fro teasingly.

They were playing their favorite childhood game: honky in the meadow. One had to hide and make all oddities of sounds. The other had to find the hidden partner while keeping one's eyes shut. The hidden partner continually roamed around, remaining out of sight yet confusing the partner with sounds that seemingly came from all directions. L'Asha had suggested it for their activity today, much to Tarsin's chagrin. He had anticipated a light stroll, followed by a romp in the grass, only to be overpowered by her strong will and forlorn expression. He hadn't had the heart to tell her no… he never could. So here he was, stumbling through the glade blindfolded, feeling rather dismayed about the overall experience. He only hoped he could catch her soon so he could kiss her and run his hands over her beautiful form.

Suddenly, the breeze carried a shriek of pure terror, instead of the sweet laughs from only moments ago. Tarsin's eyelids popped open, and he ripped the cloth from his eyes while running toward the source of the noise. All at once, their childish game forgotten, as Tarsin tried to reach L'Asha. Her screams tore at his ears, growing in timbre. A sound so desperate that he knew she was in peril—and in extreme pain. And then there was quiet.

An eerie silence met Tarsin as he crested the hill and came upon a scene so abhorrent, he was momentarily stunned. He skidded to a stop mere inches from the terrifying, hulking beast, which was as black as the obsidian blade at Tarsin's belt. It looked toward him with large red eyes, seemingly irritated by the distraction keeping it from the meal at hand—L'Asha's corpse. It snorted in anger, smoke emitting from its nostrils, before possessively hovering ever nearer the corpse.

Tarsin noted that it had taken only a second for his beloved to become scorched from the beast's hideous fire. Her body, what was left of it, lay in blackened earth. Smoke rose from its quick scorch, all hair and clothing burned away, leaving her lifeless form to be torn apart and consumed. The creature's huge scaled wings clicked the ground in cadence to its chewing.... Too focused on the meal to recognize the eminent threat.

Tarsin gave no thought to his next action. Instinctively, he reached for the curved blade at his belt and leapt upon the beast, releasing a savage snarl brimming with molten ire. Blinded by fury, he stabbed the monster deep in its neck, avoiding its foreign armor. The beast reared on its hindlegs, wings spreading in alarm, desperately trying to claw at the knife in its neck. It spun around, lashing wildly, sending Tarsin tumbling to the ground. Rising in a fluid motion, having been trained for combat since his first tottering steps, Tarsin bellowed a war cry and ran at the beast who had taken everything from him. L'Asha had been his life. He felt no fear, only primal fury. The beast, still distracted by the knife in its throat, swung its clawed wing out to block him, but to no avail. Tarsin soared past its wing, fueled by adrenaline, plunging the blade directly into the soft exposed skin on its upper chest. Jerking his blade, narrowly missing the creature's frantic snapping jaws, he felt it sever tendon and muscle, and then tear into its throat as blood spurted forth. The creature's scream was cut off just as it collapsed thrashing. Bloodied flesh clung to the animal's sharp teeth while it let out one last panging cry.

Tarsin tumbled back, avoiding being crushed as the mysterious creature's breath gave out. Silence filled the meadow, as if even the birds were paying homage to the brave hero below. On all fours, he crawled toward his love, reaching out as he came upon L'Asha's skull. Sobbing, he carefully lifted her head, cradling it. *You cannot be gone*, he wept, shooting a baleful look at the giant form of the armored beast still lying where it had fallen amidst death throes. He had never seen a creature such as this, and he was going to make sure he never did again. *That no one did.*

Years of working the earth left him hardened and resolute in his task. Shame filling him, he wiped his tears with a quick brush of his sleeve. *I failed you.*

He grabbed the pack containing his necessaries. The pick lay wrapped in cloth at the bottom. As he pulled it out from the bag, he bit the inside of his left cheek. He welcomed the pain. The iron-filled taste of blood. The work. Idle hands and time would leave him in a puddle of grief. He would see this task carried out. Properly. Then, and only then, would he allow himself to mourn. Turning away from her, he began the chore of digging the grave.

The pick struck the ground, and he moved the fertile soil easily to create space for what was left of his beloved. He wrapped her in his spare cloak from the pack, saving her yellow hair ribbon for last. She had given it to him upon their betrothal. *Carry it for luck, wherever you go,* she had said. He remembered her adoring musical voice as she had gifted it, and the kiss and wink she had given him along with the token. Emotion catching in his throat, he fingered the ribbon for a moment, feeling its soft, silky fabric. Gently, he tied it around her wrapped skull, creating a loose bow. He remembered how the yellow ribbon had tamed her raven tresses. Cradling her small form, he rocked her in a final embrace. Unable to hold back his tears any longer, he watched the tear droplets dotting the fabric holding her remains. Placing her carefully in the soft earth, he spoke the words over her.

His precious L'Asha. Gone. *I will see you soon, my love*, he promised softly. And then he wept.

The air grew crisp, and the gentle breeze grew to a steady gust of wind. Tarsin sat up with a start, disoriented by his surroundings. His head throbbed, and he felt chilled to the bone. He began to call for L'Asha, and then it hit him. The sudden emergence of memory knotted his stomach so tightly he thought he might wretch. He looked to the loosened patch of soil. He had fallen asleep upon her grave. He touched his lips softly to the earth, knowing what he must do next. He shuddered with the thought. Her father Larsel would never forgive him.

Slowly he rose to his feet, looking around for something he could use as a grave marker. He knew, if left as is, the grave would eventually be lost to the fertile meadow, and the overgrowth would hide her resting place. She would have preferred that, this having been her favorite place, but he could not let himself lose her grave too. The thought caused his soul panic, and he frantically began looking for sticks or rocks to pile up. As he searched, his eyes fell upon the slain creature, whose hulking shadow seemed to swallow up any source of light. The deep onyx scales a blemish upon the beautiful landscape.

Curiosity sent Tarsin searching his pack for his flint. He ripped his spare tunic into shreds with his bloodied dagger, starting a flame with an expert hand, light spilling forth as it devoured the shredded cloth. Tarsin had a few candles in his pack and he quickly lit two from the small fire, knowing the fire would not last long without kindling.

He carefully strode toward the beast, berating himself for feeling afraid. *It is dead!* It had been killed by his own hand, but with only the slight candlelight, the foreign beast's outline loomed. *What was it? And where had it come from?* Tarsin had heard stories of flying monsters, but never had he seen one or met anyone that had either. He thought they were mere fables told to frighten children. He only now realized the peril he was in. *What if there were more? What if they came looking for their companion to find it dead?* He quickly held the candle up scanning his surroundings, though the pitiful flame only illuminated the small space nearest him. He needed to warn the village. L'Asha had to be properly mourned by her loved ones. Cursing himself and realizing that both of their families must be sick with worry, he began to pack up.

As he did so, an idea began to form. He didn't have much time and set about his grim task with renewed gusto. Once it was done, he didn't care about his well-being, but he vowed to L'Asha that he would see it completed. Then, he would return to her and meet her in the afterlife, Creator willing.

CHAPTER 1

The Desert

"Would you hurry up already?" Darion, walking alongside the mighty unicorn Triumph, yelled at Edmond and Soren, the unicorn who had volunteered to accompany him on his quest.

The pair had stopped to inspect yet another plant down the hillside. Their effort to find any edible vegetation was commendable, but Darion's temper flared. The longer they dallied, the longer their trek through this barren landscape would take. It had taken them weeks to reach this point, and they still had a long way to go.

Darion raked his fingers through his dark, thick, unwashed hair, which was growing increasingly greasy after days of travel. His tanned skin, darker from his time in the desert, was already slick with sweat, and they had only been on the move a short while. His arm tingled, and he looked to see his Mark spreading once more, making its way beyond his elbow. It had not spread much over the last weeks, so he was surprised to see new black symbols emerging. The sight, giving him a sense of foreboding, only added to his already bad mood.

Though he considered Edmond to be his only friend, the younger boy irked him with his never ceasing curiosity and delays. Suddenly, a loud grumbling reverberated in his mind.

"You know what I mean, only human friend… my age, that is," Darion seceded to Triumph aloud, who had been creeping into his mind. "And get out of my head!"

My, my, your company is a treat this morning, Triumph said, his voice laced with sarcasm. Their bond had done remarkably little to quell the occasional annoyance they felt with one another. Darion thought that this must be what it's like to have an older brother. Though he had no doubt Triumph would die to protect him, being loyal to a fault, he also knew that the unicorn—both older and wiser—was not easily intimidated by his bonded moody teenager.

With the hard pace they had maintained since leaving Kaulter, and now having little food or water after crossing the border into the Shazla Desert, the small party's comradery was rapidly deteriorating.

Edmond and Soren, seeming to catch on to their Prince's agitation, hurried up the hillside to rejoin their companions. *He's not even winded,* Darion thought hotly as he watched his friend's approach.

Edmond's physical fitness never failed to weaken Darion's pride. Edmond, who seemed to have grown even taller and stronger—despite their lack of food—looked every bit of a Nav'Arian warrior in training. Darion felt his irritation rise ever further. He too had grown stronger and felt more confident as a fighter, especially after having fought their first Rav'Arians a few nights ago. Darion had sliced one clean through with his sword, as had Edmond. Darion's muscles had strengthened from weeks of travel and sparring with his friend. Though, looking over Edmond, he thought, *Is he sneaking some type of steroids? How much bigger will he get?*

Edmond rivaled in size many of the famous athletes Darion remembered from his past life in Oregon. *You're being an ass,* he thought to himself. *Edmond is your friend, get it together.* Shaking his head to clear his petty thoughts, he tried to focus on what Edmond had in his hands.

"Look what we found," Edmond said excitedly, shoving a speckled leaf at Darion's face. Darion inspected the unique leaf, a ruddy color dotted with green and yellow. With his heightened senses he could tell there were more below the surface, now that he knew what to look for. It seemed they were atop an entire root system of the leafy plant, its leaves preferring the coolness under ground rather than the sun's scorching rays above.

"What is it?"

Before Triumph could answer, Soren put in quickly, "I think it is the fabled Ash Plant I have read about. It is said to have healing powers and provide extreme nourishment. It is very rare. I have never seen it, so I cannot be sure, but it fits the description." Soren looked to Triumph expectantly, noting belatedly the severe glint in Triumph's eyes.

"Am I correct?"

Triumph nodded begrudgingly yet said nothing in response. Darion got the distinct impression that Triumph was annoyed with the younger unicorn. Knowing that even the mighty Triumph could get caught up in petty jealousy lightened Darion's spirits considerably.

You're too old to act like that, Darion chided him telepathically. Their bond allowing for uninterrupted communication.

Ha! You're one to talk, Triumph snorted, beginning to take on Darion's casual vernacular. Darion's emerald eyes met the clear aquamarine gaze of Triumph, and they held each other's stare for a long moment before breaking off in laughter.

Edmond and Soren simply watched them. The pair had grown used to watching Darion and his bonded companion communicate silently. Soren glowered.

"Hey, you are not talking about us, are you?" And then followed with, "Am I correct? Are these Ash plants? What is so funny? Why are you still laughing?" Edmond tried calming the sensitive unicorn, stroking his mane. He muttered that he didn't know what the two were laughing about, either. Having Soren become agitated would only prolong this whole conversation, when all Edmond wanted to know was whether he could eat it or not. His stomach grumbled audibly.

Darion's laughter finally subsided, and he wiped tears from his eyes, unsure of when he had last laughed that hard. Then he sobered, picturing Carol's face. He used to laugh like that with her. *His mom.* And he knew he had not laughed like that since he had been forever parted from her. Since the villainous traitor Narco had commissioned an assassin to try and kill the royal family but had instead killed his adoptive mother, Carol, who had heroically sacrificed herself to save King Vikaris, Darion's birthfather.

This quest was in her honor. It was in her memory, and here Darion stood wavering between brooding teenager and hysterical, exhausted traveler. Neither would do. Carol deserved vengeance, and nothing less. He felt his resolve strengthen, and that of Triumph's, as well, as they both sobered from their momentary lapse in hilarity.

Darion met his friend's eyes, knowing the boy recognized the all too familiar look of loss. Edmond knew that look well, for he had lost his parents in an attack and could empathize with Darion's pain.

"You are correct, Soren, that is the Ash Plant… Well done," Triumph's low voice boomed, causing Soren to tremble slightly under the praise. Darion smiled at their exchange. Triumph, ever the instructor, did not dole out praise unless he truly meant it, and Darion knew from personal experience the giddiness one felt when Triumph was pleased with you.

He echoed Triumph, "Nice work." Edmond beamed.

They set to work digging up the root system. The plant was at its most powerful when boiled into a tea, according to the unicorns. Because they had no water, however, they all took a few leaves to eat in hopes of staving their hunger pains. They wrapped many more leaves, placing them in their packs for later consumption.

Atop the hill Darion could make out only rocky terrain, followed by sand as far as the eye could see. He knew without water—after draining their water skins the previous day—they would never make it out of this wretched place alive.

"Let's go," Darion ordered, feeling more comfortable in his authoritative role. This quest had been his idea, and he would not give in to desperation that easily. He was the leader. He needed to lead. Triumph's presence comforted him as they began to walk again, and the midday sun beat down. They would find whatever dark source Narco had claimed those many years ago, and they would use that knowledge to destroy him.

CHAPTER 2

The Burial

"Carol—No! Hold on! I am coming," Rick started, sitting up in bed.

He caught himself as he began to reach for Carol. He yearned for the comfort of her soft arms and familiar scent. But she wasn't there. She hadn't been there in days.

He avoided looking at the empty side of the bed he slept in. His "Springflower" gone. Torn from his side. *Could she really be gone forever?* he thought, the reality too hard to bear.

He lay down, the grief crushing him as if a stone had been placed upon his chest, pushing out every wisp of air. This was the second time he had dreamt of Carol standing at the Falls. The Falls from their other life—from Oregon—from which they had returned to Nav'Aria. In the dream, or rather nightmare, she was screaming for him, as a copious, twisted black fog swarmed around her, pulling her further away from him toward oblivion. Each time, his fingers almost reached hers—mere inches away. He was so close, yet he could not quite touch her. This alone broke him.

Rick rolled over onto his side, clutching the other pillow from *her* side of the bed. He would always think of it that way, *Carol's side.* He longed to hold her, to kiss her, to stroke her auburn hair, and to see her cheerful face as she smiled at him. It had been weeks, and still he could barely breathe with the soul-wrenching weight of loss that threatened to pull him asunder.

To make matters worse, Darion had left. Fled in the night. Rick was torn between complete and utter terror, picturing his son out on his own in this unforgiving land, while also feeling unrelenting anger toward him for his abandonment. *How could he just leave? How could he leave me?*

Rick had always maintained an air of strength, and he now realized that it was a charade. His strength had been Carol, and without her, he was nothing. He needed Darion. He needed his support, and most importantly, he needed Darion so he could be reminded of Carol. Her goodness was in him.

Where could he have gone? How could Triumph have been so reckless with the Prince?

Rick pictured Darion's face at the burial. He couldn't honestly remember if he had seen him afterwards—it all blurred together. Darion had stood stone-still. This Rick remembered. Otherwise, Rick's memories of the burial were all fragmented and foggy. Clutching Carol's lifeless hand; the haunting centaur song of mourning; the smell from the lilac bouquet Lyrianna placed on the freshly covered grave; and the terrifying, vindictive fire that raged in Darion's smoldering gaze. It wasn't grief shining in those eyes... but hate. It had scared Rick, and he shuddered at the memory. Darion had left shortly after the burial. He and Triumph had snuck to the portal in the night, leaving no identifiable tracks once emerging. Darion could be anywhere. The only clue to their departure came from a hastily written note:

> *I won't allow Narco to hurt anyone else*
> *that I love. Triumph and I are going to find*
> *the way to defeat him. We'll find the answers.*
> *Don't come after us. We don't want anyone*
> *else to be hurt or... killed like Mom.*
> *I love you Dad.*
> *~D*
> *P.S. Tell ~~the King~~ ~~my parents~~ my birth*
> *parents that I'm sorry.*
> *And Triumph says to tell Elsra that he*
> *must do this, and not to interfere.*

"Where are you, Son?" Rick whispered, clutching the pillow even tighter.

***

"I know they said not to come after them, but you do not truly expect me to sit here while my son gets himself killed, do you?" Vikaris slammed his fist down on the table with emphasis. Lyrianna gasped at the mention of "kill," and Elsra *tsked* at his outburst.

Vikaris squeezed his eyes shut in frustration, trying—and failing—to calm down. *What are you thinking, Darion?*

Vikaris was furious with the boy—*his son.* The loss of Carolina had been a shock. Riccus appeared a ghost of a man, enduring his grief as a widower alone. Lyrianna, completely guilt-ridden and confused regarding Darion, thought her presence had driven him away. *Was it my fault that he had run? Did he blame me for Carol's death?* she had asked Vikaris imploringly. Vikaris hated seeing his wife and his friend suffering this way. It wasn't right. Sneaking away in the night. *The skulking coward!*

Vikaris didn't know what to feel when he tried to reason it out—abandonment, rejection, guilt, fury, anger, pride, fear—it all melded together causing his blood to boil. He felt jumpy. He needed to act. His son was out there somewhere. The hope of the land—*his heir*—was out there exposed to Narco's agents and all forms of danger, leaving Vikaris to wait like some helpless parent.

Damn you, Darion… and Triumph, he thought fuming, running his palms over his heated face. The stubble on his cheeks scratching against his callused hands. Lyrianna gently took hold of one of his hands and interlaced her ice-cold fingers with his. A shock to the system in contrast to his fiery rage. Exhaling, he opened his eyes to meet his wife's. Her blue eyes pooled with tears as she smiled at him. "He will be alright, my husband. He is our son—Rick's son—he will be alright. We must not react rashly," she spoke softly, but with the quiet strength he so loved about her.

Nodding, emotion catching in his throat as he looked upon her still recovering form, he touched his lips to her hand. Lyrianna, though still thin and scarred, dazzled like a gem amongst river rocks. Other women paled in comparison to his bride—though he sometimes found her looking far off, as if in a daze. When he inquired, she would look at him with the most haunting expression imaginable, before coming out of it. *That bastard abused more than her body. That*, he thought, *could heal with time. But what of the mind?* He longed to be able to take those thoughts from her—to carry them for her. To rid her of Narco's taint.

Vikaris' fury returned. *Darion should be here. He could have helped with Lyrianna's recovery.*

Trixon grumbled in his mind. *Yes, he should be here, but do not try to place more upon his shoulders than he can bear. He is not responsible for her recovery, though his presence probably would help. Lyrianna needs time. She must work through this pain—and overcome it. Darion cannot heal her, Vikaris, and you know it.*

Vikaris looked surprised at his friend who spoke with such vehemence—albeit, telepathically. At a loss for words, he could only nod, feeling chastised for the first time in a long time.

Where did that come from?

Belatedly he realized that with Lyrianna's return, the loss of Carol, and Darion's departure, he had not really spoken with Trixon to see how *he* felt about the matter. Vikaris had made his feelings known, but had Trixon? It was his uncle, Triumph, whom accompanied Darion, after all.

He gave his friend a bemused glance before blinking quickly to look at Elsra and then back to Trixon beside her. The truth hitting him.

"You two do not think they are in the wrong? Do you? What changed? You yourself, Elsra, had ordered search parties in all directions from the portal. Why did you call them off? What has CHANGED?" He could not keep the anger from his rising voice. Elsra snorted, and a low growl rumbled near her from Drigidor's throat.

"Calm yourself," Lyrianna murmured but did not avert her eyes from the unicorns.

"I would tell you if you would allow me to, Your Majesty," Elsra clipped with a biting tone. Vikaris felt his cheeks grow warm. He knew he had overstepped.

"Forgive me, Elsra," Vikaris said hastily, knowing that he did not need to add an offended unicorn to his mental stresses. She held his gaze for one long breath before finally nodding. There was a collective exhale in the room, and Vikaris felt Trixon's tension ease.

Vikaris watched Elsra's gaze move toward the closed door, which she had suggested for their meeting, wanting extreme privacy and security in the wake of the attacks. Antonis and Aalil, along with Cela the centaur, stood guarding the door. Antonis drew open the thick hickory door at Elsra's glance and admitted one more into the gathering. Vikaris felt a lump form in his throat at the image. In limped Trinidad. While Lyrianna's recovery was seemingly fast, Trinidad's seemed stinted. He appeared thin, deflated like an empty waterskin. The hairs along his neck had begun to grow, but his coat paled in comparison to the other majestic unicorns in the room. Without his horn, even his coat seemed to lack luster. He might easily be mistaken for a horse. Almost. Until one looked in his eyes. Their incandescent fire burned with a renewed vitality upon having reached freedom and returning to the Isle of Kaulter with the Queen.

"Welcome, Trinidad. Please join us," Elsra ushered for Trixon to make way for him. Trinidad walked up to Lyrianna and nuzzled her face. She laughed softly, caressing his cheek before he went to his mother's side.

Those two share an intimacy that I know nothing about, Vikaris realized as he watched Lyrianna's eyes sparkling with love for Trinidad.

Much like you and I, Trixon reminded. Vikaris looked to his knowing friend.

"As you know," Elsra began, drawing Vikaris's attention. "Trinidad has been spending much time in the library of late," adding quietly, "to see if he can find a remedy for his…," the words escaped her, and tears threatened to spill forth.

Trinidad continued for his mother. All present knew how she still mourned Xenia and had not much improved upon seeing Trinidad's frailty. They were all on edge.

Trinidad's voice filled the room, showing none of the weakness his frame suggested. "Yes, as you know, I plan to find the way to regrow my horn." His expression grew fiercely determined as he looked at them all in turn, challenging anyone to tell him the improbability of it. None did.

"A noble cause, my friend," Vikaris said kindly. "Please let me know if there is anything you may need in this endeavor." Trinidad held his gaze for a moment but moved to Lyrianna's. Vikaris thought he detected a small nod from her, as if encouraging him to continue.

Preposterous! Why would the Mighty Trinidad look to Lyrianna to go on? A unicorn of the Council did not need anyone except Elsra's approval to speak at Kaulter. He, Vikaris, was the rightful monarch of Nav'Aria. Elsra was the Regent of Kaulter, though she graciously allowed Vikaris the same rights here as a co-ruler. *So why Lyrianna? It is as if they are bonded. But that is impossible.* He looked askance at his wife, who bore an undistinguishable mask of calmness as she watched the proceedings. Her public demeanor was far more stolid than Vikaris's and Darion's.

Mmmhmmm, Trixon murmured into his mind, again bringing Vikaris out of his musings. *If I did not know you better, I would think you were jealous,* Trixon said chidingly.

The back of Vikaris' neck grew hot, and he glared at his companion. *I am not jealous... of my wife! I just want to know what is going on,* Vikaris shot back.

Trixon countered with, *Then pay attention. MY FATHER is explaining it all now.*

"... there is one ancient tome that made reference to the loss of a horn, and though we are all encouraged to memorize the texts, I must admit that none of the unicorns I have spoken with—nor myself—remember where the explanation can be found. And so, I search. I have two clerks helping me with the task," Trinidad looked around the room as his mother tapped her hoof, as if remembering the point of his presence. "Ah, but you do not wish to hear more about my follies," he cleared his throat, before going on, "While my clerk and I were in the study recently, we discovered something that I think you will also find interesting." Trinidad nodded to Antonis at the door again, and Vikaris watched as a thin, dark-skinned adolescent entered the room. He held in one hand a small, leather-bound book.

"This is Bal'khoa, my clerk," Trinidad introduced. The youth bowed low to the assembly. "Bal'khoa, please show the King what it is you found." At close inspection, the boy's forehead was spotted with perspiration, though his motions were fluid and showed no hint of nervousness.

Well, not that nervous, Vikaris thought, looking the boy over as he approached. *After Alice, one could never be too careful,* he thought grimly. Alice was Morta's illegitimate daughter, who had not only killed Xenia the unicorn but also Carolina. The thought of her made Vikaris scowl, and the boy hesitated his approach at his King's intensity.

Vikaris, as if realizing the boy's trepidation, nodded to him with a smile. "What do you have there, young man?"

"Vondulus' study journal, Your Majesty," Bal'khoa disclosed as he placed the small book in his King's outstretched hand. Vikaris' eyebrows rose.

"The journal of our first King, truly," he mused, turning it over in his palms before opening it. Expecting the boy to return to the door, Vikaris glanced at him again. He clearly looked as if there were something else. "Well," Vikaris prodded, "Why did you bring this to me?"

Bal'khoa dipped his head and bent to the book, opening it to the very last entry page while still in Vikaris' hands. He then gave a quick bow and stepped back toward the wall. Vikaris looked at the unicorns, each nodding their heads, before his eyes returned to the page. He scanned a jumbled page with frenetic writings cramped in every margin. Many of them explaining the day's grain counts, the weather, the health of his child, and the...

"Winged Ones?" he breathed out, hastily pointing to the text while Lyrianna peered over him to look. He read the annotation.

And though none have sighted the winged creature, tales of old remain. Tales from the first cycle read as follows:
Once the world was whole, and winged and horned creatures roamed together. Though unicorns were made firstly by the Creator, He saw fit to create companions. The Winged Ones lived for some time in harmony with the Horned Ones. As time wore on, the Winged Ones took to the skies and found new lands farther from the Horned Ones. The two councils amicably agreed that the space was necessary for hunting, thus better for both species. The two parties had never fully accepted the other, and the distance helped. It

is rumored that there was an incident between
the Winged and Horned creatures long ago.
A young winged creature attacked the
spawn of the horns and thus began the
unofficial break. The two kept to their areas,
vowing to never speak of each other again,
honoring their boundaries and common
Creation… This then, is the only mention of
them. I, hereby, seal this content with my
stamp so that none other than I, the Unicorn
Elders, and the Creator, will know of their
existence.

Vikaris met Elsra's gaze. She appeared just as shaken as he. "What does this mean? Are these something besides the Rav'Arians, then?" He felt goosebumps rising along his body, and his arm tingled oddly. Swiftly he pushed his sleeve back to reveal a now-glowing Mark. Lyrianna gasped quietly and leaned in more closely to him. Now holding her protectively in is glowing arm, he thought of how hard this must be for Lyrianna.

"We, as a Council, have deliberated on it all evening and into today, and believe—" Trinidad hesitated, looking to Elsra to confirm whether he should be the one to share. She nodded for him to continue. "We believe that *this*—this fable—is what Narco discovered past the Shazla Desert all those years ago, and somehow used it to his advantage."

Vikaris sat back in disbelief. *The source of his power.* *Winged Ones.* The thoughts collided in his head as he tried to make sense of the incoming information. "How does Darion fit into this?" His question turned to horror as Vikaris understood the implications of this revelation, and gazed into the wise, cavernous blue eyes of Trinidad's.

"How did they find this?" the King blurted out. "That is where they are headed then. Our son could be beyond the Shazla Desert by now. That is what you are telling me—telling us," he indicated to Lyrianna, squeezing her closer. Tears fell from her eyes. Trinidad bobbed his head in response. "Bal'khoa found the journal turned to this page under a stack of maps and Kingdom scrolls."

Before Vikaris could respond, Trinidad added, "I know you are upset, Vikaris. And I mean no disrespect by this, but my brother Triumph is not a rash unicorn—not like my son here," Trinidad chided, directing his gaze toward Trixon.

Trixon harrumphed in response, but no one disputed it. Vikaris knew he was right. They all did. This was very out of character for Triumph—and Soren, the other unicorn who had turned up missing.

"What, then, do you make of it? Do you believe that they are in the right?"

Elsra responded, her voice commanding once again, "I will not say whether they are right or wrong, but rather, they are on the *right* path for discovery. As Trinidad said, 'This is not the typical behavior of my son', there must be more that they found to make them think they can achieve success on this quest. Though we did not send them, they have appointed themselves to find the answers to Narco's enigmatic power. *That*, I can support. Triumph is an excellent companion for Darion. He will protect him with his life—I know that," she stated, a maternal tone creeping into her voice. Her radiant lavender eyes shone with passion as she spoke. "My son *will* protect your son, Vikaris. That I can promise you. Whether they both return to us, we must pray to the Creator. And in the meantime, we must plot Narco's demise—with or without the answers from beyond the border," Elsra said, looking pointedly at Bal'khoa, who hurriedly bowed and rushed from the room.

"And… there is more."

More, Vikaris wondered, feeling overwhelmed.

"Yes, much more to share. It seems this is a week of revelations. Please continue, Trinidad," Elsra directed.

Just as the unicorn began to speak, the alarm bells sounded.

Lyrianna had been barely listening to the group after learning of the winged ones. In a rare moment of vulnerability, her shoulders shook, and she cried, thinking of her son. *Darion, where have you found yourself?*

Suddenly, the quiet, contemplative room erupted into shouts as the unicorns and humans—and one fiery centaur at the door—lunged toward the exit to see what was happening. Lyrianna watched Antonis forcefully shove Cela back. With a strong arm and a stony expression, he made way to protect the door from the other side while the unicorns piled out, followed by their

King. Vikaris looked back to see Lyrianna behind him; she waved for him to go on ahead, nodding toward her two female guards.

Cela, Aalil, and Lyrianna filed out last, all the while Cela grumbled about men. Lyrianna and Aalil—at a different time—would have typically laughed at her grumblings, but not now. Not when the chiming of those bells raised every hair on Lyrianna's body.

As the party emerged past Elsra's audience chamber toward the hallway, Lyrianna could hear guards yelling and running, and a clash of steel. *What is happening out there?*

She heard Antonis' booming voice call out, "Soldier! Report!" His voice thundered in the wooden hallway with its rich acoustics.

"We are under attack," a panicked voice squawked, before a loud scream took place of the voice.

"Barricade this room. PROTECT THE QUEEN," she heard her husband command, before the ever-familiar scrape of steel echoed in her ears. He had drawn his sword and rushed into the fight.

"No, wait," she tried to stop him, but the door slammed, and its bolt was tightly fastened by Cela. Expecting a threat, the centaur's fierce gaze swept the room, every nook and cranny.

Aalil gave Lyrianna a half-hearted smile, trying to mollify her. *If only it were that simple*, Lyrianna thought. She sat on the edge of a divan sofa and pulled from her bodice a knife, and another from her garter. Aalil gawked at the blades. "Protect the Queen," Lyrianna balked. There could be no mistaking her. She did not mean for others to fight in her stead. She would protect herself.

Aalil nodded subtly and then began drawing her own blades.

The three females nodded to one another, and Lyrianna knew that any attackers would rue the day they entered *this* chamber.

CHAPTER 3

The Serpent

The heat seemed to have lessened the barest slip of a degree. Darion reflected that it was much like a frying pan being taken off the stove: the move may signify cooling, but it's gradual in its effect. He rubbed the tiny scar on his left thumb, where he had accidentally grabbed a pan without an oven mitt as a ten-year-old boy. He smiled sadly, remembering Carol's stern reprimand but loving touch as she had eased the pain with one of her many ointments and a reassuring hug.

Nearby, Triumph yawned and snorted loudly, standing up unceremoniously, shaking the sand and dirt from his sheer white coat. "Come along, humans," he instructed. Darion could hear the catch of amusement in his tone. They had made camp during the blazing midday heat, and it was time to continue their desert trek.

Darion rolled onto his back, nearly blinded by the sun's rays, "Aaahhh," he griped drowsily, flinging his arm over his eyes to rid the sting. Speaking with his arm still over his eyes, he asked, "Why the hurry? I thought Soren said we should rest now while he studied the terrain."

Triumph seemed to roll his eyes at him. Darion, who had partially lowered his arm, laughed. *Did you just roll your eyes at me?*

Triumph pawed the ground in front of him, snorting and shaking his mane. *I most certainly did not,* the unicorn retorted haughtily. A stone colliding with his hoof ricocheted against Darion's pack.

"But— Darion started, cut off by the unicorn's powerful voice.

"Soren did 'say we should rest', though I reminded him that you are the Marked Heir and I am your bonded steed, so therefore we do not take orders from the likes of him…".

"Oh boy," Edmond mumbled, sitting up near Darion, grinning.

It turned out Triumph had a bit of a jealous streak; they had *all* come to learn that the hard way. *Poor Soren,* Darion mouthed at his friend. Edmond snickered but kept his head down, for at just that moment, Trumph's luminescent horn appeared before Darion's eyes. Darion sneezed as the dust billowed in his face.

"Did you say something? I seemed to have missed that last part," though Triumph's tone made it clear that this was not the case.

Darion grabbed hold of the horn and hoisted himself up, patting Triumph on the cheek, not feeling the slightest intimidation.

"Whoa, boy," Darion laughed, as he fondly touched his companion's face. "I'm sure Soren knew he overstepped. Thank you for handling that," Darion looked around Triumph's head and winked at Edmond before continuing, "But why, then, are we up? Did you find something? And where *is* Soren?" Darion asked, looking around puzzled. Arid clay and sand appeared in every direction as far as Darion could see.

Triumph waited a beat before replying, exhaling loudly though appearing mollified, he responded, "He's… out."

Darion scowled at him. "Out? What is that supposed to mean, Triumph?"

Triumph nudged him slightly with his powerful neck, walking away from their sleep rolls. "He's still out. He has found something. He wishes for us to join him immediately," at that, his voice grew hard once again. "Though I reminded him—

Darion waved his hand. "Yeah, yeah, we get it. You don't want him giving orders. Honestly Triumph, you're more jealous than a middle school girl!" Triumph glared at him but didn't say anything.

Darion smiled to himself, as he hastily threw his sleep roll and cloak into his pack. He peeked at Edmond and chuckled, knowing that he had stumped them both. Though they had begun to speak less formally around him—his Oregon ways rubbing off on them, he supposed—he knew that his upbringing was something too foreign for them to imagine. He grinned, thinking of Edmond, his behemoth of a friend, at a middle school dance back home. If his behavior toward Alice was any indication—blushing at every other word from her mouth—then the shy boy would have been eaten alive by the girls in Gresham, Oregon.

Alice, he recoiled, as if suddenly remembering the vile wretch. He didn't want to think about her right now. He stood up stiffly and shouldered his pack, all traces of humor gone.

"Alright, let's go," Darion ordered with a sharp tone of voice, his hooded expression sobering Edmond's and Triumph's convivial exchanges. They both nodded, following his lead. They needed water, and Darion let his rage fester thinking on that and their mission rather than all he had lost.

The landscape hadn't changed much in the last few days. The sweeping mounds of golden sand stretched out in all directions in Darion's line of sight. Becoming more visible, however, were tiny, sporadic stretches of solid ground—a sort of red clay soil—dotted with shrubs, and the occasional tree and water source. They had lingered near one of those areas for two days after discovering the Ash Plant. They had mixed the nutritious leaves in the water and filled their bellies for the first time since entering the Shazla Desert. Though tempting as it was to stay close to the water source, Darion knew that settling there would not help them win the war. They had to press on, and so they did.

They had run out of the leaves the night before, and now Darion's stomach rumbled. It was echoed even louder by Edmond's. He gave Darion a sheepish smile but said nothing. His skin having become darkened from days in the sun, and a slight stubble growing on his chin left him with an even more masculine appearance than before. Darion just smiled. He had come to realize there was no point in being jealous of his giant friend. He had cut down a Rav'Arian during their attack days ago. Edmond was a Nav'Arian warrior now, and he looked every inch the part.

Triumph marched at the front, cautioning Darion and Edmond to watch their footing on the loose sand—as he had done on every downslope since they entered this forsaken land.

"We know, Triumph," Darion finally snapped, his annoyance growing with every instruction from his companion. "We're not idiots. We can see the *same* as you—damnit." The hidden perils below the sand slowed his pace and worsened his mood. Tripping on a stone, his cheeks flushed further. The continual exposure to the sun had left both he and Edmond scorched. Darion had more of a natural inclination to tanning, while Edmond's face reddened like a ripe tomato.

At Darion's rant, Edmond had slowed his pace just a hair, most likely in case Triumph charged at him angrily. Triumph ignored Darion, acting nonplussed, though his rigid stance and nose in the air bespoke his annoyance. Darion glanced back at Edmond. The boy was adjusting himself, and Darion averted his eyes to give him some privacy. He had been scratching his crotch not so subtly ever since they left camp.

Darion turned back to him again. Edmond had stopped walking, pulling at the fabric and scratching himself like a dog with fleas, seemingly forgetting the other two's presence.

"Dude," Darion called. "What are you doing?" The blood still pounding in his ears from his earlier outburst.

Edmond didn't seem to hear Darion. He was really scratching now, his face growing even redder with the exertion. Darion started walking back toward him, and Triumph rushed to join them. Darion and Triumph stood there for a moment watching Edmond in his frenzy, before bursting into fits of laughter. Darion placed his hand on Triumph to steady him. With the hunger, the heat, and now the wave of laughter, his body felt weak. Even Triumph's booming laugh filled the space. The boy was *seriously* scratching now.

"It's not funny!" Edmond said, his voice breaking with panic. "Something is wrong." At this, Darion's laughter ceased.

Edmond threw off his belt, pulling his pants down in one fluid motion to inspect the issue. What he found shocked them all into quiet for two heartbeats before Edmond began yelling and hopping around, terror filling his voice.

"Do not move," Triumph cautioned. "Remain still, Edmond. That is a Shazla Viper."

Instead of a little chafing, as Darion had first assumed, he saw a thin brown and yellow snake wrapped around Edmond's thigh and….

"Don't move," Darion echoed, trying to keep an eye on the snake while looking to Triumph for help. *What do we do?*

The snake encircled Edmond's genitals. His eyes bulged with the strain of not screaming or crying; his chest heaved.

That snake has enough venom to kill an ox. The scales are lined with tiny hairs that trace a trail of poison along the victim, causing a burning, itching sensation—I should have realized it! Triumph looked abashed. *It throws the victim into such a frenzy that they often collapse and do not notice the snake until it is too late. Then, once it has bitten its prey, it causes immediate death or, at the least, paralysis, before it burrows in them to feast,* Triumph shared telepathically.

Darion felt sick. "Holy shit," he breathed aloud. Triumph shot him a fierce scowl, shushing him.

"Hey guys. I know it is bad. Quit talking about it and help me here," Edmond pleaded in a voice thick with fear. Sweat trickled down his reddened face. He was slightly trembling but doing his best to remain still, just as Triumph had commanded.

For the moment the snake seemed intent on tracing itself around his leg, crotch, and over to the other leg; it was not poised to strike yet, as far as Darion could tell. Edmond's eyes filled with unshed tears. *The pain must be excruciating.* It was a credit to his character that he had not fallen over screaming.

Darion felt himself drawing into the moment. He released the breath he had been holding and allowed his senses to heighten as they had since his discovery of his spreading mark back in Oregon. He focused on the snake—he noted that it smelled fear. The venom sac in the back of its throat filling before its strike. Its fangs spread wide, and it prepared to pounce. Darion could sense its overwhelming desire for blood. To make a meal out of his friend. To burrow and feast and gorge on the warm, running blood of its prey.

"Not today, you little bastard," Darion whispered as he focused on the snake. His emerald green eyes bore into it with raging fury at the thought of losing one more person dear to him.

As if sensing a new threat, the snake ceased tracing the thigh, its head lifting to face Darion. Its eyes stared at him levelly. Darion held the stare.

No one breathed.

Darion's arm began to tingle and glow, and he shook his head once at the snake. It hissed threateningly while Darion stepped closer. The snake partially uncoiled its hold on the leg to lunge toward Darion.

Without hesitation, Darion took another step, his eyes never leaving the snake's yellow orbs. His ruby glowed, casting the snake in a pale red light. The snake whipped its head back and forth, trying to escape the glow coming ever closer. Hissing, it uncoiled further, sliding down Edmond's leg. Edmond moaned in apparent agony, slightly swaying on his feet. Darion didn't spare him a glance; all his focus was on the snake. It trailed down Edmond's bare leg and piled-up trousers as its scales slid onto the sand between the boys.

Darion then whispered one word. *Flee*.

The snake, though writhing in anger at having been denied the gorge, hissed with finality—and obeisance— before its brown dappled scales disappeared into the sand and rocks, leaving the party behind.

Darion exhaled, unsure of what he had done exactly. Somehow his senses—and Mark—had allowed him to impart a message. *Leave. This one is mine. Flee.*

Before Darion could revel in the exchange further, Edmond collapsed to the sand, shuddering.

"Edmond," Darion called, kneeling by his friend's fallen form. "Edmond, it's alright. You're going to be okay," though as he said it, he unconsciously grimaced at the red tendrils of rash that traced around his friend's legs and groin. Edmond's face beaded with sweat, his eyes closed.

It took moments to revive him, but thanks to Triumph and his telepathic abilities, he was able to speak directly into Edmond's mind, calming him and reminding his body to do its job—to heal. *Edmond, you have done well,* Triumph soothed, touching his horn to the tendrils.

After a few hours, Edmond awoke looking replenished. Darion had found a small cactus and had dribbled the fibrous milk into his friend's mouth. Triumph had stood over him, shielding him from the sun's direct rays. The shade, coupled with the barest of nourishment from the cactus, would not typically have helped someone, Darion knew, and he thanked Triumph for his assistance.

"Don't thank me," Triumph had admonished. "Thank the Creator. Had he been bitten, we would have been powerless to help him. We must keep a wary eye for any other threats." Darion gave a tacit nod.

That night the party slept fitfully, and under the still, dark sky they began their trek once more to join Soren. *Edmond could definitely use Soren's medical knowledge,* Darion thought. His friend's skin, though better, was far from healed. Triumph was not gifted in medicine as other unicorns were, so his touch could only go so far. Stoic Edmond didn't complain, but Darion and Triumph had seen the welts and knew that he still hurt from the remnants of the poisonous rash.

As they trudged over the waterless land, a thought occurred to Darion. "Triumph, that poison. You said it could kill an 'ox'. What about a unicorn?" Triumph turned hard eyes on him, trying to decipher where he was headed, when sudden understanding shone on his face.

"The poison," Triumph whispered. "We will have to discuss it with Lei when we get back, but it could certainly be the same."

Darion agreed. Now that he thought about it, he thought he had detected the same sulfurous odor wafting from the snake as it had from the poisoned soup bowls. That had to be the poison Alice used to kill Xenia. Somehow Morta had obtained the snake's venom and used it to try and kill multiple unicorns. Darion shuddered, thinking that perhaps they should have killed and kept the snake for further research. He could see in Triumph's eyes that he was having similar thoughts, but they both seemed to agree that it wouldn't have mattered. The last thing Darion wanted to do was carry around a dead poisonous snake. A reminder of what Alice had done. No, the danger had come to the Isle, and though they longed to with all their hearts, Darion and Triumph could not change the irrevocable events.

CHAPTER 4

The Hidden View

Scattered vegetation began to fill the landscape as the barren waste of the Shazla Desert spilled into new terrain. Darion looked ahead at the tall grasses intermixed with trees. Toward the east, rolling hills and what appeared to be a large meadow beckoned him and his party. He smiled at Edmond and Triumph in wonder. *Had any humans ever come this far?* The map he had seen with his father in the Shovlan Tree had only pictured the Shazla Desert. This was beyond that! Beyond what had been surveyed for the map. His skin prickled with the elation of discovery!

"We're like Columbus or Lewis and Clark out discovering new land!" Darion told them, excitedly.

Edmond looked at Triumph quizzically. "Who knows what he is talking about half the time?" Triumph said, though his tone bespoke affection for Darion.

"Never mind," Darion muttered. "They're just explorers—like us! Did you know this land was here, Triumph?" Triumph only shook his head in joint amazement.

Darion stood smiling, breathing deeply and looking around in wonder, as did his companions. The land looked beautiful in its own rugged way. Not as lush and green as Oregon had been, or vivid as Nav'Aria with its thick forests and abundant waterways. But still, it wasn't sand. It wasn't all rock. It wasn't all desert as he had imagined. It was *alive*. He could feel life all around him as he focused his senses. Birds flew overhead. He could hear the rustle of tiny padded feet in a nearby clump of grass, and a lithe red fox darted past them in search of whatever small creature scampered away. As Darion tried to recall vocabulary from his Seventh Grade Geography class, it finally came to him. "I think this is a 'prairie'."

Triumph nodded. "That sounds like a good description of *this*. Prairie," he said, testing it out.

Edmond's eyes sparkled in the excitement of adventure, momentarily losing the sullen, anguished look of one in pain. "The prairie," Darion heard him whisper.

Breaking their reverie, Darion suddenly turned to Triumph. "How on earth did Soren get so far ahead of us?" The expression on Triumph's face changed so rapidly—from evident surprise, to anger, to embarrassment, and finally to haughty reproach—that Darion couldn't help but laugh.

"Well, he's not been saddled with slow moving humans, one of whom is injured. Had I been alone, I would have cantered circles around him," Triumph boomed confidently. His large powerful build suddenly standing erect and—

Are you flexing? Can unicorns even do that? Darion carefully avoided Edmond's eyes, for he knew they could not keep from laughing if their eyes met. Triumph's and Soren's competition with one another—or rather Triumph's jealousy of his younger, talented former student—had been a constant source of humor throughout their time together.

"I wonder what he found that kept him away for so long," Darion pondered aloud. The other two didn't answer the rhetorical question. They'd all been wondering the same. Whatever it was, Soren had only told Triumph to hurry, and to follow his trail closely.

"We will know soon enough, he is just over that ridge there," Triumph directed, the light glinting off his horn as his head nodded. Darion looked straight ahead toward the ridge, where the tall prairie grasses ceased, and a rock formation loomed over them, appearing before dense pine trees. Darion felt his glowing arm tingle as they began to walk toward the massive stones near the tree line. Darion sought Soren's presence. Though his senses weren't yet fully keen, he knew there was life around them, and he could only hope that none of the activity he felt was a skulking Rav'Arian... or a winged one, whatever that was. He looked around cautiously, suddenly feeling very much exposed in the wide-open space.

"Let's go," he urged them.

Edmond winced as he quickened his steps to keep up, and Triumph fell in beside him. A shell-encased critter scurried across their path. Otherwise, they made their way to the rocks without a problem. Triumph's hooves clattered against the stone, and each echoing step sent goosebumps along Darion's skin. Something was wrong. It had to be.

It's too peaceful here, Darion thought, remembering why they had come. *What if we're being watched now? What if Soren was captured? What if we're walking into a trap?*

Calm yourself, Triumph said softly. *I would have known if he were captured. He said there is no threat, only to hurry. Whatever he found must be something good. A clue perhaps.* Darion stared at him, looking deeply into his aquamarine eyes. They were like beckoning pools of wisdom. He felt his heart rate lessen and took a deep breath.

"Thanks," Darion whispered. "I trust you."

Triumph leaned close, nuzzling his soft white cheek against Darion's in a rare show of affection.

***

"There you are. What took you so long?" Soren whispered caustically, his eyes boring into them. A growl escaped Triumph before Darion cut him off. The unicorn snorted with agitation, though when he spoke, his voice seemed calm.

"Edmond was attacked by a Shazla Viper. It did not bite him," he said quickly, casting aside Soren's spew of questions. "Darion was able to scare it off."

Soren's eyes bulged with this news. He came closer to Edmond to inspect the injuries. Darion knew they would not get any information out of Soren until the health threat was over.

"Show him, Edmond," he told his friend.

Edmond embarrassedly pulled down his trousers. The skin no longer appeared swollen or red, yet dark purple trails remained where the snake had traced itself around him.

At any other time, Darion would have sniggered to see his friend without pants while his groin was scrutinized by a unicorn. But not in this instance. Darion knew Edmond suffered from the poison. Though Triumph had done all he could, emergencies of this nature were beyond his expertise. The rash left behind by the hairs on the snake's scales had not gone away, unfortunately. Soren whispered to himself, making soft *tutting* sounds as he looked over every inch of Edmond's wounds.

"Lie down, please," he instructed him, and Edmond obeyed hurriedly.

Darion watched as Soren's horn lightly touched the skin nearest the wounds. Amazed, Darion gasped as the purplish tendrils began to vanish, leaving slightly pink skin that otherwise appeared normal. Edmond's body trembled a bit as the traces of poison upon his skin dissipated. Soren slowly raised his head, looking more fatigued than he had when they first arrived, but smiling warmly at Edmond and Darion. "Well done, boys. It could have been much worse."

Edmond smiled and thanked him; his eyes glossy with joy after experiencing the miraculous healing.

Triumph cleared his throat noisily. Soren's eyes sparkled with amusement before addressing Triumph. "Edmond was fortunate to be under your esteemed protection and care, Triumph."

Triumph stared at him, speechless, before accepting the praise. Once again, standing to his full height, Darion noted. *The fool really was flexing.*

"Thank you, Soren. I knew you could heal him fully. He is," Triumph looked pained for a moment, before continuing, "also fortunate to have your care." Soren nodded graciously.

Rolling his eyes and winking, Darion reached out a hand to help Edmond up. Edmond snickered, looking back at the two unicorns.

"Now that we got that figured out—thanks again, Soren," Darion inclined his head. "Can you tell us why we're here? What'd you find?"

Soren motioned for them to be quiet, and after Edmond had his trousers and belt done up, they moved further into the trees. Darion had no idea what they were walking into, and after what seemed an eternity of silence, he heard funny sounds. His brain couldn't connect what he was hearing until... Soren stopped at a tall grouping of trees and urged the boys to come closer and peer down.

Whatever Darion had thought he was going to see was definitely not this. His eyes widened and his heart fluttered, testosterone coursing through his body.

"They're naked," he whispered, shocked. Edmond's mouth dropped open, but he didn't avert his eyes. He stood transfixed, his eyes bulging with every second that passed.

"But... but... but...," Darion could only splutter.

Triumph peered over the two boys' heads before quickly ducking back. His chortling laughs mixing with Soren's evident mirth.

The trees they hid behind opened into a drop where a clear caerulean pool of water lay beneath them. The water was not what held the boys' attention; it was, instead, the two bare-chested teenage girls splashing around. Their long locks of hair dancing on the water's surface in an erotic swirl that opened the boys' gaping mouths even wider. If they could only see through the wet hair! And then, as if those tresses were clairvoyant, they scattered in a benevolent breeze and parted in the water, revealing pale, supple skin, accentuated by their pink nipples. Gales of laughter filled the air, though Darion could not hear much beyond the pounding of his own heart. Darion heard Edmond swallow loudly, his mouth suddenly feeling very dry, as well.

Even though it pained him to look away, he turned to face Soren. "YOU COULDN'T HAVE GIVEN US A HEADS UP?" he scolded in a harsh whisper. Soren's eyes widened, appearing almost innocent.

"I did not know their appearance would trouble you so," Soren said levelly. Triumph erupted at his words. His booming chuckles filled the space as he tried to muffle the sound, snorting and hiccupping with the effort.

Edmond stood ogling the girls.

Taking a few deep breaths before replying, Darion tried to get his muddled thoughts straight. "Yes, but… but… who are they? What are humans doing this far from Nav'Aria?"

Now that he considered it, a wave of questions flooded his mind. *Are there more humans? Did we somehow circle back to Nav'Aria? Are they the 'winged ones'?* But no, that can't be it. He was sure in Vondulus' journal, that the notations had implied a 'creature', not man. *Not beautiful naked girls, that's for damn sure.* Laughter beckoned again from the pool, nagging at Darion's focus, but he knew he needed to figure this out.

Soren and Triumph shook out their manes and blew their noses loudly, clearly enjoying every uncomfortable moment of Darion's shock.

"So," Darion growled, glaring at Triumph, before repeating his question to Soren once more, "WHO ARE THEY?"

"They are girls," Soren stated. Darion glared at him but waited for him to explain beyond the obvious.

"They have been around this area for a number of days, so it would appear." Soren proceeded to share his findings: their makeshift camp, their hunting and gathering trips in the woods, and their frequent bathing… and giggling. They appeared alone and happy.

"I have not approached them yet, for fear of scaring them off. I thought you and," he broke off chuckling as his eyes found Edmond still rooted in the same spot, "and the lovestruck boy over there, could go talk to them. They might be more comfortable speaking with humans than unicorns… since our kind has never been seen in this place."

Darion's stomach did a flip. "Talk to them?" he whispered, all rational thought vanishing. He felt as nervous—more nervous—than he had back in Oregon when he had attempted to speak with his old crush. "I can't go talk to them. Not while they're… you know…" he said, noting the sound of panic in his own voice. His cheeks felt hot.

"Go on, Darion. They won't bite," Triumph said. Soren snorted loudly, turning his face quickly from view.

After a moment, the unicorn quickly echoed, "Yes, go on, Darion. Like Triumph said, 'they won't bite.' We will be right behind you for support."

Darion looked uncertainly between the two unicorns and Edmond. "What about him?" A slow red blush had creeped down Edmond's face and neck.

"Edmond," Triumph called.

Edmond jumped at the sound, turning away from his gawking to see his three companions staring at him. His red face beamed. Darion laughed, hitting his friend on the shoulder.

"What is this place?" Edmond asked in an awe-filled voice. Darion smiled, not trusting himself to speak.

"You and Darion must go down there and introduce yourselves—do not frighten them," Triumph's voice returning to its usual explanatory tone. "And don't goggle at them, boy. Haven't you two ever seen a naked girl before?"

Darion felt his face grow even hotter and knew he and Edmond must look like a pair of ripe tomatoes. Triumph and Soren stared at them before they erupted AGAIN into fits of laughter.

"Oh, sweet Creator, this is too good," Triumph cooed, silver tears escaping his eyes. "Well done, Soren. Well done."

From behind clenched teeth, Darion retorted tersely, "That is enough out of you two. We're leaving now." Darion grabbed Edmond's arm and dragged his friend away from the still-chortling unicorns.

Away from the pair, Edmond leaned in and whispered, "What are we going to say?"

The façade of anger left Darion immediately, and he looked helplessly to his friend. "I have no idea."

CHAPTER 5

The Meeting

Antonis forcefully kicked the corpse from his sword, which dribbled droplets of blood onto the wooden floor. It had been a bloody fight until the end. Whoever these assassins were, they were skilled—and they were relentless. Vikaris, Trixon, and Drigidor guarded the one whom they had kept alive. He appeared slightly older than the rest, and his eyes burned with hate.

Antonis strode back to his companions and the soldiers standing guard around their King. Antonis looked to Vikaris for approval before beginning the interrogation. Vikaris nodded curtly.

Antonis squatted down, rolling his neck as he did so, feigning nonchalance. He really could use a massage, he thought idly. Weeks of heavy training left his upper back and neck stiff.

As he eyed the man, the captive stared boldly back at him. Antonis punched him square in the jaw. The man grimaced but didn't make a sound at the impact, only spat and continued his stare, coolly.

"Who are you?" Antonis inquired, his low, authoritative voice ringing out in the otherwise quiet corridor.

"I do not answer to traitors," the man spat.

Before Antonis could reply, Drigidor leaned down near the man's face, his horn almost touching the man's temple. "You may want to rethink how you address us," Drigidor's booming voice reverberated in the vast space, as his front leg stamped near the man, causing him to flinch. Seeing his weakness, Drigidor pressed, slashing his horn across the man's cheek. The man shrunk back in fear.

"You are not like the others," he whispered, clearly shaken.

Antonis glowered at Drigidor, taking hold of the situation. "What others? Who are you?"

The man stared wide, only just now focusing on the figure of the King behind him. "… and you? Vikaris? You are alive? You are real?" The man looked panicked… or reverent. Antonis couldn't be sure.

"Slow down," Vikaris urged, holding out a palm. "One thing at a time," he spoke calmly. "Who are you?"

The man exhaled, and Antonis felt the pressure between his shoulders lessen. "My name is Carn. I am the Commander," he paused, a hint of the glare returning to his eyes as he looked at Antonis, "Captain of the Emperor's palace guards."

Vikaris nodded as if all of this made sense. "And my uncle sent you, I am assuming?" Carn nodded slightly. "And how did you infiltrate Kaulter?"

Carn hesitated, clearly buying time. He pressed his lips, looking as if he were not about to reply. Drigidor growled, slashing his other cheek in a flash. Carn gasped.

"We found the old trails that the centaurs used with the captives," he gulped as the King's gaze hardened, and the two unicorns remained threateningly close. "I mean... the Queen, that is. We followed their trail to a hidden portal, killed the nymphs guarding it, and used the... the key we had been given."

Trixon cocked his head as the man spoke, and Antonis had a feeling he and Vikaris were discussing him.

Antonis opened his mouth to ask what key the man was talking about. There was no such thing as a key. Only the unicorns and the Marked Royals possessed the power to open the portal. And Antonis had seen Seegar open the portals using secret words from the Old Tongue, but that was it. Did he have a hidden key, as well? Antonis knew from experience, thinking back to the Falls when he had tried to lead his party back. It was Darion, along with his Ruby, Mark, and cry of "Azalt" that had allowed them entrance.

Vikaris pressed on, "When you spoke of 'others' to Drigidor, what did you mean?"

This made Antonis pause. He had not really considered that, but now his curiosity was piqued. *What had he meant?*

The man's eyes bulged, filling with fear. "I cannot say, Your Majesty. If Narco were to find out, he would kill my family. Best he thinks I died in battle," and faster than anyone could react, he quickly revealed a thin blade from his shirt sleeve and slit his throat, opening his jugular vein in one fluid motion. Those who gathered yelled and moved at once, but to no avail. The man was dead.

All but Trixon moved. "So, it is true," he mused aloud. Vikaris stopped midway from kneeling down and looked toward his companion intently. Antonis paused his inspection of the slain officer, watching them instead.

"What is true?" Vikaris asked quietly. Drigidor exhaled loudly just as Elsra and Trinidad walked up to the party.

"You will want to sit down for this," Trinidad said soberly.

***

"Ouch," Darion whispered harshly, turning back to glare at Edmond, who was literally stepping on his heels. "Excited much?" Darion taunted.

Edmond's face instantly flushed, and Darion chuckled. A squeal of laughter sent them both ducking for cover to peer through the clustered trees around the edge of the pool.

They hurried down the cliff to where they had stood with the unicorns, utterly careless of their footfalls due to nervous anticipation. Darion now realized that they were extremely fortunate for not scaring the girls away. Triumph had cautioned him in his mind to slow down, all the while continuing to laugh—*the jerk*! Darion contemplated ways to get back at him for all of his teasing. Triumph was enjoying this situation far too much for Darion's liking; however, Darion had far greater things to worry about. For instance, how to approach two beautiful girls in a foreign land, and oh yeah, they just so happen to be completely naked. *No big deal. You can do this,* Darion counseled himself.

He looked over at his companion. Judging by the dazed expression on Edmond's reddened face, he knew he'd be of no help. As if predestined, the girls swam over toward the edge nearest their hiding place. Slowly the angelic creatures rose out of the water, first revealing their chests, then torsos, then….

"Wow," Darion and Edmond both whispered in unison. Darion felt his own face flush and his heart rate skyrocket. He had never seen a naked girl before. Not in real life, at least… maybe an image here or there, but nothing like this.

Focus, you idiot! Triumph roared in his mind before exploding in loud guffaws. Darion scowled as the scene of utter perfection was rudely interrupted. While both girls were glorious in sight, one stood out more than the other. Her chestnut hair billowed around her petite frame; she glowed with joy—and mischief. Her womanly curves showed her to be older than the other. Darion found himself entranced by her beauty.

Surprisingly, it was Edmond who knocked Darion out of his revelry. "They're leaving," the boy whispered, his voice sounding desperate.

Darion observed that he was right. *What the hell am I doing?*

They had to move now. They had to say something. But what? Just as he was about to step out, the girls turned, and he received a clear picture of their firm backsides. A groan escaped his lips before he could stop it.

"What was that?" The other girl with strawberry blonde tresses cascading down her narrow back spun around with a start.

Darion froze in place, unsure of what to do yet fully aware that his indecision risked them being discovered like creeps who spy on naked girls. Though, wasn't that exactly what they were? *Get it together, Darion. You're the Marked Heir! Act like it!*

Darion coughed and knocked a few branches nearby to make it seem like he was just now approaching the scene. Edmond quickly followed suit. The two intentionally stepped into the clearing, facing the opposite direction of where the girls presently stood on the bank. Darion elbowed Edmond, pretending that they were in conversation and had no idea that two bare-breasted beauties stood mere feet away.

A feminine throat cleared behind them.

Darion paused, taking a deep breath before turning around. As he turned, feigning surprise, he still spluttered at their loveliness. "Oh-hem…." Mute stricken, he lost complete control of his thoughts… along with his speech.

Nice one, he thought miserably. *You're an idiot.*

Say something… Introduce yourself. Do not scare them away. This time it was Soren who spoke into his mind. Darion tried to clear his head and looked back at the pair, focusing on their faces only.

"Uhhh, hey," Darion started. *Not bad. It's a start at least.* The girl with the chestnut hair smiled shyly, and as she did, her left cheek revealed a slight dimple. Darion melted at the sight. Her large dark eyes seemed almost too large for her petite face and frame, but he thought they were perfect. *She's like a bird*, he thought wonderingly.

The girl arched her eyebrow at him, as if coaxing him to say more. All at once the scene, two naked girls and two embarrassed boys, awkwardly stumbling out of the forest and then stuttering like idiotic fools, was too much for him. Darion began laughing, placing his hands on his knees to brace the deep chuckles that spilled out of him. Edmond hit his arm, but Darion ignored him. Before he knew it, he too was laughing. Like a fool, he was brought to his knees by the outburst. The girls had begun to back away, but as Darion lifted his face to theirs, the dimpled smile returned.

"And what is so funny?" The girl inquired, her tone haughty but forced. Darion detected a slight accent. It reminded him of the French exchange student from his school last year. The words blended together as she spoke. The sight and sound of her mesmerized him. Darion levelly avoided looking below her neck, which proved to be a challenge since he sat on the ground.

Jumping up, he quickly rubbed his face across his shirtsleeve to stall. "Not you. I wasn't laughing at you—I promise! I just... I just thought we all looked a little ridiculous here and...," he gestured toward their nude forms. Both girls smiled at this, and Darion noted that the taller girl's face bloomed with a blush redder than any Edmond's had ever possessed.

"You *promise*?" the girl persisted. "And who are you to promise us anything, stranger?" Her tone changed with the last word. Darion lifted his hands as if to ward off her dark thoughts.

"My name is Darion… and this is my friend Edmond," he intoned as he clapped a hand on Edmond's broad shoulder. Edmond managed a smile and quick nod, but words seemed out of reach for the guy.

"I am Nala. And this is my sister Ati," she spoke softly. Her hazel, entrancing eyes seemed to engulf her face as she studied him. He was at their mercy and feared the moment they would look away. They held more than beauty, he observed: he could see wisdom in them, too. She looked as if she could discern all his secrets with one simple glance. *Not just a bird,* he thought. *An owl.*

"Nice to meet you," he murmured with only a quick glance for the sister. Edmond had that department covered.

"And… do you live around here, Nala?"

Nala stepped closer, and Darion's senses heightened. Water droplets trailed along her back, falling upon the muddy bank. The air smelled pure. Sweet.

"So… my question," he prompted. "Do you live around here?" He smiled at her, and it looked as if she were going to reply until all at once the spell was broken by a thunderous roar above, causing the party to duck and hide. The girls screamed while Darion and Edmond reached for their swords, spinning around trying to identify the threat.

The wind picked up. Ripples spread across the pool, creating small waves. Dust and leaves circled nearest the water's edge. It was as if, Darion considered, *as if it were coming from above… like a helicopter or something….*

"Winged ones," Darion shouted, grabbing the front of Edmond's tunic before standing protectively in front of the girls.

They dove behind the large boulder where their clothes were evidently stashed, madly donning animal-skin shirts and pants. Darion pondered for a moment, watching Nala and Ati. *Pants?* In a different, less danger-ridden moment, he might have asked why they wore pants. He had only seen one woman wearing pants in all of Nav'Aria, and that was Aalil… and Carol, at least initially. Though, even she had worn a dress in her final days. *Who were these girls?* But that would have to wait, for just then the winged one came into full view. Huge sepia wings filled the entire span of sky.

Darion held out his sword, though he felt like his heart might hammer out of his chest. Edmond stood with him. He may be terrified of girls, but he was the best companion to have alongside him in a fight, Darion had no doubt. Edmond was a Nav'Arian prodigy. Only he'd never had to face a foe this massive, and….

"Holy shit! It's a dragon," Darion murmured. His sword tip dipped momentarily toward the ground. The wings turned to reveal a long snaking head, a thickly muscled body, and hind legs. Darion felt as if someone had punched him in the stomach. Yes, all along he'd known they were tracking a creature called the "winged one," but he hadn't let himself imagine that it would be a dragon, like something from a fairy tale or movie from his past life. He had pictured a hefty, menacing bird. Perhaps like an Albatross, but *this*? This was unreal. The creature's yellow eyes smoldered with rage, and a plume of smoke billowed from its jaws as it searched the area close to them.

Darion contemplated his next move, when all of a sudden he heard a feminine voice calling out, "It is alright, Zalto. They are our friends."

Darion gasped in shock, turning to see Nala and Ati striding out into the open space near the water. They were unarmed... and... and smiling? Darion's eyes shot up toward the beast looming in the air.

"Wait!" he called, before dashing out behind them, sword held firmly in grip.

As he neared them, the beast lowered suddenly into the water, dousing them all in the act. Stunned, wet, and terrified, Darion stood taller, trying to take hold of the situation.

"Nala," he whispered urgently to get the beautiful girl's attention, but she was not listening. She was headed straight for the dragon. Darion began to follow but then froze.

"Yes, Father. These are our friends."

"Well, I will be the judge of that," a deep voice rumbled, causing tiny stones to tremble along the beach.

"Wait... you know him?" Darion asked in shock.

Nala turned back from her position near the creature, Zalto, and smirked mischievously as she said, "Why, yes, he is my father after all."

The strawberry blonde, Ati, burst into giggles at the sight of the boys' confusion. Darion and Edmond could only stare.

CHAPTER 6

The Chase

Porris could hear the screaming well before he entered the dungeon. He had circumspectly avoided the room until now, after a messenger had burst into his small chamber exclaiming that the Emperor demanded he attend him immediately. Porris shuddered at the thought, trying to steel himself before entering.

Curse you, Morta, he thought to himself. If the true adviser had not left them, Porris would not have been in this precarious position. Narco terrified Porris, and he had always gotten by, keeping a low profile at the Castle. Now, *he* was the personal adviser and attendant to the Emperor until Morta returned. *May it be soon,* Porris pleaded, though to whom was unclear.

His footfalls reverberated off the stone walls, and the only light revealing his way came from the few torches and braziers in the passageway. The smell of mildew… and blood, invaded his nostrils, though he tried to stem it off with a scented handkerchief pressed to his face. He shuddered again. As he came upon the entryway to the torture chamber, he stood immobile, suspended with fear while an ear-piercing scream erupted from the other side of the doorway. The two guards on duty shifted their feet uncomfortably at the sound. Porris knew they shared his feelings about Narco. Everyone did. But none disobeyed him, for if they did, it would be their screams filling the night air.

Porris took one more shaky breath before nodding at the guard to admit him. He almost gagged at the sight, and it took every ounce of will not to turn around and flee.

A man—what was left of him—lay strapped to a wooden table in the center of the room. The troll Dabor stood with Narco inspecting the corpse. The man had been flayed. His blood pooled around the base of the table. Unconsciously, Porris shivered again at the sight of Narco's feet and robes standing within the puddle. *Does he even realize he is standing in it? Does he care?* The thought sickened him.

"Does our work bother you, Porris?" Narco purred in his oily voice, snapping Porris out of his trance. The adviser sniffed noncommittally.

"He was a filthy traitor, My Lord. Just as you said." Porris felt sick but desperately sought to maintain a calm countenance—at least on the outside.

Narco eyed him coolly, and Porris avoided his gaze by looking over the man's body. It appears he had held up against the worst of it. He must have been telling the truth then. *The poor man*, Porris thought. When it had been quiet for a few moments, Porris dared look back to his Emperor. Narco stood studying him.

Porris bowed slightly under his inspection before asking, "Did you learn more of the event, Emperor?"

Narco spat and stepped away from the table, blood smearing the stone floor as his robes trailed around to stand near Porris.

"Not as much as I would have liked," Narco admitted. "He claims Carn and the other guards all attacked, and he was told to remain at the portal. He returned to inform me. Ha!" Narco laughed darkly. "It is more like he fled, the filthy coward," Narco said as his gaze fell upon the body again. "He had gleaned no new information. What use is a messenger without a message? I despise cowards," he concluded with a sneer.

From that angle, the torch light fell upon Narco's scarred face, illuminating the cheek that had been run through by Trinidad's horn. The sight of him in the shadows gave Narco a less-than-human appearance, like a demonic monster from some dark abyss. Porris shivered again, *perhaps he was.*

"Does this news displease you?" Narco said, returning his gaze to Porris. The adviser mentally chided himself for once again showing weakness in front of Narco. He knew that the Emperor didn't tolerate it and feared that he would end up on the rack sooner than later if he didn't gain control of himself.

"Yes, my Lord. The man was clearly a coward, as you say. Completely unacceptable." Narco looked skeptical but let the statement pass without comment.

"Come," he barked instead, gathering his robes and striding purposefully toward the door. "We have much to do if what this soldier has to say is true. Carn's party was unsuccessful, and Morta is still held hostage," Narco laughed at the last line, looking smugly to Porris as they reached the door. "It would appear your time as my adviser has been extended."

Porris gulped.

***

"How did you come by this place?" The owner of the low voice did not try to disguise the threatening tone.

Darion and Edmond looked at one another, deciding what to share. Darion swallowed, trying to calm his breathing. This was why they had come after all. Though, granted, he hadn't allowed himself to really consider the implications of discovering a "winged one". *A dragon! And what did Nala mean by 'Father'!?* Breathing deeply, he stared into the yellow orbs, which appeared to be penetrating his psyche. *Such wisdom in those eyes.*

"We are on a quest." Darion said. It sounded like something a hero would say. He thought it was a good opening line, until….

"A quest for what?" The timbre rising with each pronunciation. The dragon apparently did not like his response. A slight puff of smoke escaped his mouth, and the dragon's forked tongue snaked out hostilely. Edmond took a step forward, as if to protect Darion.

"It's alright," he murmured to his friend before looking back at the disgruntled dragon. Nala and Ati were both standing on either side of the dragon's lowered face, their palms patting him and speaking lowly to him with hushed, comforting words.

"Our land is at war. We come seeking answers. The man who has taken over our land has secret powers, and we believe he came here years ago and discovered something… discovered you… er… your kind… and is using it against us." The dragon's head snapped up from the girls as Darion spoke, and Darion unconsciously took a step back at the lethal aura emanating from the dragon. Smoke plumed from its nostrils, and he ignored the girls as he strode forward toward the pair, his massive bulk thundering upon the beach.

"How do I know that it is not your goal to also obtain what he 'found'… what he took from us?" At that the dragon roared and lurched forward, mere inches from the boys. Darion stood paralyzed. Nala and Ati scrambled to reach them while frantically calling for Zalto not to hurt their friends.

The enraged dragon didn't appear to hear them, so intent was he upon the boys. He sniffed at them, his tongue flicking in and out, and at one-point striking Darion's shoulder. Darion moaned with the force of the impact but did not move.

"Well? HOW DO I KNOW THAT YOU DO NOT INTEND TO KILL ANOTHER OF US?" Darion feared his eardrums may have exploded with this last ferocious and close-ranged roar. The two boys stepped back ever farther.

Darion trembled and shook his head, holding his arms out in a gesture of peace. He couldn't seem to make words, but he had to let the dragon know that this was not what they planned. Nala was screaming at Zalto now and clambering upon his back trying to calm him; Ati had collapsed near them crying.

"No," Darion tried, swallowing nervously. "We don't know what Narco did! We are here for answers, that's all. I promise. That is all," Darion managed to say before breathing heavily again, his fraying nerves making him shudder. He could smell the latest kill on the dragon's breath as its maw came closer and closer. Jagged teeth appeared, greater than any he had ever seen on a living creature.

"Narco, you said? That is his name?" The dragon stared intently, "How do I know you are not this Narco?" The dragon countered as he knocked Darion and Edmond to the ground with a swat from his wing.

As Darion lay on the ground staring up at the beast, he knew this was it. He tried crawling back but to no avail. The dragon held him in place with a front foot that pressed heavily on his and Edmond's legs. Once the dragon's mouth opened for the kill, Darion's senses heightened. His arm began to glow. He heard Nala's frantic screams as she battered the back of Zalto's head. The flesh trapped in the dragon's fangs reeked, and the wind stirred from the forest. Darion thought he could hear something, but it was all so surreal. Time seemed suspended.

The instant his arm began to glow, the dragon's eyes widened at the sight, and then two white blurs slammed into the scaled head of the dragon, causing it to spring up quickly in painful surprise. This sent Nala sprawling to the ground. The air erupted in roars... and shrieks.

Before Darion or Edmond knew what was happening, Triumph and Soren were there, and both boys quickly grabbed hold of their respective mounts before being carried away. The unicorns bearing their riders charged into the forest without delay, leaving behind a chaotic beach, two terrified girls and an enraged dragon.

It's about time, Darion managed, the trees merely a haze, Darion's speech no clearer.

We are not out of harm's way yet, Triumph cautioned. Darion swallowed, trying to focus. Triumph was right, for at that moment a giant cloud of darkness obstructed their view of the sun. Darion's eyes shot upwards. The sepia wingspan of a dragon loomed overhead, causing him to almost lose his grip on Triumph's mane. And just like that, the trees in front of them exploded with crackling flame. Triumph and Soren whinnied and skittered to a halt just before turning aside to avoid the perilous blaze. Darion could hear the inhalation of air from the dragon and knew Zalto was about to spew more fire.

"Watch out," he shouted as the trees nearest Soren's flank alit. The unicorns and their riders shifted direction again. The chase was on.

Nala's eyelids fluttered, the colors of the bright sky swirling in her vision. A dark shadow appeared overhead, and she opened one eye, squinting. It was Ati. She had been crying.

Memory returned. Nala gasped in terror, trying to sit up. Her neck and back ached from her fall, and her head felt dizzy, but she ignored it. Slowly, with help from her sister, she stood.

"Where is he?" She asked worriedly. Smoke filled the air, and the forest was aflame. *What is he thinking?*

Ati shivered and pointed toward the west. "He chases them still," she replied, grabbing their packs from nearest the boulder, where they had stashed them seemingly a lifetime ago. Nala nodded, fearing the worst. Though she knew nothing of the humans, she knew that they were telling the truth. Zalto had to see that. And then, as if on cue, she remembered what had caused her to fall.

"What were those *things* that came?"

Ati's eyes widened at the memory. "I do not know. I was crying and screaming, and then all of a sudden there were two white beasts hitting Father and taking the humans away," Ati bit her lower lip nervously, as was her habit. "Do you think they are going to be alright?" Nala had a feeling Ati's thoughts had drifted to one of them in particular. She, too, hoped they were safe... especially the dark-haired one with the piercing emerald eyes.

"We better hurry to make sure," Nala ordered, taking the pack from Ati's extended hand and heading out to follow the smoke, flames, and roars. Wreckage from their Father. Nala could not recall ever seeing him so angry, but she vowed to make sure his anger did not damage any chance of Ati and her meeting others of their kind.

"I mean it, Father," she grumbled as they ran. "If you hurt them, I will never forgive you." Ati nodded but focused on her footing. The two stumbled along the uneven forest ground, avoiding patches of flame. They both pressed scarves to their mouths to try and avoid inhaling the pervasive smoke.

A loud bellow eclipsed the twilight air, and a shriek rang out. Nala cursed and ran faster, her dizziness and worry for her own health long forgotten. Ati easily kept pace. As they approached the location of the sound, the trees cleared to reveal another pond, this one not as pristine as their favored one.

Yet, the sight was one of sheer splendor... and now terror.

Their father darkened the scene with fire spewing forth. Two white beasts reared on powerfully muscled hind legs, shrieking and skirting the flames. They had horns that illuminated the area. And between them stood a lone figure. A young man. His shirtsleeve pushed up to reveal a glowing, marked arm and a stone at his throat which shone red. The contrast of orange flame mixed with red and white light created a mesmerizing display against the evening shadows creeping in. Nala and Ati stopped stunned by the show of power and light before them.

"You will stop," the figure demanded. Nala now remembered his name. Darion.

Darion was ordering her father?

Darion stepped toward the creature. The flames had receded, but smoke curled around Zalto's terrifying face. Darion raised his arm authoritatively. He was tired, sore, scared... and truly pissed.

"I said STOP!" Darion demanded, and most surprising of all, Zalto did. The dragon slowly lowered to the ground, creating a loud crashing sound that dispelled the magnitude of the moment, and just like that, the terror of the scene dissipated.

Nala and Ati ran into the expanse, passing the two sheer beasts and their human riders before reaching their father.

"Girls," he breathed out heavily. Zalto sounded weary, and there was a deep sadness in his eyes as he looked them over. "I did not hurt you, did I, Nala?" Nala looked at him sternly for a moment, gauging his true feelings.

She held his stare as she said, "No, Father. But if you hurt these," she paused indicating Darion and his party, "visitors, I will be." She stuck her chin with obstinate emphasis.

Darion still stood his arm suspended in the air. His companions had joined him. One towering beast looking extraordinarily intimidating... and possessive as it stood nearest the strange young man.

Zalto looked as if he were going to lecture her, but she cut him off.

"I mean it, Father. We should find out WHO these ones are BEFORE trying to kill them... and before burning down the entire forest... resources are low as it is," she growled reproachfully.

Zalto looked sheepish at that, and exhaled loudly, nodding to her.

"You might be right in that, Nala." He looked away from her and her sister, toward the party. "Please sit. And tell us exactly who you are, why you are here, and everything you know of this so called 'Narco'."

Nala released the breath she had been holding and patted her father's scaled cheek before motioning for Darion and his party to sit. She took some dried meat and figs from her bag and passed them to him as a sign of hospitality and peace.

Darion reached for the food and smiled cautiously at her. Nala felt her heartrate begin to rise, but this time from a different threat.

One of her kind. A human. *A very handsome human,* she thought to herself with enjoyment.

CHAPTER 7

The Reaction

"Yes, but why did you take it? That was not part of the plan, I am sure. I thought I alone was to drink it? What will you gain from it?"

"Hush, hush, my prince. You know that I always have your best interest in mind, right?" Morta traced his fingers lightly across Narco's bare chestbone as he spoke. He then returned to kneading the knots in Narco's neck and upper back. Narco could not suppress a grimace at the tender touch, knowing that Morta would be unable to see his face. Though he owed much to his tutor, he had never fully understood their relationship... or his feelings for the man. A part of him longed to never be separated from him. To please him. To surrender to him. The other part of him—the deeper part—was repulsed by it all. But what could he do? As Morta said, without him, Rustusse would surely rule as King for cycles, leaving Narco to... to what? To wait on him and be the laughingstock of *the Meridia Court for the rest of his days? Impossible. I cannot face that future. I will not.*

Narco steeled himself to accept Morta's presence—and thereby touch—as a means to an end. He would use Morta, just as the man used him. He smiled grimly to himself, thinking of the burning fire raging inside him. A flicker of Salimna entered his mind, but he battered it back quickly and locked it away. He would not feel bad for killing the foolish youngling. It had been necessary. Just as his tolerance for Morta was necessary. It would not always be so.

He held down a shiver as the man's hands began to move slowly but firmly down his torso, turning Narco to face him. It would not always be so, he vowed.

Narco flushed with the memory, sipping his wine, and seemed otherwise nonplussed by the pair in his bed. Morta had been gone for weeks now, and surprisingly, Narco felt somewhat distraught. After all these years, and still the man had a hold on him. Some twisted, manipulative hold, yet it kept. At first Narco felt like he had been freed from bondage with the departure of his long-time tutor and… friend. He had taken multiple slave girls to bed, thrilled by the thought of a woman, especially after yearning so long for the elusive Lyrianna. And yet, now that she had escaped, Carn's search party had failed, Vikaris still reigned, and Morta had not returned, Narco felt for the first time in a long time, alone. *Weak. Vulnerable.* Morta had been with him for so many cycles. He truly did not recall a time when Morta wasn't in his life… or his chambers. Though he sometimes hated the man and the things he encouraged Narco to do, the

Emperor could not rid himself of the longing. Every great leader needed a sage adviser. He now had no one.

Glancing again at the pair, he glared, his upper lip rising in a sneer. He commanded Porris to bring him a male this time, as well as a female. Narco thought that would please him, though now as he watched, he realized the man's narrow waist and sculpted figure did not hold the allure for him. If anything, it only made Narco realize how pitiful his own body appeared. Even with his supernatural abilities, thanks to his trip across the Shazla Desert, he had grown old. Though stronger than he looked, he had not been graced with the form the vigorous man in his bed possessed. He watched the man and woman intertwined—as he had instructed them to—and grew envious. As the pair neared climax, Narco threw his glass at them and smiled as it made impact with the man's head, knocking him off course, causing him to fall beside the woman. Her groans turning to cries of pain as he fell. Glass shattered on the near wall, spraying her with glass shards and droplets of cherry wine. Sickened by the youthful pair and the now fresh blood on his sheets, he called for the guards to remove them.

Two burly palace guards barged in and hauled the crying woman and naked, dazed man from the bed.

"Tell Porris to attend me," he ordered them.

Narco hated the sniveling man. *He is all that I have though*, he bitterly admitted to himself.

A timid knock announced the useless man's arrival. Narco draped a black cloak around his shoulders. The robe had been made of rich material and intricate design.

He had commissioned all his cloaks to be embroidered with his insignia, a black and red winged crescent. He smiled to himself thinking of the enigmatic meaning behind the symbol. The unicorn symbol of old was a crescent, and by adding the wings, he included a clue to his otherwise secret rendezvous from years before. *My secret of power,* he thought smugly, placing the ruby-encrusted golden crown upon his head.

The crown had been his brother's, and before that, their mother's. As eldest, Narco deserved it. He had always deserved it. That was what Mother had wanted. Mother had just not realized the truth. He lingered for one final moment gazing upon the portrait of her that hung above his bed, before striding quickly to the door. Porris stood waiting.

"I would like to visit *her*, today."

Porris, as was his near response to everything, gulped before nodding. His eyes widening at the pronouncement.

Narco sneered at him. "Well, what are we waiting for? Take me to her!"

Porris jumped at the tone, and quickly turned to walk with Narco. The metal keys in his pocket lightly jingling as they walked through the richly carpeted corridor. Portraits that had hung in these halls for years had been replaced in an instant. Instead of images of the Meridia Marked Royals, Narco fashioned to have a series of paintings done. Images of the coup that led to his dominance. *The Fall.* He had spared one painting, of course, that of Queen Aliguette, which hung in his chambers.

Mother would be proud of me, he mused. *When I command, people obey.* He treasured the feeling. He could feel the fear radiating from Porris's stooped shoulders as he walked nervously next to his mighty Emperor. *Yes, such power,* Narco thought, gratified, feeling immensely better after discharging the two attendees from his bed.

***

Lyrianna tired of the arguing. Though she adored her husband, his obstinance could at times be exhausting... *and that of the Unicorn Council's,* she considered, arching her eyebrow at another of Elsra's more pointed remarks toward her husband.

Soon after the threat had been dealt with, Vikaris had returned to her, followed by Elsra and the unicorns. Antonis and Drigidor had taken Aalil and Cela to help with the final sweep of the fortress... and to regain order of the guards and citizens of Kaulter. The enemies had been quickly put down. However, the question still remained: *How did they gain access to Kaulter? Was nowhere safe from Narco?*

As hard as she tried, she still couldn't rid herself completely of him. The quiet of night unnerved her, yet after sleeping alone for so many nights in captivity, she sometimes awoke alarmed to find a man in her bed. However, as soon as she regained her wits, she always cozied up to her stalwart of a husband. In his arms she felt like nothing could ever hurt her.

Yet right this moment she was not in his arms, and the only feeling she had toward him was annoyance. *Why was he behaving so intolerably?*

She watched her husband retort loudly to Elsra's snide comment, both appearing to blame the other for the attack: You *should have had more guards on duty. No one besides the Marked Royals or unicorns should have ever been allowed access to the portals. The unicorns have grown lazy in their duties....*

Trixon winced as if he were caught between two rolling boulders pinning him to his spot. Lyrianna pitied him, caught between his forceful mother and stubborn King.

Not exactly the joyful reunion we had hoped for, is it?

Without a blink at Trinidad's intrusion to her thoughts, Lyrianna replied, *Not entirely.* Her mind straying to the loss of Carolina and to Darion's disappearance. Everything seemed to be falling apart.

Trinidad came to stand near her, and she leaned on him appreciatively, as she had many times during their return journey. She wrapped her arms around his stout neck, his stubbled mane tickling her arms. He nuzzled close, rubbing her shoulder and murmuring that everything would be alright. The tears fell freely upon his now sheen coat and disappeared into the fine silver fibers of hair.

"Lyrianna? What is the matter, my love? Is everything alright?" Vikaris gripped her shoulder, gently turning her to face him.

Lyrianna knew that it wasn't his fault. She wasn't truly angry at him, but she could not contain her emotions any longer.

"NO, Vikaris! Everything is not alright," she shouted, standing straight-backed and wild-eyed, her cheeks shining from the shed tears. Trinidad stood near her lifting his own head with her rising voice, as if in equal challenge.

"Nothing is alright. My son is missing. Kaulter was attacked. Narco is getting closer, and you two cannot stop your petulant bickering for one moment to admit that it's no one's fault... or it's everyone's fault. Somehow Narco is infiltrating. And it's working in this room right now," her voice grew louder. "He WANTS to divide us and break our unified alliance between man and the unicorns. You must see that! You are giving him exactly what he wants by fighting. And in doing so, you are wasting our time," she gestured passionately with her hands for emphasis as the words she had bottled up spewed forth.

"While you bicker and plan and argue and council, HE IS TORTURING SOMEONE. He is always torturing someone. He still tortures me," her voice grew soft, and she stared off into the distance for a moment as she remembered the gleeful anticipation on his face every time he thought he had broken her. Trinidad nudged her encouragingly. Her resolve hardened.

"He did not break me," looking toward Trinidad, she added, "he did not break Mighty Trinidad, and he will not break this Council. Now, be quiet," she commanded, and as she did so, she and Trinidad stood coolly, making no move to sit themselves until her order was obeyed.

Elsra and Vikaris gaped at her.

Lyrianna's heart fluttered in her chest at the reality of what she had just done. She felt near hysterics. She had just commanded the King and Unicorn Regent to be silent. She had to pinch her inner arm to keep from joining with Trinidad in his quiet laughter. She had never spoken to them like that... to anyone really. She lifted her chin smartly.

"Well, are you ready to hear what else Trinidad has discovered, or not?" If unicorns could beam, that was the best way to describe the look Trinidad gave her. She smiled up at him and patted his cheek affectionately before turning her queenly gaze upon the others.

Trixon had managed to make it halfway to the doorway before Vikaris noticed and shot him a scowl. Lyrianna did manage to laugh at that. *Poor Trixon*, she giggled to herself. *He really is caught in a room full of boulders now!*

Trinidad laughed aloud. Trixon, Vikaris, and Elsra all approached apprehensively... *and silently*, Lyrianna noted. *Blissfully silent.*

"Please, Trinidad, if you would be so kind," Lyrianna directed him with a warm smile before seating herself.

"It would be my pleasure, Your Majesty," he replied, bowing his head.

CHAPTER 8

The Labor

"... and though the night comes dearie,
I will be the last one waiting,
Until the dreams carry you,
Away, away, away..."

The evening shadows danced around the chamber, reflecting off the water in the small corner trough. The room smelled stale, and once again it would seem that the servants had forgotten to come change her hay and linens. They really were the worst at remembering. Poor Master had to do so much, being surrounded by fools. He always told her that she was special. She was the only one he trusted with his secrets. *But then why was he taking so long to come visit?* She understood, of course. Master was very busy. It was hard protecting everyone from the evil rebel. She shuddered just thinking of the monster who threatened to kill everyone and everything in Nav'Aria. Luckily Master would not let that happen.

Master will keep me safe. He takes care of me during my sick time and helps get rid of the pain. Master knows how to keep me safe. Master knows everything.

She didn't like the pain, though. It was excruciating. Master told her it was a sickness that she had had since she was born, and because of it, she had to stay safe in her room where he could look after her. *Master cares a lot,* she thought idly, looking at the pool of stagnant water at the end of the room. *He will make sure I have clean hay and water when he comes. He will come. He thinks I am special. He keeps me safe.*

She began to drift back to sleep once more. The words to the song she always sang during her sickness fading away as she drifted to sleep.

Close to sleep, she was startled by stabbing pains that gripped her stomach.

No, she thought, panicked. *Not yet. Master is not here. I need Master. Master keeps me safe.* Another pain gripped her, and she staggered to her feet. Water. *Water will help,* she thought, desperately trying to remember what Master usually did first.

She stepped toward the trough and was momentarily distracted by her appearance. Master's workers always kept a scarf around her forehead and tied it under her chin. They said that it had to do with preventing the spread of her sickness. She must have knocked it off in her thrashing. Another pain seized her, and her stomach contracted. Her eyes traveled back to her sleeping corner, and sure enough, the black scarf with the strange symbol laid where it had fallen.

Breathing heavily, she remembered she wanted a drink but was again mesmerized by her appearance. She moved closer to the water to inspect her reflection. She had always had a sore on her forehead where Master's workers put the medicine. That was where her sickness had begun, she knew. She had never seen it before, though, and now that she looked, it didn't look like a wound she had imagined. It looked… strange. Like something had protruded from there at one time. There was a small stump raised from her forehead. As another pain seized her, the door began to open, and she felt dizzy with the fear and pain and questions. Swaying on her feet, she moved toward the center of the room to see her Master. Her legs felt heavy, and she felt herself sinking down.

She fell in and out of consciousness as more pains seized her, and the fever overtook her body like it always did. The stomach pains were not the worst. She squeezed her eyes tightly shut but could not contain a loud whinny as a particularly fierce contraction coursed through body.

The door opened and closed in fluid motion, and then he was there. *Master. He had come.*

"I knew you would come, Master," she choked before another agonizing contraction gripped her.

"Of course. I had to check on my special girl. The pain is almost over. And then you can rest. But remember this is the last big part of this wave of sickness, alright. You have to push, and then it will all be over. Then you can have your special honey cake and ale. My workers are preparing it now." Master turned and nodded to a man at the door who hurriedly slipped out to fetch help.

Master patted her cheek softly. Her eyes fluttered open. She caught a glimpse of his smile. *Why did his smile never quite reach his eyes?* Then another pain gripped her, stealing away her thoughts. She was close.

"Push, my special girl. Push, Zola," Master whispered.

And she did.

***

Along with the others, Lyrianna gaped as Trinidad shared his other findings.

"There are more?" Vikaris sounded an odd mixture of fury and bewilderment. It seemed unfathomable. *How could Narco get away with it?*

After Lyrianna's commanding of the room, Trinidad had begun.

"I know my news regarding the possibility of 'winged ones' beyond the Desert came as a shock to you earlier."

Lyrianna blinked at the mention of them. That seemed like an eternity ago. *Had that truly been this morning?*

So much had happened since then. The discovery of the news, the emotions it wrought, the terror from an attack, and the odd, satisfying release that came from standing up to those closest to her. Well, it was better they knew now. She felt emboldened. She would not go back to passivity. No, she had never been the meek girl that some females were, but on the other hand, she had also never stood up to Vikaris so openly... and to the Unicorn Regent, for that matter. She still couldn't believe herself.

She turned in her seat, stifling a yawn, and caught a glimpse of Vikaris and Elsra. Lyrianna had the distinct impression that the Regent was avoiding eye contact. She smiled inwardly, pleased by the result of her tirade. *Let them squirm and wonder.*

Trinidad continued his recitation, and Lyrianna tried to focus on him.

"I know much of this is speculation, but I do assure your Majesties that I do believe I have substantiated evidence as well," Trinidad began formally.

Vikaris nodded, encouraging him to continue. Trixon took up guard near the door "to protect them," though Lyrianna had a feeling he wanted a clear escape route if things escalated.

Trinidad continued, "You have all heard that while I was captured, Narco…" Lyrianna shivered at the mention of his name. Trinidad turned his serene gaze to meet hers, so strong was the affection in his eyes for his fellow captive. "He used a paste of some kind which dulled my senses and consciousness after removing my horn."

Trindad's voice took on a steely edge. "Upon our return, I have been spending much of my time with Lei… and in the library. When I asked Lei about the medicine used, he was very interested. He explained that it would have been very difficult for Narco—and his minions—to have happened upon a successful paste without having first tested it on another. Otherwise, how could they have been truly sure I was sedated? That was my first clue."

Vikaris leaned forward, the candlelight enhancing the brilliance of his eyes. Lyrianna reached for his hand, giving it a gentle squeeze. Despite her outburst, she felt nothing but love for the man and feared what Trinidad might say. She needed Vikaris's comforting presence, especially when forced to remember the halls of the palace under their current tenant. Vikaris squeezed back, smiling warmly.

Returning his attention to Trinidad, Vikaris inquired, "And what was your second clue?"

"After Lei made this observation, it set me to thinking. As I had been in such an apathetic trance for much of my time at the Castle, it is all a bit blurry... to my great shame," Trinidad lamented, "though, there were a few instances that I heard a voice somewhere singing. Sometimes I thought I heard Narco speaking to a prisoner nearby. I never saw any other prisoners, but I knew there were more in the Castle."

Lyrianna nodded, thinking bitterly of the caged female chattel that she and Trinidad had rescued in their escape. She shuddered. Cela had become a good friend... well, maybe protector was a better word for her. She devoted herself to Lyrianna and her safety. It was comforting really, though Lyrianna did wonder if Cela had flung herself into duty so as to protect herself, too. By staying busy, Cela didn't have to sit quietly remembering *that* abhorrent day. *I wonder if she does think of it?*

Vikaris cleared his throat before speaking, pulling Lyrianna from her recollection.

"So, what does any of that have to do with the paste... or us for that matter? I mean no disrespect," Vikaris added hastily, "However, it is growing late, and I really do need to check in with my guards. Can you please get to the point?"

Elsra rolled her eyes but didn't speak. Lyrianna dropped Vikaris's hand, indignantly. *That man! What audacity*, she fumed. *Was he raised in a cave or in a castle?*

Trinidad looked as if he wanted to retort but then thought the better of it. He sighed loudly, his weariness evident in his stature. "You are right. Forgive me, Your Majesty."

Lyrianna began to interrupt, saying Vikaris was the one who should apologize, when Trixon strode over.

Glaring and snorting near Vikaris, he pushed his way through the group to stand near his father. Trinidad, stooping some, leaned on Trixon for support. He nuzzled him affectionately.

"Please, Father, continue," Trixon's low voice thundered, and Lyrianna was pleased to feel her husband flinch. Trixon's admonishment had been clear.

"As it were, there are a few occasions where I remember quite clearly seeing a cart full of hay in the hall nearest my cell. I remember hearing a servant woman say to the guard that it was for *her,* and that she needed more when her time came. Now, you can imagine that in my mental state, I had written it off as fabrication. A hallucination perhaps. Yet, after I spoke with Lei, instances such as I just described began to pop up in my memory."

Lyrianna would not give Vikaris the pleasure of seeing her yawn, especially after he had acted so insolently, yet the hour was waning. *Where was Trinidad headed with this?*

"Thirdly, beyond Lei's observation and my now returning—yet fuzzy—-memories, I also found a list of names of the missing ones after the attack at the Castle, and, well… after finding the missing centaurs and nymphs from the Castle as we escaped, it leaves me to suspect that there may be others imprisoned."

"So, what are you saying, Trinidad? Just say it out right. Who do you think Narco is housing?" Vikaris said, tersely, rolling his neck with impatience.

"It is my opinion, and that of Lei's… and my Mother's," his eyes swept over Elsra, who stood still, "that Narco has had unicorns in captivity before… and very likely still does."

Lyrianna gasped. Her head spun with questions as she tried to piece together what Trinidad divulged. Now that Trinidad mentioned it, she had heard strange sounds a few of the evenings. She remembered quite clearly hearing a young creature's cries. She had thought it came from outside. Maybe a wild bird or … but what if it had not been? What if it had been a… *No, that is impossible.*

"Lyrianna, what is it?" Vikaris grabbed her hand again, exclaiming, "Your hands are like ice. What is the matter?"

She drew a shaky breath, still so unsure of what any of this meant. "I believe Trinidad is speaking the truth." Quickly she shared how she had on multiple occasions heard a sound much like that of a whinnying foal, and as she met eyes with Trinidad, she knew he, too, had heard them.

"A foal? But why would Narco have a foal at his palace? You had said you suspected he had a prisoner, not a… a… what can this mean?" Vikaris asked.

They all fretted over this, but quick as a flash, understanding came upon Lyrianna.

"He is breeding them," she whispered, horrified. "Just like the women we found outside. He is creating a new group of unicorns, loyal to him. If he cannot get you to change your allegiance, he will make new ones that know only him."

Trinidad slumped heavily upon Trixon at this. He was nodding with her but could not say anything more. Elsra had unshed tears in her eyes.

Shock pervaded.

"Creator, help us. Let it not be so," Vikaris whispered, clutching Lyrianna's hand.

***

Zola was in the throes of sickness. She knew that if she could push a little harder, whatever was bothering her would finally pass, and she would be rewarded for her bravery. Master always said so. Squeezing her eyes tightly, she focused everything she had on ridding herself of the sickness. The tumor. *Push!*

And then it was over. The mounting pain lessened. The waves of torment slowly receded, and numbness was sure to return.

But this time it didn't. Lying there, opening one eye and then the other, she lifted her head from the damp straw.

"Master?" she whispered aloud, looking around. Her vision and mind seemed foggy from the pain, but finally her eyes and mind connected.

Master stood apart from her inspecting something in the hay, near the door. She blinked to gain focus.

What is that? She wondered to herself lethargically. There was a dark wet object lying on the ground. She didn't recall it being there before. Her eyes traveled to the two attendants nearest Master. They were bending down wiping at the strange thing with rags.

Where is my honey cake and ale? she wondered. That was part of her healing, Master had always told her, though now that she thought of it, she couldn't actually remember the taste of either. *When did they usually bring them?* As she tried to recollect the taste of said foods, the object on the ground jerked. It moved!

Zola's eyes widened with surprise. *What is that... wait, it cannot be,* she thought to herself. She felt so strange. The fact that she had this much time to think seemed bizarre. *It is not usually like this,* she realized. *Is the sickness getting worse? Is Master mad at me? Is this a trick?*

Questions swirled as she watched what seemed impossible slowly rise before her eyes.

She raised her head higher in alarm, as a tiny black creature tottered. She whinnied softly, confused, scared, and upset with Master. *What is going on?* she asked herself once more, but ceased questioning when a small, clear voice spoke into her mind.

Mama?

Her aquamarine eyes met the hopeful, coal black eyes of a tiny being. As if the word peeled back the layer of fog which had obscured her mind for cycles, it all suddenly became clear. A child. *My son...* she began to stand up, bumpily, as if her body wouldn't cooperate as her mind wished it to. *Why was she so weak?* She was a unicorn. She remembered now. *I am a unicorn... and I am a mother.* With each thought, with each breath, she felt the daze clearing away. A surge of maternal love and adoration for the little one swept over her. She had to get up. She had to move. Her eyes looked from Master to her son's. The little colt was teetering on his legs as he tested out a few steps in her direction.

"PORRIS!" Master bellowed. She had never heard Master use that tone. She didn't like it.

She quickly regained her footing and approached the timid colt. She nuzzled the small sweet face, deeply inhaling the scent of him, and felt a tiny stub at the crest of the little one's forehead, much like her own.

My horn! It is missing. Clarity dawned. *The scarf,* she realized. *They have been covering up what they did. They must have taken it from me. But how?*

As she sought mental clarity, Master dashed in grabbing the colt, yelling contemptuously at his assistant. She lurched for her son but was suddenly caught by another wracking contraction as the final afterbirth passed. She swayed in agony but continued standing. Her colt. She had to get to her colt. She ground her teeth in determination, staggering toward Master, whose eyes gleamed with… with what? Not the tender love she had always imagined there, but… something else. Something foreign to her. It chilled her.

"You idiot! You filthy vermin! You were supposed to put the ointment on her immediately after the birth! Morta always does. You imbecile!" Master screamed, dragging her colt away toward the door. Porris hurried toward her, his face whiter than her own, as he held out a tremulous hand to calm her.

In an instant she saw the threat for what it was. It was not Porris. As her eyes locked on Master's, she saw him for the first time. Master was a liar. And he was afraid.

Master is afraid of me? She balked at that momentarily, suspended with disbelief and disillusionment. *Her Master?* The man whom she had worshipped for years? He was no protector… he was the threat. And he was taking her child away from her.

"Dabor!" Master yelled.

Zola shrieked in maternal panic as a giant beast materialized in the doorway and grabbed the bulk of her son from Master's arms. Her son disappeared into the hall as Master slipped out behind them.

NO, she slammed into Porris, who hovered near her, trying and failing to press the ointment into her stub. He fell screaming as she trampled over him crossing the expanse and slamming into the door—all the while cramping seized her mid-section—the door closed seconds before she crossed the distance.

Master slammed the cell door in her face. Master had taken her child. She screamed and pawed at the metal door with more ferocity than she ever thought herself capable of, but to no avail. They had locked it from the other side.

"Master! My son! Why are you doing this? Give me back my son!"

Mama? Mama!

Zola's bereft wails thundered off the stone floor and castle walls.

I will find you. Mama is coming, she called telepathically, without a regard for how or why that was even possible. Biting off her wails long enough to reply, in hopes that the tiny colt could hear her, she continued. *Mama will save you. I promise. I promise. I promise.*

Zola's front legs pummeled the door. Never had she felt such reckless, wild emotion. Such anger. Master had kept her numb. All these years. A *sickness*, he had said. *Such brazen lies!*

Wracking sobs overtook her in her weakened condition, and she collapsed to the floor. Closing her eyes, she savored the image of the colt. *Her child!*

In a tumult of questioning, she knew only a few things for certain. For one, she had been living in a drugged state of captivity for years without recollection of much of it. She glanced back at Porris's mangled corpse and then to the bloodied, soaked hay where she had labored and passed the after birth. *How had she become pregnant? How was it even possible?*

The second thing she knew for certain was that she must see her son again. Picturing the tiny life, she wondered, too, why his coat was so much darker than hers. Unicorns possessed the silvery brilliance of the moon, though admittedly, she was not sure she had ever seen any other unicorn. The thought filled her with even more questions. *Was that how all newborns appeared? Or was this another trick of Master's?* Though she could not pinpoint it, she knew in her core that she was a unicorn, and that meant she was special and powerful. The invocation of that word reinforced her fervor. It strengthened her.

This also meant that her Master had lied to her——had been lying to her the entire time. There was no sickness. There was no rebel King trying to harm her. The only blight in this world was Master.

Maddened with maternal rage and the swirling emotions, she whispered, "I am going to kill you, Master," again eyeing the bloody mess which had formerly been her Master's aide. *I will kill anyone who tries to keep me from my son.*

And then another thought filled her with such dread and grief that she gasped. *What if there are more?* She had had the "sickness" for as long as she could remember. Truthfully, that was all she could remember. There must be more.

She tried reaching out with her mind for any nearby unicorns but only heard Castle bells.

CHAPTER 9

The Latch

Antonis slowly lowered himself onto his bed. It had been a tiresome, frustrating day to say the least. Rolling his thickly muscled neck from side to side, he heard the familiar pop.

"I am getting old," he muttered to himself, grunting with the strain of stretching his left shoulder. After the fight, he had spent much of the day searching the Fortress and grounds, organizing the guards, and collecting the whereabouts of every single creature on Kaulter. With Garis and Kragar both back at the Nav'Arian Camp, Antonis was unopposed in his authority over the King's protection, which he believed extended to protecting the entire Council, as well. He had found where the perpetrators had entered the Fortress. Two guards' throats had been slit. He grimaced at the memory as he began methodically cracking each knuckle on his right hand before moving to his left.

If Carn spoke the truth, they had used a "key" to gain access to the portal. Lei had employed many aides to scour the archives for any mention of the word *key*. Besides the unicorn horn, it was nearly impossible to gain entry—*except for Seegar*, Antonis mused, trying to recall what it was Seegar had said at the Portal. *No*, he chided himself. *Do not start pointing fingers. Seegar is like a saint around here. The unicorns have entrusted him with admittance.* He then recalled what Darion had yelled. *Azalt.* Perhaps that was the "key"? Though he made a mental note to ask the King and perhaps try the word at the portal himself, somehow, he didn't think that was it. Darion was the Marked Heir, and the royal Mark and Ruby could gain one entry. There was something here that he was missing.

"Bah," he stood up quickly. What he needed to do was sleep, yet he felt too on-edge. He needed some sort of outlet for his frustration. Quickly tugging off his tunic, Antonis got into position, as per his daily routine. "One, two, three…" he counted softly as he began his push-ups.

A knock sounded at the door. Antonis was up, striding to the door before he remembered he had no shirt on. He gripped the dagger at his belt, throwing open the door.

"Yes," he answered curtly, expecting an orderly or one of Elsra's guards, but prepared for worse if need be.

"You have kept up a nice physique over the years," a woman's voice purred.

Aalil stood nonchalantly outside his room, her tight leather vest revealing the top portion of her tanned breasts, and a small gap of skin between her tight-fitted pants. Her taut stomach peeked out from the vest, and though she had worn it all day, Antonis gulped at the sight of her. Her now unfastened dark hair cascaded over one shoulder, and she eyed him boldly, sticking out her proud chin. Antonis stood awestruck by the effect it had on him. The air felt electric. They had been skirting such desire since his return many weeks ago. It just never seemed like the right time.

"Well," she said softly. "Are you going to invite me in?" A seductive grin, one that played upon her lips, had not been there hours before when she loudly chastised one of the errant guards.

Antonis nodded dumbly. He had not had a woman in his quarters in a very long time. She slid through the doorway like a cat, and she smelled of crisp soap and rose petals. The thought set Antonis's mind alight as he fumbled with the doorlatch, turning toward her without delay.

She patted the seat near her on his bed. Averting his eyes, he instead asked, "So... uh... what brings you by at this hour?"

Aalil laughed throatily and smiled wickedly.

"I think you know." Her grey eyes shadowed by the low lighting ensnared him. He couldn't look away, practically falling over at the heat in her tone... and eyes as she slowly looked him up and down.

Carefully, he sat next to her, momentarily questioning if this was a good idea. *What does she want after tonight?* he wondered. *I am technically her commanding officer. What would Vikaris say if he found out?*

But all worry and thought of Vikaris vanished as Aalil's long fingers began to untie her leather vest. Unaware of even moving, he closed the distance between them and lifted her onto his lap to kiss her face, her neck, and her breasts that had just gloriously escaped their fastenings.

She sighed in his ear as he kissed her throat. Her skin tasted of roses, and he felt intoxicated by the many emotions filling him. He kissed her passionately, not holding back. Her mouth tasted even better, like mint leaves that she must have chewed prior to coming to his room. The realization struck him. *She came here for this one purpose.* She desired him, and that increased his own yearning tenfold.

As she straddled him, he felt her skin upon his, and he nearly crushed her when he rolled her onto the bed, tugging at her leather pants while she returned the gesture. Before either of them knew it, they were in the throes of ecstasy, riding the waves together. Without words, they looked at one another with such intense passion that it seemed far more than intercourse. An exchange had been made, and Antonis vowed that this was the woman for him. This lithe warrior with the taut stomach and stiff uppercut aroused more feelings in him with just a glance than all the other women he had encountered over the years. The one night they had spent together years ago had seemingly set them on a path for the future.

With eyes closed, she stretched languidly before relaxing into his muscled arms. They had hardly spoken at all but instead lay together in the quiet stillness before dawn. No words could explain what had taken place. Their interlocked fingers occupied one hand, leaving Antonis's right hand to trace around her chest, arms, and stomach. Antonis's eyelids grew heavy, and he felt Aalil sinking into a deep sleep within his arms.

Something squirmed near Antonis.

Startled, his eyes snapped open while his hands reached instinctively for his dagger, confused by what he saw. Until he remembered the previous evening. Entwined with him and the tangled bedding was none other than Aalil. Her raven black locks spilled across her back as she gave him a lazy smile. One breast slipping out of the covers as she reached to stroke his stubbled cheek.

"Good morning," she said, stifling a yawn. Her eyes sparkling.

"Hello, Gorgeous," he murmured, tilting her face toward his. His kiss turned into a trail of kisses, and before he knew it, she was on top of him, and the two were joined in rhythmic undulation. Her moans of pleasure filled him with pride, for they confirmed a mutual lust. This was more than a fantasy. It was...

"Ah, shit, not again," a country voice drawled before footsteps sounded clumsily, and the door to Antonis's room slammed.

"Rick?" Antonis called, turning from Aalil momentarily.

Mortified, Antonis looked back at her and tried to detach himself from her embrace. Her unabashed satisfaction said it all. *The vixen!* She firmly placed her hands on his chest and began moving her hips once more.

Antonis paused momentarily with indecision. Then his eyes rolled upwards with pleasurable anticipation as his head sunk back into the pillows. Nothing had ever felt this good. He *should* see it through. *Aalil is right, Rick can wait. This,* he matched his hips with the quickening pace of hers, *this definitely cannot.*

***

Rick knew he shouldn't be upset with his friend. He wasn't truly jealous, after all. It was just that this was something that had not crossed his mind yet. He fixated on the loss of Carol, trying to remember her every detail—and then there was that flaming anger at Darion for abandoning him. He hadn't enough time or emotional energy left to think of his *own* future. What Aalil and Antonis now shared is something that Rick would never have again. There could be no other woman. There had always been just one. *His Spring Flower.*

He shook his head, clearing the despondency which threatened to enshroud him in gloom. He needed to move on, as impossible as it seemed. He was a Royal Keeper… *a rather rotten job I have done,* he thought morosely. Since their return—which as it turned out, appeared to have been a ploy from Narco rather than the unicorns calling them back—he had been injured and fallen into a coma, his wife had been murdered, and his son had run off with a reckless unicorn. *All in all, it has been a shit-filled return,* he concluded matter-of-factly.

But today, his King had commanded he attend him, and Rick had no choice but to accept. The King had requested he and Antonis meet him in the Library. Rick was relieved by this choice, for it had been in the royal apartments that Carol was killed. He vowed to never set foot in that room again.

"Good Morning, Riccus," a familiar voice rumbled from behind. Rick slowed his pace, speaking before sighting his friend.

"And to you, Trixon," Rick replied. Then as an aside he added, "I am sorry I did not respond to the call-to-arms yesterday. By the time I got there, it was too late."

Trixon shook his head, stopping in front of Rick. "You do not need to apologize to me, Riccus," Trixon said.

Rick knew he was most likely reading his mind as well. He tried to avoid picturing his reaction to yesterday's attack when he had heard the gonging of the bell. He had sat in a corner of the room holding Carol's pillow and a dagger.

The unicorn's tone softened, "My friend. It is good to see you up and out of your room. Carolina would have wanted that, you know."

Rick flinched at the casual mention of her name. He knew she wouldn't have tolerated his moping but hearing it from Trixon stung. The unicorn didn't say it flippantly, but honestly, he knew, for Trixon had known Carol almost as long as Rick had.

Yesterday had been sobering. The warning bell had triggered everything from that abominable day. It brought up every sadness that he had been stuffing down. He even shredded Carol's pillow until there was nothing left. He cried every last tear in his body and slept on the hard floor scattered with goose feathers.

This morning he awoke feeling weak, stiff, and far sadder than he thought humanly possible. Though he was no longer incapacitated by his grief, he felt empty now. He shaved for the first time in weeks. He then bathed, dressed, and ate a small meal of pears and cheese, when the King's messenger arrived.

The messenger!

That is why he had gone to Antonis's room himself. The messenger had said he had knocked on the Commander's door repeatedly, but there had been no answer, so he had to resort to Rick.

He stopped walking. "Aaahhahahaha," Rick erupted, laughter bubbling out. Trixon's eyes widened as he paused to watch Rick.

"What is so funny?" Trixon asked with an awkward cheek twitch. Rick knew at once that Trixon had just watched the scene play out in Rick's mind.

"No answer," Rick wheezed. He clutched his stomach, which was beginning to hurt. "There was no answer because—" at this, both he and Trixon laughed loudly and without abandon. Their chuckles bounding throughout the fortress.

"Hey, what is going on?"

Rick made an unintelligible sound as his hand shot out to grasp Trixon's neck for support. He collapsed laughing against the King's steed, who now shared in the mirth.

Footsteps had ceased behind them, and Rick finally cracked an eyelid to spy Antonis, crimson-faced, bulky arms crossed, and glaring.

"What is happening here?" Antonis spluttered. "You have hardly left your room in days, and now you are out here laughing like a loon... making a scene. Is everything alright?" His commanding voice filled with concern. "Trixon, do we need to take him somewhere? To lie down, perhaps?"

"Oh, nice of you to ask. Yes, I did want to speak to you, Antonis. That is why I came to your room and walked in on... quite a scene."

Antonis's hands shot up defensively, looking around while simultaneously shushing him. "I know, I know, what you saw.... No need to tell the whole world about it." A dark flush crept into Antonis's cheek as he scowled and rubbed a hand over his goatee. "Why not knock next time?" he whispered harshly.

"Aahahahahahahahahahaha," Trixon roared now, and Rick slid down to the ground holding his stomach as gales of laughter wafted upwards.

Heads were beginning to pop out of nearby rooms. A few guards who had been at the other end of the main hall walked toward them.

"I said, 'Shhhhh'... Shut up, Rick," Antonis ordered, his voice taking on a panicky note.

Rick watched his friend stand in discomfort and genuine confusion.

"I did knock... a few times, actually. And so did the messenger who came to fetch me," Rick rasped. Despite his efforts to choke back the laughter, tears streamed down his face. "The door was unlocked."

"Oh." Antonis sheepishly paused, his hand cupped around his mouth for a moment as a look of realization hit him. "I guess I overlooked the latch." All bravado dropped.

"You must have been a little preoccupied," Trixon murmured as Antonis helped Rick to his feet.

Rick clapped his oldest friend on the back, "Yes, Trixon, I would say that he was."

A new expression replaced the look of panic on Antonis's face. "Yeah, I would say that I was," Antonis grinned with a wink. "I certainly was."

The party continued chuckling down into the musty lower level of the Fortress. As Rick entered the library to greet his King, he realized it was the first time in weeks that he had gone a few moments without thinking of Carol. He smiled at the awareness, knowing it's exactly what she would have wanted, just as Trixon had said.

CHAPTER 10

The Foray

"So, let me get this straight," Darion started, "my uncle came here and killed a... a dragon! And got away with it?"

"Yes, he killed my brother years ago. I know it was him. Salimna was drugged and gutted and left for the scavengers."

Darion sucked in a quick breath at Zalto's vehemence. After having had an hour or so of civil discussion, he had almost forgotten the wild chase through the forest. Almost. It was hard to completely forget as portions of the nearby forest blazed. Neither the girls, the unicorns, nor Zalto seemed phased by the flames, probably because they sat so near a pool of water which was surrounded by a natural rock formation. Darion supposed they would be fine, but having come from Oregon, the sight of a burning forest didn't sit well with him. Or his respiratory system.

He glanced over at Edmond, who hadn't spoken more than two words since their chase. He had eyes for one thing, Ati, the strawberry-blonde beauty. Darion rolled his eyes at his lovesick friend mooning over a girl. *Geez, he's so immature...*

"Would you care for some more, Darion?"

He smelled her presence before she spoke. Nala. He fumbled for words, watching her perfectly white smile flash before his eyes and her brown eyes twinkle with amusement. Her mouth twisted wryly, instantly revealing that left dimple. She studied him—until he nodded and clumsily thrust out the cup she had produced earlier.

The golden liquid swirled and steamed as she poured it. Whatever it was—likely honeyed water, with maybe a dash of some other flavor, heated over the small campfire that Zalto had obliged them with—it was delicious.

Triumph and Zalto exchanged more formal, yet intrusive questioning, trying to understand the other's presence.

From what they had gathered, Zalto believed Narco had crossed the Desert those years ago, luring his brother—this Salimna—into a trap. He then stole a dragon egg before drugging Salimna and carving out the beast's heart. Zalto also shared that there was a trail of blood some feet from the slain Reoul, the name that Zalto called his kind, scoffing at the casual label of "dragon." *Reoul* came from the "Old Tongue" he claimed. He believed that blood had been collected as well.

It made sense. It sounded eerily similar to Xenia's death, as Triumph had shared. Soren had agreed and relayed more of the grisly details of *that* particular murder scene. Darion shivered just thinking of it.

The dragon and unicorn seemed to be sizing one another up. Both judging... but not finding anything untoward.

"Excuse me," Darion interrupted.

Triumph gave a quick jerk of his head, trying to cut Darion off, but the teenager refused. Darion tired of listening to elders. He was the Marked Heir, for goodness sake, and had been traveling here for weeks upon end for this purpose. Answers! *To hell with diplomacy. I can talk if I want—and I will*, he shot to Triumph.

"Why then, didn't you ever cross the border? You just let him get away?" Darion asked, his question directed at Zalto.

A taloned fist slammed the earth, raking huge tendrils across the otherwise unblemished beach. "Not by choice," Zalto growled through clenched teeth.

Nala came and stood beside Darion. She placed her hand on his shoulder and gave him a solid squeeze. He got the message. Whatever it was, she was warning him not to pry.

Darion sighed. Silently, he watched the dancing flames of the campfire. No one but Ati moved. Nearest Zalto, she sat quietly speaking with him, stroking his thick, scaled neck. He rested his head upon his forearms, clearly trying to get a hold of his temper.

Darion couldn't figure any of this out, especially the girls and how they fit into it. All they had surmised thus far was that Narco had killed a winged one, which they had already had a strong suspicion about before beginning their quest. A dragon sat in front of them, and all Triumph wanted to ask about was hunting and seasonal rains. *Weather, seriously. But okay, I'm the bad guy because I want to get to the bottom of this.*

You go too fast, my Prince. You're too rash. Look at him. He is barely holding it together. He mourns his brother greatly. Your question was sound, but make sure your motive and senses are sound as well. We don't want to anger him again. The heavy burning-forest smell still hanging heavy in the air reminded them of the previous upset.

Darion knew Triumph spoke wisely, and once again he felt like the ignorant pupil. When would he ever grow up? *I'm the Marked Heir… freaking act like it,* he scolded himself.

"Forgive me, Zalto," Darion began, "I didn't mean to pry earlier. I just wondered, can you tell us the reasoning for staying here and not crossing the border? Our people do not know of your kind. Can you tell us of the truce or reason you've stayed? Or how you've come to have human companions?" Darion inquired, motioning toward the girls. He had almost said "slaves," though he hoped that were not the case. *What were the girls to the dragon? And how had he come across them?*

That was… better, Triumph begrudged.

The dragon sucked in air, as if preparing himself for a lengthy response. Darion leaned back, glad to see it.

A piercing howl filled the night sky.

Zalto smoothly spread his wings wide. "That is the alarm. We must go," Zalto ordered, "all of us. You will join us at our home to meet and discuss our leaders."

Darion and Triumph knew that had not been a request. Nala and Ati strode over to stand near them.

"We will bring them, Father," Ati replied reassuringly. Her sweet, soothing voice seemed to have a calming effect on Zalto. Something had set off the alarm, and Darion didn't need his heightened senses to see that Zalto was tense.

"See that you do, Daughter," Zalto said commandingly, eyeing the boys and unicorns, repeating to them, "See that you do."

And then he was off! The wind buffeted the beach as Zalto climbed higher and higher into the sky. With the night shadows, the fading flames in the forest, and the looming dragon overhead, Darion could not fathom ever trying to kill one of these incredible creatures. *How did Narco do it?* He shuddered knowing that the act itself had shaped Darion's entire life thus far while wreaking havoc and torture on all of Nav'Aria.

Darion grabbed his pack, and as he did, he choked at the sight of Ati kneeling down helping Edmond with his things. Though dark, Edmond's cheeks burned, and he was stuttering like an idiot. *He is gonna blow the only chance he has at impressing her,* Darion thought sardonically, preparing himself to follow after Zalto.

"Do you need help with that?"

Darion gulped. While he had been watching Edmond, his arm and shirt sleeve had become tangled in his pack, and Nala had come to assist him. Cursing himself, he forcefully pushed his arm through and shook his head.

"I got it, but thanks," he said shortly, hoping he sounded cool and confident. She tilted her head for a moment, again resembling an owl inspecting its prey. He thought he detected a flicker of... humor? Mirth? But just like that it was gone, and she became sweet and proper, her face perfectly fixed and head nodding politely while guiding them to the Reoul's home.

"This way," she called. "We have a long night ahead of us."

Nala and Ati walked ahead of the party, quietly whispering to one another. Every once in a while, Ati would look back at Edmond shyly. Nala never looked back.

Darion ground his teeth in frustration. *Who cares if she never looks back at me? I'm not here to impress a girl.*

Ha! Keep telling yourself that, my Prince.

Darion turned to glare at Triumph, though the unicorn feigned ignorance and leaned in closer to speak with Soren. Darion turned back suspiciously, knowing they were most assuredly speaking about the boys. A loud, unceremonious snort came from Soren, and Darion knew with absolute certainty that the unicorns were discussing them. He glared again for good measure, then elbowed Edmond.

"Snap out of it, dude," Darion whispered tersely, "Haven't you ever seen a pretty girl before?"

"I have never seen anyone as pretty as *her*," Edmond said, his voice sounding uncharacteristically whimsical.

Darion rolled his eyes.

Another loud snort came from the unicorns. Darion furrowed his brow and distanced himself from the lovesick youth and the chortling unicorns. As if sensing his approach, Nala turned toward him. She gave him a warm smile, and Darion felt his knees going weak. He glared even harder at that. Her smile widened as if she were the one who could read minds.

"Join us, Prince," she whispered kindly, the twinkle in her eye hinting at much more than mere civility. Darion gulped again, nodding as he joined the two foreign beauties. All thoughts of his friends left his mind as he inhaled the intoxicating scent of Nala and listened to her warm, husky voice describing her home.

As they continued their evening walk, the party rounded a bend, giving themselves a striking view of the immense sky, gilded with stars. The land had smoothed out. They had followed a shallow stream for much of the walk, and Darion was struck by the sheer volume of stars above.

"Wow," Edmond murmured nearby. The boy had apparently gathered his courage and come to join Darion with the girls. "I've never seen so many stars."

Darion looked at him, remembering the bits of history he knew from Edmond's earlier life. He knew he had grown up in the Stenlen, a forced labor community overseen by the Rav'Arians and trolls. Darion shuddered at the mere thought of it. His own life had been a dream in comparison.

Darion looked at the stars again, renewed with a sense of wonder, his friend's awe infectious. In Oregon there had been starry nights, but much of the views had been obstructed by towering trees or shaded by clouds. The sight of so many stars in the openness left him feeling insignificant as he searched skyward. He couldn't exactly put his finger on it, but he felt… well, he felt something. As if the Creator really was up there, watching him and nudging him to keep going.

I hope you're up there too, Mom.

He pictured Carol's sincere smile, with her auburn hair. He could remember each facet of her face and hoped that never changed. His fingers itched to grab his notebook and sketch right now, before he forgot any minute details of her petite image.

Darion glanced back to the others, only now realizing that Nala had been speaking.

"I'm sorry. What did you say?"

She tilted her head again silently. She studied him, opening her mouth, and then closing it again. When she spoke, she surprised him, and he had a feeling that that was not what she had initially said.

"You have lost someone? Someone dear to you?" she asked softly.

Darion bit his cheek at the verbal mention of his thoughts. Of his mother.

"Yes," he whispered. His voice, heavy with emotion, sounded hoarse in his own ears.

She nodded but kept her eyes focusing upward.

"I, too, have lost someone. I can feel your grief. It will pass," she paused, meeting his eyes, "but the pain will never go away. It will leave a dull ache in you for the rest of your days. I am sorry you have to know this pain." At that, she reached over and took his right hand, examining it briefly before squeezing it with both of her own and placing a kiss directly on his Marked finger.

"May you know peace, Prince Darion," she said in a hushed, enchanting voice. A tingle ran down his spine as her soft lips met his skin.

Darion couldn't speak. A part of him wanted to tear his hand away from her grip and tell her to mind her own damn business; the other part wanted to take her in his arms and cry all the tears he'd bottled up. He did neither. He simply held her gaze and breathed slowly, memorizing every detail of the moment. The mischievous twinkle lit her eye once more as she slowly withdrew her hands, and the moment was gone.

"We are here," she announced louder for the rest of the group gathering around.

Darion looked, startled. They stood in a wide-open landscape, but now that he looked more closely, he saw a cliffside and rocks jutting into a sort of wall in the distance. And as he looked ever closer, knowing his senses were stronger than that of his peer Edmond, who was looking entirely in the wrong direction, his breath caught. Wingbeats filled the air. And as he squinted at the rocks, though the night sky was pitch-black beyond the starlight, he could see winged ones circling. A great fire began to glow at the base of the rocks. He could make out the faintest outline of a dragon—a very large dragon—and he knew Zalto waited... preparing the others for the arrival of the humans and "Horned Ones."

Triumph strode next to Darion, comforted by the presence of his companion. And though Soren and Edmond were not bonded, they were friends, and Soren came to stand near him, also as if in a show of care and protection. Darion took a deep breath as they began to make their way toward the glowing light. Nala smiled, and Ati took off running toward Zalto.

"You have nothing to fear from them," Nala reassured. "They are very gentle creatures... overall."

However, as they came closer, glowing eyes filled the darkness, and Darion wasn't altogether sure the girl was sane. *Gentle?* That wasn't the word he would use when describing a dragon.

"Let's hope you're right," he murmured, entering the ring of light springing from the blaze.

CHAPTER 11

The Winged Ones

A mewling cry caught Darion's attention first.

The resplendent, terrifying scene overwhelmed Darion's senses. It was a wonder he could focus on anything. The crackling fire sizzled, growing taller and taller, devouring the shrubs and kindling, flames licking into the night air. Dragons soared overhead, some circling the great fire whilst others dove out of a crevice in the jutting rock. A smoky meat aroma filled the air. Darion's stomach growled in hungry anticipation. He could barely make out the image of lizards, birds, and what appeared to be a cat of some kind near the flames, charring on sticks outside the fire's heart. And despite that, one sound beckoned his attention. A desperate, pitiful wail.

Nala and Ati both shrieked, running toward the gathering dragons and the source of the sound. Zalto landed heavily, and the girls rushed to him, clambering onto his back for a better view. Obstructed by the crowd, Darion couldn't see what everyone was looking at, but as he and his party approached, a few of the dragons stepped back to peer at them. This allowed a narrow window through the scaled limbs and wings. Darion's eyes fell upon the wretched sight. A young dragon lay on its side, bloody trenches coursed down its neck and shredded wing. Though there were no distinguishable gender traits, Darion knew the creature near it could only be its mother. Her imploring eyes looked over the crowd before issuing hushed whispers as she tried to comfort her hatchling. Her evident love tore Darion's heart asunder, his emotions raw over Carol. *No mother should have to see her child dying*, he thought. His feet carried him closer before his mind processed what he was doing.

Gently pushing his way through, Darion—followed swiftly by Soren and Triumph—made his way to the pair. In the firelight, his Ruby began to glow at his throat. So intent upon his purpose, he didn't hear the murmurs of the gathered dragons and the commanding hush from Zalto.

Darion knelt at the side of the injured dragon. Completely unaware of the vehement, hissing glare the mother shot him, thinking him a threat to her young. Though, as she funneled fire at him, an invisible barrier formed between them. Darion shielded himself with his Marked arm to stave off the flames, and the fire died away, never touching his skin.

"Impossible," Triumph breathed aloud, his sentiments echoed by the crowd.

Darion's hands moved of their own accord. He had no idea how to help this invalid, but he knew he had to try. His senses beckoned him to the creature. All thoughts were centered on the young dragon, or Reoul. Ignoring everyone, including the mother, he narrowed his senses.

Hush, he whispered into its mind. *You are safe now.* The ragged divots pulsed with evil toxicity. Taking the Reoul's head in his hands and closing his eyes, Darion attempted to draw the youngling's pain into himself.

At once, Darion saw the pair, mother and hatchling, out for a test flight. He felt the exuberance of youth as young Gamlin touched down in an area farther than he had ever flown before.

This was his first hunt with his mother. He had never been allowed to roam this far. He would prove his worth this day, when he caught a bountiful feast.

Their barren land continued to withhold food from them. Their kind weakened and needed sustenance. Gamlin would be like the valiant Zalto—starting today! Just then, as his mother was circling overhead, he heard something. Instead of waiting for her as instructed, he bounced through the dense brush… right into a party of skulking Rav'Arians. His wings tangled in the thick vegetation, as if caught in a web. He couldn't free his wings before they were upon him. He yelled and thrashed. His talons ripping through one of the monstrous beaked creatures; his tail whipping at another. The third got close enough to strike, its metal weapon slicing through the thin membranes of his wings. The other, whom he had knocked down momentarily, staggered to its feet. Excruciating pain coursed through his left wing as he tried to shake the fiends off. He let out a scream from the burning, white-hot pain that seared through his neck and down the distance of his scales.

The magnitude of that pain dropped him, but before the others could finish him off, his mother crashed into them and slaughtered them with savage ferocity. Rav'Arians could never stand a chance against full grown Reouls. No, they preferred running to facing them in a fight. They must have thought they could overtake a youngling, though. Their eyes had held a feral, malicious glee until Gamlin's mother killed them.

Darion watched Gamlin lose consciousness and felt his mother's desperation as she roared her plea. She propped her hatchling up, carrying him all the way back to the Rocks-—alone. Darion could see it all. He internalized her struggle. Her wrath. Gamlin's anguish. The youngling's feelings of shame and fear. And in that instant, he understood that the Rav'Arians and the Winged Ones were long-time enemies. Whatever had been believed about evil Rav'Ar beyond the Shazla Desert was untrue. They really knew nothing about this land or these enigmatic creatures.

Darion, not taking his eyes from Gamlin-—nor his hands-—held him, soothing his thoughts and relaying peace to him. As he did so, Soren and Triumph stepped closer. Darion nodded for them to begin healing, and they placed their horns on the torn flesh.

A gasp arose from the crowd. The mother, Reki, had initially tried to stop them but was restrained by those nearest her. The Reouls watched in amazement as the strange foreigners surrounded young Gamlin. The Horned creatures glowed pure white light, and it seemed as if the dark, purulent wounds lightened in color.

Through his connection to Gamlin, Darion felt Soren's and Triumph's healing powers. Yet he knew they couldn't cure everything. Something remained. Something deep and insidious waited hidden, clutching possessively to the precious young life it held. Darion focused his senses on the evil, alien presence. He willed it to him—challenged it, just as he had with the viper.

The black writhing mass in his mind chortled. It was as if the poisonous hold that gripped young Gamlin was sentient. And while the unicorns' healing greatly helped Gamlin's condition, if this poison remained, the young one would most assuredly die this very night.

That really pissed off Darion. He felt his pulse racing and his temper rising.

You are nothing but a vile, weak coward that preys upon the young. Darion had no idea to whom he was speaking, but he felt it with his whole being. He was in a battle—albeit, a mental one.

He thought he heard Triumph cautioning him. *To seal his mind.* Darion ignored him.

YOU? You challenge me? The voice scoffed in a chilling voice. *Go back to your games and lusting, little Prince, and leave the challenges to me.*

Darion knew then, that Narco spoke. It had to be him. Fury exploded in Darion. When his arm blazed, a bright green light filled the darkness. *You!* He called. So consumed with anger, his voice took on a lethal edge. *Leave him out of it, Narco,* he spat. *I am coming for you. You have no more power beyond the Shazla Desert. And you will soon have no power in Nav'Aria. We are coming for you.*

"AZALT!" Darion shouted. Rocks overhead rumbled, and a few smaller stones clattered to the ground. His green eyes blazed with power as his Ruby shone and his Marked arm glowed even brighter, now revealing new and changing winged symbols.

Silence met him. Only the sound of his crashing heartbeat thundered in his ears. Darion trembled with fatigue and sagged slightly before Triumph was there nudging him. Arms tugged at his, pulling him upwards. Edmond assisted him, pulling him away from the young Reoul, though his eyes stared incredulously at the ground. For just as he stood, Darion saw what had transfixed the group. Gamlin slowly climbed to his feet. The shine to his emerald scales returning with every step. His mother's shoulders shook as she sobbed and let her brilliant golden wings encircle him.

Gamlin was alive.

"My Prince," Triumph whispered awestruck. "You are the true Marked Heir... The chosen one. The Marked Royal of prophecy. I am sorry I ever doubted," he ended in a hushed whisper.

And before Darion knew what was happening, everyone followed Triumph's lead: the various heads— human, unicorn, and dragon—bowed lowly before him, the man with the glowing arm and fierce stare.

Darion felt slight shock as even the powerful Zalto dipped his head. Darion noticed Edmond looking around sheepishly. He was most likely wondering if he should bow as well, but he chose to keep Darion standing erect, and for this Darion was thankful, for he didn't know if he'd be able to stand on his own. So great was his fatigue—and surprise. *The chosen one?*

Darion looked toward Nala and Ati, both astride Zalto's back, and thought he detected a smile emanating from Nala; though he couldn't see her face, he felt that it was there. And silly enough, that warmed him more than anything else that had taken place this night.

"Sir?" a small voice said, breaking the night's silence. "Who are you?" the voice bespoke innocence, awe… and hope. Gamlin's green scales glowed, completely healed where only moments ago evil had tainted them.

"This," a mighty voice interjected. "This is our salvation." And the group once more bowed as Zalto strode closer to Darion. "I fear I have much to apologize for. Please join me beside the fire. You look famished, and there is much to discuss." Snapping a quick look around, Reouls moved immediately, backing up and making way for their honored guests. Food and drinks appeared as if from thin air. Darion gladly took the drink proffered him and sat, though all he truly wanted to do was discuss the events with Triumph… and then sleep for a year.

What just happened?

Narco gaped as he was wildly thrown through the air and struck the nearest wall. He sat their dizzily, trying to make sense of the situation. *His little nephew had overpowered him? Impossible!*

CHAPTER 12

The Master

Narco sat against the wall for some time. He didn't know if he could stand.

He felt dazed. Weak. Vulnerable. *How did Darion do it? How could he do it? A stupid little boy from a foreign land—this Oregon.*

Morta had assured him Darion wasn't a threat. How wrong he had been, he realized as a tiny droplet of blood fell to the stone floor. He reached up hesitantly to touch the side of his head. His ear bled. The sticky redness surprised him, incredulous as he was. His stomach twisted, and for once in a very long time, sheer panic gripped him as it had so often when he was a boy.

Where are you, Morta? he wondered. Understanding for the first time, truly, that he wasn't the invincible and omnipotent being he'd worked tirelessly to fashion. After years of consuming Reoul blood and holding power over his minions, he was still just a weak, unmarked man.

Tears spilled, and he spluttered desperately. He pressed his palms against his eyes, willing back the tears… and the defeat. He needed that young Reoul. The abominable Rav'Arians had strict instructions to bring another one, alive or dead. It made no difference, so long as he had what the heart chamber held. The key to immortality. For though he possessed strength from his earliest taste of Reoul blood cycles ago, he found its potency had waned. Morta had promised he'd have immortality, but Narco feared the blood had expired. Left his system. He wanted more. He needed more.

Darion had taken that from him. Even worse, the mother of the hatchling killed his Rav'Arians, but truth be told, it made no difference. Narco knew that Darion was beyond the border... and working with the Reouls. His heart hammered. He remembered a cautioning tale from Morta regarding a Marked Royal's capabilities and command over the ancient species. *Could it really be true?*

"I will not relent," he said through clenched teeth, slapping his face and regaining his countenance. He stood up quickly, swaying lightly with a rush of dizziness. He returned to the Chalice. Upon a stone pedestal in Morta's tower stood an iron stand, covered in strange markings forming a swirling pattern. Atop the stand stood a bowl unlike any he had ever seen before, and within it was the black liquid. A putrid malevolence swayed and beckoned him with such force that it took an extreme sense of will not to succumb to it. He had been assured that the liquid could never spill, yet its torrential force within the bowl astounded him every time.

Narco held his breath, as Morta had taught him many cycles ago, and when the strange, magical liquid stilled, he slowly blew his breath around the bowl, claiming it. As he did so, he searched. With this chalice he could prey upon the minds of his citizens. His slaves. None but the Unicorns of Kaulter—or someone who had learned to guard their minds under their teaching—could avoid his presence, though admittedly, he wasn't nearly as talented with mind-searching as Morta. He pressed on, nevertheless.

Ah, he thought to himself. The vile liquid pausing in its small waves, taking shape in the center of the bowl. A horned creature appearing. A tiny speck of life.

Narco felt it calling for its mother. He couldn't have it disturbing Zola anymore. *This* was something he could control.

"Hello," he whispered into the vulnerable, apprehensive mind.

He felt a response. A recognition from the creature.

You are safe here. That beast is not your mother. Do not fret any longer about what you think you saw. I am here now. I will care for you. You must do as instructed. You must obey.

The shape squirmed under the pressure. Its shape shifting, glancing left and then right, unsure of what to believe. Inquiring. Pleading.

You may call me Master, he replied. *I am your only parent. The only one who cares about you. You must please me, and you will be rewarded with honey cakes and ale.*

He felt the tiny mind writhe. Images of an enraged Zola and a man in a black cloak appeared in its mind.

Narco pressed with his mind as he poured over the liquid the impression of himself: smiling, kind, safe, and a contrast to the beast in that chamber, the white creature— the enemy. It took only a matter of moments for the tiny will to shatter, and the creature gave in to him—as they all did.

Yes, Master, a tiny voice whispered. *I obey Master.*

"Good. You will be called Fourteen," Narco purred. "You will be my last pupil," Narco murmured, remembering Zola's enraged face. The shape in the liquid shifted, as did his thoughts, and for a moment, he heard a tiny gasp.

Mother?

"Fool," he muttered angrily. He had to focus. If he were to imagine two different creatures during the time of the liquid cast, he could merge the two parties in the liquid, bringing not only their minds to him, but also to one other. As quickly as he had done so, he banished the mother's panicky face, focusing instead on the small colt. It would do no good to bring mother and child together now. The fourteenth foal. It squirmed and wriggled again in the center, as if searching. Narco chided himself.

"Fourteen," he said forcefully, snapping the little one's attention back to himself. "You must rest now, for in the morning, I will come visit you and we will begin our studies. Does that please you?"

The little image of the black unicorn dipped its head in agreement. "Yes, Master," it whispered. "I am alone." The whimper in its voice barely contained. "I am... scared."

"You have nothing to fear, Fourteen. I will be with you soon. I promise. Sleep," and as he said it, he raised his hands. Using both, he grasped the edge of the chalice. It took sheer willpower to pull himself away from the vile, intoxicating hold of the liquid.

The black, swirling substance thrashed on its own, freed from his command for the time being. A shiver ran down his spine as he watched it move. This strange, dark magic. He had asked Morta once when he was young where it had come from, but Morta had only reminded him—forcefully—to never ask that which he could not understand. He remembered that lesson very well.

Looking around the tower chamber, Narco realized that he too felt scared. Morta's chambers held a multitude of muddled memories for Narco.

Narco felt his ear, confident that the bleeding had stopped, before swinging the door open. Outside the chamber door stood two trolls—Dabor and one other. Narco had not the desire to learn the names of these filthy creatures.

Striding from the room, the two lumbering figures followed behind him silently. They emerged from the spiraling staircase, exiting the tower to a bright sunny day. The sunlight blinded Narco. Again, he felt weak. Vulnerable.

I will not relent, he repeated to himself over and over while they strode toward the Castle doors. His retinue gathered in numbers as they exited the building, and even further still, as they neared the Castle. He contemplated whom he wished brought to his bed, for he never slept alone, when a messenger came riding up quickly.

The bearded man leapt from the horse, which skittered to a halt before the main gate of the Castle. Narco, still struggling to see in the sunlight, blinked away tears and shielded his eyes. Cursing himself, he forced his hands down. He didn't show weakness. He couldn't.

The man fell on his knees at the sight of him. Narco sneered.

You may have an injured Reoul adoring you, Darion, but do you have this? Men grovel before me. ME! You are nothing.

Though as he thought it, he remembered the force in which Darion had yelled the challenging word "Azalt." Narco didn't doubt he meant it. They needed to squash this rebellion swiftly. *Darion must die.*

As the messenger awaited permission to speak, Narco beheld the spires surrounding the Castle. Two heads adorned them there. Mangled and torn to bloody bits from the grazing black birds encircling them, the features were long since indistinguishable, though he recognized them as the man and woman who shared his bed a few evenings ago. *You will fear me, boy,* he thought darkly. *They always do.*

"Do not lie there all day wasting my time. Get up. Speak. Report," he snapped harshly.

The messenger jumped hastily to his feet, bowing lowly before speaking. "All-powerful Emperor, I bring a message from the northern scouting party in the Woods of the Willow."

Narco thought he might implode with the wait, and spittle flew from his lips, speckling the man's face. "Yes? What? What news?" The man didn't flinch.

"Your Greatness, we have found the Camp. We know where the rebels are…"

"AND?" Narco roared, adding softer, "Is Morta there? Is he alive?" He almost feared the answer, not wishing for his adviser's presence yet fearing a future without him.

The messenger was interrupted by the appearance of two horsemen. One hunched figure and one tall and proud astride their war horses. As the horses drew in, Narco could see the answer to his questions. A soldier accompanied a cloaked figure and assisted him from his horse.

Narco felt him, and gorge rose in his throat. The cloaked man's hand clasped his, squeezing with a force—a promise—of what was to come later. Cracked rough lips touched his hand, lingering as a hot breath whispered, "I humbly return to you, Lord." And softly, for only Narco's ears, he heard Morta's whispering voice, "I have missed you. I have greatly missed you."

Narco shuddered as the man's tongue flicked out to trace his knuckle before ducking his head and stepping away. The soldier, faceless in Narco's distracted mind, bowed and murmured platitudes.

Narco held his composure—barely. The cheerful sunlight, his throbbing head from his collision, and the breeze cooling the lingering wetness on his hand, all threatened his feigned calm.

"Welcome back, Morta," he announced for the guards' benefit. "Let us not stand here in the sun. You must be parched." He nodded to the guards wordlessly and turned on his heel.

Narco strode purposefully toward his Throne Room. He avoided eye contact with everyone around him. *This is what I wanted.* He needed Morta to help him kill his wretched nephew and his family, especially after what Darion had done with the Reoul.

But if that were true, why did he feel as if he were going to be sick?

***

Zola paced. She knew what she had seen. Her child had popped into her mind for a moment, and she had heard him. Not just a dream, but a connection. Master had been there too. She knew she couldn't be hallucinating.

Strangely, no one had come to see her—or collect the fat man's body—after the incident. After everything, now Master meant to leave her here, trapped, imprisoned, and alone to die with the knowledge of what he had taken from her? Could he be that cruel?

Upon knowing he communicated with her child, she felt an odd mix of fear and ire. And without the paste, she felt the slightest tingling where her horn should be. She thought she could hear voices. Were there others like her somewhere else? Others of her kind, besides her young? Or was she losing her sanity, having been deprived of food and sleep?

Who am I? She felt sure she was a unicorn but had no idea what that meant. What it could mean. She couldn't recall a life prior to this room—this cell. *Where did I come from?*

Her mind felt fuzzy after years in an apathetic trance, and though she couldn't remember anything, she felt the impression of something. A bright light. A nostalgic longing just outside of her grasp. An elusive, vague impression that there had been someone else. Someone who cared for her before Master. If only she could remember. She rolled her head around in frustration.

Her eyes fell upon the still and shallow water in her trough. The floating dead flies signifying that she, too, would die if something didn't change. The water had not been refilled since her sickness, and the fetid corpse only added to the pungency of the room. She needed to get out of here. Nothing good could come from waiting. Master had never taken this long, and after her tirade, she knew with certainty that she was no longer his precious pet. And he was no longer her adoring Master.

He was the enemy.

Searching, her eyes returned to the corpse, the matted, bloodied hay strewn about, the door... and again to the body. He had been a worker. She didn't recognize him. He was not like the creepy, red-haired figure who often came with Master.

She ran her muzzle around the corpse, pawing at his robes. It seemed too much to hope for, that a discarded key would be in his pocket, but then again, no one had come for him or searched his body.

Hurriedly, she examined the dead man. Kicking him onto his back, she thought she felt something in a deep pocket. Rolling, and pawing at it, she caught the glimpse of metal.

Can it be? she breathed. Her heart rate increasing as she nudged the key from the itchy, course fabric. It rolled onto the straw near the body. She quickly glanced back at the door.

This is too easy, she thought, but then again, it had been days and not so much as a person had checked on her. *It could work.*

She sniffed the small key. It would take great care not to drop it. Though no one seemed to be outside her cell, the clattering of metal could certainly change that.

Zola walked toward the door to inspect the lock, remembering forlornly that Master always had his minions lock the door from the other side. She knew nothing of locks—of anything really. Yet as despondency threatened to overwhelm her, she recalled Master's anger toward his worker. He had been angry that he hadn't locked the door. But the man was standing inside.

Hope swelled. *Two locks? Was that possible?*

Studying the door frame, she observed flat, metal squares, one atop the other. The top square appeared smooth and unmarked, yet the second square had an opening. Her eyes shot to the key and then back to the square with the visible keyhole.

She practically leapt, carefully picking up the key with her teeth. She felt strange using a human tool, but she understood the concept. *Insert the metal key in the opening to get the door to unlock.*

Stepping toward the door, she awkwardly—for the key was very small for her mouth—tilted her head and tried to line up the key with the hole. The key clanged on the metal square, and in her nervous state, she dropped it. Her breath caught as it clattered on the ground. She waited for guards' footsteps to come crashing toward her cell.

Silence.

There was no one there. Exhaling, she bent down to pick up the key again with her teeth. Her lips kissed the floor as they swept over the key. She righted herself and peered at the lock. With another tilt of her head, she very slowly moved the key toward the hole. This time it didn't clatter. It went in. *Now what?* she wondered. The key, momentarily suspended in the lock, jutted out. She backed away. *What usually happened when they locked it?* She remembered it always made a clicking sound, which this had not done. Perhaps that was because it was a different lock than what they usually used? Frustrated, she blew her bangs from her forehead. The unfamiliar sensation annoyed her. The bandage had always held her mane back. The air caused a tingling upon her stump. She paused at the feeling. As if led by an internal force, she felt her lips and teeth clasp the key, and in one smooth motion, she cranked it to the side as she tilted her head.

Click.

The heavy door creaked open. She gaped in amazement. She had done it. Her gaze traveled the room again. She raised her head proudly as she stared at the dead man. "Enjoy your prison. It is not mine any longer."

Then she peered around the doorway and into the hall. Empty.

Again, she thought this seemed too easy, although Master's foul character had been revealed. If she were the only prisoner down here, perhaps they had left her to rot. The idea caused seething hate to course through her body. She stepped into the dim hall. There had to be a way out around here somewhere. Thinking of her child, she searched the entire hall, knowing all along it was foolish. Master had taken the child elsewhere.

Though she knew next to nothing about life, unicorns, and motherhood—an innate maternal instinct drove her on. She felt it in her core. *I am coming,* she whispered.

Further down the hall, she found a massive stone staircase. Taking a deep breath at the sight, for she had never climbed anything so high in her life, she set her jaw firmly and quietly. She crept up the stairs to a wooden door that stood ajar. Peeking out from the doorway, she spied an empty courtyard. Unattended carts and hay bales were piled here. Her fodder's transport. The light gave her pause. It was the excruciating blindness that comes from being locked away for a lifetime. She felt terrified, out of breath, and exhilarated.

Zola ducked inside, breathing heavily. With one deep lungful, she poked her head out again, this time protectively squinting her eyes. No one was about the courtyard. She didn't waste time vacillating. For the moment she stepped outside, she felt a tugging presence. A connection. She felt *her* child. She jerked her head to the right. Farther down the lane stood a large wooden complex. Guards milled about.

There, she thought. She knew with all her being that her child had been taken there, and though Master had seemed to discard her, he was not taking any chances with her son. Her anger smoldered, and she felt as if she could kill every single one of those guards with her sheer rage— with or without her horn. Yet something stilled her.

Looking around, she saw an abandoned covered wagon lying on its side. Creeping to it, she stealthily obscured herself from view within the tattered material. She would wait until dark. It had to grow dark at some point, and that is when she would strike.

"I am here, Trigger," she murmured the name she had chosen for him, before her weariness led her to fade into a heavy, dreamless sleep.

CHAPTER 13

The Prophecy

"Let him be, Zalto."

Darion cracked an eyelid open at the warm sound of Nala's voice. The dusky sky had altered to a dazzling sunrise, filling with amber, violet, and gold.

Confused, Darion tried to recollect how he had come to lie here. He looked down to discover a woven mat, stuffed with grass and moss, nestled against a great stone wall. His pack lay snugly under his head. *It's pretty comfortable actually*, he thought.

Realizing he was basically camping with a bunch of dragons made him smile. *Dad would love this!*

He pictured Rick's face, suddenly wishing more than anything that he could share this experience with him. Guilt filled him as he thought of him—his father. *What must he think of me and Triumph sneaking off? I bet he's pissed,* he supposed sheepishly. A hand clapped his shoulder, stemming his self-loathing.

"You're up? Finally! I don't know what I am doing. There are Winged Ones and girls, and I could really use some help out here." Edmond appeared before Darion's eyes, his mouth chattering on, and all Darion could do was gawk. The laughter came then.

"I think that is the most I've ever heard you say, Edmond," Darion chided. Edmond creased his brow in a mock frown but couldn't keep it.

"Seriously," he added, sitting down to speak to Darion inconspicuously. "The girls insisted on watching over you last night. Between them and Zalto, I have been jumping at every noise. I didn't sleep at all. It is scary having a Reoul," he paused, testing out the foreign word before continuing, "a whatever it is watching you all night. Not that you would know, since you passed out…"

"Wait. I passed out?" Darion asked, slowly sitting up. He felt groggy, and as funny as it was to imagine Edmond sitting in the silence with Zalto and two pretty females, he needed to figure out what had happened to him.

"Yeah. You should have seen Triumph. He jumped up to check on you and growled-—really GROWLED-—at everyone to get back. I didn't even know unicorns could growl," he added wonderingly. "The Reouls were not too pleased, and before anyone knew what was happening, they all began to stand up and let out their own growls. And then everyone calmed down." And, as if an afterthought, Edmond added with a smirk, "That Nala of yours is spirited. She jumped into the middle of the circle and smacked Zalto on the tip of his… his… is it a nose? I don't know, do they have noses?" Edmond paused, scratching his forehead. "Uh, snout, I guess. She smacked him and yelled for everyone to sit down, and for Triumph to examine the Prince and report."

Darion's eyes widened. "And did they?"

"You bet they did. You should have seen the look on her face. You don't want to see her mad." He spluttered, adding, "Your Majesty."

Darion punched his younger friend in the shoulder. "Shut up. I've told you not to call me that, especially when we're alone." Though, he said it halfheartedly, distracted by feelings of incredulity and intimidation. *Nala? Mad?*

"What did Triumph do?"

"Oh, he looked you over. Must have checked your mind and assured everyone you were just sleeping, and then the girls hopped up and prepared you a campsite as if nothing had even happened. You have been asleep the whole time?" He sounded more impressed than anything else. "How could you sleep with all that noise?"

Darion squinted at him, only now realizing what the rumbling noises were. *Reouls!* What *were* they doing?

"What's going on out there?"

Edmond blinked and jumped back up, looking panicked. He now recalled his purpose. "Shit! That's why I woke you. Triumph sent me to fetch you. You are needed for their 'discussion', apparently… and Triumph said right away!" He motioned frantically with his big hands for Darion to hurry. "Zalto has been trying to wake you for a while, but Nala is standing guard over there,"

Edmond gestured toward the attractive young woman perched on a boulder near the cave opening. She was staring out toward the vivid sunrise.

Darion pulled on boots as fast as he could. He didn't need any prodding once he realized that the dragons were with Triumph—and they didn't sound happy.

They're arguing! And if he knew anything about his companion, he feared the self-righteous prick he called "friend" was most likely enticing them.

Triumph, he called out. *What are you doing? I'm coming. Don't be an idiot!*

A drawn-out pause greeted him.

Oh, you're awake? Triumph replied finally. *Do not trouble yourself. I have everything under control.... And I'm not being an 'idiot'... he is. Zalto is grating on my nerves. Actually, you should hurry. I think I angered him when I said that unicorns ruled the land from the time of creation until the Meridias. I was trying to explain our history. He did not need to get so worked up. It is not my fault they are ignorant of history.*

Darion rolled his eyes.

And don't roll your eyes. It is a juvenile habit. You must rise above such behaviors.

Yeah, you're a great example for proper adult 'behavior', Darion shot back.

"Hypocrite," he muttered aloud as he gathered his pack. Edmond eyed him curiously, but Darion only pointed at his head and returned the gesture. Edmond laughed with understanding.

I heard that!

Good! I'm coming. Now wait a minute before doing anything else stupid. And what about breakfast?

If there were a response from Triumph, Darion wouldn't have heard it, for the instant he and Edmond approached the cave entrance, Nala turned toward him. With the sun's morning rays dancing across her chestnut hair and clear complexion, she looked simply angelic. Breathtaking!

"Wow," Darion whispered.

Edmond snorted.

Darion felt the red blush heating his face. He tried clearing his throat and ran his hands through his unruly shoulder-length mop, hoping to feign nonchalance. Though when his eyes returned to the foreign beauty, he knew he had been caught. Ensnared by her aura. Her mischievous smile highlighting her perfectly pouty lower lip, dimpled cheek, and sparkling hazel eyes awaited him.

"Good morning, Darion," she said in greeting. "I hope you slept comfortably… it is a breathtaking sunrise, is it not?" She added with a wink before jumping down and asking him to follow her to the gathering.

Darion practically choked with embarrassment. He gave her no reply or greeting, feeling as if his tongue were made of rubber.

Edmond was silently laughing still, his shoulders shaking. Darion punched him again.

Girls!

As they descended the hillside, the light dazzled off the gathered dragons' scales. *Reouls*, he reminded himself. As incredible as they appeared with their shining scales, they were still a far cry from the pristine white coats and majesty of Triumph and Soren. Pride swelled in Darion's chest. As much crap as he liked to give Triumph, he truly viewed him like family. What a sight the pair made, surrounded by the vibrant green, red, orange, and violet scaled creatures that inhabited this rugged, rocky terrain.

He felt their eyes on him too, and he consciously tried to still his emotions, appearing tall, confident, and not in the least bit intimidated by the girl striding purposefully in front of him. Drawing nearer, he approached a circle of maybe ten or so Reouls and the two unicorns. His gaze traveled around the perimeter. A few other dragons lumbered about, doing chores. Gamlin was near the circle by his mother's side. And a few others circled above, most likely hunting or keeping watch. In total it could not be more than twenty dragons.

This can't be all of them?

Darion drew near the group, and as he did, a hush fell upon the arguing elders. Zalto clambered to his feet. His weighty bulk causing a small dust cloud as he shifted and welcomed Darion.

"Ah, there you are, Darion. I trust you slept well." His biting tone made it obvious that he did not enjoy waiting on the human.

Before Darion could open his mouth, Nala turned toward him and back to Zalto, glaring. "No thanks to you, Father," she admonished. "After last night—when he SAVED Gamlin—he most certainly needed his rest.

Now, everyone, make way and get him some food before you begin interrogating him."

Darion wouldn't have believed it if Edmond hadn't warned him. She really was quite bossy… and more surprisingly, they all did her bidding—even Zalto. Darion caught Edmond's sly glance and eyebrow wiggling and gave him a slight nod in recognition. He was right. *She is intimidating—and she is standing up for me. Why?*

Do not get too excited.

Darion glowered toward Triumph but was soon smiling again as Nala grabbed his hand, leading him to the circle. *Her hand is so soft!*

Before he knew it, he was seated next to Triumph, Edmond, and Soren, facing Zalto while Nala and Ati prepared divine-smelling plates of food. Zalto waited, though none too patiently. At one point, the elder dragon snorted so forcefully that smoke rushed forth from his nostrils. Nala glared at him.

"Nala," Zalto rumbled. "That is quite enough of your fuss. You have made your point. We will allow him time to eat."

Nala held his stare for a moment, then nodded and smiled sweetly, rubbing his scaled neck affectionately as he dipped his massive head to her.

"I know, Father," she said warmly, all traces of annoyance gone. Ati came over and wrapped her arms around him, creating an intimate picture of the trio.

Darion could tell that Zalto struggled. He could either appear intimidating or soak up the adoration from the two girls—he chose the latter.

What a bizarre relationship, Darion mused while he munched some expertly seasoned mutton and unfamiliar porridge.

It is not so strange, Triumph grumbled. *Do you think our bond, 'curious'?*

Darion pondered this, looking between Triumph and Zalto. *No… no, I don't. Though you are pretty grumpy a lot of the time. You and Zalto seem to have that in common.*

Triumph bumped into Darion, causing him to choke on his drink.

Pardon me. I must have slipped.

"You're ridiculous," Darion muttered aloud but smiled, leaning into Triumph. He took a few quick bites and sips, noticing then that everyone was watching them—Nala and Ati included. He gulped hurriedly and set down the plate.

"Sorry for taking so long," Darion began but then heard Triumph clearing his throat, and he heard his voice strengthening. *He was the Marked Heir and had healed a dragon, after all. The least they could do was let him eat. No need for apologies.*

"I am glad to see Gamlin is up and doing well," his eyes glancing toward the mother and son. A subtle reminder of what he had done for them.

That was better, Triumph encouraged.

Zalto relaxed. Appearing genuine, he replied, "Thank you for helping him, Darion. We are all grateful to you," his loud voice boomed across the expanse, and the other Reouls nodded.

"And yet," one croaky, aged voice chimed in, "we still do not understand who you are and why you are here." Darion looked around for the source. He felt a change in the gathering. A strong presence. The hair on the back of his neck prickled.

The Reouls rose yet kept their scaled heads bowed low.

"Tiakai," Zalto murmured with awe in his voice, lowering his own head in respect.

Darion stood to see the dragons parting for an ancient female. Her soft green scales matched the prairie landscape. Two Reouls stood on either side of her assisting her to the group.

Darion started when he saw Nala and Ati bowing on their knees.

The decrepid old dragon's milky white eyes met his, and though he wasn't sure if she could truly see, he felt that she could see *him*. See into him. His arm began to glow under his shirtsleeve.

"And you are the one of prophecy, I take it?"

The group gasped.

Darion stood still, breathing evenly though unsure of how to respond. And before he could decide what to do, the ancient dragon did the most unexpected thing of all. Her head drooped low for a moment. Darion feared she had fainted but then realized, along with the rest, that she was bowing her head—*to him*!

What in the world?

He felt Triumph and Soren begin to shift, as if they were going to bow, too. *Oh, stop it,* he yelled through his telepathic connection, scowling toward them. *What's going on?*

It was Soren that responded. *I think you will want to sit down for this, my Prince.*

Darion said the only thing he could think of. "Thanks everyone. Now that's enough bowing."

Nala's jaw fell open, and Darion bit his lip as Triumph bumped him again—more forcefully this time. "Err, I mean... thank you," and after no one spoke, continued, "I'm Darion. And you are?" he said, smiling at the elderly Reoul.

Nala's jaw dropped even further, and her eyes bulged before ducking her head again. Darion felt a slight flush growing in his cheeks. He really wished she'd stop looking at him like that, or else help him out here.

The ancient dragon's head slowly rose, and though her blind eyes stared dully, he knew she had not missed a thing.

"I am Tiakai. The Reoul Elder," she spoke in a soft yet regal voice. "Welcome to Rav'Ar."

***

Tiakai approached Darion, her eyes encompassing Triumph and Soren, who both in turn gave her a nod of respect. The two Reouls with her helped lower her to the ground. She let out a loud harrumph, wincing as she sat and murmuring, "these creaking bones."

No one spoke. After collecting herself, Tiakai's head swung around.

"Well, what are you all standing around for? Back to work. Back to your studies. All of you."

Reouls scurried off, some immediately launching into the air. The wind current buffeting off the cliffside. Darion and Edmond thrust their hands up to shield their eyes from the swirling dust. Darion listened as the wingbeats carried Reouls away, and others whispered in hushed voices as they went about their chores. What chores dragons might have was beyond Darion. As soon as it seemed the dust had settled, he lowered his arm. Zalto, Nala, and Ati remained. Darion was surprised. *They're allowed to stay when Reouls aren't?*

Tiakai must have realized this as well, for her head focused in their direction. "Why do you remain while all others have gone?"

Zalto began to inhale as if to reply, but Tiakai cut in. "I am not asking you, Zalto. They can speak for themselves," and added in a chiding tone, "You coddle them so."

Nala blushed and dropped her head. Darion enjoyed the sight, for it showed she was, indeed, human. All that intimidation had to have a limit!

"Oh please, Great Elder, may we stay? This is the first time we have seen ones like ourselves? We want to learn more about their kind—our kind—and where they come from." Ati's head bobbed, but her eyes remained rooted on her feet.

The ancient dragon's head cocked, studying the pair, and Darion was reminded of Elsra. *Both long-standing, powerful creatures. Were she and Elsra close to the same age? Seeing those two battle wills would be a sight!*

Tiakai's head swiveled to Zalto. Darion noted that he, out of all the dragons, didn't appear as intimidated by her.

He nodded his head, but his eyes held the milky whites. His expression unreadable, yet Darion thought he seemed solemn. Sad.

"We cannot keep them from this forever, Zalto. It is good they stayed."

Zalto's mouth opened and then clamped shut as Tiakai spoke, but he did not argue. Nala and Ati looked up with anticipation, and Nala smiled at Darion.

Darion was relieved when Triumph took the lead, for he had no idea where to begin.

"Great Elder," Triumph's voice resonated richly. "We have come from Nav'Aria and crossed the Shazla Desert in search of answers."

She nodded along as he spoke. Darion figured Zalto had already told her this, but it seemed like a good way to begin.

"Yes, yes, you have traveled very far," her voice cracked slightly, but she continued, "farther than any of our kind have in a very long time."

"You've been to Nav'Aria?" Darion blurted.

She sighed sadly. "None of us have traveled much farther than you yourself have traversed with Nala and Ati. Yet, our ancient ones spoke of the lands during the time of our Creation—their teachings adorn our cave walls. It is shown that our Maker saw it in His design to set us apart from them," at this she indicated toward Triumph and Soren. "The Horns roamed the North, and the Wings soared South… eventually. And so it has been ever since. The Desert was intended to separate us. Not because we were enemies, but because we were both powerful in our giftings. Too much power can lead to destruction when coupled together. That is what our ancients spoke of. And so we remain. Our hunting grounds are here." Her voice grew despondent as she concluded. "Or rather," pausing to swallow her emotion, "they were here."

Darion thought of the dry brush and arid landscape. They had seen a few scurrying creatures about, but not enough to feed dragons. He gulped, suddenly fearful of their appetites. *If they've kept Nala and Ati around, they must not plan to eat us… right!?*

"You are correct," she replied, as if she could read his thoughts. "Our hunting grounds are almost depleted. The droughts have led to severe famine."

"But why do you stay? Why don't you leave? There has to be a place where you can find better resources?"

Zalto stared intently. Darion feared he'd overstepped—again. Triumph had told him just last night that the Elder rarely left her den. It was even rarer to communicate with the ancient being.

Triumph rushed to his defense. "My Prince means no disrespect. We only seek to understand."

Zalto, appearing mollified, answered. For Tiakai's energy seemed to be withering with every passing word.

"And where would we go?" Zalto retorted. "We dare not risk leaving and jeopardizing our numbers. What if we find even less? What if we find too many of the abominations and are overcome? They grow bolder in their forays each passing season. We cannot risk it. At least here we have the natural barriers for protection."

"Wait!" Darion couldn't hold back, "You're scared to leave because of the Rav'Arians?"

"Do not call them that!" Zalto berated vehemently. "WE are the true Rav'Arians. They are monsters that have invaded *our* land. They are not natural. They are a blight upon us. Created by humans—your kin, Narco—though we do not know how or why."

Triumph murmured caution to Darion.

A soft voice filled the tense air. "They remain because of me," Tiakai shared sadly. "I cannot travel far. These old bones are almost ready to return to dust. I am their Elder, and so they do me great honor by keeping with me and protecting our teachings."

Tiakai leaned toward Zalto, who looked ready to argue, rubbing her scaled cheek against his. "It is the truth. And yet, also, this is the place of our kind. If the tribe leaves, who will know our stories? How will our young learn our histories?"

An eerie realization struck Darion.

"Wait. Where are your 'young'? I have not seen any young dra... Reouls, besides Gamlin."

An anguished expression crossed both Tiakai's and Zalto's faces.

"He is the *only* one," Tiakai whispered softly. Her cloudy eyes filling with unshed tears. She nudged Zalto.

"When your uncle came to Rav'Ar, our kind thrived. Though the drought had led to a decrease in prey, we still had successful hunts. Warriors hunted and guarded the vulnerable. We had many eggs, that is until the one was taken. Presently ..." he trailed off, watching the mottled Reouls dotting the air and landscape.

Darion followed his eyes. There were none as large as Zalto. *He is their last warrior.*

"Now those abominations have decimated everything. The entire ecology has changed. The bountiful herds are long gone. They have moved on or been wiped out. Just as we are becoming," Zalto's breath caught as he spoke bitterly. "We have not had an egg in...years. The females are not nourished enough to have them it seems. Gamlin is our last hatchling."

Tiakai's head drooped, as if in weary resignation.

Darion felt his heart sink. He understood why they chose to keep two human girls. They were young—an extension of youth that these Reouls might never have again. Their presence meant someone would remember them.

"Well, that is why we are here," Triumph picked up, matter-of-factly. His timbre rising with emotion. "We mean to find out exactly how Narco made the 'abominations', as you so aptly call them. We mean to destroy him—and their kind."

Darion interjected as a memory made its way to the forefront of his mind. "Wait. I remember Antonis telling me that there had been a Rav'Arian," he raised his hands as he said it, warding off Zalto's anger, "that attacked a centaur, and that led to the boundary between realms. Was he wrong?"

Zalto and Tiakai glanced at one another before Zalto explained. "Yes... and no."

Darion scrunched his face in confusion. "How?"

Zalto's shoulders sagged. "Though the abominations as they appear today are more recent, there have been others—similar to their kind—for generations. Not that large in number," he went on quickly, before Darion could interrupt, "but a stain of evil has been around as long as we can remember. Our stories speak to that. *That* particular beast crossed and killed a centaur. Fewer in number than they possess today, they rallied and met the Nav'Arians in battle. Our stories mention that too, but did your version also mention that *we* aided the Nav'Arians against their foe? Our mutual enemy?"

Darion gaped. But it was Triumph who added, "Excuse me? That is not in our historical records. Soren, have you ever heard this account?"

Soren shook his head. "Truthfully," the unicorn said in an apologetic tone, "we have only just learned of your kind. None else, perhaps excluding Narco, know of your existence here."

Zalto and Tiakai appeared dejected.

"Well," Tiakai added tiredly, "and why would you remember? It was very long ago. But Zalto speaks the truth. I was a young Reoul then." Her tone took on the warmth one uses when feeling nostalgic. "I remember fighting. I sprayed my fire across many an enemy and was awarded this. She smiled, lifting her wing slightly to reveal a diamond shaped symbol.

Triumph and Soren both gasped, shocked. "That," Triumph started, "That is the mark of a unicorn. Where did you get that?"

"Rinzaltan was his name. He gave me this mark as a badge of honor… for my bravery as he put it." Her scales rippled with joy at the memory. "That is why I know of your kind. I can sense him in you," she whispered.

Feeling the bond with Triumph, Darion's whole body trembled.

"Rinzaltan," Triumph whispered. "You met him? He was my father. That was the battle when he…"

Tiakai nodded her head. "A great warrior," she concluded knowingly.

Evident emotion caught in Triumph's throat.

Darion remembered belatedly that that was the battle when Rinzaltan had sacrificed himself to save the mortally injured King. Swallowing the shock and emotion, he pressed them, for he wanted all the answers. "And so why is it no one speaks of it in Nav'Aria? Why didn't we know?"

"Well, King Rustusse of Nav'Aria and our Elder Saka made an agreement to honor the border. So great was their esteem and respect for one another—the two elders—yet they also feared what could happen by combining the two dominant races in one land. It was agreed upon that in time of great need one race could call on the other, but otherwise, they would remain a secret, forgotten legend… as it had been since the early days. We thought we had defeated the threat, it seemed like a good idea. We were told to keep the truth concealed."

"That's stupid," Darion said hotly.

Triumph bumped him, but Darion carried on. "Clearly, that is a stupid deal. We need you now… and it looks like you really need us. The Rav'Arians… or abominations, or whatever the hell you call them, are destroying BOTH our lands. Don't you think it's time to forget some old deal?"

Again, Zalto and Tiakai's eyes met.

"Well, don't you?" Darion pressed. He felt flushed. Angry. Confused. They were just wasting away here, and though it wasn't their fault, he was mad. In truth, it all lay at Narco's feet. His malice—and evil cohorts—were near destroying an entire continent. That couldn't happen.

"That is not the whole story," Soren's analytical voice cut in. "There is the… prophecy, as you eluded."

Tiakai nodded at that. "There is the prophecy, yes."

"What prophecy?" Darion demanded through clenched teeth.

"Our oldest stories speak of one who will stand in the face of evil and destroy it."

Darion stared at her blankly. "And?"

"The image is of a young man with blazing green eyes and a glowing arm." Goosebumps broke out along Darion's arms. He held down a shiver. Tiakai's tone strengthened, "He straddles the desert and bridges the two lands around it, ending the border and creating one unified land."

Darion glanced at Soren. "And you, Soren? Just spit it out. Is there a prophecy in Nav'Aria like this?"

Soren whinnied softly under Darion's severe scrutiny.

"Calm yourself, Darion. I will tell you. For only the line of the First Horn may speak it aloud," Triumph soothed.

"There is a similar prophecy in our land. It speaks of the destruction of the Realms. A black, insidious force that seeks to destroy all within, and of one—of the Creator's choosing, from outside our land—who will stand against it, defeat it, and usher in a New Age."

Triumph's affection for Darion escaped his shining eyes. "I would have never believed it of you—being a moody, ignorant youngling as you are—until last night."

Darion reined in the impulse to roll his eyes.

Triumph continued, "But what you did, Darion. No other Meridia has done the likes of before. Yes, all Marked Royals have been powerful, sound leaders, and yet, you... you are something more. Something different. Your command of the elements and different ways of thinking because of your time spent in that other world will usher us into a New Age. I believe you are the Chosen One of Prophecy, brought here to save both Realms." The last notes spoken with such clear pride... and reverence.

Darion blinked dumbfounded. *Me? But I can hardly even use a sword? I'm a nobody.*

He glanced at the others. Nala's face held the mischievous grin, and Ati looked as if she were going to be sick. Zalto, Tiakai, and Edmond all just stared. *They believed it too*, he realized.

Darion's heartbeat raced, and he jumped to his feet, excusing himself. None moved. Triumph nodded, as if he understood Darion's need for quiet and a place to think.

He could hear them begin murmuring the instant he left. *Let them talk!*

Darion strode away from the sloping, cavernous rocks. The brilliance of the sun's rays announcing another excruciatingly hot day presented itself. Darion spotted a colossal boulder protruding out of surrounding sage grass, cacti, and yellow flowers that dotted the vast land. He climbed up, lying down, closing his eyes, enjoying the warm quiet. This far from the group, his senses didn't feel in overdrive. He needed to think. He needed to be alone.

Prophecy? Chosen One? Those were the types of terms tossed around in literature class or movies in Oregon. If he didn't have an arm that glowed and hadn't entered some parallel universe to which he was the heir, he would have never believed it himself. *How can I be the chosen one? I don't have some wand—some hidden powers to defeat Narco. I'm decent with a sword I guess but that's it. They're crazy.*

A tiny trickle of energy pulsed in the back of his mind at the thought. *He had beaten Narco—or at least pushed him aside—just last night.*

The grass near him began to move, breaking his concentration. He heard a bulky creature ambling toward him. *Idiot,* he thought. *Coming out here alone—without a weapon!* He searched his belt. He had left his sword behind but did have the blade Vikaris had given him. Grabbing it, he tried to narrow his focus. If it was a Rav'Arian, he would need to be ready.

Preparing to attack the intruder, he hesitated as he saw bright green scales. Searching with his senses, he caught the scent of smoke and knew the identity. It was Gamlin.

He lowered the blade just as a shining, reptilian face with bright, hopeful eyes emerged from the brush.

Gamlin stopped, his face changing and his chin dipping as he caught sight of the blade.

Darion remembered his young age and reached out his hand in a friendly gesture. "It's alright. You can come out, Gamlin. How are you?"

The dragon, still half-hidden from view within the tall weeds, peeked out sheepishly but met Darion's eyes. Darion watched the swirling orbs. The hatchling's eyes danced between yellow, green, and blue. They were mesmerizing.

"Hi," the dragon replied shyly.

"Hi," Darion said again, and then sat as a disarming gesture. "Would you like to join me?" he motioned to the rock he was sitting on, scooting to the far edge to make room. Gamlin neared the size of a black bear back home, unlike Zalto, who towered like a house!

Gamlin nodded excitedly, and with a fluid leap jumped atop the rock and into a sitting position. His wings flapped open before he tucked them in.

Darion and Gamlin were still for a moment. The silence growing. Darion had never been a fan of small talk—how did one even go about making small talk with a dragon?

"It's gonna be a hot day," he mumbled. *No, not weather!*

Gamlin only looked at him in admiration.

Darion averted his eyes, growing irritated now. He had come out here to think. What was this kid doing? As he opened his mouth to say just that, the dragon spoke.

"I wanted to thank you." The youthful voice, though soft and high-pitched, was steady. Gamlin swung his head to look directly at Darion. "I… well, my mother would have been very sad if I died. The whole tribe, really. Thank you for stopping that from happening."

Darion swallowed his moody tirade, knowing now about their low numbers and Gamlin being the last egg. He thought about what a loss like that would do to them. How it would have demoralized them.

"You're welcome," he replied, meaning it. "But… I don't exactly know what I did!" He smirked to himself, thinking about just how much he didn't know.

"Mother says you are the Chosen One. That you will save us. Everyone is talking about it."

"Oh yeah," Darion asked. "What do you think about that?"

Gamlin, to his credit, held Darion's stare. Then as he began to speak, he looked away, revealing a depth that Darion would not have expected in one so young.

"I want to believe you are. We need saving… for now, you have given Mother… and the rest of us, hope. That is a start."

Tears formed in Darion's eyes. The two sat for a time silently. Darion returned his gaze to the Reoul camp. He pictured his home in Oregon. His father's war camp. Kaulter. All the places—and people—he cared for most flashed through his mind. And he realized in that instant that he wanted to believe it, too. His mind landed on Carol's face. He didn't want any other families to be parted by Narco's wickedness.

"Thank you, Gamlin," he told him genuinely, after long moments had passed. Gamlin turned toward him, his eyes ablaze with youthful vigor and swirling intellect. Darion's breath caught. He smiled at Gamlin and thought, *no, I'm not the hope your kind needs. You are.* For in that moment, Darion knew that Gamlin, with his resilient, humble, and strong spirit, would grow to be a great warrior. *You will be the one to save your kind.*

"I hope you're right about me," Darion said casually before standing up and brushing the dust from his black trousers. As he walked back, he thought about Gamlin's eyes. Darion had the faintest impression that Gamlin had understood him. Gamlin's green scales shined in the intense sunlight as he circled overhead, casting large shadows about. Darion smiled, feeling better, though he could not really say why.

Without preamble, he said, striding up to the group, "Alright, say that you're right, and I am this 'Chosen One.' What now?"

CHAPTER 14

The Foretelling

Climbing the steep hill, Nala couldn't still her mind... or her pulse!

Who was this man who could stir her emotions more than any other individual in her lifetime? She watched his tall, lean form walking beside the sheer dazzling horned ones following after Zalto and the Great Elder.

Nala had been shocked—like the rest of the tribe—to see Tiakai leave her den. She NEVER left her den for any reason. Nala had only spoken to her a handful of times and had waited upon her even less. She honestly didn't think the ancient figure could descend the hill any longer. And now that she watched the slow procession, she knew that going up was going to be much harder on Tiakai. She had to pause to breathe every few paces. Zalto's wings and neck scraped along the cavern ceiling as he tried to stand beside the Elder, supporting her. She smiled at her Father, so respectable... *well, besides the whole forest fire yesterday*, she thought ruefully.

Her mind wandered back to the lean figure with the dark clothes and piercing green eyes. In the low lighting of the cave tunnels, his arm glowed. She wanted to grab it and study the symbols, but she thought that might be rude. Still, she did want a good look. *Why did his arm glow like that?*

Admittedly, she had very limited knowledge of humans, having grown up apart from them, and that is what made her all the more curious. Her eyes traveled over him ravenously. His dark curls trailed his neck, spilling onto his shoulders. And then there were his shoulders. He had a broad build, not like the behemoth next to him that Ati had become besotted with, but still a nice figure. He wrought emotions in her, the like she had never known before. And for some strange reason, she kept imagining herself within his embrace, with his sculpted arms around her. And those eyes looking at her while his full lips navigated her body.

"Nala. Nala! Are you alright? You look as if you are in a dream."

Nala snapped to alertness as her sister's hand clapped on her shoulder, lightly shaking her.

"What? What?" Nala said, shaking herself, only then realizing that the two humans had turned around and were facing her. He was looking at her. A small smile creased his mouth, and… he had been talking to her.

Her face flushed scarlet, and she suddenly felt grateful for the shadowed tunnel. Clearing her throat, she said, "I apologize. What were you saying?" The humans had stopped walking, for it appeared Tiakai was growing even slower. Darion grinned at her.

At once, she felt not—well, whatever that had been—but instead, annoyance. *Did he think her a petulant child, smirking at her like that?*

She scowled at him.

And to her surprise, he only grinned wider. Her pulse threatened to rise again at the sight of his alluring white smile. She forced herself to look away from the near-perfect form, waiting for his response.

He stepped closer. "I asked, where do you two sleep?"

Ah, flame it all, she thought despondently as her face warmed again. *He was thinking about where she slept?*

"That is none of your concern," she retorted hotly, pushing past he and Edmond to see if Zalto needed assistance. She murmured pardon as she skirted around the Horned Ones and disappeared from the human's sight.

"Umm… excuse me," Ati mumbled in her sweet voice, hurrying after her sister. Edmond smiled stupidly.

Darion laughed. He liked seeing Nala out-of-sorts like that. *And*, he admitted to himself, *I still do want to know where you sleep.*

After a slow progress, which seemed to take hours, the party finally emerged into a wide-open cavern adorned with art and small torches lit throughout.

Darion could hear dripping water beyond his view and knew that this must be where the Elder spent her time. She had accessible water, adoring dragons to bring her fresh kills, and her histories to occupy her. It felt claustrophobic to Darion, to think of being trapped here, but as he looked at the weary dragon, he knew that she was correct in her summation. She didn't have much longer. *This is a comfortable place to wait for death*, he thought somberly.

Art splayed across the back wall. *This*, he realized, *must be the prophecy*. For there it stood. A sketch of a human man with blazing green eyes, larger than life, straddling a natural crevice in the rock, which Darion could only interpret as the Shazla Desert—the border. Crescent moons dotted the right—the unicorn symbol. And to the left were arches—like primitive drawings of wings—which he concluded must be the Reoul symbol.

"Ahhhh," Tiakai croaked. "You have found it. There lies our history… and our hope."

Darion looked at her from the corner of his eye. She trembled, appearing close to collapse. His eyes lingered on the art a moment more. Soaking in the subtle details, before turning toward the giant woven rug in the middle of the room.

"Do you want to sit?" he asked, hoping he sounded polite. He really didn't want to upset anyone, but he also didn't really want to see the old Elder tumble to the ground.

"Mmmmm…," Tiakai hummed as she sat heavily upon the mat, her massive bulk filling much of it.

Filled with the dragons, unicorns, and humans, the cavern suddenly didn't seem as huge.

Nala and Ati went into serving mode. Gathering food and drinks for all.

As no one spoke, Triumph and Darion shared a look. Darion knew he couldn't press it, but also, that it was his duty to ask. Tactfully. They really couldn't waste any more time here.

"Thank you for bringing us here, Great Elder." Darion said after a few minutes. Tiakai's breathing had slowed, and with the nourishment of dried meat, she seemed to regain some vigor.

She nodded and looked toward Zalto. Darion understood that to mean that he should go through him. *Great,* he thought.

"Now that we know of your..." he trailed off, searching for the best way of wording things as he looked at the looming dragons.

Your condition? Triumph offered.

"...your tribe's condition," Darion picked up. "And now that you have met me, don't you think it's time to defeat Narco? Come to Nav'Aria. Fight with us, and we can end him—and the Rav... the abominations." He knew he needed to tread carefully, but he couldn't keep his tone from growing in intensity. *Narco has to be destroyed.*

"I hear you, Darion," Zalto's voice rumbled through the cavern. Darion swayed with the vibrations echoing in his eardrums. "And yet, you know we cannot."

Darion's jaw dropped. "What?"

"As Tiakai said, we stay here. Our hunting grounds are here. Our," he gestured to the walls with a long talon, "our histories are here. We will remain here."

"But... that's crazy!" Darion retorted. Clamping his mouth shut as a growl rumbled out of Zalto.

"Crazy? Going off with you—strangers to us—to defeat this Narco, whom you say is of your own kin, that is foolish. We cannot jeopardize what little we have to join you. Our kind would never make it past the Desert. You have seen how little we are in number. We cannot stand to lose any others on this quest of yours. No, Darion," he said, "this is not our fight."

Darion couldn't believe what he was hearing. His blood boiled and thudded against his temples.

"What? How can you say that? You, more than anyone, know how terrible Narco is! Just earlier you—you both—said I was the 'Chosen One'. You brought me here to see the proof... saying 'I'll defeat the evil' and all that. So, if that's what you believe, how can you just sit here?"

Zalto hesitated, his expression revealing troubled emotions. He glanced at Tiakai, who appeared to have dozed off. He continued softer than before, "We cannot leave our Elder, Darion. She will never make the trek. I will not split our tribe up for anyone—not even for a prophecy. Perhaps you can defeat him yourself and save the land without our kind as destined. We are too weak. The prophecy says one will come to destroy the evil that riddles the land of old, but it does not state that we must aid him."

Darion spluttered. "But... isn't that pretty much implied?" He looked to Triumph to back him up here. *This is ridiculous*, he thought incredulously.

"We will not fight," Zalto said in a firm voice with a tone of finality.

Nala and Ati gasped in unison, and Zalto huffed a tendril of smoke agitatedly. But before anyone could reply, Nala started.

"How can you say that, Father?" Her huge eyes bore into him imploringly.

"Nala," he reproached in a paternal tone, "You know better than anyone what our tribe is experiencing. You have seen how weak our numbers are. We cannot split up. We cannot leave Gamlin. He is our last hatchling. They will be lost without us. The abominations will come to desolate them as soon as the fighters—as soon as I—am not here to protect them."

Hot tears filled Nala's eyes, for though she knew he spoke the truth, she couldn't accept it. *There were others of her kind out there that needed help. And he wanted to stay here because some of them might die on the journey?* They spoke of a prophecy in which Darion could save them all, and they wanted to let the moment pass because of….

"That is not a good enough reason, Father. You know that either here or there many of the Reouls will die. That is not the reason at all. The reason you will not leave is because you are a coward!" Nala shouted before turning and storming out of the cavern. Jumping to her feet, she flew down the tunnel after her sister. Their quick footsteps fading away.

What ensued after that could only be described as awkward.

Darion and Edmond spent some considerable time inspecting the ground, fearing that Zalto may try to shoot flames after the girls. Triumph stood, speaking calming words, while Soren ahemmed agreeably. Zalto trembled with emotion, not meeting anyone's eyes... and the rattling breathing of Tiakai ceased as her eyelids popped open.

Her voice cracked as she drawled, "Nala speaks the truth." Her milky eyes peering at Darion, enveloping him.

"We are afraid, creatures of Nav'Aria. If we go, we might lose everything. What will remain, then?"

A long pause filled the space, but Triumph's wise, rich voice sounded, "Yes, Great One, and yet, what will happen if you remain? At least if you come, some of your kind will have a chance. As it is now, I mean no disrespect," he paused bowing slightly toward her, "what chance do you have?"

Tiakai dipped her head, for it was wisdom in which Triumph spoke. Darion could sense she felt it. Silence fell upon them, and as the torches began to flicker, announcing another day's end, Darion, Edmond, Triumph, and Soren excused themselves.

Despite everything, they still didn't have a clear way to defeat Narco.

Darion spoke softly to his friends as they left the Elder to rest and the giant Zalto to protect her, "We leave tomorrow. Narco is still terrorizing people in Nav'Aria, and we still don't know how to stop him. We need to move on."

His friends nodded in agreement—albeit sadly—and they returned lost in their own thoughts to their sleeping areas.

Creator, help us, because the Reouls certainly won't, Darion thought unwilling to concede defeat.

CHAPTER 15

The Message

"Sire! Sire, you need to see this."

Vikaris rolled over hastily, wrapping a loose linen around his bare lower half. Lyrianna lounged languidly, her hair spilling across her exposed bosom. He winked and motioned for her to pull up the coverlet and go back to sleep.

He strode across the chamber, throwing open the door. Outside stood Trixon and Cela inspecting a torn sheet with cramped writing on it in the middle-aged messenger's hands. Trixon had been on guard that night, something he insisted on regularly—as was the case with the fiery centaur. Her dedication to Lyrianna was uncanny.

Vikaris opened his mouth to ask what this was all about before he noticed the aged figure leaning against the wall.

"Seegar?" The King ran into the hall nearly naked. *Propriety be damned!*

"My friend. What are you doing here? What news do you bring?" Vikaris waved for the messenger to bring him the note. He paused when he saw the blood.

"Trixon," Vikaris yelled, panic tearing at him, for Seegar's head seemed to loll and his mouth moved but nothing came out.

I know, Your Majesty. He refused any medical care until after he delivered his message.

Vikaris knelt to cup the trusted old man's withered face. "Seegar," he whispered. "What has happened? Who did this?"

The messenger—Vikaris was at a loss for his name at the moment—knelt down beside him.

"Sire. He brought this with him." Vikaris hesitated, not wanting to tear his eyes away from his life-long friend.

Help him, Trixon. That wound looks bad. Seegar's shoulder bore a wound that was steadily bleeding. He had been stabbed.

Vikaris jumped out of the way as his companion's shining horn appeared, touching the old man's shoulder. Immediately the bleeding lessened, yet it could not be fully healed. Trixon dominated on the battlefield but was less skilled with healing. Seegar would not die from blood loss, at least, but as soon as the message was out of the messenger's hand, the King snapped for him to find help. Guards were everywhere in the hall now, scouring the Fortress for a threat. Cela was shouting orders and relaying the events as she learned them.

Under attack.

Rav'Arians and trolls- everywhere
Prisoner escaped
-Gar

The Commander had not even signed his full name, which was not like Garis. *Creator, help him!* The Camp had finally been found. Thankfully, Seegar had managed to escape to get word to him—*but what of the others?*

Loud boots thundered down the hall, catching Vikaris's attention. He held the note and stood with Trixon while he awaited his friend. Antonis and Aalil sprinted toward them.

"What is it? What happened?" Antonis bellowed as he approached the scene but quickly regained composure in his voice. "I was out on patrol but heard the shouting. There are refugees everywhere. Where did all the camp followers come from?"

"I brought them," Seegar croaked. His intelligent eyes open, and though his head still leaned against the wall, a little color was returning to his cheeks.

Vikaris swallowed. *Of course he did. At his own risk, more than likely. Just as he saved me all those years ago.*

Trixon boomed, "You have done well, Seegar. Thank you."

Vikaris agreed, helping him stand. Two guards stepped forward at their King's beckoning and assisted Seegar toward the healing quarters. Lei would take good care of him, Vikaris knew. He whispered his thanks to his friend as he was drawn away.

Vikaris's steely gaze met those of Trixon, Cela, Antonis, and Aalil. "Make sure the Portal has triple the guards tonight," he commanded. Antonis was already numbering off members gathered there to join the Portal guards.

Vikaris continued, "I must speak with my wife… and Elsra."

Trixon nodded. "I will go inform Grandmother."

"Meet in my Chambers. Get Trinidad as well."

Trixon's hooves pounded the floor as he took off. The unicorn could have communicated telepathically to Elsra, but Vikaris knew Trixon liked being in motion, having a task. He would be quick about it. Vikaris looked back to the group, surprised that Antonis had remained.

As if reading his mind, Antonis replied, "I will be guarding you, Your Majesty." Cela grumbled but didn't challenge him.

Antonis smiled at her, "You have done well, Cela. But you have been on duty all evening. Best to keep fresh eyes on our King, now that we know of the threat." Aalil stepped forward at that, clearly not intending to leave Antonis' side.

"Thank you," Vikaris responded, already stepping back toward his chamber. He needed to dress and inform Lyrianna. There was much to do.

With his hand on the gilded door handle, he turned, "Someone should fetch Riccus as well."

Antonis nodded, tilting his head for Aalil to go. She bobbed her head. Vikaris had a feeling as he watched their exchange that there was more here than simply a commander and his guard. And though fraternizing with one's officers was typically frowned upon, Vikaris couldn't fault his long-time friend. He gave Antonis and Cela a nod with orders to send the unicorns and Riccus in as soon as they arrived.

"What is going on?" Lyrianna had dressed, for which Vikaris was glad of as he made to do the same.

"The Camp has been attacked. Seegar led as many of the noncombatants away to the Portal but was injured in the act."

Lyrianna gasped, and Vikaris looked up quickly from lacing his breeches. "He lives," he assured her hurriedly, "He will be alright. Trixon helped him, and he is receiving medical care now."

"Thank the Creator," Lyrianna whispered, coming around the bed to assist Vikaris, hastily handing him his boots, and swordbelt.

"The Council will be here momentarily. We must plan our next move."

"What will you do?"

Vikaris knew she wasn't asking him as her King but as her husband.

He paused from dressing, one booted foot and one bare, he took her hands and gazed into her lovely face. "I must go, Lyrianna."

She bit her lip as he said it but didn't interrupt him. Her eyes told him what she already knew.

"They are my troops. I cannot abandon them. I fear for Garis, Kragar, and the whole Camp. This is all that was sent," he took the note that he had tossed aside while dressing from the bedside table. She took it, running her eyes over the brief message.

"Morta escaped?" Her venomous tone shocked him.

"Yes, it would appear so," he replied slowly. He honestly hadn't given that part of the message much thought. His first thoughts were of his troops... and of Seegar. It had all happened so fast. Though now that she said it, he pondered. He continued to hurry with his boots but didn't mistake his wife's changed countenance at the mention of Narco's wretched adviser.

"This is no random attack then, Vikaris," she said matter-of-factly. "Narco needs him and sent a rescue party."

Vikaris balked at that. "Perhaps it was just sheer luck. Narco is not the most loyal man, after all. I highly doubt he would go to such lengths for anyone other than himself. It is more likely that he sent a force out to patrol the Woods to find the Camp. I must get there before..."

He stopped as he saw her shaking head and creased brow. "You do not understand," she retorted. An edge he wasn't familiar with had crept into her voice, reminding him of her recent outburst. Her nerves were frail, and he knew he needed to try and calm her, not agitate her.

"What do you mean?" He said politely.

"Trinidad has spoken to me—at length—about Morta's presence and involvement with his imprisonment."

"Yes. He works for Narco. The vile man. What of it?" Vikaris regretted losing the prisoner and not killing him when he had the chance, yet he didn't see her point. Morta, as his instructor, had most likely encouraged Narco's wicked ways. But he was an old, weak man. Narco was the ultimate villain here. The one who had plunged the knife into House Meridia.

Her eyes enveloped him. His breath caught at the intensity with which she spoke. "Narco is a puppet... and Morta the puppeteer."

Vikaris felt sick confusion grip him. That couldn't be true, for it were, why had he not realized it yet? Why hadn't she said something before? The Unicorn Council had never once mentioned him as being a major threat. He had insisted in keeping Morta prisoner for interrogations at the camp, not wanting his toxic presence at Kaulter. No one had argued with that. Yet now that he considered it, his thoughts returned to Alice, Morta's apparent illegimate daughter who had killed Carolina. But Vikaris had not fully believed that it was Morta who had coaxed her into it. It was Narco. It was always Narco.

Narco IS the villain. It is Narco who sits on my Throne. It is Narco who killed my parents. It is Narco who crossed the Shazla and found dark powers there. It is Narco who lured Darion back to the dangers of this war-ravaged realm.

Lyrianna held his stare. Silently. Pityingly. As if he were a slow-witted youth. He felt like he had been punched in the gut. How had he become blinded? Morta had been with Narco during all the events that had transpired... beginning with crossing into the Desert.

"How did I not see this?" He whispered, but before she could answer, a curt knock sounded at the door before Antonis swung it open to lead in Trixon, Elsra, Drigidor, Trinidad, and a red-faced Aalil.

She handed a sheet of paper to Antonis before he turned toward Vikaris. His face also turning red, his stony gaze smoldering.

"Where is Riccus?" Vikaris asked looking beyond the unicorns to the empty doorway.

Antonis crossed the room swiftly with long strides. He held out the parchment. Antonis had crumpled it in his strong hold. Vikaris took it carefully and held it up for he and Lyrianna to read. Before he had finished reading, he too crumpled it, slamming his fist on the table.

"Like father, like son," he spat.

Riccus had left them. Fled in the night.

"But who opened the Portal?" Vikaris roared to no one in particular. He paced toward the antechamber where his party was to gather. Without a glance back, he motioned heatedly for them to join. He didn't expect an answer.

"I did," a regal voice replied coolly.

Vikaris spun so quickly on his heel that he almost ran into Lyrianna, who had quickly followed him. He caught her in his arms but had eyes only for the speaker.

"WHAT?"

The room crackled with energy—and tension.

Elsra lifted her chin stubbornly, her lavender eyes flashing. "Oh, do stop being so melodramatic, Vikaris. It is not becoming of you."

Vikaris made to step toward her, challenge in his eyes. His pulse raced with rage and confusion. Everything he had bottled up.

Drigidor stomped his hoof threateningly, and a low snarl came from deep within him as he stepped toward the King. Trixon also stepped forward, inserting himself between the two parties before a brawl ensued.

Calm yourself, Vikaris. You are no fool. Hear her out.

Lyrianna placed a hand on Vikaris's arm, squeezing it lightly. She now held out the parchment. He felt himself glowering. He was like a taut wire ready to snap at any moment. "Oh, come on," he waved his hand curtly, moving into the next room. There was a silent release of tension in the air.

Trinidad spoke next. "You should read the letter in its entirety, Your Majesties," he gestured toward both of them.

Vikaris sat on one of the plush chairs, pulling Lyrianna to his side. The two leaned close to read the hurried script. They gasped in unison as they reached the conclusion.

"But why? What does he hope to achieve?"

Though Vikaris asked Elsra, it was Trinidad—again—who spoke.

"The other day, after our meeting in the Library, Riccus pulled me aside with some questions. Beyond our revelation of Winged Ones, and Narco's new army, Riccus began to ask me about Narco's hold on the trolls—something, much like the Winged Ones that we simply do not understand." And more to himself, he added, "there are too many things we do not know."

"But the trolls? He means to travel the Nav'Alodon Mountains—alone? None of our parties have ever returned! How many more must I lose?" Vikaris glared, his anger rising once more, "And why did he not tell me? Does the title "King" mean nothing around here?" Vikaris swept his scowl across the room, blatantly finding Elsra.

"If you are keen on blame, then by all means blame me, Your Majesty," Trinidad's somber voice echoed in the room, and Vikaris winced as Lyrianna's nails dug into his arm.

He exhaled, the heat leaving him as he looked at his downtrodden friend. Trinidad was one of the wisest, most self-sacrificing unicorns there was. His father's bonded companion.

"Alright, fine. I apologize. Please, come in everyone. Be seated, and someone get us refreshments—and a map! And start from the beginning."

Once goblets and tankards had been brought in to satiate the party and all appeared calmed by the reprieve, Trinidad explained his speculations of the troll encampments… and Riccus' questions.

Riccus had come around to the idea of Darion's quest—or so Trinidad said. And instead of remaining angry with him, he had been inspired to also go in search of   answers. "If my son has the guts to go out and look for answers across the Desert, the least I can do is go find some of my own in the mountains. It is better than moping around here," Trinidad quoted.

Again, Vikaris winced. This time at the mention of "son." What a complicated relationship this was turning out to be.

Elsra continued, "And so it was yesterday, Riccus came to me claiming that he needed to use the Portal immediately—and alone."

"Yes, but why the secrecy? Why alone?" Vikaris fumed.

Elsra's radiant lavender eyes seemed to swathe the King and Queen. "Is it not obvious, Your Majesty? Riccus does not wish to endanger any more of his loved ones. He knew if he came to you, you would either say 'no', or worse, send a party with him. Riccus is consumed with guilt," she shared, her eyes glittering, "I have seen it in him. For as you know, I can read the deepest of emotions," she said softly. "Grief and shame have ensnared him almost beyond recognition. He is lonely and needs a purpose. This is the only way he can heal. He needs to feel like he is in the fight against Narco—to avenge Carolina."

"As a martyr?" Lyrianna whispered, her eyes also shining with emotion.

Vikaris felt the hairs on his neck rising. He could not lose him. Darion could not lose him.

What do you make of it?

I agree with them, Trixon rumbled. *Riccus needs this, and it may prove valuable in turning the war. Yes, no parties have ever returned from the Mountains. But you have never sent anyone like Riccus. He is tough, and he is an excellent tracker. If anyone were to make it to the trolls and back, it would be him.*

Vikaris contemplated, rubbing his stubbly jawline. Trixon—and the others—spoke the truth. Perhaps this was not the disaster or cowardly escape he had at first thought. Shame filled him.

Had he really thought Riccus a coward? *What is wrong with me?* He thought, beginning for a moment to question his own judgment.

You must question everyone. You are a King and at war. However, in this instance, it is time to begin trusting again. Riccus has not failed you yet. As you said, 'like father, like son'. You should be proud of both Darion and Riccus for taking on these quests—you can discipline them once they return, but for now, we must trust that they will be successful. For all our sakes.

Vikaris nodded at his friend's sagacity and felt sick as he recalled the account of Narco's new "weapons."

"I can see wisdom in Riccus's actions," Vikaris finally replied. "Though I disagree with the idea of him going alone."

The unicorns' voices erupted, competing with one another to speak, but he continued, firmly raising his hand to still them.

"But whom would you send? You need everyone for the fight to come. The unicorns must stand ready to defend Kaulter and face the adversary. We cannot hide out here any longer. We must stand together and fight," Drigidor interjected stalwartly. His booming voice rising.

"In that you are correct, Drigidor," Vikaris agreed. "We cannot afford to send any unicorns—I will need them for the field and to guard Kaulter. But I can send humans. A trustworthy, battle-tested human who knows Riccus better than anyone else."

Antonis had been leaning casually against the gilded door. His mind running a mile a minute as he jumped between anger at Rick, angst to be out on patrol, confusion for how quickly his feelings for Aalil were intensifying, annoyance at Vikaris for being such an ass, and....

He hadn't been listening to the last few bits of conversation, so wrapped up in his own inner monologue. Yet, coming out of his daze, he realized that all eyes stared at him.

Standing up straight, proudly, he stared back. After a moment, he grinned nervously, "What did I miss?"

He knew that look in his friend's eye. Vikaris was planning something... and it appeared to center around Antonis.

"Fancy a trip to the mountains?" The King smirked.

Antonis gaped. He was being sent after Riccus. *Damn you, mountain man,* he thought.

"Sire. But what about you? Am I not better off guarding you?" He bowed slightly, knowing he had just questioned his King in front of an audience.

Vikaris smiled at him, though his eyes revealed a sadness.

"Trixon and I will head to the Mainland to locate the Camp and prepare our remaining forces," he said, nodding toward his unicorn companion. "I mean no disrespect, but he is all the protection I need."

Antonis hoped he was right, sending up a silent prayer to the Creator.

"As you say, Your Majesty," Antonis bowed, nodding respectfully. It looked like he was off on another adventure after all. He pictured Aalil's naked body intertwined within his bedding. *I will miss that,* he lamented.

Trixon snorted loudly. And Antonis felt himself flushing as he looked at the unicorn. Though Trixon didn't meet his eye, he had a feeling he had been reading his mind. *And damn you, unicorns. It will be good to get away from your kind,* he thought.

The King and the Council were speaking again, and Antonis focused as his orders were laid out.

Lyrianna listened half-heartedly. The King and Trixon were headed to war. Antonis was being sent to accompany Riccus in a quest for answers in the mountains while Darion and Triumph had appointed themselves to find information across the border.

Where does that leave me? She had escaped imprisonment. Her only thoughts had been of surviving long enough to see Vikaris and Darion, and now they would both leave her. *Alone again*, she thought, somewhat bitterly.

I will remain with you, Your Majesty. We will assist the Council with the defense and protection of Kaulter.

Lyrianna smiled at Trinidad across the room. *And we will find a way to heal your horn,* she replied. He dipped his head slightly in acknowledgement but did not reply.

We are not weak or broken any longer, she thought, though

as she did, she remembered the news that Morta had escaped, and she felt her stomach flip with heavy foreboding.

CHAPTER 16

The Weapons

"My, my, you have been busy here."

Narco glared at the man's back. Oh, how he hated him. His condescending, judging tone. Narco knew he had made a mess of things with Zola and the chalice, but he didn't need anyone else making him feel weak. It was HE who was Emperor—not Morta, whatever the man thought. Having him gone had proved to Narco just how much he had relied on Morta over the years. That ended now. He would keep Morta at a distance... at leash. He would not succumb to the demands of an old, manipulative, one-handed man. He looked at the stub that Morta was carefully wrapping in linens. His lips formed into a smile. He was glad the man had suffered.

"Does something amuse you, Sire?"

Narco swallowed, like he had as a boy when his tutor caught him in a lie, kicking himself for showing fear again. *It ends now!*

"I do not think 'amuse' is the right word for it. I would say instead 'surprise'. I am simply surprised that you could have been captured and treated so," Narco replied, venom spewing in his voice as he continued. "I thought with all your dark powers, that you were invincible. Beyond capture. Alas, it seems we are both still human."

Morta walked over and back-handed Narco with more force than he ever imagined could have come from the man's lean frame. A pit formed in Narco's belly.

"How dare you?" Narco spluttered. Anger and bile rising. He lifted his fist, as if he were going to strike back.

"You are nothing without me," Morta purred. "If it were not for me, you would still be a sniveling brat out in the courtyard being bested by your younger brother. I made you what you are—and I can take it away just as quickly. Remember that, Emperor." Morta's amber eyes burned deeply into Narco's.

"Are you threatening me?" Narco's voice lost much of its scorn. Uncertainty gripped him. *Unmake me? He would not dare... would he?*

Let the people think of you what you want. You may be the terror in their nightmares, but I will always be the terror in yours. Remember that.

Narco's eyes widened. The man had spoken into his mind—without the chalice. *Impossible!* Sweat trickled down his spine, soaking his silk undershirt, and he lowered his eyes to the floor accepting the admonishment. Fearing what he saw in his adviser's—his "maker's—eyes.

Morta strode to the door, opening it quickly and allowing the natural light to pour into his tower chamber where the two stood. "Now," he replied respectfully for the guards' ears, "let us visit your prisoner as you wished,

Emperor," signaling for the guards to stand aside for
Narco.

Morta held the door open with his head bowed
respectfully—meekly—as Narco exited, though he knew
the man's eyes belied a different emotion than the tone he
now used. Narco shuddered involuntarily once past the
man.

What have I done?

The fetid smell assaulted Narco's senses first. Reaching
into his deep pockets, he pulled out a scented kerchief he
always kept with him. Though there was nothing more
tantalizing than the fresh smell of blood, this... this was
something different. This smelled of decay. Rot. Death.

As they approached, Morta reached for his key, then
hesitated, instead pushing the door. It swung open...
unlocked.

The smell was repulsive.

"NOOOOOO," Narco cried.

At the same instance, Morta screamed, "She's gone?!"

Inside the cell was not the broodmare, Zola, as
expected, but instead a decaying, fly-ridden corpse.

Porris.

"You idiots," Narco roared to no one in particular.
"No one thought to check on the prisoner? For days?"

With the death of Porris and the absence of Morta, no
one had been given specific orders to check on her, as it
was from the adviser directly that any interaction with her
was allowed. Narco ground his teeth, knowing this,
dismayed. Morta shook visibly with rage.

Narco needed to make sure he didn't erupt here in front of the guards. Or ever.

"To the holding," he commanded, turning on his heel so hastily that he almost tripped on his voluminous cloak, hurrying away before Morta.

His guards, apparently not wanting to spend any further time than necessary in the sickening room, rushed after their Emperor.

Only Morta didn't follow. Narco didn't know whether to be glad of this or not. He turned back to see Morta standing in the doorway, analyzing the scene before making a tsk sound and turning to follow Narco.

Outside felt better than the cramped, enclosed hallways from moments ago. Typically, Narco preferred the refuge of his chambers and Throne Room, but with Morta back—and angry—a little space felt safer. Morta trailed behind the guards. Narco stood up taller. The man would never challenge him directly, in front of the guards at least, though he had come close in the prisoner cell.

How could I forget Zola? Narco should have had someone go in and perform ablutions after her labor.

Narco remembered that peculiar night. Perhaps the paste had expired, or she had developed a tolerance to it? Narco would have to discuss it further with Morta—when the man was rational.

Two unicorns had escaped their clutches. *Was Morta losing his power? Was something else pulling the unicorns out of their holds?* The thought quickened Narco's pace. Darion had returned and was mingling with the winged ones presently... *what else might he be capable of?*

Narco's familiar smoldering rage returned, banishing his fear of Morta's wrath for the time being. The guards in his party grew as he approached the holding. The large wooden barn stood fortified at all times by his command. Though he had overlooked Zola's imprisonment, his weapons were another matter. Surrounded by a clump of towering conifer trees behind the Castle stood the impressive site, unknown to all in the Kingdom save for the Castle guards and staff.

As he approached, he could hear soft whinnying and smell the ever-present hay and alfalfa. Guards surrounded the building. Some leaned down from the watch tower and balconies atop it. All bowed to him. He soaked it in, standing erect, basking in their worship. Murmuring to a guard, he ordered him to gather a search party to locate the missing prisoner, but to do it quietly. The guard bowed low until Narco passed and then hurried to do his bidding.

Zola couldn't have gotten far. She had spent her entire life practically in that cell. She would be easy to locate. A dazed, weak broodmare, nothing more. Her horn had been removed, and without it, she could never utilize any gifting, or so Morta had assured him.

Zola had been the main producer of stock for years. Fourteen to be exact. There had been two other females, but each had died in the birthing process. That left his numbers at seventeen. Zola had been his best to breed by far. Morta had said it was because she came from the First Horn's line. She was stronger than the rest. He hated to lose her but didn't spend too much time worrying over it.

He was confident that she, unlike the wretched and traitorous Trinidad, would be found.

A bulky troll saluted before pulling the chain from the door and opening it to admit Narco and his party. The iron stalls each held a unicorn in varying degrees of age and strength, all sharing one unique commonality. They had black coats and horns, glistening like freshly polished obsidian blades. Another of Morta's tricks.

Master, he heard whispered throughout. *Master has come.*

He smiled at them, pausing at each stall to greet his weapons. *His unicorns!*

Morta came up beside him smiling wickedly. Narco knew that this place energized them both. Seeing what they were capable of and dreaming of what these younglings would do to Vikaris's numbers was extremely satisfying.

As he neared the back of the building, he saw the newest member of their holding. Only days old but already standing. Its horn grew in length each day.

"Hello Fourteen," Narco whispered, pausing outside the stall gate.

"Mama?" the tiny being squeaked.

Narco felt his smile faulter as the word tumbled out of the infant's mouth. He purposely avoided Morta's gaze, for he feared that the man would lash out once he realized just how muddled the entire birth had been.

"No, Fourteen. I am 'Master'. You must call me such. It is I who will care for you and keep you safe."

"But ..." the young one began again, "I want Mama."

Narco squeezed his fists, trying to keep his face neutral, knowing that all the unicorns' eyes were on them. "I am 'Master'," Narco repeated. "There is no one else to care for you. There is no 'Mama'. I am Master. Do you understand?" He could not keep up the feigned calmness for long, and the last words left a biting tension in the air.

The young colt began to tremble. It nodded yet said nothing. Its eyes pooled with tears.

"Leave this one to me, Your Excellence," Morta murmured softly. And Narco knew that Fourteen would rue the day he had whispered, "Mama" aloud.

"Very well," Narco replied smoothly. "But first, we must discuss the Camp and our battle plans." Narco nodded toward the upstairs where a large compartment had been designed for this very purpose. Narco had ensured every written scroll or piece of information on unicorns was brought to this room. One entire wall had a painted Nav'Arian map, and it was there that he prepared to strategize against the enemy. His War Room, he liked to call it.

"Please, join me," he said in as kind a voice as he could muster, for there was an audience, of course.

Morta bowed, gesturing for his Emperor to lead the way.

As soon as his back was to his guards and unicorns, Narco began to nervously chew on his upper lip. He feared his failings—and Morta's retribution.

Zola watched Master enter the barn. The wicked red-headed man had returned. This did not please her, but she knew she would be breaking into that building whether he was here or not. Master could not have Trigger. If she could manage it, he wouldn't have any of them.

CHAPTER 17

The Humans

"What is it, Triumph? You've been quiet all morning. Do you think we're doing the wrong thing? Are you mad at me? WHAT? Just talk!"

"No, it is nothing like that. Are all humans as insecure as you? By the Creator, you are a dolt sometimes." Darion scowled at Triumph, who walked beside him and kept his eyes on the rugged terrain to ensure he didn't twist a leg, or so he claimed for the last hour or more. He wouldn't meet Darion's eyes, and it was driving Darion nuts.

"STOP," Darion yelled, and moved to stand right in front of Triumph.

Edmond and Soren had been further behind, again identifying plants and the like.

"Seriously, Triumph," Darion whispered tersely, holding Triumph's face so he'd look at him. "What is your deal?"

Triumph tried to lower his head further, and for a moment Darion thought he was mocking him, making as if to charge. The sun glinted off the piercing horn just inches away from Darion.

"Come on, man, stop it," Darion chided. Triumph looked up, and Darion could see tears in his friend's eyes. Darion's anger vanished at the sight.

"Triumph. What is it?" Rubbing Triumph's cheek affectionately as he spoke.

They had made their departure with the dawn light. Triumph had gone to speak with Zalto, and the Reouls had gathered to bid the party goodbye. Zalto had murmured his understanding at their haste, and Darion had thanked him—though he still felt bitter that they intended to do nothing and have no part in the war for Nav'Aria, even with the belief that Darion was the one from prophecy. Not being able to personally say their goodbyes to the girls was another source of disappointment tainting the morning's exit.

Darion felt hurt. He thought Nala had at least cared for him as a friend. She didn't even have the decency to say goodbye. The knowledge of that stung.

Zalto had shaken the question off, muttering that the fool girl had ordered everyone to leave them alone, and refused to speak to anyone... especially Zalto. His exasperated tone revealed that he too felt hurt, and Darion remembered the wounded look in his eye when Nala had called him a 'coward'.

Darion had asked for Zalto to extend his goodbye to Nala, and Edmond had echoed similar sentiments for Ati—with a blush, of course.

With that, they had begun their trek. No destination in mind but knowing that staying would not defeat Narco. They needed answers, and until they found them, they had to keep moving. Gamlin had clamored over to Darion spreading his wings wide, trying to block his path, until his mother, ordered him to move. The youngling had flown over them for some distance before hovering in the air and calling a final goodbye. Finally, he circled back to join his mother and the remaining Reouls at their home.

Triumph hadn't seemed bothered by any of that, taking their need to continue all in stride. *So, what could his problem be now?*

What is wrong?

Triumph rubbed his cheek against Darion's palm, returning the affection. Clearly struggling to formulate his response.

I don't… know, Triumph eventually replied choking on some sadness. Darion could not remember ever hearing him sound like that.

Did something happen? My family—is everyone alright? Darion felt the familiar panic setting in as he pictured Carol.

"Yes, yes. To my knowledge everyone is fine," Triumph hurried to say. "It is just…" he paused.

Darion held his breath.

"I had a dream last night. I… at least, I think it was a dream. I heard a voice… It was…"

Darion waited. This was clearly difficult for his companion. He nodded to him encouragingly, waving away a fly before it landed on Triumph's neck.

Triumph lifted his head so that he gazed into Darion's eyes.

"It was Zola, Darion. I don't know how to explain it, but I dreamed of Zola. Not as the child she was, but as an adult. Why would I envision her in this way?" And then he added inaudibly, "Why does the Creator taunt me? Reliving her loss today is almost more than I can bear."

Darion felt his eyes welling with tears for he had known such grief. He would give anything to have his mom back. He too had had dreams of his mother, and then had awoken to find reality. She was gone—forever. Just like Triumph's family. His Zola.

"I'm sorry," was all he could say, and he wrapped his arms around Triumph's quivering neck. The sheer white coat as soft as silk along his bare arms.

"Thank you," Triumph said after a moment attempting to return his vestige of self-control. "I am sorry to bring it up," he mumbled.

Darion gripped him tighter, whispering, "Don't ever apologize to me. You are my family now, Triumph. We have both lost, and I'm glad you told me."

Triumph's neck bobbed. Darion released his hold and did what felt like the most natural thing in the moment. He kissed Triumph's cheek before letting go.

"Did you just kiss your unicorn?"

Blood rushed into Darion's cheeks. He swung around to see Edmond and Soren standing a few feet away.

Edmond grinned happily, clearly not having recognized that the two were having a very emotional conversation.

"Shut up," Darion shot at his ignorant friend.

"… and just what do you mean by 'his unicorn', boy?" Triumph's voice thundered.

Edmond's smirk vanished, and his cheeks reddened. Darion laughed before motioning for them to keep moving. Darion looked over his shoulder and winked at Triumph.

Triumph nodded his head ever-so slightly in acknowledgement.

Darion smiled before grabbing his pack and heading toward the large clump of trees ahead. *He'll be OK. Together, we'll get through this and beat Narco. We have to.*

As the sun's afternoon rays beat down, the oasis that Darion had begun to suspect was a mirage finally appeared. They emerged into an immense forest. The trees were unlike any Darion had seen before. Taller and narrower than what grew in Nav'Aria. A kind of pine, perhaps.

Basking in the shade, the group decided to make camp. The heat and emotions of the day had worn them out.

Soren and Triumph wandered the area, nibbling grasses, flowers, and berries as they searched for water. Darion and Edmond pulled out the dried meat and fruit Reki had made sure they packed. Darion felt gratitude toward her.

The hardest part of this journey, in his opinion, was the lack of certainty. There was no guaranteed food or water source at the next stop. Something he had greatly taken for granted in his former life.

Sitting back and chewing the tough meat, he pondered this, thinking of the Reouls. No hope. They were simply wasting away. *That is no way to live*, he thought sadly. He closed his eyes, enjoying the calm shade of the forest and the rich, smoky meat. He was famished!

Darion's nostrils filled with a toxic odor, his eyes popping open a moment later. He looked quickly at Edmond, wondering if the smell was coming from him or…. Suddenly, he recognized *that* smell.

"Rav'Arians," he yelled, jumping up and fumbling with the sword at his belt.

Just as he unsheathed it, a black-clad figured appeared from the trees and darted toward him. He kicked his pack out of the way and spat the meat from his mouth, preparing his stance for the enemy. His arm glowed, and his ruby shone brightly, casting red dancing rays across the verdure. The small clearing cramping their movements.

Edmond drew his sword expertly, moving to Darion's left.

Darion gave a quick glance, sighting two more enemies emerging from the trees. He felt claustrophobic. The safe refuge of the forest was gone. They had been ensnared in an enemy's trap. How many more lurked out there?

Triumph. I need you! Darion called out frantically.

No response.

Dread filled him but he tried to push it aside as his towering adversary, who had paused outside the reach of his sword, suddenly lunged with a bloody, curved blade.

He noted the blood, wondering whose it could be, but pushed it from his mind. He would worry about that after the fight.

Darion's senses immediately took hold, all other thoughts cast out as he became one with his sword.

If someone had told him a couple of months ago that he'd be in a sword fight to the death against a hideous monster, he'd have told them they were crazy. But now? This moment? This was his new reality.

Working with the blade for the past month made the skill more natural. His calloused hands gripped the hilt expertly, and though he had only experienced one actual fight thus far, he and Edmond had continued their sparring and training throughout the journey. He hoped it would be enough.

Darion heard the clicking of the Rav'Arian's maw, the whooshing of its blade; he smelled the pervading odor that clung to the repulsive 'abomination'. He heard Edmond grunt as his blade struck his opponent's.

Darion hammered aside the blade that was aimed at his chest. He gripped his sword, thinking of Barson's teachings, just as he did in every fight. *Think Darion. Focus. Breathe. Move your feet. Duck.*

The Rav'Arian had two blades, the first thrust having been a ruse, for as Darion harried it away, the creature swiftly jutted a shorter blade out toward Darion's shoulder. But Darion was faster. His senses had already caught the motion of the small blade, and Darion jerked his sword back in time to block the cut. The Rav'Arian cried out angrily with frustration. He heard Edmond grunt again, and Darion knew he needed to finish off his opponent so he could aid his friend. As the creature reeled from the force of Darion's second blow, it was knocked to the side for a moment, and Darion used the surprise to his advantage. He feigned left, and as the creature began to block, he spun out of its reach, then swiftly lunged. His sword tip cut into the Rav'Arian's arm. The guttural cry caused the hairs on Darion's neck to stand. He narrowed his eyes, removing his sword before the creature had time to react. Darion thrust his sword into its chest with deadly accuracy, striking its heart—*if the bastard had one!* The Rav'Arian dropped heavily, and Darion began to withdraw his blade, but before it was fully freed, he heard the swift clicking of another enemy behind him. Just as he jumped out of the way, his sword grip gave way. A black sword blade swung in the space he had vacated. A wicked sound spilled from the creature.

"No sword," it cackled, moving closer toward Darion.

As the sword swung toward him again, he ducked. And having no other weapon, he remembered his training. "Use whatever you have," Triumph had taught him.

With its sword arm pulled back to slash again, Darion barreled into the unsuspecting Rav'Arian, tackling him to the ground. Its sword fell as its talons reached for Darion's face and neck.

The revolting smell overwhelmed Darion. Its potency burning his eyes. As the two hit the ground, their struggle ensued. Darion tried to reach for the blade at his belt, but it took all his strength and focus to keep the Rav'Arian's talons from ripping out his throat. Darion's arms were bloodied, though ironically while so in tune with his senses, he could see more, hear more, yet he felt no pain. The Rav'Arian rocked on its shelled back, swaying the pair in their struggle.

Darion roared in anger as he saw in his peripheral Edmond knocked to his feet and a Rav'Arian standing over him, its blade preparing to plunge into his friend. He had to move.

"Ahhhhh," Darion yelled, punching the unsightly beaked creature as it turned its head, striking it in the temple. Darion's arm glowed a bright green that exposed the Rav'Arian's mottled skin beneath its cloaked hood. The skin, though varying in color, was strangely... scaled. Even more unsettling were its eyes. Darion recognized fear in them. His focus gripped them while his aura illuminated its core. It was a writhing, confused, spiteful being. It was fear that stayed its frenzied attack.

Darion grabbed his knife and slashed rapidly across the Rav'Arian's throat, thinking it almost a mercy for the abominable monster. Black blood spurted out, splattering his face. Darion didn't notice it, nor did he wait to watch it die. Instead, he peeled around to see the sword dropping in mid-air above Edmond. The creature pinned his friend in place to cast a killing blow. Darion's blade connected first.

His toss caught the beast in its face. Its arms froze; a gurgling sound escaped its mouth. As it tumbled backwards, the sword dropped haphazardly near Edmond's leg, bouncing off the jutting tree stump nearby.

A horrible wheezing, cackling sound came from the creature. It collapsed to its knees, its talons scrabbling with the wooden hilt. Oddly, though it was clearly dying, its sounds—and the aura emanating from it—which Darion keenly sensed, didn't appear like fear. This one seemed… amused.

Darion attempted to piece it together. His breathing came fast as his senses informed him of a greater threat.

His fingers groped for his sword, for he knew the fight wasn't over. The trees rustled, and even as the wretched beast died, a multitude of clicking talons filled the forest, and a fetid odor permeated the air.

"We have to get out of here," he shouted, turning to help Edmond up.

Edmond winced as he arose, shaking his right leg a few times, rubbing at his knee. There was no time to ask if he was alright. They needed to run.

Triumph! Triumph, where are you? It wasn't like Triumph to leave him in danger like this without a response. That terrified Darion more than anything. Was Triumph alright?

He turned toward the direction whence they had entered the forest only a short while ago, but found it blocked. Five Rav'Arians approached. He spun to find figures coming from the trees in every direction. They were completely surrounded by ten or more of the monsters.

"Shit," Darion said, his pulse climbing ever higher.

Edmond didn't say anything, but he stood back to back against Darion. As the duo did so, the creatures cackled, their hoods shaking as their mirth escaped....

"Ok," Darion whispered softly. "Barson did say together we'd make a damn good fighter."

Edmond replied even quieter. "No matter what, Your Majesty, I will protect you. And if you have a chance, run. Leave me." Darion was about to argue, but just then the first Rav'Arian attacked. Its companions' blades quickly followed, swinging from every direction. The two fighters blocked, harrying right then left.

No blades struck home, but Darion knew the Rav'Arians toyed with them. There was no way they could defeat all of them. Even if they were the best swordsmen in Nav'Aria, which was unlikely.

Triumph! I need you. Where are you!?

Triumph's head throbbed. What happened?

He could feel the uneven ground, with its roots, foliage, and small rocks poking into him as he lay on his side on the forest floor.

How did I.... Darion!

Triumph's mind, though foggy, searched for him. His eyes fluttered open, trying to comprehend. *Where was Darion? Why couldn't he hear him? And what was Soren doing?*

As Triumph shook his head slowly, he saw a glimmer of something catch the light. Craning his neck around, he saw a thin, long metal instrument jutting out from his chest. The motion of looking down swayed him, and he was forced to close his eyes for fear he'd be sick. Everything was blurred and slow.

He cracked his eyes again and saw Soren reared up on his hindlegs and kicking a bunch of trees. He closed his eyes again....

NO, not trees... Rav'Arians!

Soren was surrounded and screaming in panic, rage, and anguish.

All at once Triumph remembered. They had been grubbing, eating anything they could and exploring the area surrounding their camp. Soren had called for him to look out, and then everything went black. The object protruding from his chest must be the cause for that blackness. Hurriedly, he tried to jump up to aid his friend but realized belatedly that he was also bound and netted. *Like a fish—like they did to Trinidad.*

None of the beasts guarded him for they had all encircled Soren. Jagged cuts appeared on him and blood trickled down Soren coloring his coat. Triumph watched in horror. His friend was tiring. He was running out of time.

Soren's back kick knocked a Rav'Arian's blade askance, but there were too many of them. He was an academic, not a fighter. There were at least fifteen closing in on him that Triumph could hazily make out. He had to help him. He had to get there before....

A high-pitched scream erupted from Soren before his body collapsed with a thud upon the ground.

Momentary silence reigned until the excited clicking and raspy speech of the demons swelled as they moved closer toward the fallen unicorn. A huge gleaming blade caught the sunlight as the Rav'Arian nearest Soren's head made to stab him or cut off his horn. Triumph knew not, only that the blade never hit its mark.

At the sight of his friend's collapse, Triumph exploded with rage, then released every emotion of guilt, shame, and self-loathing at having been incapacitated while Narco's wretches killed his family and took over the Castle years ago. His friend was down; Darion's whereabouts—and safety—was unknown. Supreme power unlike he had ever known before coursed through him, and with a mad slash of his horn and hooves, and a sheer flexing of will, the bindings and netting fell away. His lips clasped the instrument jutting from his lower chest and he angrily pulled it free with his teeth.

As the Rav'Arian's blade began to fall, so too did Triumph fall upon the enemy.

"Get away from him, you fucking monster!" Triumph roared and didn't give the creature any other notice before his horn slashed open the creature's torso, its blackened, putrid guts spilling out. He didn't wait to see what came of the Rav'Arian, for at that instant the others had overcome their shock and were encircling him. Their blades drawn.

What they didn't know was that Triumph, though serving as an instructor now, was of the First Horn's blood. And with that came incredible strength, tenacity, and vigor. What they would learn was that he was still a warrior. And they had just killed his friend. They were going to know his wrath.

Triumph's enraged screams blasted them. His ears flattened against his head, and his eyes rolled around wildly. His back hooves shot back to pummel the two Rav'Arians at the rear. He swung his gory horn across the throat of another in front.

In his peripheral, he caught movement toward his right. Quickly, his head turned toward the motion, and he ran full force into the oncoming Rav'Arian. His horn pierced through its hooded face before he threw back his head with such force that the corpse soared overhead, knocking into its fellows.

Their dwindling numbers didn't deter them. These were creatures with a limited mission. Death. Destruction. Pain.

Triumph knew that. They were products of Narco's malevolence.

Triumph shook his mane and pawed the ground fiercely. *Fuck Narco.*

Charging the three who loomed ahead of him, he speared another with his horn, knocked one on its back, impaled on its comrade's sword, still poised erect in the dying Rav'Arian's grip. He kicked his front leg out to catch the third between its legs. As it fell clutching itself, Triumph stamped his hoof straight through its chest. The creature ceased its struggle immediately. Triumph had always been told that Rav'Arians' exteriors were extremely difficult to penetrate. Apparently, that was a lie, but no one stood a chance against one of the First Horn's descendants.

The unicorn was wild. Feral with rage. If they did anything to Darion, he would kill every single Rav'Arian that still breathed.

He couldn't let his mind think on it yet. He had to focus on the enemy... on their utter annihilation. As he pulled his hoof freely from the corpse, it caught in the creature's ribs. He felt a stinging slash strike his flank. A spear had skidded off his rear, and he bellowed with rage. He ripped his leg free from the corpse so forcefully that it tore open the victim's chest cavity and bloody gore splattered his lower half. He turned slowly to eye the remaining party, glowering at them.

The Rav'Arians clustered together just feet away from Soren's body. As he spotted his friend, who had not moved since his fall, Triumph's blood smoldered with intense molten rage.

He flew at them, leaping over his friend's body and hammering them to the ground with the power of his build. Slashing swords bounced off his thickly muscled chest and torso. He moved too fast, swinging his horned head at all of them. None could angle their swords quick enough to stave off his blows. One tried feebly to cut at his neck. Triumph's horn slashed at the creature's elbow. Its taloned hand gripping the sword fell clear away from its body. The creature clutched its bloody stump in agony.

Triumph slaughtered them. Stamping and stabbing until none moved. He panted heavily, breathing, snorting, grunting, growling. He needed to get to Darion.

His gaze roamed the area, until he saw a swath of black fleeing into the trees. One had gotten away.

Triumph was no stranger to dense and tangled forests, for he had grown up in the Woods of the Willow, on the Isle, and among the trees surrounding Castle Dintarran. He had always loved forests and had grown very capable of traveling swiftly, even through the thickest underbrush. Trees and twigs scraped at his side, but he paid them no mind as he dashed after the treacherous beast.

The creature in front of him swerved suddenly and then spun around. Its hood catching on a tree branch revealed its hideous face of slightly reddened scales, mottled skin, an unsightly beaked maw, wild human-like eyes, and tiny wisps of red hair standing straight up from its foreign, unnatural skin.

Triumph reared, preparing to trample it. The creature pulled a glowing orb from a cord around its neck. It glowed with a yellow-red liquid. It held it out toward him, as if warding off his attack.

Triumph paid it no mind as he lowered his head and rammed full force into the wretch, jamming his horn directly into the creature's armpit. He sliced through the creature's upper body and throat. It fell away gurgling, writhing in its final death throes.

Triumph regained his footing and stomped through the creature's head. As he did so, his back hoof collided with the orb, smashing it.

Suddenly, he could hear Darion's panicky voice calling for him.

"Darion," he breathed, swinging his head around trying to identify his location. The device had blocked their communication. He would give it more thought later. First, he needed to save Darion, his Prince.

"I'm coming, Darion," he roared, charging the area where he could now hear the clashing of swords.

Darion and Edmond had so far kept the enemy away. They had no opportunity to strike offensively: they were completely outnumbered, in a poor position, and their only hope was to defend themselves long enough for the unicorns to show up or for the Rav'Arians to tire from their frenzied blows.

A screeching Rav'Arian dove at Darion.

He prepared his sword to stave off another blow, but it never came. The creature was knocked aside, struck by an enormous wild beast of the forest.

The Rav'Arians ceased their attack on the humans to collectively face this new threat.

Black gore and red blood trailed its body. Its once aquamarine eyes burned red with raging ferocity. The air crackled. The ire and energy radiated from this new threat. A bolt of lightning shot down from the heavens, and the earth split apart as Triumph reared before them. His huge muscles bulged and flexed, ready to spring at any moment. Crashing to all fours, he lowered his head, exhibiting his horn, blackened and dripping with Rav'Arian blood. Small scrapes and scratches dotted his sides, his legs a mucky brown.

Darion gaped, staring at his formidable friend in relief… and terror. He knew now what Antonis had been talking about when he had told him to never enrage a unicorn.

Triumph met his eyes only for a moment, and though Darion knew it was him, even he feared the mighty unicorn. His friend had transformed into a warrior. A savage beast about to decimate the Rav'Arians. Darion could feel it... and he knew the Rav'Arians could, too.

They gathered together nervously, squawking, chattering, and pointing at Triumph.

Triumph roared challengingly, as he pawed the earth and ran into the Rav'Arians without pause. Cutting, slashing, kicking.

Edmond and Darion only hesitated for a moment more before stabbing at the distracted enemies.

Darion pierced the side of a Rav'Arian nearest him. His sword didn't plunge into the tough exterior as hoped, but it did knock the creature off course. As it began to fall, he moved his sword arm upright with both hands, just as Barson had instructed. His blade penetrated its chest and it fell lifelessly to the ground. He kicked the corpse from his blade and swung around to attack the next enemy, as did Edmond. The pair remained back to back as Triumph went ahead into the heart of the melee.

In a matter of moments, the three swiftly finished off the Rav'Arians. A bloody, foul tangle of corpses lay scattered. A blight upon this otherwise pristine forest.

As the final creature fell from Triumph's horn, he reared and landed heavily on it. Bones and shell cracking and breaking under his might. He angrily hammered the creature again and again and again. His hooves drove the bloody mush of flesh and guts into the ground.

Darion and Edmond stood wide-eyed and stepped back. Triumph was crazed.

Darion had never seen him like this… had never seen anyone like this.

Darion started to say something to try and calm his friend then stopped looking around. And then he understood.

Soren.

"Triumph," he yelled with more force in his voice than he thought he could muster, all things considered.

Triumph ceased his pummeling. His chest heaved as he swung his head around searching for the next threat, and then he met Darion's eyes. His shoulders slumped.

"Triumph, it's okay. You saved us. They're all dead. But you need to stop now. Where's Soren?"

By that time, Edmond must have realized it too, for he was already walking around the area—limping slightly, his eyes darting to and fro in search of his friend.

Triumph blew noisily from his nose and walked up to Darion. He threw his arms around his unicorn companion—uncaring if there were remnants of dead Rav'Arians splattered across the once sheen coat. He felt Triumph shudder and knew he was near collapse from the fight, or sorrow, or both.

"Triumph," Darion whispered. "You have to take us to Soren."

With his rage subsiding, Triumph looked worn, tired, and somber.

Darion didn't ask any further questions. He grabbed his things, sheathed his bloody blade and kept his arm on Triumph's side as the unicorn ushered them toward a different clearing. A battle scene.

They neared closer and Edmond gasped.

There were bodies everywhere. Many more than they had just faced.

Darion turned to Triumph, his stomach tensing. "You guys killed them all? Where's Soren?"

Triumph shook free of Darion's grip, and his ears flattened. His voice reverberated with anger... and something else. It was haunting. Darion felt goosebumps rising on his arms.

No. I was too late to save Soren. I killed them... after.

Triumph nodded his head toward a larger heap of bodies. Edmond stumbled ahead on his twisted leg and hopped over dead Rav'Arians, narrowly avoiding the pools of blood and guts spoiling the ground. And then Darion saw what Edmond was running toward. A swatch of white peeked out from under a pile of black, bloodied robes and bodies.

"Oh no," Darion whispered. Understanding his friend's wrath... and anguish.

He started toward Edmond but turned back to Triumph who had instantaneously gone from a hulking beast to a grieving friend.

"This is NOT your fault, Triumph," Darion said strongly, for he knew exactly what his friend was thinking. "This is Narco's fault. You saved us. YOU did that, Triumph. Now lie down. You need to rest." Darion rubbed his friend's cheek. He could see Triumph's lower body trembling with fatigue.

Triumph only nodded. His body a heaving mass of muscle and Rav'Arian gore.

How many had Triumph killed? Singlehandedly? Darion wondered as he jumped over the foul scene to assist Edmond with the clearing of bodies. It was a nasty business. Three corpses lay near or across Soren.

Removing the Rav'Arian remnants exposed more of the unicorn's white coat. He too was speckled with cuts and slashes. A puddle of blood pooled underneath Soren. His lower half no longer white but red.

Edmond fell to his knees. "No," he cried in pain, his palms digging into his eyes as if to prevent the image from taking hold.

Darion's heart broke for him. Though only the Marked Royals could bond a unicorn, the two had willingly paired up to accompany Darion and Triumph. Their bond, though perhaps not "official," was still closer than most. Their bond had been the truest of friendship, and Edmond's shoulders shook as he succumbed to grief.

But Darion wasn't ready to give in to sorrow just yet. For as he beheld Soren, he thought he detected something. A tiny thrumming upon his senses. He knelt beside Soren's great neck and felt for a pulse.

There.

His heartbeat was slow and infrequent. But it was there. A moment more and he might have missed it.

"Triumph," Darion called desperately, not turning back for fear that he'd lose Soren.

Triumph had not heeded his order to rest, so it appeared, for he nudged Darion's hand aside. His grimy head appearing to inspect the wound. He must have also realized that his friend was still hanging on to life—if just barely. He gently touched his horn along the entrypoint of the chief wound.

Soren's neck trembled underneath Darion's hand. His eyelids fluttered but fell still once more.

The wound, Darion observed, no longer gushed blood as it had been, though Darion knew Triumph was not a healer. Soren was. And Triumph was exhausted.

These days in the desert had shown Darion the importance of preserving every last unicorn. He now understood Vikaris and Elsra's decisions not to unleash the unicorns in full force against Narco. Yes, their might would desolate the enemy, but at what cost? If the unicorns were lost, think of the wisdom—the giftings—that would also be lost. Soren brimmed with knowledge. He had the gift of healing, of medicine, of information, and of course posterity. Nothing could be worth losing that. The loss of unicorns would ultimately mean the loss of wisdom—of civilization.

Darion's eyes closed, and his hands moved of their own accord as they had with Gamlin. He breathed out all the thoughts and emotions that would distract him from his purpose. He needed to focus. Concentrate on one focal point. Soren.

He could sense a beautiful and pure life essence in Soren. Yet there was something dark there too. Something hidden and insidious.

Darion's attention narrowed. The dark poison commonly found on the Rav'Arian's blades and talons and had once threatened Rick's life now coursed through Soren's. He had lost a tremendous amount of blood, and his remaining blood cells fought a battle of their own against the toxic poison traversing his bloodstream. If Darion didn't stop it, they would lose Soren.

The poison. Oh, how he hated it. It didn't belong here in a creature of beauty. In a creature of innocence. Much like the Shazla Viper didn't belong upon Edmond.

Darion whispered, "Flee," just as he had with the snake. He noted the moment the poison stopped and became alert to danger—a more powerful threat.

Darion's arm glowed and tingled as he focused in on the poison. He whispered again for it to flee. Rid itself. Depart. For Darion was coming for it, and it would know true fear then, as if it were a living being. Slowly, he moved his hand toward the deep wound, just as Triumph had. His gesture mimicked the pooling and extricating of the toxin.

Soren's body shuddered, and a low moan escaped from his muzzle, but Darion was not swayed. He pulled slowly. Intently. Tugging at the invisible agent. And once he was sure it had all been withdrawn, he cast it far off to the ground. Where it fell, the forest floor darkened as if it had been scorched with fire.

Darion leaned back, exhaustion consuming him as if he had run a race.

Triumph nudged him preparing to speak.

Soren's eyes blinked open. His visible eye stared at Darion's, and a lone tear traced down his cheek. "My Prince," he murmured.

Before any of the males could speak, a feminine voice rang out into the stillness. A voice Darion recognized.

"You killed them. All by yourselves?"

Nala, Darion thought in a culmination of shock, joy, and fear.

He, Edmond, and Triumph all turned—startled.

Nala and Ati stood surveying the scene. Small packs upon their shoulders and looks of worry creasing their brows. In her study of the scene, Nala's eyes landed on Soren. "No," she cried, and she and Ati ran over, hurriedly unpacking their things with skilled hands.

"Sit—all of you," Nala ordered curtly. "We have herbs that will help."

And just like that, Darion again found himself bossed by this sparkling-eyed beauty. He had never been gladder of anything in his life. He knew Edmond, whose eyes were trained on Ati, felt the same way.

Triumph didn't appear to have the energy to laugh at him. He lowered himself slowly to the ground next to Darion and fell asleep, while Darion lightly rubbed his neck, regardless of the dried blood.

CHAPTER 18

The King

Vikaris stared into Lyrianna's eyes.

They had said everything they needed to last night—their bodies sharing what their words did not. They had been reunited. Lyrianna was safe. But the war waged on, and Vikaris could not sit idle at Kaulter while his forces fought—and died. He had to return to the Camp. He feared what he would find, after receiving Garis's short message and seeing an injured Seegar.

While Vikaris boiled with rage, he also felt a renewal of hope. His Bride was safe, and that is what mattered to him most. Well, that and the safety of their son, for which he could only pray to the Creator. Gripping his wife's soft hands, he could feel her small finger jutting out. Narco had broken it, but he had not broken her. Vikaris believed that fully as he stared into her crystal, clear blue gaze. She had a proud, lovely face, and the set of her jaw steadied him. She would be alright no matter what. She was Queen of Nav'Aria, and she would stand in his stead, if anything were to happen to him, until Darion returned and took his place.

"Lyrianna."

Her lips parted as he began.

"Sire," Trixon's voice boomed. "We must go while the Portal is open. It is not safe to leave it so for too long."

Vikaris cursed. He knew this, of course.

Lyrianna gave him a tearful smile reaching for his neck, and as he bent to kiss her, he felt all the passion and aching love they had shared last night and that he would carry with him always. She was the loveliest woman in existence. He wrapped her in his arms, allowing his tongue one final taste of her, in a warm, full kiss before pulling away. The breeze blew, carrying her honeyed scent. He ran his hands through her long, golden tresses before planting a final parting kiss upon her forehead. Her eyes were full of unshed tears, but she stood tall to meet his stare.

"Come back to me, husband." She said in a hushed voice, though so full of authority that he knew it wasn't a request, but a command.

He swallowed the lump of emotion. "I will," he replied brusquely. He gave her hands a final squeeze, kissing her palm. "Protect Kaulter. I leave you in charge here in my stead. You—and Regent Elsra, of course," he nodded respectfully to the unicorns grouped away from the Portal entrance, a deep pooling shelf at the waterfall that glowed green with the unicorns and Marked King so near.

And with that, Trixon and Vikaris strode into the shallow pool, Vikaris's eyes never leaving Lyrianna's. As the water beneath him began to swirl and writhe, tugging him toward the Woods of the Willow, he saw Trinidad and Cela approach Lyrianna, standing to each side of her. His heart knew peace then. She would be safe with those two watching out for her, away from Narco's clutches. "I love you," he mouthed to her, and then nodded in thanks to her companions before he found himself lying against a mossy tree in the Woods of the Willow. Back in Nav'Aria, blue sky and jubilant chirping birds greeted him with the dawning of a new day.

The Portal was strange.

From Kaulter—and it sounded like this Oregon place, according to Darion and the Keepers— one had to enter a designated pool to access the Portal, but on this side of things, one only needed to find one of the great moss-covered trees. The nymphs and unicorns of long ago had designated them, and though the nymphs couldn't access them without a unicorn or Marked Royal, they guarded the ancient trees. Moving between the four that existed within the Woods, never settling in one place, the nymphs remained ever vigilant for movement in the forest.

Trixon rose, glancing around the area. Vikaris got up slower, the burdening emotion of leaving his wife tiring him more than he wished. Trixon came to him knowingly. He rubbed his cheek upon Vikaris in a rare show of affection. "She will be alright," he said in his rich, steady voice.

"She will," Vikaris agreed, taking heart from his friend's assuring tone. "They will," he added, smiling at his friend. For Trixon had been consumed with worry and grief over Trinidad's imprisonment, just as Vikaris had been over his wife. They did not have to carry such worry any longer. Their loved ones had escaped, and that comforted them more than anything else.

Vikaris tried to orient his bearings. They were in one of the far northern clearings in the Woods. If their Camp was where it had last been, it would be southeast. They had a big walk ahead of them and there was no time to delay.

"Time to find our people."

***

"Me? You wish for me to go? Why would I ever do that?" Narco asked incredulously, thinking Morta insane. "I cannot go and jeopardize everything here. I will not go. I am the Emperor, not some uneducated swordarm."

Morta snorted but didn't reply, for the guards behind the door could most likely hear their tones, if not make out the words.

"Yes, My Great Lord, you certainly are," Morta intoned calmly. "Yet it is my advice that you lead your forces out—with our fresh weapons—to face your nephew in battle to end this conflict."

Narco trembled at the thought. *The gall of the man! Absurd!* Though as he contemplated the preposterous notion, he couldn't deny sage advice when it was given. Morta, vile as he was, did offer good counsel, most of the time—though it usually came at a cost. Narco shuddered, taking a sip of wine from his goblet in order to stall and ponder. *Perhaps it was time to unleash his pets. They had been trained for this very mission for their entire lives.*

With the help of Morta's strange, dark powers—for Narco didn't exactly know what was in the needle that Morta used to inseminate Zola each term—all her young were born midnight black and wholly obedient to him. He delighted in the contrast from Zola's typical sheer white coat. Also unique to them was their inability to communicate with other unicorns or have innate giftings such as telepathy, healing, or commanding of the elements as the First Horn's line typically did. This had always surprised Narco since Zola was of that line, but Morta assured him, as he did with all his "creations," that he had taken care of it. They were simply *weapons*. Powerful, loyal weapons that would wreak havoc upon Vikaris's forces. They had been properly indoctrinated to believe the others were the enemy. The threat. Monsters who wished to harm their Master. And they would vanquish them!

Even with this, was it truly time?

The two men sat facing one another, the stunning map wall drawing his attention. Narco let his gaze travel over the painting, resting in the West near the Woods of the Willow. Many day's ride from here, somewhere out there, Vikaris and his rebels lurked. Morta's rescuers had killed some, yet before more troops had arrived, the Camp had moved again. Vikaris hadn't been present, but Narco knew he wouldn't be able to stay away after an attack. *But why must I go?*

Narco rubbed his right forearm, thinking of the Mark that did not decorate it. *Curse the Creator*, he thought angrily. This all could have been avoided had he been born with the Mark. As the eldest, the throne should be his by birthright. The ridiculous tradition of a Marked Heir would soon be forgotten once he eliminated the last living Marked Royals.

Turning back toward Morta, but not quite meeting his eyes, he continued, "I agree with your wisdom. It is time to use our... pets. But, why must I lead them? You, more than anyone else, know that I am no war leader." At that, his eyes flicked up to meet Morta's beastly stare.

Narco hated sounding weak, but Morta knew all his weaknesses already, and this was nothing new. Narco had never done any real fighting. He dispensed men to do that.

"Yes, but for the pets'—and troops'—morale, you must go. They must see their Master strong and proud. Whether you actually do anything or not is beside the point. Your presence is the key. Your officers can do the rest."

Narco made to interrupt, but Morta held up his one remaining hand as if Narco were once more the student—and Morta the tutor.

"I do not mean that you must fight. Not all leaders fight like the... reckless rebel King," he paused smirking, and Narco hated him even more in that moment. The differences in leadership between Narco and Vikaris were all too apparent. Vikaris' people loved him, while Narco's feared him. But he needed their fear. They deserved to fear him. No one had ever loved and worshipped him as Vikaris' ragtag troops did, all because of an idiotic birthmark.

Narco had seized power just as a true leader should. He had taken it! He had been strong with Salimna's blood coursing through him. He flexed his arm at the recollection. He had shown them. He was strong then— and he still was in muscle, but not in spirit. He would be again. This time for good.

Vikaris would die, and Narco would bathe in his blood in his Throne Room while his people celebrated the end of the rebellion. Basking in the blood would prove HE was the magnificent and omnipotent Meridia they desired. And when Vikaris was dealt with, Narco would sit upon his Mother's Throne with finality. Lyrianna would be his Queen, and all would worship him as the true leader of Nav'Aria.

As Narco envisioned his grand status, swirling his wine cup in hand, Morta continued, "You can remain behind the lines, overseeing the battle. You need only be present, and they," Morta indicating to the unicorns down below with his stub, "will do the rest."

"Yes," Narco replied, his thoughts lingering on Lyrianna and her full bosom. "I think I will. Good counsel, Morta." He began to take a sip of the velvety wine he had made especially for his cellars.

And yet, just as he was beginning to enjoy his revelry, he remembered the boy. Spluttering on wine, he spat nervously, "But what of Darion?"

"Leave him to me," Morta said softly. Narco shivered at the menacing tone, but then smiled gleefully at the thought of Vikaris and Darion both killed.

Morta laughed and reached his hand over to grip Narco's knee, slowly moving his hand up Narco's leg....

"And now," Morta whispered, coming closer, grabbing the wine goblet and setting it aside, his hot breath upon Narco's exposed face. "How will you thank me for my wise counsel?"

Narco's face froze. He tried not to show his distaste for the man whose hand began to rove over him, pulling him down to the lavish carpet.

Narco now knew why Morta had whispered to the guards to not enter for any reason. Morta wished to take him here and now. To claim him only feet away from his pets and guards, taking ownership of the Emperor's body again after being away for so long.

He knows, Narco thought worriedly. Someone let it slip that Narco had visitors in his bed, and now Morta was going to show him what he thought of such disloyal coupling.

Narco longed desperately for tomorrow and the chance to be rid of Morta again. He considered calling for the guards, but he knew, as Morta did, that he could not defeat Vikaris and Darion without him. While Morta was away, he had lost Lyrianna, Trinidad, and now Zola. He was incapable of ruling without Morta, and so he had to endure him, as he always had. For now.

Morta removed his pants and robe, carelessly tossing them aside before kicking Narco onto his stomach. Narco closed his eyes, picturing his hands around Vikaris's throat and his naked body pressed against Lyrianna's warm, curvaceous form, instead of against the robed man who was mounting him into physical submission.

**

"What do you make of it, Trixon?" Vikaris murmured quietly, walking beside his friend. The moss-covered ground covering their footfalls.

Trixon peered around them. Together, their heightened senses could only make out a humming sound… and the cloying scent of Rav'Arian filth.

The unicorn turned his head sharply and Vikaris knew he had found the trail.

"Get on my back," Trixon ordered, and Vikaris didn't take the slightest insult from the command. He knew that it was something serious, for the unicorns—even those bonded—rarely had riders, unless they were in battle or a dire situation. One must be asked to ride a unicorn, even the King of Nav'Aria.

Vikaris expertly took hold of Trixon's strong neck and mane. He squeezed his knees to remain upright as Trixon tore into the forest. Gripping his sword hilt, Vikaris watched for any skulking enemies in the dense trees. Coming upon an area of clustered rocks, trees, and tree stumps, Trixon slowed his pace. It was rougher land here, and the rocky footing could be dangerous. Trixon still searched though, his head swiveling from side to side.

And then Vikaris could sense it. Wingbeats. That was what the humming had been.

They rounded a massive fallen tree, and as they neared it, four nymphs popped into view, bows raised. At once, they dropped their guard, falling to their knees, bowing and apologizing as they immediately recognized their King and his steed.

Vikaris hastily jumped from Trixon's back. "Rise," he called soothingly. He didn't recognize the four, though he could tell the females had been crying. Tears streaked the youngest one's face, and her shoulders bobbed as she tried to gain control of herself.

The nymphs were a secretive clan and kept their young hidden in the trees and apart from the fight until they were of age. However, once the Nymph Elders deemed them old enough, they were thrown into the front lines. No initiation. No introductions. They simply appeared.

It irked Vikaris, for he liked to know his troops, but he had been taught, what seemed like ages ago by his Father, that some of the clans were more private than others. Being a ruler of Nav'Aria meant knowing when to pry and when to respect the different cultures. So long as all were obedient to him in the end, he allowed them their customs.

The nymphs, merfolk, and trolls were extremely private. Though in Vikaris's mind, now that the trolls fought on the side of Narco, their privacy was null. They were traitors. They deserved nothing but death. At the thought of the trolls, Vikaris sent a quick prayer to the Creator to watch over Riccus—and Antonis and Aalil. They were all separated again, and he hated it. But there was nothing for it.

Vikaris blinked, his focus returning to the nymphs. Their wings hummed softly, keeping them aloft from the ground.

As he bid them to rise, the male did so.

Trixon reminded him the Woods of the Willow nymphs preferred to be called "guardians" for they were entrusted to guard the portal entrances. Their recent failure in this respect would be discussed with the elders later on. He knew they were a proud clan and so followed his friend's counsel.

"Guardians. Thank you for your protection. Please report."

An anguished cry escaped the doll-faced young female.

Vikaris tried to decipher her response. The loss registering as he smelled the tainted air. Lowly, he asked, "Where was the attack?"

The Rav'Arian's putrid odor was fading, but only a bit... like a skunk that passes in the night, its foul-smelling presence still lingers.

The male spoke. "Your Majesty," his melodic tenor voice rang out. "I am Bertin, and these are my sisters," he nodded to them, "We were too late. We have failed you... and her. We arrived in this place, headed to the next Portal, where you must have come from." He asked with a look of question and dismay in his eyes.

Vikaris felt his arm tingle. "Her?" he inquired quietly.

Trixon had already begun moving, and a growl escaped him as he rounded a heap of rocks.

Bertin's head drooped. The nymphs landed and walked softly beside the King to the spot holding Trixon's gaze.

There, Vikaris almost wretched.

A female, or what was left of her, lay discarded. Her wings had been torn and left in the near brush. Clawmarks slashed her upper arms, and her lower half had been mostly eaten away.

Vikaris grunted, grinding his back molars in sudden rage. His green, fierce gaze riveted upon the terrible scene.

"We must bury her," he said in a steely voice.

Bertin and Vikaris took turns speaking the burial words over Flora while the sisters cried what tears remained.

After Vikaris deemed it appropriate, he asked them to accompany him toward the Camp. They needed to move. As they walked, Bertin explained what had transpired during and after the attack.

"It is not good, Your Majesty," Bertin said nodding his head respectfully but pressing on. "Commander Garis was grievously injured. Many of the Camp scattered, so overtaken were they, and so we have been out searching for survivors." His chestnut eyes hardened, and Vikaris saw his obvious pain as he spoke, "Unfortunately, Flora is not the only deceased we have come across."

The younger doll-faced nymph, Ida, sniffled as Bertin shared the tragic news.

Ida flew between the other two nymphs, Lula and Adelina. All three looked alike. They shared the same lilac tresses, with grey eyes, pale, translucent skin and glossy rosebud lips. The only variation in appearance being their shimmering wings that varied in size and degrees of pink. They wore minimal clothing common to the nymphs, revealing more skin than many humans would deem appropriate.

The nymphs, Vikaris remembered, had always viewed their bodies and dress differently. He would not cast shame on their customs. Bertin fell silent at the sound of young Ida's sniffles, and a somber silence overtook the party as they continued in the direction Bertin led.

I will kill him, Trixon boomed suddenly in Vikaris's mind, causing him to almost trip on an unearthed tree root.

Vikaris didn't need to ask who Trixon was referring to. He too had the same strong desire to remove his uncle's head from his body.

If only the coward would show his face, Vikaris mused.

And if he does not? Bitterness dripped from Trixon's every word. *We must flush him out. I cannot take seeing another young victim eaten alive by his filthy barbarians. The things he and his kind have done are… are… atrocious! He must suffer as he has made others suffer.*

You are right, my friend, Vikaris agreed coming to walk closer to Trixon, resting his hand upon the mighty neck as they spoke telepathically so as not to be heard. *The time has come. Once we organize the Camp, we will march for Castle Dintarran…. We will send word to Drigidor to rally the unicorn warriors, and he will meet us for the affront.*

Vikaris again pictured the image of Lyrianna and Trinidad standing near the Portal as they bid farewell. *And make no mistake, Trixon,* Vikaris added, a lethal edge to his voice, *I will be the one to kill him.*

Trixon shook out his mane and whinnied in response, but he didn't argue. The time for hanging back was done. Vikaris would face his uncle now. He was done hiding.

The smell of cooking meat filled the air, abating his smoldering rage. The Camp was close.

CHAPTER 19

The Stragglers

After the forest skirmish, they had spent the day tending to the injured unicorns and clearing the Rav'Arian corpses. They had piled them, and Triumph, using his horn as a flint, struck it on a stone to set them aflame. Darion's eyes and nasal passages had burned from the acrid smoke and wretched smells.

Before the last corpse had been piled, Darion and Edmond had decided to strip it. They had never seen a Rav'Arian unrobed, and Darion had a feeling that their enigmatic, alien form should make sense. It was connected to the Reouls he knew, but how? They certainly weren't dragons. *So, what were they?*

Triumph had explained them as best he could when they had been in their studies at Kaulter, yet without examining one, Darion had never quite believed him. They had killed the others they'd encountered so swiftly before moving on in search of reinforcements. Darion and his party had been severely fatigued and dehydrated crossing the Shazla. There had been no time for inspections.

They wound torn strips from their shirts around their heads to block the smell, though the material did little good, the smell having saturated everything.

Edmond grabbed a small knife and cut away the creature's robes. They had seen one's face during the fight when its hood fell away, as had Triumph apparently.

The naked corpse was worse than anything Darion could have ever dreamed up!

The creature's blackened skin—for lack of a better word—was mottled with a red scale-like texture. Its back appeared like the loose image of a shell which spread into two parts as if it were wings. Since the Rav'Arians didn't ever fly, at least that the party knew of, they assumed the wings must not function. Its face was something else! *Hideous doesn't begin to explain it*, Darion thought. Nightmares were made of this type of stuff.

The scaled, mottled skin covered a protruding beak, though now that Darion saw it, it was more of a maw than a true beak—unlike that of a bird's. The mandible was large, and Darion could see how they could devour their prey, ripping it apart with their strong jaw and jagged teeth. *That must be what makes that horrid clicking sound,* he thought as he looked at the rows of teeth. *That and its poisonous talons.*

Darion inspected its limbs. Even though it walked on two feet and used its arms, it wasn't fully proportionate to a man, being much larger and stouter. And strangely, Darion spied a stumped tail. He had never noticed it because they wore long black robes. The eeriest part of the creature, though, were its eyes. For there, it did resemble a man.

Edmond thumbed its eyelids, revealing amber eyes. Red hairs stood erect around the top of the creature's otherwise bald head. The tiny hairs growing out from the crevices between the scales. The entire being seemed wrong. Unnatural. As if Narco had somehow taken the DNA of multiple species and created a new one. No wonder they hid behind cloaks. They probably hated the sight of themselves as much as he did, Darion thought, feeling disgusted.

"I think you are right," Triumph murmured. "Its origin and ancestry is still unknown to us, but this specimen would appear to be multiple species in one." Triumph's voice sounded hollow. Darion knew he still felt unwell and responsible for Soren's sorry state.

Darion stared at the corpse. Somehow this being had been created, and they needed to know how. And with what?

He shuddered with a final look before nodding for Edmond, his strong friend, to add the body to the heap. Edmond easily lifted the massive abomination and threw it atop the pile before it was consumed in flame.

That had been hours ago. Still, the revolting smell lingered in his nostrils. Unfortunately, they simply had to bare it. They were unable to move from the area because of Soren's incapacity.

The rise and fall of the sleeping unicorn's chest appeared steadier, which brought comfort to Darion. There was nothing to do then but wait. They had cleared the corpses as far as they could while the girls tended the camp site and unicorns. Ati had a small fire going, and in a tiny metal pot roasted herbs that were not meant for eating but rather to clear the air. Darion wished they worked faster, for though he could detect the sage aroma, the toxic odor prevailed.

Darion sat near Nala, unable to hold back his biting tone. "Yes, but why did you come?"

His emotions felt raw. He felt fear, anger, exhaustion, joy, hope. Too much for him to process. He stared into Nala's eyes, drinking in her image as one might drink from an oasis pool. He would gladly look into that pool all the days of his life, yet fear pulsed through him. *What if she had been injured like Soren?*

Nala smiled fondly at him, leaning closer. "We came to find you, of course."

Darion's heart fluttered, as she said it so matter-of-factly. But he couldn't give in to foolish, adolescent feelings. He vividly remembered how angry Zalto had been days before, when he had set the ground on fire that fateful meeting. His eyes darted to the sky overhead, where the first evening stars were announcing the night.

She laughed. A warm, husky sound. She intimidated the hell out of him… and he never wanted that sound to end, but he had to ask.

She touched his arm briefly, speaking with sincerity in her entrancing accented voice. "It is alright. Father understands. He is not angry—well, he may be disappointed in me, but he is not angry with you." Her smile faltered and her gaze drew away toward the fire. He noted how the firelight brought out the red in her chestnut hair and lent an even greater shimmer to her hazel eyes. His pulse rose.

"Yes, but… why come? It's dangerous," he noted, stating the obvious and waving his hands toward the charred remnants of the Rav'Arians yards away.

He looked across the fire at Edmond, who was fumbling for words as Ati knelt beside him, most likely asking him if he were hungry. Edmond looked as if he had never heard the English language. Ati giggled and Darion smiled at them.

Nala once more touched his arm, drawing his attention back to her. "I wanted to be… with you," she said, adding quickly, "with my kind," before a deep rose blush bloomed in her cheeks.

Darion grinned like an idiot. He couldn't stop himself. "I'm glad you came," he said quietly, trying to assure her, though as he said it, the fear throbbing in his stomach remained.

The twinkle was back, and though her blush had not fully faded, she winked at him before continuing in a stronger voice. "Yesterday, when Tiakai spoke of the Prophecy. I was very upset, as you know," she shook her head slightly. "I have never spoken to Father that way, but I was so angry with him. He… all of them should help you, especially if what they say about you is true." Her eyebrows rose questioningly.

"Why do you call him Father? We still don't know your story. How did you end up living with dragons?" At her look he stuttered, "I mean... umm... Reouls." He had heard enough of the stupid Prophecy; he wanted to learn more about her.

Her smile faltered and she stared into the flames. Darion didn't think she would answer him and worried he had offended her. He waited. He wouldn't apologize for this. She knew so much about him, and he needed to understand this. He felt, as he did with the Rav'Arians, that these events and meetings were connected.

His gaze drifted as well, welcoming the silence as she decided her next move. Triumph slept near him. The firelight casting shadows upon his grimy, battle-worn form. Covered in dried blood, he looked more demonic than majestic.

That is quite impossible, Triumph rumbled in Darion's mind. *Unicorns cannot be evil. It goes against every law of nature. The Creator made us near his image—our bright, sheer coats are like moonbeams upon the land. We are pure, clean, powerful defenders of the Realm and the Marked Royals. We could never be 'demons'.*

Darion rolled his eyes. *Leave it to Triumph to ruin a moment,* Darion thought.

Ha! You did that all on your own, my Prince, then added in an admonishing tone, *You mustn't pry with Nala. She will tell you when she is ready.*

Darion muttered something inaudible under his breath.

"Did you say something?"

Darion swallowed what curses he had been about to direct at Triumph. "Me? Ummm... no," but at her skeptical glance, he added, "I was only checking on Triumph." He nervously ran his hand through his shoulder-length hair at her inspection of him. He knew he needed a bath. He must look as bad as Triumph. And stink!

Hey!

She glanced at Triumph and back to him. "You two can communicate, though I have not quite figured out how," she commented as one might comment on the weather.

She's extremely perceptive. He needed to remember that around her. She saw everything, though in this case he was glad. Triumph, annoying as he was—*I heard that!*—was the truest relationship in his life presently. He and Triumph were bonded, and he knew that whatever came, Triumph would be there with him. He had proven that today, when he slew over twenty Rav'Arians by himself to get to Darion.

"Triumph and I are bonded," he shared with her, surprising even himself for being so forthcoming. "I don't really know how it happened, but I guess all the Marked Royals have bonded unicorns. We can share... well, we share a lot," he stopped, unsure of what else to say.

"And those two?" Nala questioned, gesturing in the direction of Soren and Edmond.

Darion shook his head. "They're friends. The unicorns are able to communicate telepathically—though it is rare for a unicorn to partner with a human like Soren has with

Edmond." He smiled at his friends, feeling such relief knowing Soren was going to be alright. He knew Edmond felt the same. For it was those two who had secretly partnered up in Kaulter to come looking for Triumph and Darion.

"You care greatly for them, don't you?"

"Of course, I do," he retorted hotly, wondering how she had now become the one prying. "They're my friends. I'm loyal to my friends—especially friends who are injured because of me."

He squeezed his fists in an attempt to calm down. He felt awash with guilt for snapping at her… and for letting his friends down. For letting Carol down.

He should have been able to protect them. He should have been able to prove to the Reouls that he was the Chosen One and convince them to travel with him to save Nav'Aria. It should have happened that way. Instead, he had told his friends to leave and they had trusted him. Now look at where that had gotten them.

Soren had nearly died, Triumph was exhausted and sliced up, and Edmond… Well, Darion paused, *Edmond was doing alright, all things considered.* He looked at his friend, who was becoming the color of a ripe tomato as Ati carefully pulled off his boot and proceeded to roll up his pant leg. While she examined his hurt leg, Edmond fidgeted. You would think she had offered a lot more than a footrub to make him squirm like that.

Darion smirked at him.

Triumph spoke surprising him.

"Darion," Triumph said aloud his voice intoning paternal affection. "You did the right thing… you are leading us valiantly—and wisely—for one so young. The Reouls would never have joined us," Triumph surmised. He tilted his head as if in apology to Nala before continuing. She nodded sadly but didn't deny it.

"We have learned much on this journey, but we have still not found a way to defeat your uncle, therefore it was time to move. If anyone is to blame, it is I. I should never have left you unguarded. Soren and I should have detected the Rav'Arians. They reek. There is no excuse for my grievous error. Soren almost died because of *me*."

Triumph's haunting eyes held such utter sadness as he looked across the firelight toward Soren. "My friend," he said so softly, Darion almost didn't catch it.

For all the grief he and Soren had given one another over the journey, Darion knew that Triumph was extremely loyal. He would take this personally. Darion could understand this, for that loyalty—and self-loathing—was something the two shared. Darion felt familiar misery gripping his own heart. Who might they lose next?

"Would you two stop it?" Nala's voice pierced the night air, surprising them both. "None of you are to blame. This is *their* fault," she waved her hand toward the smoldering embers. Her eyes blazed fiercer than the flames.

"You asked why I call Zalto 'my Father'? Well the truth is, it is because I can barely remember my Father. My real human Father. And it is because of them," her chin jutted toward the smoking pile as her eyes filled with hot tears. Darion and Triumph both sat silent, afraid to further enrage the foreign female who spoke so vehemently with her hands waving emphatically.

Ati started at the sound of her sister's voice and came to sit next to Nala, grasping her hand.

Ati's sweet, clear voice took up the narrative as sobs cut off Nala's for the moment.

"I cannot remember his face, but I remember his voice. It was a kind, soft voice. 'Stay quiet, stay safe,' he used to say. We were wanderers. We lived off the land, avoiding those monsters. We were…" she pursed her lips, grasping for words. "I think we were running from something… or toward something. I do not know. But one day, Father told us 'stay quiet, stay safe,' and so we did. We always did. For two days we sat quiet. I was a small child, though," she glanced at Nala, who had stopped crying and now stared steadily into the center of the campfire.

"I awoke hungry. Nala was asleep, but I could not sleep anymore for the hunger pains…" at this she bit her lip, again looking to her older sister as if for permission to continue. Nala leaned into her and squeezed the hand she still gripped.

Darion felt sick with worry. Clearly this was traumatic, and he hated to see Nala hurting. *Both of them hurting*, he realized. But he had to know. He dared not breathe, not wanting to upset the moment.

Ati recovering her lapse, continued, smiling shyly at Edmond, who by this time had joined them on this side of the fire. "I remember the sky that day. It was a clear blue day, like today. Not a cloud or shadow in any direction. Everything was quiet. So peaceful. I remember leaving Nala there sleeping. And I started to wander. I think I was looking for our Father because I remember calling out for him, forgetting his command to 'stay quiet'. And then, the shadow came. And I screamed for Father louder and louder. I was so scared." She paused to catch her breath and Nala picked up the story.

Her husky, more mature voice drew in Darion's attention ever further.

"I awoke to Ati's screams. I remember running to her, and then the sky was blocked out, and there was darkness overhead. I remember looking up, and that is when we met... Zalto." She smiled, sardonically. "He had scared Ati, not on purpose of course, but human children are not accustomed to seeing Reouls, as you know. I ran to Ati, who I glimpsed nearby. She stood frozen in terror. I remember hugging her and covering her face before I pushed her behind me. I had picked up a stick and was waving it around at the flying 'beast'."

Darion could imagine the scene. The strong female, brave even as a child, rushing to protect her sister whilst standing up to a monster.

"Zalto landed near us. After a while our curiosity beat out our fear, and as he spoke to us, we listened. He said that he had sad news of our father. There had been an attack by the evil abominations in the land, and that Zalto had gotten there too late. He had seen the whole fight from the air, and after defeating them, he sat with our father while he took his last breaths. Our father told him to find his girls and protect them. To become their father, and never let them return to…" Her voice cut off, and bit one of her knuckles in contemplation.

"Return where?" Darion prodded, sitting forward, the hairs on his neck prickling. "To Nav'Aria? Why would he trust Reouls more than humans to raise his kids? That makes no sense."

Triumph groaned in his head, and Darion winced. He knew he must sound so heartless.

Nala shook her head sadly. "I wish I knew. Father—I mean our human Father—died before he could say. Zalto then flew around until he spotted Ati and me. After he spoke with us, he told us that he would take care of us. We have been with him ever since."

Darion finally exhaled, trying to comprehend such a fate. That must have been a decade, or near a "cycle" ago, as the Nav'Arians called it. *They had spent most of their lives living with dragons!*

"Thank you for sharing, Nala… and you, Ati," Triumph said formally.

"Is that why you're here now?" Darion found his voice.

"Yes," the two girls replied in unison.

Nala pressed on, "We have to know. We have to know if there is something else out here, or if we can find any other remnant of our father. I know we came from this direction, though I do not know any specific details. But I have a…" she trailed off, thinking, her brow wrinkling in consternation.

"What is it?" Triumph asked, being a seasoned expert at drawing information out of people.

"I have a feeling, that is all," she said. "It is as if when I saw you all that day on the beach…."

Darion colored with the memory of that glorious day when they had first spotted the girls in the pool.

"It sparked a memory in me. I remembered seeing other human faces. I had not thought on it for years, but when I saw yours," she said gesturing to Darion and Edmond, "I remembered."

"And so did I," Ati whispered softly.

"There are others of our kind out here somewhere, or at least there used to be. Perhaps there, we will find answers."

"But what about Zalto?" Darion forced himself to keep his eyes on Nala instead of searching the sky overhead.

"He forbade us to ever leave the tribe, of course, but after that day with Tiakai, he knew. When he came to tell us you had left, it was as if the fight had fizzled out of his body. He did not try to stop us. He appeared to know we must follow you. That we were destined to follow you," she concluded inaudibly.

Darion's expert hearing picked it up, and he felt a strange tingling on his arm. He pulled his shirt sleeve up to reveal a strange winged pattern emerging on his upper arm. It looked like the Reoul symbol from the cave wall.

Ati gasped. Nala's eyes widened as she pointed at it covering her mouth.

Darion met Triumph's eyes. The unicorn didn't say anything, though Darion could tell Triumph was trying to figure it all out. Whatever it was, it could be the turning point in the war. He just knew it.

***

"Come on, Gus, we best be on the move," Rick grunted, as he tugged on his horse's reins.

Gus was a good horse, all things considered. He just had a mighty appetite and getting him to stay on task was proving to be a challenge—and Rick had trained and worked with horses all his life. "Just my luck," he grumbled as he jerked on the reins sharply and dug his heels into Gus's sides.

Rick's head thundered. He had been traveling with this dumb horse for days, and all he had to show for it was a sore back from sleeping out alone. *Oregon made me soft*, he cursed himself. He was an outdoorsman. He didn't need a bed or pillow; he just needed his saddle roll. Though as he reached the base of Mt. Alodon and stared at the looming peaks of the Nav'Alodon mountain range, he wondered if that were really true.

Fortunately, he had packed his thick fur lined cloak that Carol had sewn for him upon their return. He remembered mocking her in their familiar way, that it wasn't even winter, and he'd have no use for it. Oh, what he wouldn't give now to thank her. It was as if she had foreseen his need of the garment, making him treasure it all the more.

Rick had no idea where he was going, led by instinct instead of a set path. He knew the trolls lived far in the mountains, though most Nav'Arians had never frequented the area, even before the wretches turned traitor. The mountains were cold and treacherous... why risk it, when you could stay in the safe, abundant land of Nav'Aria? He had always preferred the plains and forest himself, good for tracking and riding. He tried to trick himself into believing that this solo journey would be fun. *Put his tracking skills to good use*, but he realized it for the lie that it was. He was running. Just as Darion had.

"Damn hypocrite," he mumbled as he tugged on Gus's reins again, trying to keep him on the straight path, instead of diverting to the edges where ferns and wildflowers crowded the trail.

"You certainly are that," a loud, familiar voice called out from behind.

"Gus," Rick drawled, not turning around. "I think this is the part where I officially lose my mind."

"Shut up, you wanna be cowboy, and help me down. You know I hate riding... no offense, buddy," the familiar voice said as it patted something.

No way. Rick had frozen at the sound and dared not turn for fear that it would all be in his imagination.

"And while you are at it, help me down too. Give me a sword and a good pair of boots any day, this thing stinks!" At the sound of the other voice, Rick did turn, Gus, grateful for the distraction stood lazily in the pathway stretching his neck out toward the wildflowers.

"How did you find me?" Rick did not know whether to be impressed or upset. Had he grown that lazy with his tracks?

Antonis's booming laugh filled the dead space and warmed Rick more than he'd ever admit.

His big friend jumped down in one fluid motion. For all his griping, Antonis had not risen to the rank of Commander without being an expert rider. He turned to help Aalil, who rolled her eyes and hopped down just as he had done.

"You are full of surprises," Antonis teased her grinning ruefully as they approached. Rick climbed off Gus, allowing the slow-witted horse to graze.

Antonis wrapped Rick in a bear hug—whether Rick wanted it or not, apparently. Antonis clapped him on the back, and as he drew back from the embrace, he peered into Rick's face. "Are you okay?" He asked him in a low voice.

Rick shook free of his friends' hands and gave one curt nod of his head, before greeting Aalil. "You must be thirsty?" he said turning quickly to his saddle roll and wiping his eyes on his shirtsleeves before the two saw him crying like a fool. He cleared his throat gruffly and spat before turning around.

Though Antonis and Aalil stood feet apart from one another, they radiated sexual tension. They were a couple... beyond what Rick had accidentally intruded upon. He could tell by the way Antonis stood partially facing her, and by the way she kept glancing at him when he didn't see her looking. The look she gave him was like the look Carol had once given Rick. An all too familiar lump formed in his throat... he stuffed it down. Carol would want him to be happy for their friend, and that is what he was going to do. *My friend.* He had not realized how alone he had felt until this moment.

Drawing the horses away from the trail, the three gathered to sit and share a midday meal of nuts, jerky, apples and an oat flatbread. They washed it down with ale from Kaulter. It was fresh. Antonis mockingly smacked his lips, savoring the flavor.

Rick cocked his head. "How did you two find me? And so fast?"

Antonis looked at Aalil sheepishly before grinning at him. "Well... we had some help." The big man's shoulders seemed to tense as if expecting an attack. Rick raised an eyebrow, waiting. Aalil pursed her lips, as if in distaste.

Antonis cleared his throat, "Help from the ummm... nymphs in the area of the Western Portal... they helped us find your trail."

"Yeah," Aalil cut in, appearing unable to hold back. "They were only too happy to help," the stare she shot at Antonis could have cut glass.

Antonis raised his hands in a "what can I say" gesture.

Aalil slugged him in the arm before continuing, causing Antonis's ale to slosh over the rim of the cup he held, "I let them know when we had had quite enough of their help, and could take it from there," she smirked as she flung her dark braid over her shoulder. Antonis winced at the recollection.

Rick watched the two, taking in their body language and story. And then he burst out laughing. "Damn, I missed you," he chuckled, lightly punching his old friend's shoulder and wiping his eyes.

"Alright, alright, have you both had about enough?" Antonis jested, feigning injury and crossing his massive arms. And then, after taking a hearty swig of ale, Antonis added, soberly, "I missed you too, Rick. What were you thinking, leaving without telling me? Telling anyone?"

Rick blew his dusty bangs from his forehead, knuckling the knot in his chin. "I... had my reasons," he replied obstinately.

"Had?" Aalil pressed.

Rick glowered at her.

"Yeah... I had them. They just... do not seem as good anymore," Rick admitted.

"It is alright, really," Antonis continued. "Vikaris understands—it took some convincing, but eventually the entire Unicorn Council believed you were on the right track—no pun intended, huh?" Antonis winked.

Rick felt relief flood him. He had wondered how Vikaris—*the King!*—would feel about his trek. "Well, I am glad to hear that," Rick drawled, as he took another swig of ale. "But why are you here, then? I thought you were protecting the King, back in your old role?"

Antonis stared at him levelly. "I was until you decided to go galivanting across the mountains all humble hero, taking this quest upon yourself... Gee, I wonder where Darion gets it?" Antonis sounded off.

Rick cursed. Antonis was right. He had been so flaming mad at his son—Darion—and yet, when the opportunity presented itself, he had done the exact same thing.

Antonis smiled at him then and added, "So, once I heard you were going to defeat Narco's mysterious hold on the trolls, I figured I needed to come... ya know, protect you."

Aalil snorted but didn't respond.

Antonis scowled stroking his goatee, "Well, something like that. Vikaris ordered us to find you and assist you, but," he raised his hands to ward off argument. "I would have come anyway. I want to kick some troll ass as much as you do." He grinned, leaning back.

"Are you always this chauvinistic?"

"I guess you will find out," Antonis grinned at Aalil to reveal his perfect smile. She only rolled her eyes once more in response.

Yep, Rick thought. *Sexual tension. Not awkward at all.*

CHAPTER 20

The Unicorns

"Nothing has turned out as I imagined," Lyrianna murmured listlessly as she brushed her windblown golden locks from her shoulder, biting her cheek to prevent herself from crying.

"Nor I," Trinidad agreed softly, nuzzling her face before moving to inspect a bumblebee buzzing the flowers where he lay.

Lyrianna exhaled. Vikaris had left that morning, and though she knew he had to go, it only reinforced her feeling of inadequacy. *What was she to do here?* Vikaris was gone. Darion had runaway—*from her*! One by one her loved ones were disappearing, and all the while she remained.

She and Trinidad sat near a leafy Elm tree, and at its base little wildflowers dotted the hillside, overlooking the cliffs of Kaulter. As she stared out upon the blue swirling waves, she spotted a dolphin fin here, or a merfolk tail there. At one point, three heads popped out of the water, and as the party looked toward her perch, they all waved.

Lyrianna waved back, her despondency momentarily forgotten as she thought of the merpeople. *How must they be faring in wartime?*

She knew that those who had been trapped in the River and Lake near Castle Dintarran had suffered terribly. Many out there must be longing for their loved ones, suffering from survivor's guilt. She made a mental note to inquire about the merfolk to Elsra, to make sure those here were well cared for. She had had limited interactions with them in the past—being such a private clan—yet still, she felt it was her duty as Queen to ensure their welfare. They had learned so much from the freed nymph and centaur captives regarding Narco's hold on the Kingdom; which included the horrid treatment of the merfolk left behind.

"Ohhhhhh," she grumbled, standing up suddenly and brushing the grass from her linen dress. "This is ridiculous. I am the Queen. I cannot waste time with this childish behavior. I have Nav'Arians to care for." With squared shoulders and a lifted chin, her path was now clear.

Trinidad stood hurriedly. With a freshly washed coat and the sun's rays upon him, he seemed more and more like the mighty Trinidad of old. Though he lacked his horn, the good meals and medical care at Kaulter had greatly improved his sickly appearance. He was filling out.

Lyrianna thought he looked brilliant in the light. She smiled affectionately toward him.

"What will you do, my Queen?"

Before she could respond, Cela rushed into view, her hoofbeats thundering upon the ground. She had been scouting the perimeter, of her own volition, being Lyrianna's self-appointed bodyguard and all.

Cela's cheeks appeared flushed, and a light sheen of perspiration graced her pale forehead, only making her all the more lovely. Her bright red curls draped down her voluptuous frame, spilling into pure ivory coated legs. *No wonder Cela had been a hit with the young male centaurs at Kaulter,* Lyrianna thought.

Cela had knocked many of the males down in the practice arena too, or so Lyrianna had heard. This had only gained her more attention. A fierce, stunning warrior…. She and Aalil had made quite an impression with the troops. She smiled thinking of Antonis and Aalil. Whether he knew it or not, *that* woman had gotten her hands on him and would not be letting go.

Lyrianna smoothed her skirts, awaiting Cela. She truly did feel well protected and cared for with Trinidad and Cela around. She knew it was not bad news, for Cela was radiant. A huge smile brightening her face.

"Your Majesty," Cela greeted with a quick bow.

"What is it, Cela?" Lyrianna began to feel her pulse rise.

"Elsra has requested your presence in the Fortress, her messenger just gave me word."

Lyrianna felt herself frown, "Alright, but why the big smile?"

They were already beginning to move down the slope toward the bridge that would carry them into the Village.

Cela was practically bouncing in jubilance now, her hooves clattering on the stone bridge.

"It is the frieze, Your Majesty. Elsra thinks it has to do with Darion. He has had success... or so she thinks."

Lyrianna turned toward her, surprised. "Darion?" She quickened her pace.

Cela didn't reply, but instead sealed her lips tightly, grimacing, as if she had spoken out of turn.

Darion. Lyrianna started to run. Her son? Why hadn't Cela just spat it out? The centaur and unicorn easily kept pace with her, and the three dramatically entered the Village. Passersby jumped out of the way, murmuring greetings—and warnings to watch out—as they passed. Cela only had to knock one out of the way; at Lyrianna's scowl, Cela only laughed.

"He had it coming, your Majesty," the centaur joked and grinned mischievously. "He is a poor loser. I beat him at cards the other night, and now he will not leave me alone. Says I cheated him," she laughed, tossing her red curls as she added, "can you believe that? Me?"

Lyrianna didn't reply, for she was feeling embarrassingly winded compared to her four-legged companions, and she could most certainly believe it. She had heard Cela had a bit of a gambling problem, and quite a bit of luck. Lyrianna—through Vikaris—had even heard that some of the guards whispered that the gorgeous centaur tricked them by using her womanly virtues as distraction. She was gaining quite the reputation in the barracks. Upon reflection, Lyrianna laughed aloud, grinning at Cela in return. *She cannot help being beautiful and good at cards.* Shame on the player for getting distracted amidst a heated card game. That showed weakness, and Cela was an expert at exploiting weakness in the arena, and at cards, apparently. *Or was it just in men?*

Cela gave her a cat-like grin as if she could read her mind, before pushing ahead to get to the door before Lyrianna. They had arrived outside the massive wooden fortress. Cela's chest heaved, bosom at eye level with the young human guard who looked like he was going to either faint or cry from the sight, an idiotic smile warping his face, as Cela elbowed him out of the way and opened the door herself for the Queen. Bowing her head respectfully, Cela was the picture of propriety.

Lyrianna felt near giggling herself, her affection for her bodyguard growing with each and every exchange. But she quickly forgot the cards and the centaur as she strode into the huge rotunda.

Guards lined the walls, and in the interior of the room stood the dazzling Regent and her mate. All other furnishings and creatures looked plain when faced with such splendor. Elsra's entrancing lavender eyes studied the upper wall. Elsra spoke as Lyrianna approached, though she did not cease her focus of the frieze.

"It began at the top of the hour. Bal'khoa noticed it first."

Trinidad approached the party with Lyrianna, and he nodded, murmuring praise to Bal'khoa, his young assistant, who stood clutching a notebook apart from the Council. Lyrianna smiled at him briefly before focusing on the frieze.

She had never spent too much time studying it. She knew that it told of the history of Nav'Aria—and thereby, Kaulter—and of the various species of the land. There were sections devoted to the First Horn, Tribute, and the unicorns. Some for the centaurs, the nymphs, the merfolk, and even the trolls. Great sections held the Castle Dintarran and symbols and images for each of the Marked Rulers, beginning with Vondulus. It had stopped with King Rustusse. No images had ever come since. It was strange. Old magic from the Creator, the unicorns explained it. None had created it themselves, it just "appeared". Typically, after a large occurrence or event, such as the naming of a new Marked Royal, the creation of the new species, or a victorious battle. It had been cycles since Rustusse's image had been etched into the ligneous frieze.

"It looks like... wings," she said softly, at the same moment, Trinidad breathed, "Winged Ones."

Gooseflesh covered Lyrianna's arms. *Winged Ones? Darion!*

For so it was. As they stood, an impressive winged creature appeared on the frieze, with tiny winglike symbols dotting the area above it. In between it and the crescent moon symbols to the right which were also materializing, a figure emerged. An invisible hand guided the wood carving, meticulous in its design. It looked like a man. A young man, judging by the face, with a Marked arm clearly risen for all to behold.

"What can this mean?" She felt giddy and terrified at the same time. Lyrianna turned toward Trinidad and Elsra. "What has happened to Darion?"

"He has passed the Tests," Elsra said softly, her voice sounding reverent. Tears glimmered in her eyes as she finally looked away from the frieze and deeply into Lyrianna's.

"He is the Chosen One," Trinidad's familiar voice enveloped her. He sounded awestruck, just as Eslra did. "He... This..."

Lyrianna's eyes widened, staring from her friend and back to the frieze which was growing in detail. The figure, of Darion, she now supposed, straddled the land between the two parties. Lyrianna had never heard Trinidad like this. He spluttered. Speechless. Her pulse jumped at the unknown connotation, and she wished more than ever that Vikaris were here.

"But, what does it mean? 'Chosen One'?"

"Your Son," Trinidad's chest heaved with emotion, and he bowed his head to her before continuing. "Your Son is the true Marked Heir, Your Majesty. He has met his tests valiantly—and he has passed."

"How can you be certain?" She knew something of the "tests". Bonding and gaining admittance to the Shovlan Tree had been two, but what were the others?

She gasped, suddenly remembering the other tests. *Valor, fair judgment, and full use of the senses.*

"Is he alright?" She asked, feeling more and more unsure of the situation as she glanced from the awestruck unicorns to the strange art. Too often, she knew those tests were met in battle or upon an injury. Oh, she hoped he was safe, and if he had faced the enemy, that he had come out unscathed. *Where are you, Darion?* she wondered again.

Elsra's strong voice rang out. "He is more than 'alright', Your Majesty. He is our Marked Heir. The True Marked Heir."

Lyrianna wanted to say that she had already known he would be but thought better of it as Elsra continued. "Yes, he has faced the enemy and come out victorious. For this to appear could only mean that he has also met the Winged Ones."

Goosebumps scoured Lyrianna's body again at the Regent's words. She wanted to ask how she could be so sure.

"This..." Elsra continued steadily, "This is Prophecy. This image is of something that will come to pass. We can only conjecture at this point, until we receive word from Darion—and Triumph."

Trinidad and Bal'khoa's heads were together speaking in hushed tones.

"What is it?" She whispered to him when he had finished, after Bal'khoa had been sent out on some errand.

"I need my horn," Trinidad whispered, his eyes revealing the fervor in him that this event had extracted. "If the final fight is upon us, I must be in it. I must be ready and able to communicate with them. I have always had the gifting of communication. I know with my horn I would be able to reach them. It is imperative that I can regrow it to aid our Marked Heir!"

By this time Elsra and Drigidor had gathered with them. Drigidor, who had up until now been silent, spoke, his voice booming and filling the expanse. "Trinidad is correct. He must discover this truth—for he has a part to play in the coming events. As do I," his dark eyes glowed like hot coals as he looked into Elsra's.

Lyrianna stepped back to give them a moment of privacy, but the unicorn's words were too loud to miss.

"I must rally the troops, Elsra. This is it. I can feel it. I will join my King, as he has requested. We leave at dawn."

Elsra inhaled but didn't reply. Her wise eyes spoke the words she could not. Lyrianna knew all too well the emotions she was feeling. Pride in choosing a strong, brave partner, and utter dread at the thought of losing him.

Surprising even herself, Lyrianna put her hand on Elsra's pure white mane and neck, and as Elsra was unable to speak, Lyrianna did.

"Rally the warriors, Drigidor, and join my husband on the field. I, Queen Lyrianna of Nav'Aria, wife of the true Marked King and mother of the true Marked Heir, give you my blessing. We," Lyrianna paused, patting Elsra's velvety coat, "We will safeguard Kaulter and assist Trinidad in his quest for his horn."

Lyrianna let go of Elsra and took Drigidor's giant head in her hands, purposely stepping to the right so his gleaming horn wouldn't pierce her. Gently, she planted a kiss at the base of his horn. "May the Great Creator guide you and keep you safe," she said formally before whispering softly, "Bring me Narco's head."

Drigidor's eyes glinted intensely, and she knew that a promise had been made.

Elsra inhaled behind her, and Lyrianna turned toward the Regent. "Prepare the troops," Lyrianna commanded spinning on her heel.

Regent Elsra nodded her head slightly, gazing at her with the oddest of expressions. Trinidad and Cela quickly trailed Lyrianna toward the doors.

"Well," Elsra purred, leaning into Drigidor as the chamber cleared of soldiers running to do the Queen's bidding. "We have a Queen at last."

Drigidor rumbled in agreement before murmuring his desire for Elsra to join him in their apartments for their final moments together.

Elsra scrunched her eyes at his words. One silver tear escaping her. Returning her gaze to the frieze, she observed that the invisible artist had stopped. The image was complete. "Long live the Marked Heir," she whispered, staring at the foreign image of the winged ones near the figure. Then she turned slowly, leaning affectionately upon her husband. She had already lost one to this fight. *Creator help her, she could not lose another.*

***

Zola glowered at the men leaving the pavilion. Master and his entourage. *Oh, how she hated them.* She had been living in a trance for years, and coming out of it, she realized how vandalized she had been. They had taken everything from her. *Her horn, her freedom, HER CHILDREN.* She wanted to watch Master suffer. But not yet. First, she needed to find a way to get into that building and free Trigger. She assumed the others were housed in there and could only hope she'd be able to save them too.

Cowering in the broken cart and drapery behind the castle, she hid. For the past couple of days, and only when she was sure it was clear, she scrounged the area for food and drink from the puddles of rainwater left from the evening downpour, before returning to the refuge of the wreckage. Having been kept like a pet all these years, she had not realized how hard it was to forage and find adequate meals. Her stomach rumbled, having never gone without a meal. At least, not until Trigger's birth. She felt weak and tired and angry.

As she watched them through the torn fabric of the cart, she saw the hooded figure—Master's friend who always helped with her "pains." He was scanning the area as if searching for something. For someone. She ducked, her heart beginning to race. He couldn't sense her. He was only a man. That would be impossible.

But she remembered his eyes. Those creepy yellowish-brown eyes that, even though entranced, had always left her chilled. She tried not to breathe as she heard footsteps approaching the rubble in the courtyard, praying her rumbling stomach didn't give her away.

Soft footfalls fell upon the gravel. She held her breath, daring not to move. She tried to think. If someone tugged on the fabric, what would she do? *Fight*, she realized, tensing her muscles to spring upon her discovery. If she could attack before the person could react, she might be able to make it to the treeline. She had seen that the soldiers surrounding Master wore blades, but if she were fast enough, they wouldn't be able to touch her. She wondered if she could run that fast. Hesitation and fear gripped her. She had never actually run—never exercised properly, having been imprisoned all these years. *Could I make it to the trees?* As she began to secondguess her plan, the footsteps arrived outside the cart. From one of the small tears in the side of the canvas, she could make out the black slippered toe of the approacher.

She heard the person draw a deep breath. Closing her eyes, she braced for what was to come.

"Sir," a young voice called. Hurried footsteps approached the slippered individual outside her hideaway.

"What is it?" the haunting voice of the hooded man said.

Zola's eyes bulged. *The hooded man.* She felt a longing to drive her hoof through his skull and a desire to escape. Run as far as possible from his evil presence.

"Emperor Narco bades you come at once," the young voice squeaked before gulping loudly. Clearly this guard was as terrified of the hooded man as she.

She shut her eyes, wishing more than anything to be away from here.

She heard the man draw another long breath, as if he were sniffing the air. Tasting it. Her large bulk lay sprawled out atop the broken cart floor. All it would take was a glance. If he happened to kneel down and peer into the torn canopy, she was done for. She dared not look around for fear of shifting the wood. She listened, frozen.

"Does he now?" The chill in his quiet voice sent a tingle coursing down her whole spine. The stump on her forehead began to throb. She shuddered involuntarily and then froze once more, terrified he may have sensed her movement. "We must not make him wait then," the man retorted.

Her eyes were still screwed shut when she realized the footsteps were striding away from her and had rejoined Master's party near the Castle entrance many yards off. She waited, painstakingly quiet, until finally she let out a relieved sigh and chanced a look through the torn fabric. Empty. They were gone.

Her pulse lessened now that the threat had passed, but she knew he'd be back. He suspected her. He would be hunting her now. She had to move.

***

Triumph jolted awake, springing to his feet.

"What is it?" Darion asked groggily.

Edmond met Triumph's eyes, then grappled for his sword checking the perimeter. Edmond had been on watch.

Triumph shook his head, dazed. He observed Soren and the girls still sleeping undisturbed.

He didn't know what had awaken him. *A nightmare?*

Triumph thought he had sensed Zola, ridiculous as it may seem. Many years had passed since her murder. *Why dream of her now?* He felt disconcerted. He had a sense that she was in great peril, and his skin crawled as it often did when Rav'Arians were near. He searched around their encampment with his mind. He couldn't sense any living presence—especially another unicorn beyond Soren. And he didn't smell the putrid beasts. *So why do I have this sinking feeling?*

"Triumph," Darion stood up, placing his palm against Triumph's neck. "What is it?" Concern filled his voice, but Triumph didn't know how to reassure him. He couldn't explain it; he only had a feeling that they needed to move. Immediately.

"We need to go."

All the noise woke the girls, and Soren, though lying still, was coherent.

Darion made to argue, and as Triumph prepared to defend himself, Soren spoke. He had hardly said much since the attack.

"I sense it too," Soren whispered, a tremor of fear escaping.

Edmond stood over the girls protectively as his eyes scoured the treeline. Darion was strapping on his sword and gathering his things.

Triumph felt his pulse escalating.

"Sense what?" Darion asked looking around.

"Something is out there," Soren said, his voice growing stronger. He began to stand up on shaky legs. The girls were up in a moment attending to him.

"Soren, no. You need to rest," Darion started, but Triumph didn't let him finish.

He knew Soren spoke truthfully. Whatever it was that had disturbed his sleep was not abating. It was growing. Triumph shivered. It felt as if there were eyes on him. Something was… searching for them. *Narco?*

Triumph pictured Gamlin, when Darion had pushed the evil force from him. He had explained it as Narco using him—the young Reoul—as eyes. Narco had been there, Darion had told him. Triumph didn't how that could be possible, but it would certainly explain the disquietude.

"We need to move now," Triumph repeated in a commanding voice. He walked toward Soren, inspecting his friend's wounds. They had all healed, except for the final gash that had scabbed over. The skin had repaired itself, and the girls' poultice seemed to have sped up the healing. Triumph sniffed the wound. It didn't smell infected.

"Can you walk, my friend?"

Soren lifted his head proudly, the moonlight shining off his horn, and though he was still covered in blood, mud, and muck, Triumph felt his heart swell with pride. Soren was a unicorn. The mightiest species of the land. He—and Triumph—would not let this new threat harm the Prince.

Resolve wakened in Soren's eyes. "Let's move."

Triumph shot a fierce look at Nala, who looked like she wanted to argue. She grumbled, sullenly, but set to work. The humans packed the campsite quickly, and before the first morning rays lightened the sky, the party was on the move again.

***

Trixon couldn't stand still. Though they had made it safely to camp hours ago, he felt anxious. Something was coming. He could feel it, and though he had had Vikaris and Garis triple the guard, he still paced. Something unidentifiable, but evil, was happening. The foreboding, it seemed, had reverberated through the five unicorn warriors at camp.

What are you doing?

Trixon turned to see Vikaris approaching, his face a picture of annoyance and vigilance. He had left Garis's command tent. The centaur had recovered from the previous Camp attack. His note had been short because he had needed to react to the enemy, having only moments to dispatch a messenger—Seegar.

Trixon and Vikaris both had been relieved at finding Commander Garis and Lieutenant Kragar, safe. Vikaris had met with his officers well into the night, and all the while, Trixon had stood guard.

Vikaris had been perturbed that Trixon did not join the War Council… and by the look he was giving Trixon, the unicorn had a feeling he still was.

Trixon shook his mane in agitation. *You may be my King, but you are sure dense sometimes.*

Did you just insult me?

Trixon blew out hot air before answering. He peered at his King, whose ruby and Marked arm glowed in the moonlight. There were few stars out tonight, a hazy fog creeping into the forest. The whole thing drove Trixon mad. He knew Vikaris had every right to be annoyed with him, yet he felt… something.

"Something is there," Trixon alleged lowly, the other unicorns he had been marching with, gathered in a circle around the King and himself. Guarding the pair from whatever threat was coming.

"What is there?" Vikaris responded, his fierce green eyes piercing into Trixon's. "I feel nothing. Is it Kaulter? Is it Lyrianna? Darion?" Worry pervaded the King's words, and he creased his brow as he continued to stare intently at Trixon.

"No." Trixon shook his head, thinking. *What is it?*

"I do not know how to explain it, but…" Trixon trailed off as the unicorns surrounding them began shifting and pawing the earth.

Vikaris broke eye contact, startled, looking at the others who were whinnying and stamping the ground. The unicorns' eyes rolled around wildly, and in the low light they looked almost possessed. Feral. They were wild with fear or rage, or both. Trixon stamped his own hooves in response. His skin crawled. Something evil was on its way.

In moments, the whole camp was aglow. Garis, his russet coat gleaming in the torch light, approached, his bandaged forehead creased with concern, followed by the steely jawed Kragar and a nervous contingent of guards. Myrne's braids clicked loudly as she hurriedly left her nearby tent to join them.

"What is it, Your Majesty?" Garis's voice boomed, as he flexed his sword arm, his own hooves seeming to stamp the earth of their own volition.

Vikaris paused. "I do not know, but I trust Trixon in this matter." The King looked to him for guidance.

Trixon beheld the uneasy unicorns, and the gathering soldiers—man, centaur, nymph.

"Make ready the camp. We need to march." And to Vikaris only, Trixon added, *The final battle has come at last.*

Vikaris did not react outwardly, beyond a slight widening of his eyes. He nodded at Trixon.

"You heard him," Vikaris shouted, "We march at dawn. Prepare to move. Prepare—for war!"

***

"Oh no," Trinidad whispered, fear seizing him. Only moments ago there had been laughs and gaiety in the Queen's compartments as Cela regaled them with another story of her victory in the practice arena against a cocky male opponent.

"What is it?" Lyrianna spoke just as softly. The candlelight enhancing her beautiful radiant skin. The corners around her blue eyes creasing with worry.

"The moment has come. Narco is releasing *them.*"

"Who?" Lyrianna followed Trinidad as he hurried toward the door.

Trinidad's serious gaze brokered no argument. They didn't have time for explanations. He needed his horn. The time had come, and he had wasted another evening. *You fool!* He chastised himself.

After spending hours in the library with Bal'khoa, he had decided to sup with the Queen and Cela. *To spend the evening laughing? What was I thinking? While I relax, Narco and his minions are plotting our downfall.*

"I must visit the Shovlan Tree."

Lyrianna gasped but didn't question as they came to the main hall. Cela had pushed past them to ensure their safety as they emerged into the passageway. All traces of humor had left her face, and she was once more the most terrifying female warrior—well, besides Aalil—that Nav'Aria had ever seen. Her toned arms flexed as she prowled the halls in search of any lurking threat.

Trinidad felt something. It must be the trapped wretches Narco had kept. He had to regain his horn now if he ever hoped to be a help in these final events. Whatever had pushed Narco to act meant that he was on the move. The enemy was coming, and Trinidad was helpless without his horn. He feared for his son, Trixon, and for the King, as their force would also be on the move to meet the enemy.

Hooves clattered on the wooden floor.

They paused. Trinidad spun, knowing who he would find.

"You felt it too?" Drigidor's voice boomed. Lyrianna inhaled, and this time Cela drew her sword, her eyes devouring the space around the Queen.

"I did," Trinidad replied. "I must go to the Tree."

Drigidor, and the unicorns arriving from all directions, nodded.

"Do so, quickly, Trinidad. We need your wisdom if we are to win this fight."

Trinidad swallowed, emotion filling him. Though Drigidor was not his father, he did not loathe him as his hot-headed brother did. He nodded in agreement to the powerful warrior.

"What will you do?" Lyrianna's voice held only the slightest tremor. "Is the King safe?"

"We ride for the Portal now, Your Majesty," Drigidor bowed, his voice reverberating loudly. "We will join your husband as he rides for war."

Lyrianna lifted her chin regally, and spoke, "Go then, Mighty Drigidor. Protect the King—and Nav'Aria. May the Great Creator bless you and keep you all," as she spoke, Trinidad watched her gaze upon the gathered unicorns. His heart swelled seeing their heads rise valiantly under her watchful gaze. Many murmured their thanks and assent before following Drigidor toward the fortress entrance.

"Drigidor," Lyrianna called, and though she didn't say anything more, Trinidad had a feeling he knew what that look meant. Drigidor's gaze became so smoldering that Trinidad knew it was Narco they were thinking of.

Trinidad could not delay any longer. "Your Majesty, I must go."

Lyrianna gave the departing unicorns one final nod before she began walking ahead. She paused, turning back to Trinidad. "Then, come along," she replied authoritatively.

He shook his head sadly. "Your Majesty. You know that you cannot. Only one baring the Mark can enter the Tree."

She strode back to him, making up the distance alarmingly fast. She came right up to his face, mere inches from him.

"We stay together, understand?" She said fiercely. "You and I are bonded, whether formally or not, it makes no difference," she said passionately and then lifted her hand to stop him from dissuading her. He had never seen her like this—at least toward him. His heart soared at the word *bond.*

"We are bonded," she said again through gritted teeth. "You never would have lost your horn if I had not run off that day," her cheeks flushed red with her speech. "No one else knows what we have been through," she looked at Cela, and nodded, "Except we three. Together, we will go to the Shovlan Tree and find your answer. You will regrow your horn. Cela and I will help you."

Trinidad stood, shocked. How could he argue with her? But it was impossible. None besides the Marked Royals had ever entered the Tree.

Cela smirked at him, planting her hands against her sides and stamping an ivory coated leg with emphasis.

Lyrianna gave him a pat, much like a mother would with an unruly child who had been redirected.

"Whatever you say, Your Majesty," was all he could muster before continuing down the hall toward a side door in the direction of the Tree's last sighted appearance. As they continued on silently, he realized that he had never tried to access the Tree without his horn.

Would it still recognize him as a unicorn? *Maybe I do need them.* And as he walked, a chill ran down his spine, his stump tingling. *They are coming.* He needed all the help he could get if he were going to be able to face the enemy in time. They all did.

CHAPTER 21

The Release

Narco glared at the troops assembled in his Throne Room—below his dais.

He reveled in the feeling as he watched them kneeling to him. This was *his* Castle. He would defeat Vikaris and end the looming challenge of succession. The last Marked Royals would die by his hand.

The men, in their black and red uniforms baring his winged insignia, stood instantly at the flick of his finger.

He could feel Morta's toxic presence beside him, but he ignored it. In the face of his troops, he was invincible. *Omnipotent. NOTHING can stop me. And once Vikaris is killed, I will no longer need Morta's interference.*

Narco sipped from his goblet to mask his smirk. It would do no good letting Morta know of his intentions now. He needed to play the game. He was still the meek student when alone with Morta. But oh, how that would change. He purposely had to keep from closing his eyes as he pictured Vikaris's bloodied head dripping from where it had been torn from his body and planted on a spike. He would sit here soon and bask in his peoples' worship. He and Lyrianna—his Empress. He grasped the vial upon the cord adorning his neck. The orange and red liquid swirled. This was the last of it. He could not use it up—not yet.

A throat cleared, interrupting his thoughts, as a pale hand gripped his shoulder.

No, I will not use it yet. I will need the vial if I am to rid myself of Morta.

Narco shook the man's hand off from his shoulder as he stood. A bowing servant taking the proffered glass from him.

Narco knew he looked magnificent in his red and black tailored clothes, a fitted chest plate—the handsomest of its kind—adorned his chest and belted at the waist. Having glimpsed himself in a mirror, he had for the first time felt like a warrior. He possessed strength, thanks to the idiotic dragon from years ago. He had an army behind him, and as his emblem blazoned across Nav'Aria to meet the rebels in the field—and destroy them—he would stand out among the rabble. The sun would glisten upon his chest plate, and his ornate cape would billow in the wind as he rode one of the largest of his pets, the midnight black unicorn. All would stare in wonder.

For a moment his face contorted into a grimace as his thoughts turned to unicorns. One in particular and the scar he had left him with. *Trinidad.* That unicorn would pay with his blood.

Morta assured Narco the scar made him look powerful, yet Narco feared it revealed his weakness. An opponent had gotten close enough to wound him.

Fortunately, his strength from the dragon blood helped him heal… it made him downright immortal.

"Move, you fools," Narco barked at his troops. As the men jumped to obey, the Rav'Arians and trolls that lined the far walls began filing out, and Narco turned to give Morta one final look.

"Guard *my* Castle, Adviser," Narco ordered loud enough for the soldiers in the back to hear. "I will return to *my* Throne with Vikaris's head—and his bride for my own."

Morta bowed humbly, which Narco knew was an act for the spectators, but all the same, it left him feeling empowered. He laughed wickedly.

Narco strode through the large Castle gates, cape blowing behind him. He thought how majestic he must appear. *Mother would be proud. Rustusse never had this much power.*

The sun had not yet risen, leaving the gathered soldiers in the eerie dark alongside creatures from a nightmare. The fog swirled around their legs. These ghost-like emanations accentuated the unnaturalness of the scene. Unicorns as black as night stood in a row, pawing the earth, and growling in challenge to their keepers. The frightened guards holding their harnesses tried to steady the beasts—unsuccessfully.

Narco paused before the line, and the creatures ceased. He smiled, a genuine, wicked beam tugging his scarred face. "Good, my children. You make Master very proud."

At his words, the pets' heads all lifted higher, their horns sparkling, but in such darkness, only their eyes shone—unless one looked closer at their faint silhouettes amidst the fog.

Oh, the power indeed.

They would sneak upon the enemy and slaughter them before the rebels even knew the Camp was under attack. He and Morta had spent hours in the night using the chalice to scour the Woods for the Camp. The murky liquid had swirled madly as they swept across the land. They had found their target. Narco knew exactly where Vikaris was hiding, and his nephew had no idea what was headed his way.

Narco strode up to the bulkiest unicorn. Dabor, his faithful troll, assisted him up onto the tall animal. Narco squeezed his knees, feeling the powerful rippling muscles underneath him and the saddle. Only a Marked Royal and his bonded Unicorn could use a "war saddle" in dire need, and even then, to his knowledge, no unicorn had ever been harnessed before. They were more than capable of directing themselves. Narco fumed remembering the smack he had received from his father when he had suggested that Mother use a harness with her unicorn, Trinity.

No unicorn needs a harness, you fool. They are the wisest of all creation, unlike a mindless horse… or you, Narco remembered his father's scornful remark.

Flinching at the memory's harshness, Narco shook it off. These wretches didn't know that. They were chattel, just like all the rest in his Kingdom. Commodities for him to exploit. He couldn't wait to see Trinidad's face when he was taken alive, saddled and bridled like the most common of horses. Without a horn, he was nothing more than a horse anyway, Narco mused. He still vacillated on the question of killing or maiming Trinidad. *Choices, choices.*

Narco patted the beast he rode on its thick neck, its black mane speckled with silver hairs that stood out in the moonlight. "I will call you Silver Seeker," Narco patted. The unicorn didn't respond, save for a jerk of its head. "Remember your duty, Silver Seeker. Your training. Take me to the false King. Our enemy. And help me destroy him. You are the lead unicorn, and if you make me proud, I will bond you."

At this, the unicorn shrieked and leaped ahead. Narco pulled on the reins to steady him but smiled at the creature's obsessive need to obey.

"Azalt!" He cried before kicking Silver Seeker and leading the troops—mounted and on foot—toward the bridge. They would cross into the Stenlen, where the remaining villagers would load his supply trains, before continuing north to attack Vikaris near the Woods of the Willow. He knew Vikaris couldn't stay hidden any longer. His officers—and Morta—had assured him that they would catch him off guard.

His troops cried "Azalt! Azalt! For Narco!" He laughed mirthfully as he caught sight of his other pets, shaking free from their keepers and tearing across the field to surround him and his steed. Feeling aroused with all the primal power around and beneath him. *I am the Emperor. And I am coming for you, nephew!*

"Yes, fly, oh powerful one," Morta whispered, chuckling. He stood atop the Castle ramparts, hidden in the still dark night as he watched the procession of thousands of humans, Rav'Arians, and trolls in motion heading to battle. Morta's amber eyes glowed in the darkness.

His plan was unfolding perfectly, and the foolhardy Narco had no idea that he had just been duped. How he loved toying with his Emperor. But now he turned toward the abandoned wooden structure outside the Castle. There was still one lone unicorn to deal with. This creature would be his pet. Zola's last foal had been born while he was away, but he would now come to know Morta as Master.

He laughed as he flung the exit door open and hurried down the stairs. His guards following at a hearty distance.

Morta knew Zola was near. He could sense her. Yet she was nothing without her horn. Let her fret upon her son while he claimed him as his own pet. This unicorn would grow to be the most powerful, and Morta would ensure that he was loyal wholly to him.

**

As dawn broke, the party emerged through the last of densely forested land, emptying into a lush landscape. Darion wondered if they had somehow entered back into Nav'Aria overnight, but Triumph assured him that this land felt foreign, and that he had never been here.

Soren confirmed this, commenting on the unknown vegetation. The scenery changed from a prairie lined with forests to a marshland.

Darion's heart felt at peace. Hearing Soren's analytical tone identify and observe plants alongside Edmond assured him his friend was not going to die from a mortal wound as once supposed. The girls, too, recognized some of the plants but not all.

Darion and Triumph walked apart from them to discuss events. So much had happened since he had come to Nav'Aria. He and Triumph discussed it all telepathically. Darion felt himself pouring out his soul to his friend, discussing his confusion over his place here, the loss of Carol, the meeting of Vikaris… and Lyrianna. In only a few months, Darion's entire life had been upheaved. He had gone from never seeing a sword, to now training with it daily and using it in battle. He had gone from longing for his identity and his family of origin to losing his mom… and becoming a Prince.

He wasn't mad at Lyrianna—exactly. He didn't know why he felt such confusion over her. She had been imprisoned. It was her undying love for him that had called him home. She had been his focus. Yet, now he realized, thanks to Triumph's observation, that he had unconsciously been blaming her for Carol's death.

You know, my Prince, Triumph explained, *that grief has stages. You lost someone dear to you. I know how that feels, believe me.*

Darion nodded in agreement. Triumph, more than anyone, knew loss.

And yet, you must not let anger cloud your judgment. Lyrianna is one of the kindest, most beautiful women I have ever known. She is a terrific queen, and she does not deserve to be blamed for something not of her doing. Your anger is misplaced. Narco is the ONLY villain here. Do not let your emotions rule your mind. You know, when you think rationally, that Narco is responsible for Carolina's death. No one else. Let that anger fuel you, but do not spend any more time wishing ill upon Lyrianna.

Darion paused. He didn't wish her ill. *But… won't I be betraying my Mom if I allow myself to love Lyriana?* He asked, adding ever so softly, *I'm afraid I'll forget her.* Though they spoke telepathically, Darion knew his voice quivered.

It was Triumph's turn to pause. The sun's morning rays brilliant upon his sheen coat. "Is that what you are worried about, Darion?" Triumph's voice, so tender and loving, caused Darion to lose himself for a moment, and he felt hot tears escaping.

Triumph rubbed his muzzle and cheek upon Darion's, catching his tears, and Darion comfortingly threw his arms around his friend. He knew he should feel embarrassed, but he couldn't stop the torrent of emotion erupting from him. His shoulders shook as he sobbed, and Triumph murmured words of comfort.

After he cried every last tear, he stood back, hastily wiping his face and runny nose upon his shirt sleeve and beginning to worry about Nala seeing him cry.

"Now, my Prince. Do not let your heart worry so. Carolina will always be your 'Mom', as you say. It is not betraying her, to love Lyrianna—who is your true Mother."

Darion made to interrupt, but Triumph stamped a foot in warning. "In life, we have the ability to choose whom we love. It is written nowhere that you should limit your love, Darion. Carolina loved you fully, and you her. But that does not mean that if you embrace Lyrianna as your mother, that you will be betraying Carolina—or forget her. Her memory will always linger. She was your Keeper, and her sacrificial love should propel you to love fiercely. We have no guarantee of future days," he turned to look back toward Soren. "You saw how quickly we almost lost Soren. Our days are a gift, and those that we can and should love are also a gift from the Creator. Do not deny your Mother love. You know Carolina would not have wanted that."

Darion recoiled at the casual mention of 'sacrificial love' but soaked up his wisdom, nonetheless. For someone who had lost an entire family to speak so of love was profound, and Darion knew this was a lesson he would remember. A partial smile tugged at his lips, but he didn't speak. He couldn't speak.

Triumph tilted his head, then stepped closer, as if he had just decided something.

"This," Triumph murmured softly, "This will be your memory of Carolina." Triumph dipped his head, his horn lightly pressing upon Darion's chest.

In any other instance, Darion would've been terrified to have a piercing horn—much like a blade—pressed upon his person, and yet his senses felt calm. Warm. Loved.

His eyes widened as he felt a tingling upon his skin, where his heart was. At once, a picture of Carolina bloomed in his mind, as if fastened there, and Darion had the pleasurable realization that Triumph had locked the image of her in his mind. He need not fear ever forgetting her face. He could see her. Sense her.

As Triumph moved away, his horn glittering like a diamond in sunshine, Darion tugged at his shirt collar and pulled his shirt down to reveal a small etched flower upon his skin, above his heart. A spring flower... like his dad had always called her.

He barreled into Triumph, hugging him tightly. "Thank you," he whispered fiercely, meaning it from the very depths of his soul.

The party plodded along for the rest of the day.

Ati's giggle carried across the wind. The girls' company lightened the mood considerably. Darion had spent much of the afternoon in conversation with Nala, and she had told fascinating stories of her adventures living with dragons. *What a life*, he thought.

As twilight emerged, she gasped and turned back to her sister, who was walking with Edmond.

"Ati," she called breathlessly. "Do you recognize this?"

Ati ran up, and Darion watched as Nala's sister dropped to her knees. They stood gaping before a purple flower. It grew from a strange yellow-green plant, and the petals drooped long and low to the ground. It was an ugly flower, to say the least. Darion had no idea what was so special about it.

"Yes, I do," Ati whispered.

The party stopped and watched the girls both kneeling and smelling the strange flower.

"But... what does this mean?" Nala whispered.

Darion looked at them confused. "What do you mean? What is it?"

Triumph gave him an odd look, and Darion felt dumb for asking.

"I have seen this before."

Darion stood there. It still wasn't registering. "Yeah, and?"

Now, Nala looked at him as if he were dumb. "This flower does not grow near the Reoul tribe. This means we have been here before."

Understanding slammed into Darion. "Your home?" he breathed excitedly.

Nala's face crinkled in anguish for a moment. "I... I think so," she breathed out in her husky voice, her voluminous eyes gazing upon the verdant landscape, surveying it like an owl.

Darion wanted to give them a moment to recall their past. Perhaps the flower would help them remember other things. He drank from his waterskin and let his senses wander. Letting go of his thoughts of the girls and the ugly flower, he inhaled deeply. He could smell all at once the tangy scent of the flower's pollen, the smell of sweat upon he and Edmond, and the Rav'Arian blood and muddy refuse upon them all. How he longed for a bath... or a shower! As he let his senses wander, he thought he detected a sound. A choppy, staccato sound. He searched for it, closing his eyes and focusing solely upon his senses. He smelled the earth... and something more. Southeast of their position the scent changed. He turned that way, moving apart from the group. Smelling and listening and feeling it all.

And abruptly the light breeze that had been cooling his skin now left him trembling.

Rav'Arians.

Though far off, he identified the clattering sound as the clicking mouths of the Rav'Arians snapping their jaws and talons in speech… and hunger. He inhaled deeply, knowing what he would find. A cloying, toxic odor filled his nostrils, burning them. He spluttered on the water he had been swallowing, coughing, and opening his eyes to find his friends watching him.

"Rav'Arians. They're close. A lot of them—that way." He pointed in their direction, speaking quietly.

Nala and Ati stood. Edmond's hand moved expertly to grasp his sword hilt, and both Soren and Triumph's noses lifted to the air, as if testing it for themselves.

I do not sense them. Perhaps they are too far for my senses? Triumph replied after a moment. *But I trust yours. What do you want to do?*

Darion paused—thinking. He closed his eyes again, and as he inhaled, he caught another odor. Much like the Rav'Arians, but new on its own. It was a stronger, deeper odor.

"What is that?" He wondered aloud.

"What is what, my Prince?" Soren asked inquisitively, still sniffing the air.

Against his better judgment, Darion knew they had to find them. The other aroma was part of the conundrum surrounding the Rav'Arians. *Was it their secret lair?* He knew there were a lot of them. Darion could sense it. They had come so far… he had to find out.

"We have to see what is over there. Let's rest first and eat."

The girls paled with worry, but no one argued as they found an area to make camp.

Darion fretted. Could they leave the girls here while they went? Darion couldn't imagine fighting Rav'Arians while worrying about the girls' welfare. And then he remembered Soren. They had marched much of the day. Soren looked thoroughly worn and in desperate need of rest.

As Darion contemplated splitting up, Nala interrupted his thoughts. "Do not even think about it," she said sharply.

Darion gawked at her. "What?" He asked, unsure if she was even talking to him.

Her severe gaze held his own as she pointed her finger in his face. "Do not even think about leaving us behind. We have our own answers to find, and we are not leaving you."

Darion, unsure of how Nala had known what he was thinking, looked to Triumph for guidance.

The unicorn just sighed, shaking his head at Darion.

Darion took his meaning but was still unsure. "But—

"I mean it, Darion," she said tersely. "Ati and I are not the helpless girls you think we are. We have grown up here, and we know how to fight—how to survive."

"Yes, but—"

"As do I," Soren growled. "Do not pity me."

Darion had never heard such fervor in his usually placid friend. "I mean no disrespect, my Prince," Soren continued, "But I will not be left behind either."

Darion looked at them all and scowled. *So much for me being in charge*, he thought dejectedly. Triumph snorted but again said nothing.

"Well, fine. Have it your way. But we have to move fast—and quietly. There are too many there to fight. We'll sneak up on them just to check it out. They can't find us."

The heads around him bobbed in agreement.

After they had eaten and drank their fill, Darion stood. "I guess it's time to go spy on some monsters," he announced.

Edmond jumped upright. His eyes almost giddy at the prospect. Darion was pretty sure his friend dreamed about killing Rav'Arians.

"You're crazy," he chided as they gathered their packs.

Edmond smirked. "I'd rather deal with Rav'Arians any day compared to…" he let his words trail off as Ati approached. Her feminine beauty accentuated by the warm evening glow of a setting sun. The air blew her long, strawberry blonde locks around her tall, lean frame. She looked like an angel. Edmond gulped.

Darion laughed. "You got that right," he muttered, catching Nala watching him from his peripheral.

Girls! He thought. *Headstrong girls.* Just what he needed.

Don't forget, the headstrong unicorns too! Triumph added.

Darion exhaled forcefully, running his hands through his hair. He was surrounded by the oddest group ever. It wasn't like this in the stories. Usually the leader was brave.

Invulnerable. Tough. And respected. In this case, all Darion had was a couple of unicorns and girls ready to question his every move.

Great, he thought sarcastically. *Just what I always wanted.*

Triumph blew air out noisily, shaking his dazzling mane in the evening light. But it was Nala who spoke.

"Lead us, Prince Darion," she said in her warm voice.

The sight of her in the shining light caused his breath to catch. He glared. She only smiled that familiar, mischievous twinkle… and then she winked at Triumph.

Darion muttered under his breath about his disloyal friend communicating with the enemy.

Triumph raised his chin haughtily in the air, pointedly ignoring him.

"Fine. Let's move," Darion commanded gruffly, before quickly setting off in the direction of the pungent smell and threat of the true enemy. *Narco's abominations.*

CHAPTER 22

The Hidden Creatures

"You two need to move faster," Aalil barked, climbing further ahead.

They had set the horses free a while back, after the rocky terrain became too steep and there had been a near rockslide.

Antonis and Riccus glared, but both were too winded to retort.

Aalil felt a deep desire to prove to them that she was the tougher of the three... which was becoming a pretty easy contest. She had to remember that the two men had been sent away for the last cycle or more. *To this Oregon place, wherever that was.* They hadn't spent much time navigating the wild... like her.

Aalil turned back to the slope she was climbing. She had spent her time training, growing as a warrior, and proving to every damn Nav'Arian that she deserved to be a part of Vikaris's military because she was the best. Her taut arms gripped the cliffside she was scaling. Antonis had jokingly asked where the harnesses were. *What were those?* She had simply ignored him, heading up first. With her bow and quiver of arrows strapped to her back, she had a big loop of rope tied around her, and the plan was that she would secure it at the top and help them up.

"Soft," she grumbled. Though, as she reflected on it—and the last night they had shared at the fortress—she had to admit that Antonis was anything but soft. The thought warmed her, and she smiled inwardly.

"Be careful," Antonis called for the hundredth time.

She rolled her eyes. "You old ninny," she muttered sarcastically. *Maybe he was a little soft.*

As she thought about the two nervous men below, while their eyes scrutinized her every movement, she began to grow uncharacteristically nervous. Without thought, she glanced down. This was a big mistake, and the glance cost her her equilibrium. She experienced a nauseating wave of vertigo. Gulping, she felt perspiration break out upon her forehead. She cursed herself. *Antonis better not have seen my eyes. Who is the soft one now, Aalil?* She chided herself. "Get going."

Without waiting to catch her breath, wanting to maintain her brave face, she reached for a far overhang. And as she released her grip, she belatedly realized that it was not an overhang at all, but instead a clump of soil shadowed by the towering peak. As she gripped it, the dirt crumbled in her fingertips, and she felt herself beginning to drop.

"Watch out," Antonis shouted from below.

It all happened so fast that she barely had time to register what she was doing.

Instinctively, she grabbed her blade and dug it into the earth as she descended quickly. Her blade cut right through the dirt and she continued to fall, but just as a scream mutinously escaped her lips, her blade, which she held now with two sweaty hands, caught on a very thick root of an unseen plant.

She felt the blade beginning to pull her down, cutting through the root, but she didn't allow it time. As a seasoned climber, she noted her surroundings, noticing a small enclave in the cliff she had been climbing moments ago. It looked like the opening of a cave. She had heard that the trolls sometimes traveled through large caves and tunnel systems in the mountains. She shuddered. But she would worry about trolls later. Right now, she needed to grip something beyond her blade.

Her feet found crevices that lessened the gravitational pull considerably. Teetering there and not quite trusting her footing, she reached for another protruding knotted root. She tugged on it cautiously. It seemed to hold. She looked for another grip and found one just near the knotted root. Tenuously, she gripped the knot and followed suit with her other hand. Still carrying the blade and trying to grip was awkward, but she feared sheathing the blade just yet. She glanced again toward the right. As she began to move slowly, she saw that it was indeed a cave opening. More knotted roots and embedded stones in the mountainside aided her climb.

Aalil heard the men's relieved sighs as she reached the cave. Replacing her blade, she leaned out of sight against the entrance, momentarily catching her breath. Her hands unsteadily wiped her mouth and face. She had a small water pouch at her belt, and she drank from it thirstily.

"Aalil?" Antonis's concerned voice rang out.

A rueful smile tugged at her lips. She knew she shouldn't, but she really liked the sound of concern in his voice. Having grown accustomed to living alone, being alone, this was a new sensation. A part of her mind warned her not to give in to that voice. She didn't need a man. Hadn't she just proven that by saving herself?

And yet, as she crept to the edge, peering below, her eyes met Antonis's. She knew that her feelings for him could not be ignored.

She watched his shoulders sag in relief when he sighted her. Riccus clapped him on the back, just before moving to secure their packs and possessions prior to their own ascent.

"I will secure the line," she called down.

Both men nodded. Riccus gave her an odd gesture with his thumb raised in the air.

Aalil left her bow and quiver but kept her pack as she crawled back in search of a hold. This would be difficult in a cave. She began moving backwards, and as she moved further into the cave, the sun's rays didn't accompany her. She was alone in the dark. She moved by feel. Instinct.

She cautiously tested out the ground before her with a toe here and a step there, always keeping a hand on the cave wall. She had hoped to scale the mountain and reach the top, where she would most likely find a tree or stump to secure the rope. They hadn't even considered a cave entrance... *what would hold the rope?* She could feel it secured across her breast. Antonis had enjoyed looping the rope around her.

Her breath caught. *What was that?* She froze.

There it was again.

She reached for her blade, but her unsteady hands felt like someone else's. She fumbled with it, cringing as it clattered to the ground. And then the mountain exploded.

At once, shrieking, flying creatures fell upon her.

Falling to the ground covering her head and neck as best she could, a swarm—greater than any she had ever encountered—of bats flew out of the cave in a torrent. Thousands of tiny feet and wings brushed past her; she felt small scratches tugging upon the fabric of her coat. Fortunately, an earlier argument with Antonis convinced her to wear it. She and her unexposed arms thanked him silently. She rocked herself in an attempt to calm her nerves. The sound was deafening, and the wingbeats cast a swirling dust cloud. It took her a moment to realize the colony was gone. Her breath came in fast gulps in the cold cave, and she finally uncovered her head and ears. She felt for her knife. It was inches from her left foot.

As she picked it up, she stood carefully and began her push forward again. She knew Antonis and Riccus would be worried for her, but it would cost them all more time if she went back to the entrance just to wave hello. They would have to trust her.

She continued further into the abyss. The rotten smell included a mixture of mildew, earth, and bat guano. Her nose crinkled in protest, but she pressed on. Her toe stubbed something jutting from the floor. Kneeling, she reached out and found a solid mass growing from the earth. She had heard of spiked growths within the caves and was relieved to have found one at last. As she felt around it and pushed on it to and fro, she decided it was sturdy. It would have to work.

She looped the rope around the base of the stalagmite and expertly knotted it—even in the pitch dark. Every soldier learned their knots before they were given a weapon. She prayed that the thin rope would be long enough to reach the men. She hadn't realized how far she had walked into the cave until she had to retrace her steps.

Unwinding the rope as she went, the light finally became visible. There she stood, momentarily blinded, with her hands over her eyes at the entrance. The sky blooming before her was so bright compared to the black hole from which she emerged. Her eyes brimmed with tears from the pain of the light.

This time Antonis threw both his arms up in the air.

Maybe she should have come back after the bats. Oh well, it was no matter. She had been successful, and they could argue about it once he was firmly standing next to her.

Her eyes slowly adjusted, and she tossed the cord toward them in a wild fling. As it fell, the light glistened upon the unspooling rope. Intermixed with the other fibers were unicorn hairs—on Elsra's authority. Any discarded unicorn hairs after groomings of their manes and especially their tails were used to strengthen the ropes. The secretive magic of unicorns once more proving powerful. Even the hair shed from their bodies held power. Unicorn-enhanced ropes were the best in Nav'Aria. They were incredibly strong and allowed for lighter ropes to be made. Only an obsidian blade could cut a unicorn's hair, it was said. She thought on this—and on the brutalized Trinidad—as she waited for the men. It made her blood boil to think of anyone taking a blade to one of the majestic beings.

Riccus, followed by Antonis, cleared the cave—after a long, harrowing, curse-ridden climb, both men's chests heaved, and their hands burned. Aalil rubbed a balm into each of their hands as they sat and drank.

Soft, she thought again, looking at the red rope burns on Antonis's hands. The man didn't even have fully formed calluses!

"Well," Riccus drawled after they had sat for a moment. "Best we see what other hidden treasures this cave holds."

Thinking of the bats threatened to expose the chink in Aalil's armor. Antonis tightened his grip on her shoulder. Though they had not spoken much, she knew he had been worried for her. She leaned into him for a moment, savoring the masculine scent of the man before jumping up to assist Riccus.

Antonis grumbled a bit about how they were overdue for a meal. But she didn't pay him any heed, for she watched Riccus light a torch from some fabric wrapped around a thick stick. *Where did that come from? I could have used that earlier,* she thought forlornly, shuddering with the memory of the bats.

Riccus held the torch to two candle sticks he also produced from his pack and handed them to Aalil and Antonis. He winked at her and set off. She knew the light wouldn't last long, and she feared being in the dark again, but what other choice did they have? They needed to see where this cave led, and so they followed the Keeper into the darkness of the Nav'Alodon mountain cave.

***

"We have to stop," Ati's sweet voice held a desperate, plaintive edge that Darion had to acknowledge. These girls were not pushovers by any means, and if they said, "Stop," it would be ignorant of him to ignore their wishes. They were, afterall, very tough. Living with dragons would do that. He had learned in short order that Nala and Ati were willing to walk harder and faster than any of the rest of them, and so it was not out of weakness, but necessity, that Ati spoke. Still, Darion scrunched his face in consternation, taking a deep calming breath before he turned around.

The pull of the beasts was so strong now. He had to know what was out there. This had to be Narco's secret hold.

Yet as he turned, he saw the truth in Ati's eyes. Though Soren would never complain, Darion could see how his head drooped wearily and he had begun to drag his back leg as he walked. Edmond stood proud, erect, though his cheeks were flushed, and perspiration dripped from his forehead. The leg he had twisted in the fight dragged a little too, but he seemed oblivious to it. He would not stop unless Darion commanded it. Triumph also stood proud, and Nala and Ati looked as if they could continue.

"Damnit," Darion mumbled softly. They were all looking to him...well, except Soren, who seemed as though he was beginning to fall asleep still standing.

He whispered to Triumph, who gladly obliged.

Triumph strode toward his fellow unicorn, murmuring for him to lie down, and though Soren protested, his weary legs shook. He had been mostly healed by Triumph's horn and the girls' aid, yet he needed rest, which he had had very little of.

Darion looked at him guiltily. They had fought Rav'Arians and then walked unceasingly across Rav'Ar. The night sky filled with millions of shining stars loomed overhead. Maybe it was better for everyone to get some rest before they approached the enemy camp. They were in a field of wildflowers and plants, interspersed with small, stout trees unlike any he had ever seen. He felt exposed. He didn't like this spot, but it didn't look like Soren was going to be able to leave it for some time.

He grimaced at Triumph, hoping the unicorn would decide for him.

Triumph only stared at him solemnly. Waiting. Just as Edmond and the girls did.

"Shit," he whispered.

Nala arched an eyebrow at him but did not speak. He ran his hand through his dark, sweaty hair. He had kept it tied back earlier but had taken it out once the night air had cooled him further. It now warmed his neck. *Be the leader, Darion. Come on.*

"Alright," he spoke. "We'll make camp here, but no cookfire tonight. We eat what is in our packs, and two at a time will stand watch. We move before first light. Edmond and I will take the first watch, and then Triumph and..." he trailed off when he looked at Soren. He bit his lip, contemplating.

A feminine throat cleared nearby, and he saw Nala cross her arms in a gesture that made her point very clear. "And Nala and Triumph will stand second watch." Darion's eyes lingered on Nala's beautiful mouth a heartbeat too long. He couldn't spend the watch with her. He'd be way too distracted.

"And what about me?" Though Ati didn't quite match her sister's skilled scowl, she came close.

Darion coughed noncommittally, trying to buy himself time. "You... umm... you're in charge of Soren. Please help him get comfortable... and make sure he eats something." She lifted her nose in the air and made as if to argue, but then must have caught Edmond's eye, for she blushed sweetly. Her face breaking into a beautiful smile as she replied in a much gentler tone, "As you wish, Prince Darion," and turned to dig in her pack before looking to Soren.

Darion's gaze fell back on Nala. She still exuded annoyance. Her chin jutted out, as if daring him to try and command her.

Wow... that girl has mastered the scowl.

Triumph rumbled nearby, and Darion knew he agreed... and found humor in it!

It was an uneventful watch. He and Edmond spoke very little, not wanting to wake the others, but as Darion guessed it had been a couple of hours, he spoke into Triumph's mind.

Your turn, my friend.

A low growl escaped the unicorn. Darion rolled his eyes. Triumph, though much older—could match any moody teenager's outrage at being awoken before he intended.

As he turned to frown at his companion, he caught Nala's eye. She was lying on her side facing him, her face nestled upon her pack. She stared at him with an unreadable expression. Darion felt his stomach do a flip at the sight of her in the nightfall shadows. She was the prettiest girl he'd ever seen. He wanted to turn back, but now that she was staring at him, he stood up and brushed himself off. He moved toward her carefully, not wanting to disturb Soren's contented sleep. He knelt beside Nala to tell her it was her watch, but something in her eyes stopped him.

"Are you alright?" he whispered, growing worried as he now saw tears brimming in her eyes. She nodded slightly, sitting up. As she did, a tear escaped, and without any thought to his action, his thumb smoothed away the tear. Darion's hand continued down the side of her face and through her hair before resting on her shoulder. His senses took in her sweet smell and the silken chestnut hair. He squeezed her shoulder softly. "Are you sure?"

She only smiled at him, a few more tears escaping which she wiped away with her sleeve. And then she did something he would have never expected. Out of nowhere her two small palms touched the sides of his unshaven face and her soft, beautiful lips met his own. He sat there like a dummy, his eyes surely bulging out of his head. She trailed one finger down his face and held a palm against his chest for a moment, where she surely felt his heart hammering. She didn't say a word, and he for damn sure couldn't. And then she was gone.

She went and sat next to Triumph; he heard the two whispering softly. Edmond pumped a congratulatory fist at him before lying down. Darion walked to his own sleeping spot as if in a daze. He felt as if he could run a marathon! *She kissed me!* He smiled dreamily until sleep finally took him.

Though his eyes were still closed, Triumph's telepathic nudge awoke him. Darion lay still, conversing with his friend.

Triumph told him the evening had been uneventful. He also told him that Soren needed to stay behind. Darion knew it was true but cursed, nonetheless. He hated being separated, and worried over whom to leave behind. He had no idea what he was about to walk into. Perhaps it was best to leave the girls and Soren as he had originally wanted to do before they all went head-strong crazy on him. He cracked one eyelid, then two, rubbing away the sleep.

Unexpectedly, a shadow materialized in front of him. Nala's face peered into his own. Her owl-like eyes enveloping him, and her sweet-smelling hair a canopy blocking the morning sun.

"Good morning," he mumbled behind his hand, staving off a yawn.

"Good morning, Darion," her husky voice cooed. His heart began to hammer again.

She leaned back then, allowing for him to sit up, but spoke before he could get a word in.

"I will go with you and Triumph," she announced matter-of-factly. "Edmond and Ati will watch over Soren. It is all worked out." Her smug expression caused his heart to speed with a new feeling—annoyance.

"No," he blurted, pushing her aside gently.

He felt better standing near her, as if his extra inches would make her back up. If anything, the opposite occurred. She only stood taller herself, and though nearly a foot shorter than him, she tilted her head and carried on. She would not be intimidated.

"Yes. Like I said, 'it is all worked out'."

Darion risked a glance at Triumph, who seemed very interested in a nearby flower.

He caught a glance of Soren speaking with Edmond and Ati. Edmond only had eyes for Ati, and Darion then questioned whose idea this had been. He glared back at Nala. She raised her eyes, her face becoming so oddly neutral that he realized she was feigning innocence.

Darion grinned. "Ha! You're no better than that big lug," he teased, gesturing at Triumph, whose interest in flowers had seemingly developed overnight. "You both suck at acting."

Triumph's head shot up, and his eyes blazed, but none more so than Nala's.

Nala might think she's in control here, but she's not, he assured himself, stretching. The thought cheered him up considerably.

Triumph snorted.

Darion wished he'd quit doing that. He looked back to see the smug look had returned to Nala's face.

Creator, help me! He ran his hands through his hair before replying hotly, "Fine. You two will come with me, and you three will stay here. Edmond," Darion paused seriously. "You're in charge while I'm gone."

Edmond nodded solemnly.

"If something happens…" he trailed off, looking in the direction his senses were leading them.

"It won't, my Prince," Edmond assured. "We will wait for your return. I will keep them safe."

Darion clapped Edmond's muscled shoulder, knowing that they had crossed another threshold in their training… and relationship.

Before, he had hated being called "Prince," feeling embarrassed or undeserving. But now that their numbers had grown and they'd been battle-tested, Darion knew he needed to move into that role. He needed to allow even his friends to treat him for what he was, the Marked Heir.

He took Edmond's hand in a firm grip, just as he had seen his father do with his officers. As he turned to break camp, he caught Nala's eye. The smugness faded, yet she remained unreadable.

They left the group moments later. The men and unicorns looked away as the two sisters bid each other farewell. If all went well, the parties would meet back up later that day, but if it didn't….

Darion didn't want to think on that. Ati had cried, and though Nala had maintained her composure, Darion could sense the disquiet in her soul as they walked away. He realized that they had most likely never been apart from each other. He left her to her thoughts and took to his own, heeding his senses. They needed to be alert, and he couldn't spend any more time thinking about females… or his friends.

Edmond had agreed that if Darion and his party were not back by tomorrow—or if forced to flee—Edmond would take them north. Soren could guide him. Edmond had initially protested, but Triumph had assured him that he and Soren would be able to locate the other.

There were Rav'Arians nearby. With every passing step the smell became more prevalent. Triumph had long-past sensed them. Threats lurked, and they all needed to be on guard. Darion would not have anyone die for him out of sheer stubborn will.

After a couple of hours, the mid-morning sun blazed, and the humidity seemed to thicken the air. The marshy vegetation enclosing them. The clattering, clicking teeth thrummed.

Triumph, though rigid and alert, tried to walk as stealthily as possible, allowing for the strange plants to shield much of his body. They had slowed their pace considerably. Darion and Nala crept. They both had blades drawn—if you could call hers that (it looked like animal bone). Darion feared for her, but he couldn't worry about her, for in that instant, his senses erupted with a burning, pungent odor.

Creeping forward, Darion spotted a cluster of undergrowth and stout trees. He gestured for them to make for that spot. They had agreed that they would not speak aloud but, instead, use hand signals—and telepathy.

Yet, as they edged forward, Darion was given the first vantage point over Hell.

The smell seared his eyes and nostrils, and his mind reverberated with the demonic clattering and clicking of the teeth, beaks and talons of the hatching Rav'Arians. For that is what they were. Darion discovered a pool of black liquid encasing huge floating—and cracking—eggs.

Tar pits, Triumph breathed. *The Rav'Arian breeding grounds.*

Darion's skin crawled. The smell he had been unable to identify: tar pits.

The ghoulish sight of the small figures emerging from their eggs and floundering in the tar sickened him. Many of them escaped their eggs, only to plunge headfirst into the thick slop. Heads bobbed all around. The beings treaded the thick tar, and the black substance seemed to soak into their initially pale skin... or scales. Darion couldn't be sure.

Darion heard gagging. His head swiveled from Nala to the tar pits and back, panicked. He glared at her. The scent was terrible, but she had to get a grip. He shook his head at her. If she started puking, they'd certainly hear it below. Her hand covered her mouth, but her eyes raged. He shook his head at her again. *Seriously, she was mad because he was trying to keep her alive? Rude!*

We have never been sure how they reproduced... or where it happened. This is huge, Darion. Triumph spoke quietly in his mind, his tone reverting back to that of a scholar. He had been an instructor for years, and the new knowledge, though exciting, was also terrifying... and confusing. *I wish we could confiscate one of those eggs. Learn what exactly is in it. If only Soren or Lei could get one to examine....*

Darion ignored Triumph, for he was certainly not going to let any of them get close enough to steal an egg; instead, he hesitantly reached out with his senses, fearing what else he might detect there.

He sensed the hatchlings. The tar must cause the cloying pungence that clings to the creatures even years after. As he watched, the tiny beings dipped in the thick liquid. Bigger ones, what Darion could only suppose were adolescents, floated nearer the surface. On the very edge, larger Rav'Arians crept out of the tar like demons.

The tar dripped heavily from the beasts. The four emerging stood tall and erect. Their backs showing the ridges of where the wing-like shell encasing would form. Their ribs protruded—a sign they had most likely not eaten yet. Due to the tar, Darion could make out little more beyond their profile and extremities.

Two robed Rav'Arians with swordbelts cackled and clicked to their new recruits. He couldn't make out any intelligible words, which he found strange, for he knew some could indeed speak. *Maybe that was something they learned later on, as well? But who taught them?*

Darion's eyes enlarged as he noted tails dangling between their legs. He couldn't recall seeing one on the corpse he and Edmond had inspected. But there was that stump.

The two robed Rav'Arians motioned with their thin arms and long talons for the four to lie down. They did as commanded.

Darion watched in horror as one of the Rav'Arians grasped a huge scythe and proceeded to chop each creature's tail from its body. The Rav'Arians writhed in agony but stayed put in complete obedience while the discarded tails were thrown back into the tar. To his even greater horror, the bobbing hatchlings savagely clamored over one another to reach the parts, then tore into them with razor-sharp teeth wickedly lining their beaked maws.

Nala dry heaved loudly in response.

One of the adult Rav'Arians began sniffing the air, looking around. Darion cursed silently, preparing to tell his companions it was time to go. He tried to imprint the sight in his mind so he could accurately relate this abominable scene to his Father.

Darion leaned forward for one last look. He must not have been as hidden as he thought, for the Rav'Arian who stood sniffing suddenly zeroed in on their position across the tar pit.

Its robed arm pointed wildly as it released the most terrifying sound Darion had ever heard.

CHAPTER 23

The Discovery

The Rav'Arian howled, raising all the hair on Darion's body.

He spun, running from the trees with his friends. Triumph's hooves pounded the earth, yet a new sound, more beastly and terrifying than anything Darion had ever heard, assaulted their eardrums.

Triumph skittered to a halt, turning in the direction of the noise.

"Get on my back! Both of you! Hurry!" Triumph beckoned them, the note of sheer panic chilling Darion to his bones.

Darion swung up on Triumph's back, pulling Nala up behind him. She squeezed his torso so tightly, he could hardly breathe. He gripped Triumph's mane and yelled for him to go.

As they tore off, heavy footsteps hammered behind them.

Darion stole a glance, spotting the horrendous creature tearing across the landscape in pursuit of them. The vile image soiling the otherwise beautiful land.

Nala looked too, screaming in terror. She swayed slightly, and Darion gripped her arms around his torso, fearing she might faint.

The hideous, dark, scaled beast was no Rav'Arian. It was unlike anything Darion had ever seen. Its reptilian body lumbered toward them, wings outspread, allowing it to glide a few yards with each leap. Its globular head and stout legs looked more like a troll—at least, as Darion pictured them—than a dragon. Its eyes glowed red, and yet, as it opened its protruding, cavernous mouth to roar its challenge, spittle flew. He detected many rows of teeth.

What the hell is that?

Darion encouraged Triumph, who practically flew over the ground, though the pursuant continued its charge. Darion glanced back. It was gaining on them. And then he knew what it reminded him of. An alligator. It was as if an alligator, dragon, and troll had all been mixed into one.

But how could that be? He didn't have time to think on it, for the snapping jaws were gaining on Triumph's hindlegs.

Nala, to her credit, didn't faint. From her precarious position at the rear, she whimpered softly. Darion needed to free his sword but didn't want to accidentally knock off Nala in the event he had to begin fighting while upon Triumph.

Triumph, what do we do?

Triumph screamed in outrage at the pursuit.

Darion knew Triumph felt terrified also. Darion realized that the unicorn's fighting would be encumbered with two riders. Darion glanced again to see the creature mere feet away. Its talons reached for Triumph's tail and Nala's longs strands of hair. The odor it emitted was so strong, Nala swayed, and Darion knew that she was losing consciousness.

"Triumph!" Darion yelled. "We have to fight!"

Upon his words, Triumph looped around in a tight circle to face the threat, Darion, having only one option, grabbed Nala and jumped from Triumph's back.

Darion heard rage building in Triumph, as well. Nala clung to consciousness, barely.

"Stay here," he demanded, drawing his sword from his belt and running into the fray.

The abominable beast had slowed its rush and now paced to face Triumph. Its red eyes searched its opponent. Saliva trailed from the gaping orifice.

Triumph pawed the earth, whinnying, growling, scraping, and barking.

The beast hopped from foot to foot, pounding the earth with its vast bulk. Quicker than could be imagined, it swung in a circle, its scaled tail lashing out at Triumph.

Triumph reared, narrowly missing being knocked askance. The beast bellowed in challenge, thrust forward, and snapped its jaws at Triumph. Again, the unicorn skirted the danger, making a wild swipe of his own. His horn struck the creature's arm but didn't penetrate it.

The creature wore a metallic chest plate and bands along its forearms. Triumph's strike glanced off the strange metal.

Darion could see the panic in Triumph's eyes at the realization that its armor, and thus, much of its thick scales, were impenetrable. Triumph backed away, avoiding another swipe from its arm, looking for another opening.

As the creature lunged again toward Triumph, Darion ran at it, slashing with his sword. It felt like he hit stone. The blunt force twanged up his arm. The beast roared almost gleefully at having another opponent.

Darion, blade raised, came to stand near Triumph.

"Darion! Get out of here! Take Nala and join the others."

For whatever reason, that statement, above all else taking place, really pissed off Darion. As if he would leave Triumph, and for him to even suggest it made Darion's whole body shake with fury. He wouldn't run. He was no coward. He was bonded to Triumph, and this monster was going to die. End of story.

Darion bellowed his own war-cry, releasing all the energy, fear, anger, and rage he had stored up. And strangely, that exhale caused the creature to stop its menacing steps forward. Its wings billowed out to catch itself as it was blown back a few feet.

Its predatorial gaze stopped. Looking between them, his focus narrowed on Darion, deciding he was the stronger opponent.

Again, Triumph urged him to run. "Go, my Prince. Run, now!"

Darion looked at his friend and wiped his sweaty bangs from his brow before shouting, "I WILL NOT RUN ANYMORE!"

And then he charged.

Swinging his sword, Darion's arm shone brightly, tingling with all the energy, anger—and power—that his Marked status held. His Ruby blazed, but what Darion could not see himself, was the way his eyes burned a brilliant green and scorched into the creature's own demonic orbs.

It stopped swiping at him and crashed backwards, shielding its eyes between intermittent steps and glances.

Without hesitation, Darion rushed the beast, all his repressed fury at the loss of Carol, his bastard uncle, the Rav'Arians hurting Soren—it all fueled him to a point of cutting clarity.

Darion was one with his senses. He was in a sensory vacuum, claiming the moment. He rushed the creature, stabbing first its underbelly, then its armpit, and as it began to slow its defenses, he thrust his gleaming sword at its throat. Darion could sense every vulnerable spot on its body. *Metal chest plate be damned.*

The beast wasn't wholly invulnerable, as they'd initially supposed. He could sense each soft area of skin that the scales hadn't fully encased, and the armor narrowly missed covering it completely.

Darion could sense its incontrollable anger—and fear. He could sense the repulsive desire within it to taste their blood. To please its master. To gorge on their flesh. And then, to Darion's horror, he sensed its realization that one of them wasn't armed. Easier prey lay nearby. It could still wound the green-eyed man.

"Nala," Darion breathed.

In a flash, the creature hopped yards away, assisted by its wings, to the side of the combatants where Nala crouched. It roared in victory as it landed upon her so suddenly that she could only let out a startled cry.

Darion and Triumph ran. But it was too late. Even if he killed the monster, it already sat atop where she had been. Its head clacking, crunching, gorging.

"You bastard!" Darion screamed as he flew upon its back.

In one swift motion his sword cut through the thick membranes and bones of one wing, completely removing it from its body. Darion clung to the other wing as the beast screamed in agony.

Triumph thundered into its side, no longer using his horn, for that would not work upon its exterior, but now relying on his brute force to knock the beast further off balance.

Darion used his Marked arm to saw his sword against the other wing. His left arm barely maintained its grip upon the bloodied, protruding bone where the other wing—another sensitive spot—had been attached only moments ago.

The sounds emitting from the creature would haunt Darion for years to come. So unnatural. So terrifyingly loud and… wrong.

The creature hopped around, swinging itself wildly, trying to knock Darion off as it howled in pain. It crashed to the ground, and Darion leapt before being crushed. He dropped his sword in the leap. He jumped back as the creature splayed itself in sheer agony and crazed anger.

Darion ran to where he had last seen Nala. Terrified, he dared not risk a look if she were dead, knowing the grief might consume him. But just as he gave up hope, she sat up, dazed.

Blackened blood streaked her front. Her long, bone-like dagger clutched in her hand. Her eyes burned with anger. She jumped up, and though one of her arms sagged and trailed red blood, she was definitely alive. She threw off her woven pack, which now resembled tattered rags.

Triumph's cry brought Darion's attention back to the fight. The rolling beast, still unaware that Darion had jumped off, was lashing out with his tail, slashing at Triumph.

Darion searched the ground for his sword.

The creature recklessly charged Triumph, who staggered from the blow of its tail.

Without thought, Darion again gave into his senses completely, running at the creature. Before it made contact with Triumph, Darion raised both of his hands and yelled, "STOP." His voice resounded.

Darion's eyes aglow and ruby blazing alit the beast. It suspended its lunge, held captive by Darion's attention. The Prince focused his energy and senses, this time funneling into the beast's heart. He could feel its pain from the wounds, and even more, the fear of... what its master would do if he let these ones escape.

Anger coursed through Darion's entire body. He strode up to the beast, who still didn't move, as if frozen by Darion's supreme attention. As he walked, he saw through his peripheral the light gleaming upon his discarded sword. Swiftly, he grabbed his sword before he charged the creature, whose movements seemed delayed. In one final leap he slammed his sword all the way up to the hilt into its throat. Because it was so tall, Darion dangled from the sword momentarily, and with one final motion, he jerked his arm twisting it before jumping down.

Dark blood spurted from the wound, and the being collapsed, gurgling in challenge until its very end.

Darion stood there, chest heaving, watching it die, ensuring that it truly was dead. Before he knew it, another force slammed into him.

Nala.

Her feminine smell filled his nostrils, carrying away the rotten filth of the slain beast. She ran her hand over his face, through his mop of hair, and gripped him again in an embrace.

"I was so worried," he admitted, their foreheads pressed against one another before leaning back to look into her eyes. Later, he might be surprised by his honesty, but not now. Right now, it felt right. He had been terrified that he had lost her, and that realization only hammered home the importance of telling her. Her huge eyes gleamed with unshed tears, and she laughed a little. A tremulous smile brightening her face. "I though I lost you," he whispered, and before he knew what he was doing, he took her face with both hands—having discarded his sword—and kissed her. A full, deep, passionate kiss. His first kiss, truthfully, and he knew it was hers too. As they broke contact, slightly breathless, he heard a grumble off to his left.

Nala laughed throatily, turning to the unicorn.

Triumph stood there, panting from the exertion, looking a little worse for wear with the shallow cut on his side.

"Don't worry about me, I'm fine," he chided.

Darion grimaced.

Triumph walked toward them, gently nudging Darion's back.

As he did, Darion gained a full view of the bleeding wound on Nala's arm. Darion felt worried and abashed.

"You're hurt!" he blurted.

She raised her shoulder in a characteristically casual way. She still hadn't spoken.

Darion knew in that instant that he loved her. She was a warrior. There she was bleeding out before him, but she paid it no attention. Darion was her sole concern. He had never loved a girl before. When he saw Triumph's tender touch of his horn to her arm and her tearful pat of his cheek in thanks, Darion's heart filled.

Mom would have loved her, he thought, but in the same thought wondered, *will Lyrianna?*

Above all, he knew his mother was a fighter too. He had a feeling his birth parents would approve. *They would have to,* he thought. As he smiled at Triumph and Nala, he heard footsteps.

"We have to go," he insisted.

The beautiful, dimpled smile falling from Nala's face.

"No, it is alright," Triumph spoke soothingly, not taking his gaze from Nala's arm.

Darion frowned, but as he looked around, Edmond emerged, trailed by Ati and Soren.

Darion had never been gladder to see his friends.

Ati squeaked words of praise and admonishment for Nala as she looked at her arm. Newly healed—thanks to Triumph—blood still coated it and her torn shirt. Ati pulled her down to a seated position to inspect it. As the girls chatted, Triumph and Soren examined the corpse of the slain beast. Darion had to finally tell Edmond to shut up and quit apologizing for not being there. He had been ordered to stay and guard Ati and Soren, which he had done.

Once Soren's inspection of the beast was complete, and Ati had administered her balms to Nala and Triumph, Darion ordered them to move. They were vulnerable here. He began to feel uneasy, as if there were eyes upon them. Triumph and Soren whinnied, shaking their manes in agitation, and he knew they felt it, too.

Are there more of these? he wondered, eyeing the colossal corpse. *Whatever they are.* He shuddered at the thought. *The Rav'Arians were bad enough, but an army of these. They would destroy Nav'Aria. He needed to tell his father.*

"Okay, let's move," he called, and all obliged quickly.

Darion feared making camp anywhere near the Rav'Arian secret home, but by the time the moon was high overhead, Triumph urged him to stop. It had been a silent march throughout much of the day.

Darion's feet were sore—blisters had long since popped—and he knew the others must feel as wearied as him. Ati and Nala appeared to be supporting one another. Soren's back leg had begun to drag again, and even stalwart Edmond's shoulders slumped with fatigue.

Triumph and Darion held up the best—and they had been the ones in the fight. Darion wondered about this as they made camp.

Triumph?

Yes, my Prince? Triumph's sleepy voice rumbled.

Does our bond make us stronger?

They were supposed to be sleeping. Edmond had agreed to take the first watch—they would have three watches total this evening.

Triumph smacked his lips before responding, clearly annoyed at being awoken. *In a sense, yes. No disrespect intended, unicorns—when in full health—are stronger than other races, humans included.* He continued before Darion could interrupt.

Yet in our case, you are an exception. You are the Marked Heir—the Chosen One, and with this position comes great power. Together, with our unique strengths, we are more resilient than others.

Darion pondered this.

It made sense. For though they had been in the Shazla for weeks now, he still didn't consider himself of great fitness—not when he thought of Edmond's huge biceps—and yet, even after fighting and walking all day,

Darion could have continued. Edmond, however, appeared near collapse.

As sleep drew ever nearer, he asked even softer, *you said 'power'. Do you mean magic—like you? I thought only my senses could detect more than others, but after Gamlin, and now this, I… I'm not a sorcerer or something, am I?*

Triumph, knowing not what that term meant, only said, *All I know is that you seem to have more giftings than once supposed.*

Darion thought he detected a sliver of shame in Triumph's voice. He recalled their meeting in the Library and their time together in Kaulter. It seemed like a lifetime ago. It was crazy to think that he and Triumph hadn't gotten along well at first.

Now, let me go to sleep, or I will start disliking you once more. Our watch will be up before we know it, Triumph murmured grumpily.

Maybe it wasn't so crazy afterall. Darion had to go bonding the cranky and prideful unicorn.

I heard that!

Good, Darion retorted, smiling inwardly. Whatever he was, he was Darion's companion, and Darion loved him. Thinking on love, his thoughts shifted to Nala, who lay mere feet away, and wondered if her thoughts lingered on him.

Go to sleep, you besotted boy.

Shut up, Darion snapped, annoyed at the intrusive unicorn, yet smiling as he drifted to sleep.

***

The centaur exhaled for the thousandth time—that hour.

"Must you really keep doing that?" Lyrianna asked, and though she said it in a sweet voice, her facial expression couldn't hide her annoyance.

Cela grimaced and dropped her head in admonishment. "I apologize, Your Majesty."

Lyrianna felt guilty. They were all growing snappish. They had been standing near the Shovlan Tree for hours each day with little to no result.

She craned her neck upward, for she could see nothing but a cloudless azure sky. Neither could Cela, but Trinidad insisted he could. Lyrianna stared overhead and counted to ten. This *was* awful. It seemed like wasted time, yet Lyrianna felt sure she needed to stay near Trinidad. They had gone through something horrific and come out on the other side. She came here each day with him, and then he accompanied her with her administrative duties at the fortress, checking on the wives, widows, and families of the troops. Many had spouses on the mainland headed to fight alongside her husband. The least she could do was serve as a beacon of hope by making it a point to visit them.

Yesterday, she even descended a steep cliffside, one that led down to the pristine beach, to speak with the merfolk in the bay. They had certainly been gladdened by her appearance. Twelve had gathered to speak with her, and their stories were tragic... just as she had unfortunately expected.

They had been separated from their loved ones, cycles ago, during the coup. No news came from those left behind in Lake Thread, and so most of the merfolk had swum to the refuge of Kaulter. It seemed that no portal was needed for the merfolk. When asked about it, they had looked at one another nervously. *We know of the way between the worlds*, the oldest merman, Jazzeet, had shared. He looked uncomfortable, so Lyrianna didn't press them. She knew the ocean swirled around Kaulter and must lead to Nav'Aria, somehow. She was sure Vikaris knew this.

What else does he know that I do not? She vowed then to take a more active role in the leadership of Nav'Aria, caring for the people within it.

Trinidad exhaled, pulling her away from her thoughts.

The unicorn stood looking up and skirting around the area in what she assumed was the circumference of the Tree. All she knew was that the Shovlan Tree was made of crystals and could only be seen by Unicorns and the Marked Royals. Though a royal herself, without the Mark, even she was left out of the secret.

Another secret, she thought, frustrated. *So, why come here each day?*

Trinidad stomped a hoof in uncharacteristic frustration. His growing mane and freshly cleaned coat made his presence known. He was a unicorn—with or without his horn.

Though for whatever reason, he could see the Tree but couldn't gain admittance. His worst fears had been realized that first day.

Lyrianna knew he was losing hope. He believed the answers he needed to regrow his horn would be found inside Shovlan. He needed a horn though, to gain entry. When pressed, he finally admitted that it had never been done before—to his knowledge. It was known throughout the Council, that ever a unicorn turn traitor, the penalty was the loss of their horn so that the punished could never gain admittance into the Shovlan Tree. Apparently, Vondulus and Tribute had declared it from the very beginning. *Why had they declared such an abhorrent practice?*

But Trinidad was no traitor. Narco was. He had had his brutes torture Trinidad with their special obsidian blades. A small stump, no larger than one's nose, stood out atop Trinidad's forehead.

As Lyrianna began to reassure Trinidad, she froze. Terror gripped her heart and she gasped.

Cela and Trinidad, who had not been looking at her, both jumped to her side now. The humming of Cela's bowstring sounded in the air as she smoothly nocked an arrow and spun searching for the threat.

Lyrianna couldn't speak to tell her it wasn't a threat— at least not here. Her heart pounded in her chest, and she sat with the magnitude of the realization. She felt *him*.

She could feel the evil that threatened her son. It must be him. For in that instant, she saw Darion's face. He looked much tanner, stronger, and older with his dark hair swept around his forehead and shoulders while charging an unseen enemy, sword blade drawn. Darion was plunging headfirst into darkness.

"Lyrianna. My Queen! What is it?" Trinindad's anxious voice called to her, and without request or waiting for her response, he touched his stump to her. He also let out a gasp.

Lyrianna's teary gaze searched his. He, too, had seen it through their touch. Facing the perils of the Shazla, Darion was in grave danger. Just as quickly as it had come, the image faded away. She gulped air as only a nearly drowned person would.

What was that? Is he alright? Her maternal instinct and worry consumed her and all she could do was fret. What could she do for him while stuck in Kaulter? He was in Shazla... without her. He needed her, and she wasn't there. That thought, more than anything else, tore at her heart.

She was his mother, and she had missed everything up to this point in his life. She was still missing it! She would not miss out on anything else. She couldn't lose him. Certainly not now, without getting a chance to know him.

This dire circumstance gave her the clarity needed to solve the problem in front of them. And yet, though it had never been done before, on that sunny day, even as the dark blight of the Shazla threatened her son—the Marked Heir and hope of Nav'Aria—she gazed into Trinidad's solemn eyes, and without thought, as if guided by the crystal spirits above, pressed her palm upon Trinidad's stump, whispering, "Denont."

And as Trinidad started, shocked by the event, she added, "Trinidad, I bond you before all the spirits and as Queen of Nav'Aria."

"It is not possible," Trinidad stammered, yet as he spoke, she knew it was indeed possible. For it had been done. She had bonded a unicorn.

All at once, their bond took them to a depth never before known to her; the scene completely changed overhead to a looming, illuminated white tree with dangling crystals of varying sizes and sheens. The blue sky hidden by the curtain of dazzling crystals.

A huge smile broke out on her face. *So, this was the Shovlan Tree.* This was the Tree that her husband had frequented so often during their marriage.

"Now," she commanded as if this were the most ordinary of happenstances. "We need to get your horn back."

Cela looked dumbfounded and squinted up in the direction where Lyrianna was gazing.

Trinidad couldn't speak. He couldn't explain any of it to Cela—or himself. He only spluttered unintelligibly.

Bonded? Me? How can this be?

As he stared at Lyrianna, whom he had grown to love more than any other—beyond his son, Trixon, of course—he deliberated. *Whatever had made it possible had to be her strange connection with her son.* Darion was indeed the Marked Heir and child of prophecy. Perhaps his connection and powers were so strong that they could rub off on his mother—an unmarked woman? Or was it that her love for him was so strong that it had given her supernatural power where none other had been successful before?

Trinidad knew this would require much study, and there would be repercussions from the Council.

Though at that moment, as he gazed at the radiant, headstrong Queen, stunning with her sunlit golden locks below the glimmering crystals, he knew he had gained much more than a friend in captivity. He had gained a companion. Lyrianna was his Queen, and he was her bonded steed. And though he would never have allowed anyone to know the deep, hidden secret, he had always felt a miniscule sliver of shame for being overlooked by Vikaris. He knew the King had made the right pick bonding Trixon, his son, but not even being considered had at one time, long ago, hurt him. His bond had been stolen from him when Rustusse was slain. That pain had nearly driven him mad in his younger years. He had feared after the coup, and then again in captivity, that he wouldn't live up to his father Rinzaltan's legacy.

Trinidad acknowledged his ignorance, knowing that he had not been intended to bond any other besides Rustusse… and the beauty that stood under the Tree. Pride filled him, and with it, hope.

Now, Trinidad thought, pulse racing. *Now, I will regain my horn.* There was magic at work here, he could feel it. The Creator had led them to this place and would not leave them in this dire time. As he exhaled, Lyrianna looked at him, her expression indecipherable.

"Can I try something?" She asked, and without his response, she snapped for Cela to stand just so under the Tree. Lyrianna scrambled upon Cela's ivory coated back, balancing precariously and extending her hand toward the crystals.

"Lyrianna, no!"

Trinidad, dazed from bonding, slowly understood what she intended. He didn't know of anyone ever touching the crystaled branches and feared what might happen. As he yelled, her fingers clasped one low hanging crystal, and a blinding white light eclipsed the sky.

CHAPTER 24

The Watchers

Edmond trudged along beside his friends, feeling ashamed.

Darion could have died while Edmond sat babysitting. He looked at Ati walking beside him. Just the sight of her made him nervous. He had never really been around females before—besides his mother. Growing up in the Stenlen hadn't provided much opportunity for socializing. The thought only enhanced his bad mood. *Why am I wasting so much time thinking about her? I am supposed to protect the Prince.* And while, yes, Darion could protect himself— he had certainly proven that—Edmond still felt he owed the Prince his total attention. He could not stray from focus... from his mission.

He flexed his sword arm and rolled his thick shoulders as they walked. He and Darion had not sparred for days, and that left him feeling edgy. He had not used his sword since fighting the Rav'Arians days ago. Cleaning the blackened blood from the blade had been a nasty chore.

Edmond glared around him. As they moved north, back in the direction of Nav'Aria—so the unicorns assured them—the landscape shifted again. The swampy, dense vegetation had disappeared as they moved on, and the landscape looked more and more familiar. Grassy rolling hills, wide expanses, and smatterings of trees he again recognized.

Ati babbled beside him. She must have asked him something, for she touched his arm lightly. He flinched at her touch, and she removed her hand quickly, as if stung. Looking perplexed—and a little hurt—she added sweetly, "do you think so, too, Edmond?"

He ignored her. He couldn't waste any more time on girls. He needed to protect Darion—*his Prince!* He felt that he had let him down and, thereby, let the King down.

The honied voice that had for days caused his pulse to quicken, grated his nerves. *Why was she so cheery?* His family had been killed by Rav'Arians. The Prince had almost been killed by Rav'Arians. This was war. Not a good time for distractions.

He grunted and picked up his pace to walk beside Soren, leaving the girls a few paces behind. He grimaced as he looked back once at Ati's crestfallen expression. *Don't look at her,* he chided himself. *Forget about her.*

Darion studied his friend but didn't say anything. Edmond seemed off since the attack. He made a mental note to speak with him—privately, when they took a break.

His friend's moodiness wasn't going to bring him down, though. Darion beamed as a fat swallow chirped at its friends in the trees. He had missed the sound of birds. He didn't know if they were officially back in Nav'Aria, but his heart felt gladdened all the same. They must be close… Soren and Triumph both seemed unsure of their exact location, being so far from any area they had ever traversed, and yet Triumph had said he felt a presence. He believed they were most likely nearing the Kingdom. They kept a vigilant guard, but they had seen no other Rav'Arians in the past two days of marching.

Coming to a stream, they were surprised to see fish leaping and swimming within it. They made quick work of it, and before the frenzied fish could get away, Edmond had caught three large, yellow-scaled fish with a net from his pack. He gutted them, and after a moment of indecision, Darion allowed them to make a small fire.

After days of only nuts, berries, and dried meat, the fish—seasoned with some of Ati's herbs—were delicious. The four humans shared the fish, eating greedily and moaning with pleasure, savoring the flavor of a warm meal. Soren and Triumph munched the wildgrasses and flowers around the area, not letting the humans out of their sight for a moment.

Leaning back and yawning happily with a full belly, Darion watched Edmond. He looked miserable. His shoulders were slouched, and his stony expression left no doubt. Something was bothering him, and Darion wanted to get to the bottom of it.

"Dude," he whispered. Noting how Ati and Edmond seemed to be avoiding one another's eyes, though Ati's glance darted over between whispers with Nala when Edmond wasn't looking.

Edmond turned to him, not quite meeting his eyes.

"What is your deal?" Darion whispered tersely.

Edmond pressed his lips together firmly, clearly not wanting to talk, but after a moment replied dully, "What do you mean, my Prince?"

Darion rolled his eyes. "Quit that. You know you don't have to call me that when we're just talking alone."

Edmond dipped his head slightly but still didn't reply.

"Like seriously? What is it? Is it Ati? Are you guys fighting?"

Edmond jerked his head, his eyes glistening. "Nothing is wrong, my Prince." And as he said it, he wiped his greasy fish fingers off on his breeches before jumping up. "I will bury this," he replied, his hands already moving to the discarded scales and fish bones.

Darion was about to tell him they'd just let the fire finish them off. He knew it was best to bury your leftovers so you don't have bears sneaking around your campsite, but this was nothing like that. This wasn't a camping trip in Oregon. They'd be on the move in a matter of moments. Darion and the unicorns couldn't sense any lurkers nearby. It really wasn't necessary, but Triumph cut him off.

Let him be, Darion.

Darion turned to Triumph, who gleamed anew in the sunlight, having asked (actually, commanded) Darion to groom him in the stream. It hadn't been a perfect job, but with a wetted old shirt and a brush provided by Nala, he had been able to at least give him and Soren a good rub down. All of them had taken this opportunity to rid themselves of the stink and remnants of battle.

But what's his deal? Did they get in a fight? Did she reject him? Darion couldn't believe that last part as he saw Ati looking after Edmond longingly. *He wouldn't have rejected her... would he?*

Darion watched the behemoth skulk away with his implements. He went much farther than needed, and Darion could only guess that he required a little space.

Darion didn't think Triumph would answer him, but as he heard him approaching softly on velvet feet, he whispered, "He feels ashamed, Darion."

Darion gaped at his companion. "What? Why?"

Triumph's glinting eye bore into Darion, willing him to shut up.

Darion snapped his mouth closed. Irritated. *Why does Edmond feel ashamed? He did everything I asked him to.*

"He places a lot of pressure on himself, Darion. He regrets not being there at the tar pits. Not fighting in your place. He fears that he let you down... Prince Darion," Triumph added, punctuating the title.

"Oh, geez," Darion mumbled. It would be just like Edmond to go all selfless Nav'Arian on him.

Triumph stepped in front of him.

"Let us give him a moment. For even if you do not understand, he has spent his whole life searching for meaning. He carries not only the weight of the attack on his shoulders—but also the deaths of his parents."

Now that really pissed off Darion. "What? He couldn't have stopped them. They were monsters killing grown ups. He was a kid, and he had his little brother—who he saved! It's not his fault. He shouldn't beat himself up over something he had no control of…"

"No," Triumph murmured, "no, he should not."

Darion had a feeling they were no longer talking about Edmond. He bit his lip, breaking eye contact with Triumph. He rubbed a hand over his face and scratched his cheeks at the unfamiliar sensation of stubble that had long since given way to the beginnings of a beard.

Considering the group, he realized they had all lost someone. For though Soren had not mentioned it, Triumph had told him that Soren had lost his siblings at the start of the war. The girls had been orphans raised by dragons…. None of them could continue to hold on to their losses. They were the victims in this, and it did no good to blame themselves. That would not bring their loved ones back. They were not responsible for what happened to them.

Darion patted Triumph's neck. "You smell way better," he quipped with a wink.

Triumph grunted. "So do you, human," Triumph replied, and though his tone was haughty, he rubbed his cheek against Darion's in one of his rare shows of affection.

Darion looked back at Edmond. He was bent low, and his shoulders were shaking. *Ah crap. He's crying.*

Darion crossed the clearing to where Edmond knelt. As he approached, Darion heard the spade shifting dirt. Edmond wasn't crying… he was working.

"Dude," Darion called. "I think that's far enough. It's just fish."

But as he got closer, he could see that Edmond had long ago forgotten his initial purpose of burying their dinner. Instead, he was digging up something. A giant skull appeared from the depths of the earth. The empty cavernous eye sockets boring into him. *What is that?*

He heard the others approaching. Soren moved closer and touched the skull with his horn in inspection.

"Reoul?" he questioned.

Nala made a sound in her throat, as if to disagree. "That is not possible," she said with confidence. "Reoul have never come this far." She said it so matter-of-factly that Ati nodded in agreement. "This land is not known to us—or the Reouls. Zalto told you they stay near the caves."

Darion recalled the conversation. But as more of the perfectly white bone was revealed, he found it hard to deny. *It sure seemed big enough to be a dragon. Could it be one of the beasts Zalto had spoken of?*

They had discussed it on their march. The beast from the attack the other day had to have been one of the *other* 'abominations' Zalto had spoken of. Narco clearly had made various hybrids. Darion shuddered.

"Quick," he called out, "we need to get it out."

And on his cue, the girls knelt down and began clawing at the soil around the enigmatic skull with their hands.

Darion knelt to do the same. Edmond continued to shift the fertile soil in huge clumps. A heap formed to the side.

As they dug, more of the skeleton revealed itself. As Darion pressed his hands in the earth, he breathed in deeply, his senses awakening to this discovery.

The rich scent of earth mixed with the sweet smell of fresh grass and unearthed roots. Millipedes, beetles, and worms fled the humans' hands as they dug further. Darion could sense the bones. And he thought he detected something deeper within.

Darion cursed the fact that they didn't even have a real shovel. The unicorns did their best to assist them by pawing the earth with their front legs. As they worked through the rest of the day, they had mostly unearthed the enormous skeleton of a dragon—a Reoul.

"Here," Ati cried suddenly. "I feel something else."

The unicorns came over to inspect it. Apart from the huge hole in the earth that they had created, a blackened stake stood in the ground. The sight of it caused gooseflesh to appear on his arms, and Darion shivered, knowing what they would find underneath it. The twilight cast shadows on the ghastly skeleton and grave.

Darion's ruby glowed, as did the mighty unicorns, which cast light upon the digsite. Darion ordered them to carefully dig under the stake. It didn't take long, for what was buried was much smaller than the dragon.

Nala gasped as her fingers tugged on the ancient cloth.

Darion felt sick. He knew. His senses told all. He reached down wordlessly and lifted the bundle that lay beside the dragon. As he carefully unwound the fabric, the others gasped.

A human skull.

A pale-yellow ribbon wrapped the petite skull in a loose bow. The tattered rag suggested it had been buried for ages. Darion lightly lifted the ribbon, catching a lingering odor of smoke. He closed his eyes, dizzied by the truth.

A Reoul had killed this human, and whoever had buried the human—he assumed it was a she because of the ribbon—slew the beast, leaving it's remains there. The land must have changed greatly for so much soil and earth to cover an entire Reoul skeleton.

No one spoke as Darion set the bundle back down into its grave and sat back to stretch his aching muscles. He twined the ribbon in his fingers, thinking. He could not say why, but he felt like this discovery was the key.

Was this land now in Nav'Aria? Or Rav'Ar? Why would Zalto say they never made it this far? This is obviously evidence that they did.

It was, without a doubt, a dragon skeleton. It did not have the abnormalities of the other Rav'Arian beasts they had faced.

Nala and Ati were crying softly. Darion ignored them, thinking. *Why would a Reoul kill a human? And who killed the Reoul?*

Awash with questions, it took him a moment to realize that a light was coming toward them, not of their making.

Triumph nudged him, and a low growl escaped his lips. He and Soren stood serving as shields from the unknown threat.

"No trouble. No trouble, Horned One," a voice croaked in the darkness. A torch blocked the stranger from sight.

Edmond leapt at the sound, sweeping up his sword from his discarded belt with his dirt covered hands. He waved it menacingly at the stranger, and with bloodshot eyes and sweat-soaked shirt, he looked half crazed in the torchlight.

"No trouble. Hear me? No trouble," the voice croaked louder, coming closer.

Darion squinted at the light.

He stepped up beside his friend and put his hand on Edmond's shoulder, willing him to calm down. Edmond didn't look away from the person, but his sword ceased swinging.

"Who are you?" Darion called. He could sense it was a human. What he didn't know was whether the person was friend or foe.

How could someone sneak up on us out here? In the middle of nowhere?

And then suddenly the pale arm moved the torch, revealing an even paler face... as if this human had never before seen sunlight. Translucent skin practically glowed in the moonlight, and the skin had a greenish tinge. The person, whoever she was, did not look healthy. White wisps of hair stood on end.

Darion relaxed. It was just an old woman. No threat. "What are you doing out here alone? And at night? It's not safe."

She gestured with her arm and turned. Her hunched form, wrapped in a forest-green shawl, began walking slowly the way she had come.

Darion scoffed. *She's crazy.*

Soren and Triumph both spoke at once. "Let her go," Soren replied as Triumph whispered hotly, "I do not like her. She gives off a strange feeling. She is not Nav'Arian."

Darion searched their eyes. Confused. *Not Nav'Arian?* He, too, could recognize that she was odd. Strange. Psycho maybe. But now that he paused, there was something else there, below the surface. *Let her go? After what we've just discovered?*

He didn't believe in coincidence. It just seemed too strange to find a couple of graves and then have an old lady in the wilds between Rav'Ar and Nav'Aria sneak up on you at night.

"We should follow her," Darion announced, strapping on his swordbelt and leather pack.

The girls were already on their feet. Edmond didn't argue, thankfully.

I do not like this, Darion, Triumph boomed in his mind.

I don't either, Triumph, Darion snapped. *That's the point. She's a weirdo that just shows up like a ghost in the middle of nowhere. This has to be related. This is why we're here. To figure out Narco's secrets. Maybe that lady has the answers we need.*

Moving toward the torch, which had suddenly ceased its progression, Darion sensed the light and knew they would follow. It slowly began shining ahead, and on they continued.

I really hope you are right, Triumph mumbled. *I have a bad feeling about this.*

Good, Darion retorted. *I do too.*

Then he spoke aloud to include the others. "Keep your eyes open, and get your weapons ready," he looked hard at Nala. She nodded, determination in her expression. She already gripped her dagger, and her huge bird-like eyes combed over the shadowed landscape.

The topography shifted, once more leading toward a dense wood. The sight of the thick trees in the still, dark night caused the hair on Darion's neck to stand. The scene reminded him of the Rav'Arian attack only days ago. Yet the woman skirted around the trees, as if avoiding the forest.

Darion had tried to get information from her but had stopped asking questions when she continued muttering, "No trouble, no trouble, no trouble."

A rambling old woman. Darion hoped he wasn't making a big mistake. *What are we doing following her?*

As Darion contemplated abandoning her, the crazy old hag stopped, her torch light flickering in the sudden breeze. She stood in the middle of nowhere. Stones, trees, stumps… nothing out of the ordinary.

She wheezed, moving closer to him. Darion shuddered as her features appeared in the torchlight. A few red hairs sprouted from moles on her cheeks. She had no eyebrows, her eyes pale yellow. *Is she blind?*

"Come, come, come, come, come. No trouble. Come, come, come...." She began to move toward one of the boulders near the base of a large mound, as if she were going to crawl over it.

What a nut, Darion thought, reaching for her arm for fear she'd hurt herself. As he did so, he reached out with his senses. What he found floored him. He dropped his hand. Spinning around, his eyes scoured the earth.

You sense it too? Triumph asked quietly.

Darion looked at him, nodding.

Soren spoke then, *I think you are right, my Prince. This has to hold the answers we seek. I fear your being here though. Perhaps I should stay behind to inspect it while you all get away?*

Edmond and the girls huddled together. Edmond's sword arm still held out in a protective stance, unexpectedly drooped as he gawked.

Darion and the party watched the old woman walk toward a stone and then disappear from view.

In a moment her white-wisped head peeked back out, lit by the torch. "Come, come, come, come...."

Darion, ignoring Soren, moved closer to find that what appeared to be a rock was really a door that had been opened from the inside. A door that opened into the earth. "What the..." he breathed as they reached it.

Edmond pressed his hand firmly against Darion's chest, pushing him back. "I will go first, my Prince," Edmond said roughly, brokering no argument.

Triumph and Soren nodded, standing on either side of Darion, as if protecting him.

Edmond strode through while Darion listened. He didn't hear any sword clashes or cries. He followed after, as did the unicorns and then the girls. The door fit their bulk easily. As soon as they entered, a beam expelled the darkness.

Darion saw Edmond standing a little farther ahead, near a motley group of humans, all as pale and unhealthy looking as the old woman.

"Come, come, come, come," croaked the woman who stood in front, motioning and muttering as she had during the walk.

"Who are you?" Darion asked, completely shocked at finding not just an old woman, but an entire hidden community.

"We watch. Watch. Watch. Watch. Come. Come. No trouble. We watch. Watch. Watch…. We Watchers."

Watchers, Darion shivered. *Watch for what?*

CHAPTER 25

The Leader

Noises filled the night air. Men yelled, women screamed, babies cried… and Narco reveled in it.

The shining terror in the eyes of the Stenlen slaves demonstrated his immense power. *They fear me... and my troops,* he conceded.

Narco had commanded his forces to gather supplies upon reaching the Stenlen. They were needed for their main assault on Vikaris's traitors.

He stood near the horse pens, now brimming with horseflesh since the soldiers had taken over the village. Torches from the watchtowers lit the hellish scene. As he spoke calming murmurs to Silver Seeker, stroking his muzzle, he watched as his Rav'Arians and trolls had their way with the villagers. A good leader shared the spoils of war with his troops. He showed his pleasure in his army by allowing them to pillage and plunder—and rape—to their heart's content, so long as they were on the move tomorrow.

Narco wouldn't need these villagers any longer. Now that they had used them to stock his supply trains, he cared very little for what happened to any of the vermin. There had been far too many uprisings and rebellious traitors in this community over the years, or so Morta had informed him. Unlike his perfectly conditioned Kingdom populous at home. *Obedient, thanks to my might… and the Callers,* he thought sardonically.

Better to show the Stenlen what housing traitors looked like. He could always replenish their numbers with the rebels he would soon have in his clutches. After defeating Vikaris, he would really be supreme! *No one will challenge my rule… not even Morta.* He would set up even more slave communities to work the land beyond the Stenlen… into the Woods of the Willow, and even farther south toward the Shazla. This land boasted vast resources, and now he would have access and control of them all! Vikaris would die; Lyrianna would be his bride; and Trinidad would pull a wagon until the day his brittle bones wore out.

Narco chuckled as he stroked the midnight black unicorn's soft nose. Silver Seeker's eyes gleamed wickedly in the torchlight. Horses milled around, keeping clear of the glorious unicorns that surrounded Narco. He didn't need any of the despicable, treacherous Kaulter unicorns. He had created his own! And they would pay for not acknowledging his rule cycles ago. Maybe they would all serve as packhorses.

Growing tired, he nodded to his guard and they began moving toward his war tent. As they moved, a soldier ripped a wailing swaddled infant from its mother's breast, throwing it to the ground. The mother's shrieks pierced his ears as he watched, riveted. Her wild arms reached for her now-still infant as she was dragged off by the bulky man. Behind her a troll ran by, scooping up the child. Narco shuddered involuntarily, turning away. He moved hurriedly toward his tent, where a pair of Rav'Arians stood watch. Narco grimaced with distaste at the pile of dismembered body parts which lay a few feet from them. Apparently, they had kept some on hand in case they needed an evening snack.

"Get that filth away from my tent," he snapped. "I do not wish to smell it all evening."

One of the Rav'Arian's heads nodded, its eyes glowing from behind its cowl. It moved toward the pile, and instead of moving it, it clucked to its partner and the two gorged on the bloodied remains. Narco felt their hidden eyes on him. They were challenging him. He had not said how exactly to rid the pile.... For an instant he felt a tremor of fear. Kept safe behind the castle walls for so long, he had never been on the move like this. The Rav'Arians were Morta's charge. They couldn't turn on him—could they?

He swallowed, hardening his gaze, jutting out his chin and standing proudly upright. His chest plate gleamed and his cloak swirled as he entered his tent. The two human guards stayed behind, though he heard how their feet shifted nervously eyeing the abhorrent Rav'Arians.

Once inside, Narco breathed heavily. The screams of the night intensified, and he knew he would go without sleep. *The price of leadership,* he thought mockingly.

***

These Kingdom soldiers are young, untested fools. They have never fought anywhere... wherever you pick, we will be victorious, Vikaris.

Vikaris smirked at his companion. While he appreciated Trixon's confidence, he wasn't sure he agreed. Secret imprisoned unicorns loyal only to Narco made his skin crawl, and he knew it enraged Trixon. They were in his command tent with Garis and Kragar.

Garis towered over the map, the candlelight shining gold upon his russet coated legs. The centaur wore a dark green jerkin, his thickly muscled arms left bare. Multiple scars lined the centaur's visible flesh. A warrior. Standing erect, he glared at the map, arms crossed.

Vikaris knew his Commander was a force to be reckoned with—he and the steely-eyed human, Lieutenant Kragar. He completely trusted these officers and valued their counsel, along with Trixon's. Both had been furious that their camp—*his Camp*—had been overrun as they explained the brazen attack. They had lost good soldiers that day, as well as a lot of resources, including many of their mounts who had been released from their stalls. Vikaris knew they wanted vengeance upon the Rav'Arians.

Rav'Arians. How I loathe them. Vikaris had faced them in many battles... always victorious. There had not been a battle in months, he considered. This caused him trepidation. For every time he had faced the enemy over the years, they had risen in number... and intelligence. He could remember some of the earliest battles... it almost wasn't even fair to call them that. The creatures had fallen beneath the might of his sword, and yet now, they had learned to defend themselves—and many of them fought back. In the last battle some had even snuck behind his force using a hidden trail. That single-handed tactic reminded Vikaris that he could not write them off as mindless fodder any longer. A wise leader had to take the enemy seriously and consider their various motives.

This time is different. Narco was up to something, causing Vikaris to feel apprehensive. The last battle had come, and his son tread far beyond his protection. This maddened Vikaris. He had the stronger force. Thousands of troops had amassed, with more pouring out of Kaulter and back into the mainland every day. Drigidor and his entourage of veterans had arrived just last night. *Yet, if Narco had truly unleashed the unicorns, what else might be coming our way? What if any of his agents fell upon Darion in the Shazla?*

He is safe, Vikaris. He has to be.

Vikaris squinted at Trixon towering over the table, making Garis look of average size in comparison. Vikaris held his gaze. He knew Trixon could not be certain, but in this—just as with Trinindad and Lyrianna's captivity—he had to trust his companion.

Returning his attention to the map, he and his officers began to discuss the path Narco's forces would likely take. It was expected that they would load up at the Stenlen.

Vikaris gritted his teeth looking at its placement on the map. Ever since the boy Edmond had escaped from there and shared his horrific maltreatment, in addition to that of the escaped nymphs and centaurs from the Kingdom, Vikaris felt his blood boil with rage. Narco was slaughtering his own people. Treating them as slaves— chattel. That all would end soon. Nav'Aria would soon be freed from Narco's tyranny.

"Here," he announced strongly, tapping his pointer-finger on the map.

"Sire," Garis interjected, just as Kragar cleared his throat noncommittally.

"That is…" Garis paused as Vikaris raised an eyebrow challengingly. "You mean for us to extend our force… that far? To make the first advance? But we have never gone such a great distance into the Nav'Arian plains. All battles have been fought near the Woods… our refuge. Our supply lines. What of the portals?"

Vikaris allowed for his Commander to voice his concerns. He was a sound General and judge of military tactics, but he played it safe on far too many occasions.

Trixon's eyes resembled smoldering coals in the glimmer. Vikaris studied him. Trixon understood. They couldn't hesitate again. They couldn't play it safe any longer. There would be no retreat. The time had come to be rash. Reckless. Offensive. They were going to war… and Vikaris was going to start it!

"I wish to be on the move in the next two hours."

Garis's stern face had returned to a neutral expression, though there was a slight widening of his eyes before he bowed his head. "Upon your command, Your Majesty."

Kragar bowed wordlessly behind Garis before the two strode from the tent to prepare the troops.

Trixon walked to stand beside him, and as he peered at the spot Vikaris had pointed out, he touched the map with his horn. A small crescent moon appeared on the sheet.

"Here we make our stand for Nav'Aria. The fate of all will be determined on the Nav'Arian Plains."

Vikaris's mouth set in a grim line. He could only pray that his decisions—his leadership—would be enough. His shoulders felt weighted with the immense pressure of this decision and of what it would mean for his people. *Fighting on the Plains, warring unicorns on both sides? How had it come to this?*

***

"Stop being daft," Aalil called.

Antonis grumbled, again. He hated how the damn woman could get under his skin. *She was so… so… stubborn,* he thought. Yet even as he thought it, he couldn't keep a slight grin from his face. *That's what makes her so damn irresistible.* He still felt annoyed, though. Much of this trek had been comprised of he and Rick standing and waiting while Aalil ventured or climbed ahead… putting herself in peril, all while he stood by.

The trio had come through the cave system in the mountains and ended up finding another cave opening to exit. The daylight had been blinding, but Antonis vowed then and there that he would not go into another cave. Between the musty smells, the utter darkness, and the creepy little flying bats constantly tickling his face and neck, he had had just about enough. And so here they sat on a sheer cliff, watching another of Aalil's impressive descents with her unicorn-strengthened rope. Her thick fur-lined coat hid her womanly virtues, yet Antonis still felt extremely aroused by the sight of her. So strong and capable.

They were much higher up in the mountains by this time, and though they had not run into any trolls yet, Rick continued to say they were getting close. How he knew, or thought he knew, Antonis wasn't sure. There had been no tracks, campsites, or sounds. It was really quite peaceful up here, if you didn't think about the creepy bats and the many ways one could die, never to be seen again.

He glowered. Aalil dangled from the rope that Antonis and Rick were slowly lowering, both men wearing their leather gloves this time around.

He had insisted on going first, but Aalil, true to her nature, had shot him down immediately.

Antonis huffed from the exertion and frustration. *Has she ever heard of insubordination? Because that is exactly what she is doing.* For some reason that thought led his mind back to the magnificent evening in his Kaulter chambers, suggesting perhaps they were long past insubordination. He would need to address her disregard for his authority.

"Quit your grumbling. You are worse than a teenager. If you are going to pick an independent woman to love, then you just have to let her be strong…" Rick said in his straightforward way, without even looking back at Antonis.

Though as he said it, Aalil called up commanding the two old men to hurry up, which got a curse and a grumble from Rick. Antonis thought he heard him mumble something about "stubborn woman."

He couldn't reply though. Rick had said 'love'. That isn't what is happening here. *Is it?*

Finally, he felt the rope pull and tighten. He knew she had reached the bottom safely. She quickly found a place to secure the line. Since Rick didn't weigh much more than Aalil, Antonis instructed him to go next, after he had secured the rope to a solid tree behind them.

Inhaling deeply, he almost choked on the cold air, his breath visible as he exhaled impatiently. Antonis's fingers felt slow and numb, but he secured the knot, putting up with Rick's scrutiny of it before he agreed to climb down. As Rick cleared the edge, Antonis stood looking over and staring down into Aalil's smug face. With her narrow form bundled up and her hair blowing freely in the wind, she looked like some maiden warrior from a story—or his adolescent fantasies. *How is she real?* She was horribly stubborn—Rick was right about that, but she was without a doubt the sexiest, toughest, most loyal woman Antonis had ever known. He watched his friend hurry down the steep cliff to drop down next to her. Antonis smiled, relieved.

"Ah, to hell with it," he mumbled to himself. "Maybe I do love her." And as her face stared up at his, he thought, *I am going to tell her, just as soon as I get down there.*

He waved, signaling his intent to climb. Her face screwed up in response. *What was her problem now?*

He squinted, trying to read her expression. It looked like… terror. Her mouth opened to cry out as her finger pointed behind him. He spun around, cursing himself as he heard the thump of heavy boots.

As he whipped around, three trolls dropped from an overhang. He considered trying to climb down, but he didn't think he had time to get into position and feared them finding Aalil. No, he would fight.

The trolls towered over him, a rare event given his height. All three appeared to be male—bulbous, tight, and grey-skinned against their large, bare torsos and exposed arm. They each carried huge spiked clubs, and they were laughing, grinning teasingly as they plodded toward him.

He didn't give them a chance to keep it up.

He drew his sword in one smooth motion, his numbness long forgotten. Years of wielding a blade prepared him for instances such as this. Antonis sliced the air nearest the closest troll. It bellowed as the tip of his sword connected with its thick skin. He had been testing its reflexes. Slow, just as he'd expected. *Perfect*, he thought.

Snarling, he leapt forward, slashing and hacking the troll. Its bloodied body crashed to the ground, and its club fell from its palm. Antonis heard a yelp and a crash and prayed that Aalil was alright. He could not afford to divert his attention, for as the one collapsed, the other two moved in sequenced steps. Clubs swinging, yellow jagged teeth bared in challenge. He ducked, narrowly avoiding one club before jumping over the other. He slashed his sword through its thigh. Spinning around, he stabbed them both in the back of the legs. *Slow* was putting it nicely.

He needed to get to their vital organs to finish them before they drew the attention of any others. Their bulk, and this narrow, rocky platform created a challenge, though. Shards of rocks clattered around and off the edge from the commotion.

Both trolls appeared crazed with anger and pain, and Antonis knew he wouldn't be as lucky in this next charge. As the two headed for him, he thrust his sword into one's side, but he lost his grip on his sword hilt as the other grabbed him forcefully and threw him against the rock wall.

Antonis's head slammed against the stone, and he blinked rapidly. Everything looked blurry. Fuzzy. His head throbbed. As he sat up, he could feel a slight wetness on the back of his head. His sword protruded from the other troll's side. The troll crouched to its knees in an effort to reach it and remove it, but to no avail. *Good*, he spat, getting up and positioning himself into a fighter's stance. That left the one who'd thrown him.

It prepared to swipe its massive club, the grin appearing again on its distorted face. Antonis felt his resolve turn to steel. He was going to wipe that imbecile's smile clean off its face. He ducked and rolled to the side. The spiked weapon collided with the stone wall, causing disrupted earth and shattered rock to rain down on Antonis. He grabbed the short blade hidden in his boot. Leaping back to his feet, he charged the troll as it tried to remove its embedded club from the mountain side. Antonis felt his knife tip enter its stomach. The troll howled. Antonis hastily removed the bloodied knife, jumping back, preparing to strike again, but as he did so, something unexpected struck his already sore head from behind.

Darkness came.

"NO!" Aalil screamed.

Rick clasped a hand around Aalil's mouth, pulling her back. For just as they had been able to see Antonis stepping away from the third troll, seeming to have things in order, a half dozen or more troll heads and bodies appeared from another nearby cave opening.

Rick swore. He was supposed to be the tracker. He should have inspected the area first. He should have let Antonis go before him.

As the trolls grew in number, Rick knew that there were too many to fight. He dragged Aalil, who squirmed and writhed every inch of the way, behind an eroded boulder that was surrounded by dried brown grasses and shrubs.

Positioned behind it, Rick kept a hand on Aalil's mouth until she bit down. He cursed and grabbed her arm tightly, keeping her from going back. "Knock it off," he growled.

Aalil glared, opening her mouth as if to argue.

"Now, you listen to me," he whispered, his tone icy cool with warning. "That is my best friend up there… the only person I seem to have left, so do not look at me like that. We cannot fight off that many… not right now."

She stopped trying to pull her arm away as he spoke. She was a soldier, afterall, and could see sense. He motioned for her to stay down and quiet.

With a cursory glance he could see the trolls inspecting the cliffside by the rope. A number of them were moving though, and he spotted Antonis dangling unconsciously from one of the lumbering beast's shoulders.

"Shit," he whispered, ducking and silently trying to signal to Aalil what was happening. Once quiet, he told Aalil the plan.

They were going after them, of course… they just needed to be more stealth. No more screaming.

She nodded silently. Her seething yet stoic anger suited Rick just fine. *I am not going to lose anyone else. Tony, you better be alright.*

CHAPTER 26

The Legend of Tarsin

"Oh, back to work everyone. Go, go. I will lead."

A squat woman with a greying strawberry blonde bun atop her head stepped forward. Her face seemed kind enough… compared to the croaking psycho that was still muttering. With an air of authority, she waved the onlookers away.

Darion and his friends found themselves standing in an earthen tunnel as the strangers filed out. "No trouble, no trouble. We watch… watch…watch."

I do not like this, my Prince, Triumph spoke sharply, breaking into Darion's mind.

Darion didn't look at him directly but could tell he and Soren were both agitated and unable to stand still. Darion also knew that Triumph never liked anyone upon meeting them. The woman ushered the last stragglers out before turning to them with a smile that didn't quite reach her eyes.

Darion's skin crawled. He didn't like it here either, but he could sense… something. He wasn't about to leave yet until he knew exactly what this place was, and how it all fit in the Shazla/Narco puzzle.

As her eyes searched them intensely, the woman smiled wider, revealing decaying yellow teeth. She stepped toward them. Darion got the feeling that her smile was forced. He wanted to turn and run under her scrutiny, but instead he squared his shoulders.

"Hello… and welcome to the Mound," she cooed. "I am Tav'Opal." As she spoke her eyes traveled over them, lingering an instant longer on the girls than the rest.

He felt Nala stiffen as the woman spoke in a distinct accent similar to Nala's and Ati's. *Could this be where they came from?* If that were the case, no wonder her dad left. *This place is creepy.*

Darion longed to ask Nala in private, but knew he'd have to wait.

"Hello," he said, trying to sound composed, as if it were all perfectly ordinary to discover a hidden community of people in a foreign land, living underground. As he introduced the unicorns, he thought sarcastically, *Sure. Totally normal.*

"Join me this way, if you please. I will find you a more comfortable place to sit and wash." Tav'Opal couldn't have seen their hands in the low lighting, but somehow Darion had a feeling she knew they'd been digging in the earth. He longed to pat his pocket to ensure the ribbon still remained safely tucked away. He refrained, for whatever was going on, he didn't think he needed to go about sharing all their secrets just yet.

"You can put that away now, boy," she snapped, her convivial facade breaking momentarily, as she eyed Edmond's sword.

The unicorns rumbled in warning; Triumph stepped forward, slightly blocking Darion from the woman.

Vanishing quickly, Tav'Opal's scowl was replaced with a smile. She raised both her hands in a gesture of peace. "You are very safe here. We have no weapons in our community. No need. I assure you, you will not need *that*. We wish no trouble. No trouble."

Edmond chanced a look at Darion, since it was up to him as leader.

"It's fine, Edmond. Put it away."

Tav'Opal smirked. Her eyes tightened around the sides, as if it were a struggle for her to maintain that expression for long. Darion had a feeling she was used to being obeyed.

Darion took a moment, listening, feeling for any slight sense of what this place could be. Any sign of hidden danger. He sensed wrongness, though nothing in his mind screamed "run."

I don't like this one bit, Triumph repeated, as they began to move farther into the Mound.

Darion tried to ignore him as he halfheartedly listened to the woman, trying to focus more on their surroundings. He needed to be on guard—and so did Triumph.

Quit complaining and pay attention, Darion snapped.

Tav'Opal wiped her hands, smoothing the olive-green apron that was tied around her thick frame, accentuating her tight chocolate-brown dress.

The few people he had seen thus far wore muted colors of greens, browns, and greys. As if they wished to blend into the earth. Upon leaving the small opening, they arrived at a larger one. Darion saw at once that it held many offshooting tunnels. They stood in the center, and Darion tried to memorize the tunnel's appearance, distinguishing it from the rest. *If we could just find a way to mark it.*

Tav'Opal chose a section to the right. The unicorns had to duck the entire way. Eventually, the tunnel began to lighten considerably, and Darion was relieved to smell fresh air. But where were they? And why?

Beyond cautioning them to watch their step, the woman had been quiet in the passageway. As they finally emerged from the tunnel entrance, Darion found that trees loomed overhead. They crawled up the stone laden steps that emptied into the forest.

Hidden from view, he now noted small wooden huts encircling the tunnel entrance. Clothes lines, small cookfires, and other signs of life—yet there were no people. It was an empty camp.

"We are not used to outsiders," she continued, "Follow me. You will be fed and washed." She directed them toward a round complex at the end of the row of houses. Darion felt like he was being watched, but as he looked around, he saw no one.

"This place…" Edmond trailed off as Tav'Opal whistled sharply.

Two red-headed adolescents, whose skin possessed the same sickly pallor as the rest appeared. They, without a word, handed out wetted cloths before passing around bowls of an unidentifiable green porridge. As they set diligently to work, Darion observed the wide berth they gave the unicorns. He surmised they'd rather be hiding in their huts like the rest of the villagers.

The trays they carried had already been filled with bowls of porridge and wooden cups of water… as if they had been expecting the group. *Super creepy.*

Once seated, Darion couldn't take it anymore. The disturbing villagers, the hidden community, the silence! It was like a scene from a horror movie.

The woman watched him coolly, the immense trees shading her face partially from view.

"So… who are you? What is this place? What did that woman mean 'watchers'?"

In the shadows, Tav'Opal's smile looked more like a snarl. Perhaps it was one.

"Tav'Maya misspoke," she said in a firm tone, implying there would be no further questioning.

She is lying, Triumph snorted hotly.

And freaky, Darion shot back.

Soren cleared his throat, which Darion took for agreement.

Speaking aloud for Tav'Opal, Darion began again. "Forgive me. But I don't think that's the whole truth. Who are you watching for? Why do you live here?"

The stout, uncanny woman cocked her head, reminding Darion of a hawk intent upon its prey.

"Before I answer you," she said in a gentler voice, the smile returning once more to all but her eyes, "I wish to ask you questions. Since you are our first visitors in many, many years."

Darion didn't doubt that from the way her people were reacting—hiding from them or looking as if they had just sprouted horns. *Well, I suppose the unicorns do have horns... maybe they are afraid of them? They couldn't be afraid of humans— could they? And why are they staring at Nala and Ati?*

It was so oddly quiet. He looked at his friends' faces; the girls avoided eye contact. He didn't like any of this, and he knew they didn't either. It was his idea to follow the old hag though, so he'd better at least try to gain some information.

"We're not from here," Darion began. "We're looking for answers."

The woman continued to peer at him. After an awkward pause, she finally responded. "And what information is it you seek?"

Darion hesitated. *What should I tell her?* He didn't trust her at all and feared revealing too much.

Triumph then spoke, for which Darion was glad. This was the first time the unicorn had spoken aloud, and the woman's cool posture gave way to goggling eyes while the two serving girls froze in mid-step.

Darion tried to hide his smile.

"We come form the North, Tav'Opal, in search of information that will explain some of our land's history. Perhaps you can be of assistance with that? If you would be so kind as to tell us how long you have been here—and why—that may help us in our quest. And then we will be able to carry on our way and leave you all to your...

community affairs," Triumph concluded stiffly, sniffing as he spied the serving girls hurrying away to hide behind a nearby tree.

Darion studied Tav'Opal as Triumph spoke, for her expressions changed rapidly between what he could only guess was fear, surprise, anger, and... pleasure? Though just as quickly as it had come, her face shifted again, returning to the forced smile she had maintained during their visit. *What was that about?* he wondered.

She inclined her head and parted her lips as Triumph finished.

"We have been here since the beginning, One of the Horn," she told Triumph. "We have lived off this land quietly and privately for generations. We do not trouble anyone. We simply... watch." Again, the cool smile.

"Yes, but," Darion interjected, "Watch for what?"

The hawk-like stare swiveled its predatory glance to him. "For outsiders, of course," she said simply.

"And," Darion swallowed the tremor in his voice, berating himself. *I am the Marked Heir, and she is just some creepy woman.*

"What do you want from the outsiders you watch?" The hair prickled along his neck and forearms as he waited for her to reply.

Again, she took her time with responding. "Nothing. We also wish for information. That is all. We are a quiet community. You are safe here and welcome to stay," though her lip sneered as she looked at the boys' swordbelts. "Now, I will leave you to rest. You must be tired from all of your… findings," she purred in that strange, slurring accent. "We will speak later."

It took force of will for Darion to stay his hand, desiring to reach for the ribbon. *Was it still hidden? She knows*, he thought worriedly.

Rising surprisingly fast, despite her heft, Tav'Opal brushed the pine needles and leaves from her dress before striding off without a word.

Darion looked around. The eyes. He could feel them. They were certainly being watched. "Let's go inside," he suggested.

Once inside the thatched hut, there was an audible sigh from his companions. Nala and Ati sagged, looking pale. The unicorns each placed themselves near opposite windows to stand guard while Edmond's hand returned to his swordhilt. He looked ready to spring into action at any moment, with his sword arm flexing and a vein bulging in his neck as he frowned anxiously.

This place definitely couldn't be more uncomfortable. But what should they do? This mysterious village might have the answers… or it could all prove an enormous waste of time. Tav'Opal had skirted their questions. They still knew nothing about this community.

"We need to get more information, and then we'll go," he told them. And though no one spoke, he felt that they agreed with him.

His eyes fell on Nala and Ati, who were whispering in such hushed voices, that even with his heightened senses, he couldn't quite make out their words. He went and sat near them. "What is it? Have you been here before? That lady kept looking at you both."

Nala's haunted eyes focused on his. She nodded slightly, "I think so," she said in her low, breathy voice, her eyes revealing far more than her words.

He grimaced. It couldn't be good. "What do you remember?"

"I..." she trailed off frowning. Contemplating. "I think we come from this community. It was long ago. Remember how we recognized those flowers? We had to have been near here. And the way she looked at us! It felt like her eyes were burning straight through me," she shivered, wrapping her toned arms around her knees. Her tan animal-hide pants a contrast to the dress Tav'Opal had worn.

Darion hated seeing Nala like this. From what he had seen, Nala was no chicken. Even when faced with the monster outside the tar pits, she had fought. Then why did this place stir such fear in her?

He paused for a heartbeat before pressing, "Do you remember why your dad left?"

Ati's eyes glimmered as she spoke up. "I do not remember my father... not much that is, being that I was so young. And yet, I remember the *feeling*. The feeling here makes me remember. I do not think he left. I think he ran—and took us with him." She added softer, her words chilling Darion, "I think he escaped from here."

Darion chewed his thumb nail thinking it over, as he inspected the hut. *It is hella creepy here, but what would they be running from?*

I do not like it, Darion. We need to leave—now. With, or without, answers. I have a really bad feeling about this place.

Triumph didn't turn to look at him, his gaze remaining out the window. Darion swallowed nervously. *It must be bad if Triumph is acting this worried.* Darion toyed with the ribbon from his pocket. Thinking.

Narco had come here years ago. Everyone knew that. Zalto had confirmed it, sharing how Narco had killed Salimna, cutting out his heart and fleeing across the border… The border. Darion paused considering it. *A skirmish years earlier had created the border. And yet, Zalto explained that that had not been of the Reouls' making. That an earlier "abomination" had lived in Rav'Ar. But how could that be? How could there have been evil Rav'Arians before Narco's trip?*

Darion scrunched his brow and rubbed his temples as he tried to make sense of everything they had learned. *Then there were the Tar Pits. We found the Rav'Arian breeding ground.* He shuddered thinking back to that horrific scene of the young hatchlings fighting to the death with one another to consume the tails of their own kind! And then there had been the larger beast that had chased them. Darion was positive it emanated the same malevolent feeling as the Rav'Arians. *Like this place*, he realized.

And as he rubbed his temples, he felt something tickle the exposed skin on his hand. Opening his eyes, he saw that the ribbon still dangled from his fingers. *And then there's the gravesite, and this community? How does it fit?* He wanted to yank his hair out in frustration.

I think you are right, Darion. It is connected, though even Soren and I are struggling to piece it together. One clue still evades us.

Unexpectedly, a knock sounded at the door and it slowly creaked open.

The serving girl, her pale, sickly skin surrounded by locks of red hair lent her ghoulishness. She kept her eyes downturned. She stepped in warily curtsying as she hurriedly set a basket inside. "For the festival," she whispered before scurrying out.

"Wait... what?" Darion called after her, but the door closed. "What festival?" He strode to the basket and found garments—strange garments—feathered masks and head coverings, with a note set atop the pile.

We will celebrate our new friends under the orb.

The handwritten note scrawled across ripped parchment wasn't signed.

"Darion, I do not like this," Triumph repeated, this time to all of them. The girls stood, mouths agape as he lifted a mask. The snarled, bird-like faces looked like a terrifying costume.

"Do you recognize these?"

Nala and Ati both nodded, looking faint. Nala's arms wrapped about herself even tighter.

Darion knew they still had a few hours until the moon was at its zenith. *Perhaps we should go now?*

As they deliberated, another tap came... from the window nearest Soren. The unicorn whinnied in surprise.

Edmond drew his blade expertly, expecting an attack.

Darion wasn't sure what he had expected, but it wasn't this. As he advanced toward the window ledge, he saw another woman with a small boy in tow. She motioned for them to follow her. *Ridiculous.*

Darion could feel the eyes watching the hut. The door stood exposed, and as it was, the unicorns wouldn't be able to leap from the window. He reached out his senses. She seemed different than the others.

Do not even think about it, Triumph growled.

Darion blinked, surprised. He wasn't even sure he had been thinking about it. But now that Triumph said it, and as he looked into the woman's worried eyes, he could tell she differed greatly from Tav'Opal. She looked terrified… and she had a child. *I have to go,* Darion voiced, and smoothly opened the window.

Triumph moved to cut him off, but Darion leapt out before his companion could reach him.

"Darion!"

I will be right back.

Edmond and Nala jumped out before he could stop them.

Triumph's face and piercing horn leaned out the window. He glared with murder in his eyes.

Watch Ati and Soren, Darion told him, trying to sound calm.

If anything happens to you, I will kill every last one of them. I will give you a few moments, and if you're not back, I'm breaking out of this hut and coming after you… this simply is not right!

Darion gulped. He had never heard Triumph's voice so… worried. He gave him a subtle thumbs-up, *I'll be alright,* he said following the woman and child into the trees.

As they rounded another bulky tree stump and found themselves completely in the shadows, Darion began to reconsider. Nala pressed herself against him, clinging to his arm. Edmond stood close. His sword drawn.

Suddenly two pale faces popped out of the trees.

"Please," the woman said softly. "You must go now."

Ice coursed through Darion's body. "Why? Who are you?" The questions tumbled from his mouth.

A pale hand reached out, and Edmond made as if to grab it, but Darion jerked his head signaling him. The hand gently caressed Nala's cheek next to him.

"I am your mother's sister, child. I would know your face anywhere."

Nala gasped, squeezing his arm even tighter. "My mother?" she asked dubiously.

"Yes, Tav'Nala," the woman's reedy voice spoke so quietly that Darion had to strain his ears to hear. "It is not safe here you all must go—now." Her hazel eyes were made visible in the emerging moonlight. They glistened with tears.

"But why?" Darion interrupted. "Where are we? What is going on?" He asked plaintively. "We need answers."

The woman shuffled her feet nervously and surveyed the margins. "Not here," she whispered and waved for them to follow her deeper into the forest. The little boy stared with big umber eyes but said not a word.

Triumph? Darion tested.

I am listening. If anything changes, I will be there in an instant. Keep up your guard!

Furtively stepping around a fallen tree, the group arrived at a small hut. It appeared less gloomy than the ones by the cave tunnel. Woven yellow curtains hung from the windows, and a small lace and floral wreath adorned the door.

The woman waved them inside, anxiously glancing around.

Once the door closed, the woman lit a few candles, revealing a pleasant room with a table, four chairs, and a small cot in the corner, piled with a few blankets. A painting of a sunrise hung over the cot. That image alone surprised Darion. He doubted many in this community had ever seen the sun. Where had it come from?

She motioned for them to sit. The little boy bounded to the blankets, where he withdrew a small wooden horse. He flopped onto the cot, toy in hand, and happily cooed to himself as he played.

Without preamble, the woman began. "Our community has not always been like *this*... at least, that is what my grandmother told me, and what her grandmother told her." Her honest eyes twinkled in the candlelight, and her dark chestnut hair warmed her pale face.

"We are the people of Tarsin. The watchers."

At the mention of the name, Darion's arm began to glow underneath his shirt, glimmering under the tattered fabric. The woman's eyes widened, but she didn't pause her recitation.

"Long ago it is said that Tarsin was one of the leaders' sons in our community. We were a strong, hard-working village. We traded with nearby communities and lived peacefully off the rich land."

Darion started at the mention of 'communties', yet as if reading his mind, she continued sadly.

"Those other villages are gone. We are all that remain."

"Yes—but why? And why did you say we needed to leave? Who are you?" Darion blurted.

The woman blushed, breaking off from her story. "Oh, my apologies. I am Tav'Raka, my sister was Tav'Alora... your mother," she said again softly, looking at Nala.

Nala frowned slightly but didn't speak.

"Nice to meet you, Tav'Raka. I'm Darion, this is Edmond, and you know Nala."

She smiled kindly. She turned toward the tiny boy lying on the blankets, trotting the carved horse around, and giggling to himself. Her maternal love for her son made clear by her expression. "This is my son Valon."

Darion watched Nala's eyes widening with understanding. The woman smiled and reached for Nala's hand. "Yes, Tav'Nala. This is your cousin."

Though Darion couldn't say what changed, the woman's smile seemed to faulter at the word, and her face filled with sorrow. As if breaking from a spell, she looked around at her windows and door.

"You must go," she said again, her reedy voice filling with panic now. "They are coming."

Goosebumps covered Darion. "Who?"

"We are watchers... for them."

Darion had no idea what she was talking about. *For who?* Nothing was making sense. Without thought, he drew the ribbon from his pocket, his shirtsleeve sliding up to reveal more of his Marked hand and wrist.

She looked astonished… and crestfallen. "So, it is true? You have come at last?"

"What?" Darion was growing ever more frustrated with each word. "Who?"

"You are the one who will save us. The one he wants."

Darion hoped without interruption she would continue, so he pressed his lips together, firmly stemming his questions.

"Long ago, Tarsin—one of us—slew a great beast that had killed his fiancé. He was never the same after the attack and vowed that we must "watch" for more. But as my grandmother told it, somehow the story became muddled. We went from watching out for the flying beasts, to watching out for… humans. My grandmother told me this, even though it was not to be spoken of. If Tav'Opal ever heard me sharing it, I would be punished," she bit her lip, worriedly glancing at her son.

Darion pleaded for her to continue.

"Our community has changed in my lifetime. We now watch… for you," she paused eyeing his arm. "Darion, you are not safe here. We have been instructed— according to Tav'Opal—to send word to *them*, when one of your kind—or the horned ones you journey with—ever cross this land. They are coming."

And then meaning took hold. Darion could smell them. He could sense them.

Rav'Arians.

In a flash, he was upright and standing. "You…" he started menacingly. Mistrust filling him. The little boy began to cry, and the mother held up her hands to shush him.

"No, I do not serve them like the others," she pleaded, wringing her hands as she spoke. "Our community consists of four of the old families. Mine—ours—has never served them. We wanted to get away when they first started appearing years ago, but we were caught." Her eyes brimmed with tears, and Nala reached for her, her eyes desperate for the information she had always longed for.

"Your mother was betrayed by Tav'Opal, Nala. Her 'friend' told her family, and the night we made our escape, your mother was shot in the back with an arrow. Knowing she was dead, I screamed for your father to run. I knew what they would do to you girls had you stayed," the tears began to fall freely as she looked over again at her small son. "I… we… were not so lucky."

She looked back at them. "My husband, Burn, was taken. They still have him—after all these years—down below in the tunnel, where he mines and sits in the dark holding chamber."

Darion knew they needed to move, but his feet felt like they were glued to the floor.

"They said I would bear the memory by living here alone. I can visit him only once a year. That is how he…" she gestured toward her son.

Darion felt his face flush with understanding.

"So, you see, I cannot leave. I love Burn, and I will not leave him here to suffer alone. I will bear his 'holding' too, until I can free him. But you must go, NOW! Tav'Opal serves them and has sent a runner to tell them of the outsiders. They will be here any moment. You must flee," and as indecision flickered on her face, she went to scoop up her young son. "And you must take Valon. This is no place for a child. No place for anyone," she said hauntingly.

Darion knew they needed to go. The cloying odor wafted closer. Stronger. He couldn't hear them yet, but knew they were drawing nearer.

Triumph. Rav'Arians are coming!

"Come with us," Nala said, grasping her aunt's hand.

The woman let out a moan in her despair.

"What will they do when they find out you helped us? You cannot stay here. Please," Nala begged as the woman shepherded them toward the door. "I will be alright. I cannot leave my husband," she said, quickly wiping the tears from her niece's face. "But my son. He deserves better than this. I will not allow him to worship those… beasts. I worship the Creator. He will protect me, and you will protect my son. Promise me… please."

Nala sobbed but nodded her head before grabbing the woman and child in a fierce embrace.

"I promise," she whispered.

Darion closed his eyes, overcome by the senses and emotions of this meeting. The picture of the mother passing her son to another for safekeeping resounded so heavily within Darion's being. He realized that this is exactly what Lyrianna had done with him, when she had handed him off to Carol.

Tav'Raka opened the door and ushered them out, leading them silently—save for Nala's sniffles—back toward their hut. The first licking flames of a fire disrupted the black night near the cave entrance.

"The festival is beginning," Tav'Raka whispered worriedly.

Bodies emerged in the darkness, masked behind hideous facades of bird-like beasts. Feathers spread billowing as they moved. In the firelight, a drumbeat punctuated a steady rhythm, and the bodies thrusted and jolted to the music. "They are preparing for the ritual."

"What ritual?" Darion asked softly.

"Sacrifice," she murmured. "Your sacrifice—the outsiders. Leave now. They are close. I can feel them. Take my son and get away from here, this way," she pointed through the trees behind their huts, "Fast!"

Ati leapt out the window of the hut suddenly, and as she did, Soren and Triumph appeared. Darion knew they needed to go, but he couldn't help asking one more thing. "Who does Tav'Opal report to? Who are you watching for?"

The woman looked so panicked but answered understandingly. "For Tarsin."

Darion blinked. *The man who killed the beast?* That had to have been centuries ago, but he didn't press her. She must be overwhelmed with emotion.

He only nodded and kissed her cheek before moving away in the direction she had indicated. Valon, perhaps lulled by the strange drumbeats, had fallen asleep during the walk.

"But how will you find us?" Nala spluttered.

Tav'Raka placed a gentle kiss on her boy's brow before pushing Nala's arm gently to go. "The Creator will guide me—now go!"

Darion protectively wrapped an arm around Nala and Valon, guiding them away.

Tav'Raka sat on her cot staring at the small painting of the sun. One day she would see the sun, and it would be brilliant. She could almost feel its warm rays upon her skin.

Her hut door creaked open, but she didn't turn. Her tears had all been shed, and she sat upright holding the tiny horse that Burn had carved for Valon.

"You have made a very poor decision this night, Raka."

Tav'Raka closed her eyes. She wouldn't see the sun for a long time, but she would see Burn. They would take her to the 'holding' chamber, just like they had taken Burn. She knew it.

Abruptly, pain gripped her, and her eyes widened as she looked down to see a blade jutting out from her front. Blood spurted. The pain was excruciating. Dazed, she turned to look. Tav'Opal stood behind her, wiping her hands upon her olive apron.

"Why?" Tav'Raka asked weakly, a trail of blood dribbling from her mouth.

"The sacrifice must be paid, Raka. You knew this. We watch. And we called them... but the outsiders got away. This would not do. The sacrifice must be paid."

Shadows loomed in the doorway, and the tapping of heavy boots sounded before excited clicking sounds filled the tiny hut.

"No," Tav'Raka whispered, gurgling on her blood as she collapsed on her side.

"It has to be so, Raka," Tav'Opal's arid voice sounded as if it came from far off.

Tav'Raka was losing consciousness.

"We watch... and we obey. It must be so."

Valon's wooden horse was the last sight Tav'Raka's eyes beheld before life left her and the Rav'Arians crouched over her still-warm body.

CHAPTER 27

The Trigger

He has been in there too long. He knows I am here. I must kill him. I will kill him. Dark thoughts tormented Zola as she peered at the entrance of the towering barn.

Narco had left with the other unicorns and his mass of minions days ago, and only Master's friend remained. The pale, red-headed man with the eerie amber eyes. He had the barn surrounded from sun-up to sundown, and all throughout the night. It appeared more heavily guarded now than it had been previously. Zola cursed her bad luck. How was she to free Trigger with this huge contingent of guards, not to mention the villain himself who made a point of visiting the barn for hours each day? She longed to know what was happening inside. She yearned to go to Trigger and comfort him. What was he doing to her son? If Narco's wretch was hurting him she would kill him too!

He knows I am here, she thought again darkly. That day in the yard, he had felt her presence. He baited her. She knew it, yet what could she do? She couldn't leave—she wouldn't leave without her young colt. She hadn't heard his voice in days, and that worried her even more than the evil man. Why had she been unable to communicate with him? What had severed their connection? She tried to reach out to him telepathically again, to reassure him. She met silence.

She decided to forage, since it seemed she would be here another day, and she needed to keep up her strength. She spent the rest of the afternoon exploring away from the barn and castle. Trying to find enough to eat while staying hidden proved a challenge. She had rolled in the mud to try and blend into her surroundings. Her appetite, she realized, had not been satiated since her escape, but she cared little. Having the knowledge that she had been kept penned up, sedated, and well-fed like a house pet— *nay, a slave!*—infuriated her. Her hatred for her Master and his soldiers consumed her. But her new sense of love for Trigger… that is what sustained her. What fueled her! The sensation had completely overtaken her, and she had thought she could hear voices. Sweet, pure singing. Though the sounds had long since gone quiet, it nagged a part of her memory. Some part of her had been regained when that sensation took hold. She knew she needed to free her son and find other unicorns. They could help her—and Trigger. She may not have a horn, but that sensation had filled her with such positive energy and warmth that she knew restoration would happen. She felt it in her very bones. She would regrow her horn, and she would kill Master. He would never hurt her—or another unicorn again!

Trigger felt confused.

The pale human who sat speaking to him chilled him, but he was all that came. The young colt thought he could remember another Master, one with a scarred face. His first days a blur, and being so small, he couldn't remember anything except the shadowed face of the man, and the urgent maternal voice of another. Maybe he had imagined it. He couldn't hear her anymore, whoever or whatever it had been.

The tiny unicorn stood still as the man sat in his stall brushing his ebony coat. He didn't like the man. Not the look or the feel of him. Most of all, he didn't like what the man said.

"You, my pet, will be the mightiest of all. I have seen to it. I took extra care with your creation. You will be the strongest, most powerful of my creations. You will bring down the Kaulter beasts. Narco is a fool, and once he kills Vikaris, or is killed himself, I will claim the Throne for myself. None will live past this battle. None save you and me. We will wash the world in blood and come out of it as victors."

A tingling sensation ran down Trigger's back as the man's words washed over him and his maniacal laughter filled the empty barn. Trigger wanted to pull away, to cry out, but he had done that before. He had been punished that day. This scary man caused Trigger to tremble at his touch. Though he dreaded the man's appearance, he feared the silence of his departure even more. He cried every night, hoping someone—anyone besides this scary

human—would come for him. No one did. He didn't
know what this man was talking about. He only knew that
he seemed to like hurting people—hurting Trigger—and
that frightened him. Upsetting the man scared him more
though. He tried to keep from trembling as the man's pale
hands ran the brush over his already emaculate, glossy
coat. The man never touched his horn though, which
made Trigger curious. He knew he looked different from
the man, and one time, the man had used the word *unicorn*.
Trigger assumed that was what he—and the other *pets*—
were. He didn't know why he had a horn or what his
future would be. He only knew terror, isolation, and
dread.

Zola watched the man exit the barn after being in there
most of the day. A flock of uniformed men followed him
toward the Castle where he would retire for the evening.
The same predictable routine as the previous night.

The superb full moon began to crest the horizon, and
Zola knew it would not be long until the moon cast the
land in its silvery light. She watched it climb in the sky.
There was something magical about moonlight. She
bathed in it, hidden in the trees and wreckage surrounding
the castle; she loved how it had twinkled upon her sheer
coat, though not tonight, for she could feel the caking
mud stiff on her body. She had never seen the moon so
large before. The moon assisted her, like a friend. *This is a
sign*, she thought excitedly. *Magic is in the air. It is time to free
Trigger.*

A mewling cry erupted in the stillness. Her gaze flashed back toward the barn. Her son! The sound of his cries tore at her heart, torturing her. She decided to move closer to inspect the building.

A new troop of guards had come on duty once Master's evil friend had left. Skulking through the dense trees behind the castle and outbuildings, she could see the guards' faces from the emerging moonlight flooding the area around the barn. Two men close to her hiding spot stood speaking in hushed voices. One of them puffed on a pipe, cherry tobacco smoke filling the air. She crinkled her nose at the unfamiliar odor. But it was their words that filled her with fear.

"Did you hear today's Callers?" a gruff voice drawled.

"About the Stenlen? Or the rebels?" A younger guard's voice said softly.

"The rebels, you daft man. Who gives two fucks about the Stenlen? They are traitors. Everyone knows it."

"Yes," the younger voice paused, sounding nervous. He looked around before speaking even softer.

Zola strained to hear his words.

"But, the whole village? Just gone? The Callers say they turned traitor...but," the man shuddered. "You know what happened to them?"

The older man looked around anxiously, "Quiet! Of course, I know what happened to them," he whispered tersely. "And unless you want to end up in a Rav'Arian's belly too, you will never speak of it again. We believe as the Callers say. We obey. The Stenlen villagers turned traitor and were dealt with, just as the rebels will be. Got it?"

The younger man stood silent for a moment, chastized by the older guard. Yet he couldn't stand still. He looked agitated.

The older guard puffed his pipe, and his eyes swept the area. "What is it?" he asked quietly.

"Well," the younger guard gestured with his hands, "but what of the rumors? Of the real unicorns—not just these," he gestured toward the barn, "What do you think they will do when they see what the Lord Emperor has done?"

The older man scowled furiously, mopping his forehead with his shirtsleeve.

"Damnit, Gerald. You are going to get us killed," the guard growled. "Now shut up. There are no real unicorns left... you know that. Those are just filthy rumors. The Callers speak the truth. We obey, just as the Lord Emperor says."

"But—"

"No, no Gerald. You listen to me. You do not stay alive in the Kingdom by listening to rumors. We listen to the Callers. We obey the Emperor. That is it. The rebel in the Woods will be killed—just like the traitors in the Stenlen," the older guard continued even softer. "You do not want to be next, do you? Now shut your mouth, before we end up strung up like the latest pair on the ramparts." The older man cursed, tapping the butt of his pipe on his boot, emptying it and then tucking it away in his jerkin.

Before the younger guard could advance his argument, the desperate wails took up again. A yowl disturbing the night's stillness. Zola's heart lurched at the sound.

The older guard growled. "I cannot do it. I will not listen to that mewling one more night. I am going to shut that beast up."

The young guard—Gerald—grabbed the older guard's hand. "No, Ander. You cannot go in there. What about our orders?"

"I know the orders. Just like I know not to talk about rebel rumors, but it appears we are doing both this evening. That sound grates on my nerves."

And with that, the grizzled older man stomped off toward the entrance, growling for the guards at the door to let him in.

Zola's pulse quickened. She crept closer, keeping an eye on the younger guard while trying to watch the older guard. He appeared to be arguing with those at the front, but after a moment, one of them relented, handing the older guard a torch before allowing him to enter the barn. The cry increased in volume as the door swung open momentarily. Zola felt desperate.

Abruptly, the cries shifted from despair to pain. She heard a crack in the air and realized it was a whip. She had seen a man working an ordinary horse with one a few days ago and had recoiled each time the man whipped the poor creature's rear.

The cries inside stopped, and instead she heard panicked squawks intermixed with whip cracks and yells. The human was whipping her son.

She leapt from her hidden enclosure in the trees. Approaching the lone guard, she punched her left front hoof through his face as she reared up, dropping him in an instant. No other guards stood on this side of the building. She could hear the old guard's growling voice above the whip inside, along with her son's painful cries. She hustled around the building, colliding with a guard who had been inspecting the area. His sword was almost out of its scabbard before he, too, was dropped. She ran him down without delay or hesitation. *I am coming, Trigger.*

The man's moans of agony were muffled by voices coming from the barn. Her front hooves felt sticky with blood, but she cared not. Three more guards stood near the doors. They looked startled when she approached, seemingly from out of nowhere.

In the moonlight, she could only imagine how the mud and bloody hooves made her look. She used the surprise to her advantage and ran at them. Drawing their swords, these guards had more sense than the others, apparently. One attempted to flee. She chased him down first, kicking and pummeling him with her front hooves, just as she had with the younger guard. His crumpled form fell with a thud.

Breathing heavily, she snarled, spinning to face the new threat as she heard boots crunching on the gravel. One of the guards crept toward her, sword extended. In turn, she extended her back leg into a rear kick, striking his shoulder and knocking him off his advance. Before she could finish him, a shadow leapt out near her neck. She danced out of the way as a steel-edged sword sliced the air in front of her. The clean metal shining in the moonlight.

Backing up, she shrieked as she felt a stinging on her back leg. It was a shallow cut. She could still use her leg, but her fury burned. In a mad frenzy, she spun and stomped her foot through the felled man's chest in a quick motion. His raised arm with the bloodied dagger stopped in midair. Knocking his corpse away, she turned to see the other man backing away from her. She charged him, turning her body just so as she slammed him into the building. He crumpled against the wall, sliding down, and leaving a thin trail of blood upon the wooden barn. She didn't check to see if he was breathing or not, for the door stood cracked and her son needed her inside. She ran in.

The darkness inside surprised her. The interior was pitch-black, lacking windows, save for the small torch light coming from the back stall. It reminded her of her prison cell, enraging her all the more. Then, the sight of the man standing over her son triggered something in her spirit.

"Stop!" She said in a low voice.

The man spun around. His eyes widening. At his feet lay a tiny black shadow. It was trembling. It was her son.

Her eyes burned, and she darted for him.

"You?" the man whispered.

"Unicorns are not to be beaten," she hummed, eyeing the whip in the man's hands. "You will learn that today."

He gaped, drawing back his whip. He retreated from her shadowy, bloodied image, which his pupils reflected in the dim torchlight. Finding himself in danger, he suddenly didn't seem as tough. He whimpered.

Zola sneered as he backed toward the stall, feeling for the edge but keeping his eyes glued on her.

She stalked his every move, coming closer. As his hand moved down to reach his dagger, she bounded forward, kicking his leg. He screamed in pain as the bone splintered through his pant leg and he dropped to the ground.

"No," he pleaded. "Please…"

She laughed deep within her throat. Stepping forward as the man writhed on the ground, she saw his bone protruding from the skin. Blood pooled. He had dropped the torch. It fell upon the straw, igniting it instantly.

"No," he begged, rolling around pathetically, attempting to crawl.

"How does it feel when someone stronger than you hurts you?" She growled.

Stepping down with her other hoof she heard more bones snap as her hoof collided with his other leg. He shrieked in agony.

Maddened with rage, she had almost forgotten her son. Yet as the flames spread in the stall around the man's writhing body, she saw her son's big, innocent eyes. In the firelight, they reflected her lethal image. She felt ashamed. The colt shook but remained otherwise still as the flames drew closer.

"Trigger," she said, leaving the thrashing man, who now had rolled over and frantically tried to pull himself away from the fire. With both legs broken, he wriggled like a worm.

"Come here. It is me. Mama. That fire will hurt you." She could feel the heat from the flames growing.

Luckily, the torch had not fallen on Trigger. She cursed her carelessness. She nudged his face, encouraging him to get up. He lay still, paralyzed with fear.

"Trigger," she cried, panic filling her voice. "I am your Mother. I am safe. That bad man will never hurt you again, but you must trust me. That fire will. It is not safe. We have to leave." She could hear a bell tolling. The remaining guards had gone for help.

Still he hesitated, as the blaze grew. "But... he will be very mad. Master says I am his." He shook with fear, seemingly more afraid of *him* than he was of the fire.

Zola's rage turned to molten ire, though she tried to keep her voice level. "You are mine. You are my son. That man has no claim on you." Her last words coming out in a possessive snarl.

The little unicorn's eyes blinked as he saw the flames licking near his hindlegs, sense appearing to return to him. He didn't respond to her, but he did achieve a wobbly stance and made to follow her.

The man had crawled some distance. His voice no longer gruff but pleading.

Zola didn't give him a second glance. She could just make out the doorframe from the blessed moonlight. She cautioned Trigger to wait as she poked her head outside. The guard tower became a din of yells, footsteps, and clambering.

Master's guards are too slow!

No one moved in front of the door. She and Trigger stepped out of the barn. She glanced back to see the flames growing—eating up the straw, wood, and hay at the back of the building.

The guard had made a considerable effort to reach the door, but he wasn't quite fast enough. His eyes met hers as he realized her intent. He grunted with even greater effort and scrabbled on his forearms to drag his unwilling legs behind. He, too, was slow.

Nudging the door with her head, Zola closed it behind them, pushing across the bar to lock him in, just as she had seen other guards do countless times before. The man screamed.

Zola smiled in the darkness. *No one hurts unicorns,* she thought before urging Trigger into the trees. Together, they snuck away in the darkness.

Guards, blood, and flame were all behind them. Zola had her son, and for now, that was enough. *I have beat you, Master,* she thought triumphantly.

***

"They are close," Trixon murmured aloud.

Vikaris sat astride him on the leather war saddle. He wore a forest green jerkin baring his royal crescent. The King kept his muscular arms exposed, as was his habit. His Marked arm glowed brightly with symbols; his ruby sparkled in the early morning light.

Garis, towering over most men, strode near the King and Trixon, at eye level with both rider and unicorn. Together, they led their amassed force toward the Plains. Thousands had come—from the Camp, and from the refuge of Kaulter. Their lines spread for miles. Warrior unicorns and centaurs, mounted calvary and foot soldiers, followed by supply trains, armorers, fletchers, and the few brave camp women who served as laundresses, cooks, and medics, having refused to leave their husbands—or their King. Vikaris gritted his teeth at that. He hated having civilians here but prayed that they kept their sense, and their word to him to stay back beyond the supply trains until the fighting was over. Nymphs flitted by, through, and around the trees. Serving as scouts, they carried messages to the troops and relayed word of Narco's location.

Vikaris closed his eyes momentarily feeling the dawn's early light warming his face. *This is it. There is no other way. Narco's tyranny is almost over.*

Drigidor rumbled in concurrence. Whether to Vikaris's thoughts or Trixon's words, the King did not know.

The King eyed the unicorns that surrounded him. At no point in history had this many unicorns gone into battle. When they did fight, he and Elsra restricted their numbers. They had never allowed every able-bodied warrior to fight at once. To do so jeopardized everything. Without the unicorns, Nav'Aria would be nothing. It was too great a risk… until now.

But it is worth the risk, Trixon spoke. *Risk is the only palatable option. Everything else means defeat.*

Vikaris wasn't surprised that Trixon knew his thoughts. Their tight bond intertwined their minds. He didn't respond, only patted Trixon's thickly muscled neck.

Their front lines were awash in sunlight as they left the refuge of the forest behind, making for the Plains south of Mt. Alodon. Vikaris could see the peaks in the distance. He hoped Riccus and his party were safe there. He smelled the sweet fresh air, but as he drew a deep lungful, he could also detect an approaching filth.

Rav'Arians advanced, Vikaris knew. His heightened senses, much like a unicorn's in a number of ways, allowed him to detect the enemy before many of his human counterparts.

They would meet this day. He looked to Garis, "Prepare the troops. We will make for that slope and mobilize. I want the higher vantage point. Tell the archers to be ready."

He needed not tell Garis, for the Commander had already gathered the nymph messengers. Vikaris couldn't help it. This was his war.

CHAPTER 28✦

The Lake

Zola felt him more than saw him. Thankfully, Trigger's dark coat blended into the night. They could not be found. All evening they had walked, barely resting, though she knew her son's tiny legs could not keep this pace. Hers barely could, she thought angrily, having been kept prisoner all her life; she knew she didn't possess the muscle typical of her kind.

Yet they had to keep moving. The pale man with the amber eyes would be searching for them. They couldn't rest. She wished she could carry her son. All through the night she spoke soothingly to him. They had walked through the forest, avoiding the Castle grounds. She was drawn forward. North. They could have gone any direction, but she followed the tug, as if a magnetic force pulled her toward the bright star in the sky. *Magic*, she thought again.

The trees grew sparse, and she knew morning was close. The wondrous moonlight had dissipated as the sun prepared to rise. She could hear birds chirping, greeting the new day. She exhaled again, turning back for the thousandth time to ensure Trigger was still there. He had begun to slow considerably, and whenever they paused, he leaned upon her for support. He had not spoken to her, though. She would worry about that later. For now, she would be the fortress supporting his weak limbs. Nothing had ever given her so great a feeling. It propelled her. The pale man and Master could not deny her this feeling. If ever she lost this child that had been returned to her, she knew she'd go mad.

Small stone homes and huts dotted her view. Though no one moved outside, they needed to be extremely careful if they were to cut through the Kingdom inhabited by humans. She was too weary to fight. But if they waited, they would lose their advantage. The pale man might find her. Detect her presence. And that could not happen.

A tangy smell filled her nostrils. She had never smelled the like and tried to identify it. As she squinted, she could see a shining surface beyond the homes.

Zola rubbed her velvety nose on Trigger's cheek. His eyes had closed, nearly asleep as he stood leaning against her. "Come, my child," she said softly. "It is not safe here. We must keep going."

A small sigh escaped him, but to his credit he blinked his eyes open and shook out his mane.

Pride swelled in her breast. Her son. *A brave unicorn.*

Zola tried to see, hear, and smell everything around her. She bid him to follow her toward the shiny surface. The sun cresting the horizon hastened them. As they moved toward it, the scent became more prevalent. It smelled… interesting. They passed soundlessly through the village, moving from grass to cobbled stones, to now a strange grainy substance. Her hooves sunk into it as she and Trigger plodded along. It pulled her feet downwards and required more of their effort. Approaching the shining surface, she realized it was water. A lot of water… more than she would have ever thought possible. *What is this?* she wondered.

Land appeared on the other side, much farther away than she had thought. But that was the direction she needed to go. She could feel it. Panic filled her. *What do we do? Could this strange water be crossed?* She turned, fearful, as she heard a dog bark in the distance. *The homes.* The village would be a hive of activity once light came—she knew that from her days studying the Castle and the movements outside its walls.

Casting aside her uncertainty, she stepped one foot into the water to test it. It was cold but not unbearable. She nodded for Trigger to do the same. Still mute, his large eyes looked from the water to her in trepidation.

It couldn't be that deep. They could walk across, though as she stepped forward a few more paces, the water swelled around her ankles, then forelegs, then knees. *How deep is this?* she thought frantically, as more village dogs began to bark. *It would be over Trigger's head in just a few steps.*

She stomped her foot angrily. The sticky muck at the bottom of the water glopped as she moved. She wanted to whinny with terror, frustration, and rage. *So close.* She knew she needed to go north. She had freed her son from the barn but not from the Kingdom.

"Hello," a male voice whispered through rippling water.

Zola gasped and looked around startled. She thought her eyes would pop out of her skull. A human head had emerged from the depths of the water.

Trying to step back quickly, she bumped into Trigger, who was also struggling with his hooves in the squishy substance.

"Shhhh, stay quiet. I am here to help you."

Zola stopped her struggle and peered at the man. He raised his bare arms in the air as if signaling peace. His skin had an odd, greenish tinge to it.

"Who are you?" She snapped, turning her body to shield Trigger's from the stranger.

The man's eyes, a seafoam green, looked deeply at her.

Without explanation she lowered her guard. He was safe. His eyes were not like the guards'—or Master's. They were different. His eyes appeared kind.

His face broke out into a magnificent smile. "I am Shannic. And you, Horned One?"

She almost scoffed. *Horned one?* She had no horn, but then she realized he knew what she was even without her horn. *He must know about unicorns!*

She heard a door creaking open, and boots rang out on the cobblestones. *The village! The humans are waking up!*

"We need to get across," she said, her panic returning.

"Yes, I can see that," he said, his head tilting to peek curiously at Trigger. "We will assist you."

We?

Before she could ask, heads broke the surface all around them, and a loud splash sounded from a fin nearby. She almost jumped out of her skin at their appearance.

"What… are you?" she asked peering at them curiously. Their skin looked so different from the other humans she had seen. She could sense that Trigger was trying to see around her, too.

"We are Merfolk," Shannic replied. "And we do not have much time. We will always serve the Unicorns—and the true Marked Royals of Nav'Aria. Now, hurry. I know not how you came here—or ended up in this position," he said, indicating her missing horn and young colt, "but the beach is not safe for you, especially in the daylight. We must go now. We will carry you."

She almost laughed. *Carry her?*

Suddenly, firm hands grabbed her from all around. It took all her will power not to shake free of them. Her eyes met Trigger's as she saw that he too was being drawn farther into the water.

"It is alright, Trigger. Stay quiet. They are going to help us."

Just then, her voice was cut off as a huge fin splashed from the water. *Where are its legs?*

"You are not human?" she asked.

Shannic, who swam freely beside her, laughed. It was a warm, melodic sound. His eyes twinkled.

She felt ignorant.

"No, Horned One, we are merfolk. Creatures of the sea," his voice faltered. "Of the water, that is."

Nothing made sense, but looking into his merry face, she decided her only option was to trust him.

"Please," she said, "I have been imprisoned for years. I know nothing… of you or the 'rebels', or where to find other unicorns. I only know about Master. Please tell me what is going on."

Shannic's face turned solemn as he listened to her and looked over at Trigger. As the merfolk carried them slowly across the water, he unwove the tale of Nav'Aria. It stoked both awe and fear. The dozen or more merfolk kept them submerged as they swam. Shannic explained that with the daylight, they need to stay hidden as much as possible, and only their heads could stay above water to breathe. They couldn't be spotted by a patrol, or else. Zola only wished they would go faster.

As the sun rose, she found herself immersed in more water than she would have thought possible. *A lake*, he had called it. She only hoped that the merfolk's arms wouldn't tire keeping her aloft. She feared the murky water.

She looked at her son, whose head was now beginning to droop from fatigue and overwhelming stress. Far more than any uncertain water, she feared losing him. "Hold on, my son," she whispered to him. "Freedom is near."

***

"We have to free him," Aali snarled.

Riccus glared at her, rubbing his chin in thought, again ignoring her.

She had listened to Riccus when Antonis had been taken. *Why had she not screamed louder? Warned him? Fought for him?* She had just stared and pointed while trolls surrounded the man she loved. The thought sickened her. *You coward.*

She realized she was in love with him... *I should have told him.* Aalil couldn't imagine losing him a second time.

She and Riccus had followed the trolls, silently stalking them for a day and a half now. Once the trolls had examined the hillside, they returned to the cave, leaving their dead but taking Antonis. Surprisingly, they had also left the rope. Riccus had commented on their stupidity, and Aalil had thanked the Creator for this small gift. After waiting for quiet, the pair made a much more harrowing climb up the rope, following after Antonis's captors.

The trolls had gotten a good lead on them, but Riccus—true to his reputation—was an expert tracker and picked up their trail quickly. They had been following them at a distance ever since.

The trolls had now stopped, and Aalil felt sure they needed to capitalize on it. If they were resting here, something was happening. They couldn't let the trolls draw Antonis or them further into the mountains, for this large cave tunnel seemed to be more frequented than any others they had seen. This meant more trolls. They needed to act. *So, what is he waiting for?*

This expansive torch-lined cave bustled with trolls going to and fro with messages and shifting of the guard. Riccus had directed them to a natural rock ledge, just wide enough for two humans. They climbed it and were given a vantage point over the tunnel, where they sat waiting. Watching.

Far inside the depths of the tunnel, three trolls guarded a sleeping captive. The captors had brought him here, where they conferred with more trolls. Riccus believed that the opposite opening led to their stronghold in the mountains. He insisted they find out what lay beyond that entrance.

But not without Antonis, Aalil had countered.

She knew their mission was reconnaissance in the mountains, but it did not include abandoning her Commander. Her friend. Her soon-to-be husband. She decided right then and there, as she saw him propped against the stone wall, tied up and gagged, that she would free him... and marry him before he ever had the chance to leave her again.

They had watched the changing of guards three times now. Riccus was sure that the only way they'd be able to free him would be to exploit that vulnerable time. For just as the new guards entered the cave, the others left his side to go mingle a bit before returning to their positions.

Riccus rose, crouching, signaling for her to quietly follow him.

She felt annoyed with him, but knew Antonis trusted him with his whole heart, so she tried to do the same. It was hard though. *One wrong decision and we will lose our advantage and get caught. Or worse, yet, Antonis might be killed. That is not an option.*

Edging further, they spotted barrels below. Riccus signaled at them, and she could only guess that they were their target. They would hide there until they could free Antonis the moment the trolls appeared distracted. After that? Aalil assumed they would fight their way out, not seeing any other option.

Aalil felt the soft crunch of brittle stone beneath her feet. Small shale gravel and pebbles slid off the edge. She had left her bow and quiver outside the cave, hidden by some underbrush, for which she was glad as she leaned against the buttress of the cave wall. This high up, they were fairly obscured from view, but if any of the trolls grew curious and spent much time inspecting the area, she knew they'd be sighted. Riccus had warned her to tread carefully on the brittle stone, which she knew he was thinking as she caught his glare.

Glaring back but feeling less confident, she continued after no shouts arose. Directly across, Antonis sat bound against the wall. She stifled a gasp as she saw his eyes fixed on her. The trolls near him sharpened their blades, none seeming aware of him—or what he was looking at.

He shook his head with a quick jerk. He looked worried, and she knew it was not for himself. He was the bravest fool she'd ever known. *What did he think, that I would just leave him?* She scowled at him and caught an eye-roll in return.

That vexing man, always wanting to be the hero. Well not this time, she thought heatedly. *This time I will do the saving.*

Aalil felt Riccus's eyes boring into her. She returned her attention to their path. Riccus was indeed staring at her. He waved his arm angrily at her, and she knew she was too exposed across from Antonis and the trolls. She moved and bit her cheek to keep from cursing as a significant chunk of brittle stone crumbled off the ledge. Her eyes darted toward the trolls, one of whom stood looking around. She ducked down, lying completely flat, her body pressed against the cold, stone wall. She prayed that the torchlight wouldn't reach her here.

"Hear something?"

A giant shadow loomed as the troll stood peering around.

Antonis chewed his lip in consternation. *Damn woman. What is she thinking? What is Rick thinking? They should run, continue the mission. Leave me.* But, as he sat there, he knew that wouldn't happen. That is why he loved those two people more than anyone else—well, besides Darion and Vikaris. And yet that is what was so agonizing about this predicament. He couldn't lose them, and he feared what might happen to them if captured.

He refused to give their presence away by looking where Aalil had last stood. Instead, he watched the troll's feet turn in a slow circle as it monitored the cave happenings. Antonis prayed it would not see her.

"Sir," a warbling voice called, as footsteps thudded near.

Antonis looked up, startled. So did the trolls on guard.

The one standing glowered at the youngling. The young troll stood shorter than its towering elder but held his angry glare.

"What?" the troll boomed.

The youth, its pale grey-like skin flushed under the elder's scrutiny. "Orders," the youth swallowed loudly before continuing, "follow, sir. You… prisoner… to lake."

Antonis dared not look at Aalil for fear of exposing her, but he prayed she didn't do anything stupid. *Stay put,* he thought desperately as rough arms pulled him upright and slung him heavily over one of its shoulders.

The trolls grumbled but didn't hesitate. Hurriedly, they loaded their weapons and moved toward the entrance.

No, Aalil thought frantically, eyeing the ledge, pondering the quickest way down.

Riccus made a *psst* sound, wildly waving at her. She looked from him to Antonis, who was draped over the lumbering troll headed for the cave opening.

Cursing, she followed Riccus. He whispered to her the new plan. Rocks protruded out from the cave wall here. The two would climb down once the trolls left. She only hoped that they could follow him… and that she didn't have to kill Riccus if this plan went awry!

CHAPTER 29✦

The Battle

Vikaris gazed across the sea of men, centaur, unicorn, and nymph. They all gathered for him. For the common cause—bringing down Narco.

Too long had these men gone without homes of their own and without the assurance that they would have a place to raise their young. Too long had this land gone without an annual harvest, a semblance of stability, a King. *How long had the realm gone without peace? What would that even feel like?*

Feeling the sun's warm rays shining upon his already tanned skin, Vikaris smiled, thinking of the joys he'd had growing up in the Castle. He had loved his parents. Rustusse had been a noble King; Vikaris tended to grow despondent when he thought of all the ways he had already failed him. But that ended today. Narco and his vermin would no longer be a scourge upon the land.

Casting his gaze across his forces, he noted grey in some of the men's beards. Then there were young boys who had not even the first inklings of stubble on their chin. The smile faded from his face as he took in the faces of war. It sickened him.

It is worth the risk, Trixon boomed again in his mind.

His unicorn—his friend—stood valiantly upon the Plains, with sunlight gracing his pure coat.

Atop Trixon, Vikaris towered over most of his soldiers. Nearby, Drigidor stood, equally impressive in stature as Trixon. They had arrived at the place of their choosing. They stood in their formations. Vikaris had his archers lined upon the ridge that overlooked the spilling grasslands and fields below. The slow rolling hills and flat Plains were something that Vikaris had almost forgotten; he had not been this far East in years. He had been hiding. He saw that now.

Trixon grumbled loudly.

Alright, not hiding, but you know as well as I it has been too long.

Trixon whinnied and stomped a foot in agreement. *That changes now, for here he comes.*

Vikaris knew his companion was right. He could smell the fetid odor which clung to the Rav'Arians.

Garis towered over the left guard. Vikaris could just see him across the great field. Kragar led the right, and Vikaris took the center. They would launch a three-prong attack, spraying the enemy with arrows as his forces stayed safely out of range until their charge. The humans and centaurs in the front lines held pikes, ready to trap the first enemy soldiers. Vikaris had tried to keep the youngest soldiers for the rearguard, yet it could not be helped. Too many of the soldiers were young. *Where did one draw the line?*

"Members of Nav'Aria," Vikaris yelled. Trixon moved so they faced the troops. Having led his soldiers in many battles, Vikaris knew the effect that a speech could have on his troops. He spoke loudly, his Ruby sparkling and Marked arm gleaming as his hand lightly rested upon the sword at his hip.

Trixon, knowing full well what Vikaris desired, paced before the troops, allowing for more and more to hear their King.

"Long ago, my father and mother were slain in their beds. Long ago, your families and friends were likewise slain. Our Realm plunged into utter darkness, the likes of which has never before been seen in Nav'Aria. I am here to promise that it will NEVER be seen again!" He paused to allow for cheering, "Today, we make our stand… to Narco! To the Rav'Arians! The trolls… and any other enemy that opposes the Marked King of Nav'Aria, and the Unicorns of Kaulter! Today, we remember those we lost. We carry the weight of their absence upon us. Let it fuel you. Let vengeance swell your chest as you think of all that these beasts have taken from you. Our families will sleep securely tonight. We can rest knowing that our wives, our children, and our children's children will be safe tonight… and every night! Because we fought here, on these Nav'Arian Plains. We defeated a tyrant. A usurper. A murderous traitor whose sole intent has been to spread disunity and chaos. But that ends today!" Spittle flew as his empassioned words rang aloud: "Today we conclude the usurper's reign! I will face my Uncle… I will take my father's crown from that bastard's brow and wear it proudly, just as the Marked Kings and Queens have done since the beginning. Mark my words, soldiers. Today we remember! Today we fight! And today, victory is ours!" The cheers swelled ever louder as he shouted over the tumult. "Let us finish this! For Nav'Aria!" Vikaris's sword gleamed in the light as he drew it fluidly.

Trixon ran up and down the ranks encouraging the troops, as Vikaris gave them one final salute.

Garis bellowed a war cry, slamming his gauntleted fist upon his chest, and the other Centaurs—old Myrne included—yelled their savage howls.

The sound was thrilling. Vikaris knew they would not hesitate today. Today they'd be reckless. As he ran back toward the center of the lines, he caught the swirling dust from the approaching force. To make such a dustcloud meant that there had to be thousands on the road, and they were coming fast.

"Make ready," he told the troops around him, including the majestic unicorn warriors he wished did not have to be here.

Drigidor and the other unicorns stood at the center, pawing the ground and whinnying at the sight. Vikaris waited patiently for his uncle to draw near. After long moments, the opposition began to frame its battle formations across the field. Vikaris sucked in his breath when his eye caught the gleam of metal. In the center of the party, a man in brightly shining metal armor rode atop a black unicorn.

So, Vikaris thought darkly, *he too rides a unicorn.*

The unicorns nearest him—Trixon included—mauled the earth, their eyes roiling madly at the sight.

*"*What cursed beast would allow him on his back? And to be bridled like a common horse?*"* Drigidor sneered at the foreign unicorns.

Those beasts, either slaves or traitors, would not be spared this day, Elsra had told Vikaris back in Council at Kaulter. Though the idea of any unicorn slain made all their skin crawl, it was simply non-negotiable. The Kaulter unicorns and the Nav'Arian forces came first. Simple as that. War wasn't pretty, and much blood would have to be shed this day to end it.

"Let them come," Drigidor growled as his massive chest heaved with adrenaline.

His words seemed to encourage the others. Before long, even Trixon's hooves stepped in place, anxious to be off and charging the enemy. Vikaris agreed. Just seeing the vile man—who had not shown his face in cycles—made Vikaris want to let go of every rational battle tactic he'd ever learned and charge off alone to kill him. Instead he yelled, "Steady," in a calm voice.

He didn't feel calm. He felt... ready. Rolling his shoulders, he closed his eyes and offered a prayer to the Creator. All knew that if he was to fall today, Darion was to be named the rightful King immediately. There would be no surrender. They would not lose, but if... IF... Narco's forces seemed to take the upper hand and slay Vikaris, they were to ride for the Shazla Desert, find Darion and Triumph, and name his son "King."

Creator, let it not be so, Vikaris prayed.

With his eyes closed, he breathed deeply, his heightened senses picking up the tension from the troops across the field. He could smell the sweat on men and beast alike, and the sweet fragrance of the soft grasses and flowers dotting the landscape. As he opened his eyes, his gaze lingered on a violet flower. *A spring flower,* Riccus's name for Carolina, though he wasn't sure how or when the pet name started. Looking back at his uncle, Vikaris thought of Carolina and all the rest he had lost. *This is for you, Carolina… and for you, Darion.*

The gleaming figure's arm rose and fell, signaling the charge. In an instant, the calm grasses were ripped apart by the charging hooves of maddened unicorns, war horses, lumbering trolls, and scurrying Rav'Arians. All left their position… all but Narco, atop his black unicorn, and a small contingent of guards. He held tightly to the reins, as even the beast seemed to judge his cowardice, longing to be in the fray with its kind.

He is a coward, Vikaris thought darkly. "I am coming for you, Uncle," Vikaris whispered, challenge filling his voice.

Trixon shook his mane and reared back on his hindlegs, his horn sparkling like a diamond in bright light.

"Archers," Vikaris shouted, and his orders were relayed.

The battle had begun.

Immobile, Narco watched. He had never been on a battlefield, and he felt elated with anticipation yet paralyzed with fear of what would come. *What if Vikaris comes for me?*

A small part of him wished he would. Then he would best Vikaris in front of both armies… but a prickle of fear trudged up the memory of his defeated duels time and time again with Rustusse as a boy. He shook himself; this was no time for nostalgic fancies. He was the Emperor. He smiled, cooing calming words for Silver Seeker, who was electric with energy.

His pets had been bred for this moment. They were told all their lives how those snowy beasts were the monsters here who followed the rebel leader. Monsters who roamed the Woods, making it unsafe for his pets to walk freely. Their Master had to keep them locked up for their own protection. That is why there were so few left— or so he told them. Because the unicorns across the field had long ago challenged for rule of Nav'Aria, killing many—including his pets' families in their wakes.

Silver Seeker begged Narco for the opportunity to kill alongside his brothers and sisters. He desired the enemy unicorns' blood more than anything else.

"Shhhh, be still, Silver Seeker. And let us see how this plays out. I assure you, you will not be left out for long," Narco murmured, stroking his black gleaming mane. His coat lustrous, his piercing horn directed at the unicorn and rider straight across the field. *King Vikaris,* Narco mused, looking upon his nephew.

He had chosen well, so it seemed. Trixon was the largest unicorn present, besides his own steed. Though far, he could not mistake the glow from Vikaris. He literally shined in the sunlight. *His blasted Marked arm bared for all to see. That might be a problem,* Narco brooded. He had made his Callers tell the people for years that the man was a fake—that the real Vikaris had been slain, along with his parents, by the rabble who had fled north. Narco had been the true victim, as the Callers shared, left alone and unmarked to govern a realm at war as he grieved the loss of his family. Many of his seasoned troops knew the truth, but not the commoners… and certainly not his pets. *No matter, they were loyal to a fault.* Morta had seen to that with their… unique… creation.

Narco watched as his pets—black stains upon the earth-trampled ground—gained a considerable lead upon their mounted counterparts as they rushed toward the unicorns.

Narco couldn't help but think there was something so tragically beautiful about the white and black unicorns coming together in challenge for the first time. A collision of supernatural making. He longed to see them up close. But he was the Emperor. He needed to watch the battlefield, along with his rear guard and the leaders of the supply trains wheeling up behind him. He would be safe here. He had no intention of fighting, whatever he told Silver Seeker. His pets had been groomed for this purpose. *Find the leader atop a unicorn and kill him.* None of the other unicorns bore riders, so Vikaris was easy to mark. As his unicorns tore the expanse, he saw how they made their own formation—like a horn ready to pierce the force where it would hurt the most. By robbing these traitors of their Marked King.

Narco continued to stare as the unicorns drew ever closer. Why didn't Vikaris move?

None of them had moved an inch since his forces launched the attack... and then he saw the archers appear from their hiding spots atop the ridge, where they'd been covered by the tall grass. Arrows filled the sky as the archers loosed one and then two and then three volleys in the blink of an eye. And just like that, the battle truly begun.

"No," Narco wailed. General Norder had warned him of this happening. But Narco had insisted on sending the full force. To show Vikaris his might. He had even called Norder a coward and commanded that he lead the troops onto the field instead of sitting with Narco to watch the battle unfold, as had been their initial plan. Narco now watched in horror as the field erupted in screams from wounded horses and falling riders. It looked as if the unicorns had escaped the volley unscathed, but still the arrows rained down. A troll thumping by many of the horses fell in mid-stride, knocking over a horse and rider, causing two others to collide as he thunderously collapsed to the ground.

Narco began to sweat, and as Silver Seeker renewed his anxious stepping, the Emperor wondered for the first time what would it feel like to charge into battle. He watched the blackness scour across the land, and finally he saw Vikaris raise his sword, still standing in place. At once his force roared in unison and challenge at the oncoming charge.

Narco could only marvel at their uniform and well-disciplined lines, for though thousands of men and beasts came tearing toward them, they stood steady. *To Vikaris's credit,* Narco thought jealously, knowing that he was no Commander like his nephew.

Send them all to crush any and all opponents like a hammer hitting an anvil, he vividly recalled telling Norder. He briefly closed his eyes to fight off a wave of nausea. Opening his eyes, Narco snarled as the first of his pets charged toward the King. Perhaps it would still be worth the risk. *Here comes the hammer!*

Once the land was rid of Vikaris, Narco would be the best. There would be no one left to challenge him. Though as he thought this, he saw Vikaris's frontlines raise their pikes, holding steady to face the oncoming charge.

Horror stricken, he heard the two forces meet like a thunderclap. The shrieking and war cries only grew in calamitous volume. He tried to keep his eyes on Vikaris, but the man was obscured from view. Thrown into battle as the front lines were pounded by the rushing soldiers.

Vikaris bellowed his war cry, just as his fellow soldiers shouted theirs!

His sword arm swung freely, so accustomed was he to gripping Trixon's heaving sides with his strong legs. With his left hand he gripped Trixon's mane, and with his right he fought for his Kingdom, as did his loyal soldiers. Vikaris had been raised to believe that if one was to lead, they had to be willing to be the strongest and most capable leader possible. This absolutely included one's role on the battlefield. Rustusse had taught him that. Vikaris was the rightful king, and that coward out there was a tired old man who needed to meet his end. Vikaris slashed and cringed as he saw the Kingdom unicorns joining the tumult. He hadn't wished it to be this way. And he could feel the tremor of doubt in Trixon. His movements seemed off. Jerky. *It is worth the risk,* Vikaris urged vehemently.

He felt Trixon rise to his shared thoughts. Trixon's head reared and he roared at the charging midnight black unicorn headed their way.

Beyond anything Vikaris had ever experienced, being atop a unicorn fighting another unicorn had never been in his training. It was so tragic and terrifying, but he knew that he could not give in to the feelings. He let his training guide him, as did the warriors who fought at his sides.

As Trixon charged the beast, Vikaris's sword slashed at the approaching unicorn, connecting with the flesh in its thickly muscled neck. Though it appeared shallow, the wound still startled the creature, and its crazed eyes glowed red as his Ruby shone upon it.

It kicked wildly at Trixon, rearing in outrage.

Trixon was much larger—and much more skilled in battle, however. His companion had already anticipated his enemy's move, and just as the unicorn lifted off the ground, Trixon jutted forward, slashing expertly with his horn across the unicorn's throat. Blood sprayed out, and the unicorn dropped heavily, earsplitting cries erupting from its muzzle.

The front lines held—barely.

The bodies piled up in front of the pikes, while the press of human and beast from Narco's forces continued advancing at an undaunted pace. This caught those in the front between their pressing comrades and the bloodied, sharpened pikes. Narco's back rows still harried by the archers' arrows.

The forces looked crazed with bloodlust. With no order, they all rushed. It was a neverending mass of bodies.

Vikaris knew that Garis and Kragar would begin pushing forward to sweep around the sides of the enemies' haphazard battle formation, encircling them with Nav'Arians. That meant Vikaris and the unicorns had to hold the line.

Drigidor's familiar voice thundered as a shriek filled the air.

One of ours, Vikaris thought, anger clutching his heart.

In a moment, the pristine white coat of Tabar turned swiftly to red, and then fell victim to black hooves and the press of troops filling the space.

Rage filled the King. *No,* he thought. *There has to be another way.*

He fought on, all the while feeling his uncle's cowering presence across the field. *I have to get to him, Trixon. We have to end this.*

CHAPTER 30:

The Answers

"Yes, but do you think he will mind?" Lyrianna asked as they stood around the large stone table, eyeing the vast map collection strewn about inside the Shovlan Tree.

Lyrianna stood facing Elsra and Trinidad.

Cela, much to her chagrin, was still not admitted to the Shovlan despite what had happened.

Elsra's serene lavender eyes searched Lyrianna's face. Though she had acted outraged when she first learned what transpired, after discussing it with Trinidad, she had acquiesced. *It must be linked to the prophecy,* Trinidad had concluded.

They believed Darion would become a great and mighty Marked King, and the prophecies spoke of one who would defeat the evil of the world. Though how that could be when he was not on the battlefield with his father, none knew. They could only hope that he had found answers in the Shazla Desert and would return to them soon… her connection to him, and her ability to bond Trinidad, had to be part of that prophecy.

Lyrianna's fingers traced the faint silver diamond shape now cresting her forehead. The Mark had been left there when her fingers touched the crystal from the Tree. Waking up on her back to see her friends' concerned faces peering into hers, not to mention the reflection of a mark in Trinidad's eyes, had created quite a shock. Cela had rushed to get a mirror so Lyrianna could inspect the Mark while Trinidad called for his mother. They had been in the Tree ever since.

Strange events had occurred below the Tree's crystals. Lyrianna could now sense Trinidad's feelings and thoughts, not solely from his expression, but as a part of her. They were connected. Their bond created a strange, wonderful, unique attachment that she had only thought possible with a spouse or a child. To be so wholly connected to Trinidad seemed completely ordinary after everything they had experienced together in captivity. Yet, at the same time, it also seemed completely insane.

Not only had bonding Trinidad allowed the crystal tree to materialize before her, but upon touching the crystals, she was left with a Mark—one that had gained her access to the Tree. It had transformed into an overgrown Maple with fiery red leaves, and Trindad had suggested she try.

Apparently human and unicorn had two different ways of accessing the Tree. The Mark upon her forehead allowed her to access the unicorn's entrance into the tree simply by touching her forehead to a specific knot on the trunk. Lyrianna's cheeks colored thinking of it.

Cela, not having been permitted to see anything of the Tree, could only see her Queen hesitantly bending to place her forehead against... air. Her chortles had irritated Lyrianna, who had chastised her and told her to go guard someone else!

She felt a momentary pang of regret for reacting that way... but not much. She knew Cela was happy to have a reason to go inspect the barracks. The red-haired beauty was probably playing a round of cards this very instant.

"Vikaris is a great King," was Elsra's only response.

Lyrianna sighed. She only hoped she was right, and that he wouldn't be too angry—or turned off—by her new appearance. *It would appear I am also now a Marked Royal,* she mused to herself. Regardless of the changes, she knew he would love and support her all the days of their lives.

Trinidad had looked fit to burst with inquisitive energy. He longed to search Vondulus's old scrolls and journals to see if there was any mention of a non-marked human having the ability to bond a unicorn... He was fascinated by it!

As was she. But she knew this was not the time. He needed to regrow his horn. That was why they were here today. Elsra had come to lend her aid as best she could. Trinidad believed that there was an answer here in the Tree. When Lyrianna had suggested that he, too, touch a crystal, he'd gasped as if he'd just seen a ghost.

No, my Queen, we have been told for generations that the crystals must not be touched. They our our ancestors' spirits, and

*they must be honored. It would be as if we went and opened up your
kind's graves.*

She shuddered. She had touched the crystal. She didn't
remember anything besides a bright light and a soft,
melodic hum. If she closed her eyes, she thought she
could hear it. She prayed she had not upset any of the
spirits. She had not meant to be disrespectful. Trinidad
assured her that, since she had been Marked, it was not
disrespect. Instead, she had been found deserving and was
honored. *Take it as a gift from the Creator,* he told her.

Yet that still left Trinidad.

"Let us search. I know the answers are in here. I can
feel it." Trinidad spoke so confidently that Lyrianna felt
tears come to her eyes.

She nodded and smiled warmly at him. "Yes," she said
softly, "I can feel it too. The answers are close."

The three set to inspecting every crevice of the huge
Cavern of Creation… the lowest level of the Shovlan
Tree. The Cavern spread farther than she'd ever imagined,
despite Vikaris's descriptions. In it, there were shelves and
trunks full of old writings. Somewhere in here lay their
answer.

***

Aalil kept her eye on Antonis as they crept along the
mountain trail. The cool air and bright sunshine were like
a slap in the face after being within the cave. They could
hear noise, which meant a huge gathering, Riccus had
warned her.

Following the trolls that were almost out of sight as they rounded another bend, Aalil gritted her teeth. They should set upon them now.

Riccus continued to disagree. Before revealing their presence, they needed to see where they were and what the trolls were planning.

She knew he was right, of course, but oh, how it tore her up inside. She had seen the troll smack Antonis soundly across the face before hauling him away. Antonis, dwarfed by the enormous creatures, had hung limp.

Aalil continued to crouch, watching her footing on the unsure mountain side. While she wanted to save him, it wouldn't do him any good if she walked off the cliff while lost in a daydream. *Focus!*

A hand grabbed her forearm, and she blinked.

Riccus held a finger up to his mouth, quieting her. They were nearing the bend, and the sounds had risen, echoing off the mountains. Guttural roars and cheers rose.

What is happening? Her sweaty palm gripped the dagger in her hand even tighter. Slowing to a crawl, they both carefully peeked after the trolls. What they saw around the way startled them both beyond anything they'd ever seen before. Aalil felt like she'd been punched in the stomach.

Nestled between snow-capped peaks, a crystal blue lake filled with the cleanest water from the snowy mountain run-off lay before their eyes. But it wasn't the lake that took their breath away; it was the small island within the lake, and the dark towering creature that bellowed, pounding its chest as if preparing for battle.

Aalil gasped. "What is that?"

At the same time, Riccus prayed softly, "Creator, help us."

They could see hundreds of trolls gathering on the beach around the lake, staring out at the island where a beast—the size of three or more trolls combined—paced, madly raising a war club and pounding its chest as he issued a slew of croaky, rough commands.

Aalil spied the cages he seemed to be guarding. *Trolls.*

They didn't look like the male warriors Aalil had formerly had the displeasure of seeing. They looked much smaller; it was clear they were the female trolls—with their young. They were in hefty, wooden cages, sitting quietly, raptly listening to the demonic beast as he called out toward the onlookers.

Aalil clutched Riccus's arm as she watched the troll carrying Antonis, making his way down to the beach, where a flat-bottomed ferry sat ready to take them across. "Oh no," she breathed. They were taking Antonis... to him.

Riccus's worried eyes met hers, and she knew in that instant that he had no idea what to do next.

That thought worried her more than anything else so far. Riccus always had a plan... or she did. Their eyes revealed the truth. They had messed up. They had lost their opportunity to save Antonis.

We should have freed him when we had the chance. Now, with so many trolls around, they'd never have the chance again. Tears formed in her eyes. And caring not about appearing soft, she let them fall freely as she watched the man she loved lowered to the ferry and taken across the lake. He would soon be in the grip of that demon.

***

"Nala, you can't be serious," Darion implored, fear and anger churning within him.

He thought of her as a woman now, and of himself as a man. Though in another world he had been treated as a minor, in this world they had seen too much to think of themselves as children any longer. This was the woman he loved. And she was leaving him.

Nala held a crying Valon in her arms. Darion watched his little pale face nuzzle into her neck. He had cried for hours, ever since waking. And still they had run, fearing the Rav'Arians just behind them.

The changing landscape and distance, over the course of that night and much of the next day, spawned changes in Nala, too. She had slowed her pace and had begun sneaking whispers with Ati, who herself looked resigned.

"I have to, Darion. My father needs to know what we have seen. Our tribe needs to know. We cannot sit by and let you fight alone. I will tell my tribe, but I cannot abandon them. Zalto *is* my family. He deserves to know."

She had declared at midday that this was as far as she, Ati, and Valon would be going.

Edmond, for all his acting tough and nonplussed a couple of days ago, had not left Ati's side since the announcement. She had spoken softly to him, and he to her, and they had walked much of the way hands held.

Triumph and Soren had both pleaded with Nala, but ultimately they understood and agreed with her decision. *If* the Reouls truly believed Darion was the Chosen One, then they should join them. And furthermore, the Reouls needed to know of the Watchers and the Rav'Arian breeding ground. What if the Rav'Arians pressed west?

"But it isn't safe! You'll be out there—with them again—and alone." Though he didn't say it, he wanted to add, *without me to protect you.*

Nala's eyes, though teary, were resolute. She called for Ati, who came and took Valon from her. She took Darion's hand to draw him aside. "I must do this, Darion," she replied.

"But…" he trailed off, squeezing her hands. "But… I love you." There, he said it. He couldn't believe he'd said it, but it was out there.

She smiled, and a pleased sound escaped her throat as she gently pulled his face down to hers and kissed him sweetly. She ran her fingers through his shaggy hair, before her hands came to his chest, pushing him away. "And I love you," she said so softly that Darion almost missed it.

She turned then, and he wanted to grab her arm and drag her in the opposite direction toward Nav'Aria.

You have to let her go, Darion. She has the spirit of a warrior. She will take care of them, and she will warn her tribe. She will make an honorable partner. But you must let her do this.

Darion looked at Triumph startled, and back at Nala. He wanted to sob, to yell, to hit something. Instead, feeling gutted, he simply stared.

Partner? If only I knew if I'd see her again, he thought. He watched Edmond's crestfallen expression as Ati, too, walked away.

We must continue, Darion. I can feel the pull from the north. They are in danger.

That snapped Darion out of his heartbreak, and as difficult as it was, they continued on. He looked back occasionally to see if Nala, headed in the opposite direction, did so too. She never looked back.

Pressing on was a challenge.

They had been running ragged for weeks. The only respite they'd had in the Shazla had been at the Reoul camp. Beyond that, they'd faced enemies, exhaustion, dehydration, and hunger. *What I wouldn't give for a cheeseburger right about now.*

His parched mouth felt like he'd swallowed dirt. Still they pressed on. They were near the border, Triumph and Soren assured him. Nearing Lake Thread, and beyond that, Castle Dintarran… Darion's rightful home.

They had to be watchful as they neared this part of the Kingdom, for it would be a calamity if Darion were to fall into Narco's clutches. Triumph assured Darion that he'd slaughter anyone who tried to take him.

They continued, and Triumph began looking around, swinging his head as he walked and sniffing every few steps like a crazed hunting dog.

Darion knew they needed to be on guard, *but this*? It seemed a bit over the top. "What are you doing? You look ridiculous," he derided, that is until he met Triumph's eyes. Hollow, overbearing sadness manifested in them.

Zola, Triumph lamented.

Darion knowingly patted his friend's neck. Though his heart broke for them, Zola had been dead for years, since the start of this war. There was nothing Darion could say to comfort him, and they needed to keep going.

They were heading toward the edge of the Lake nearest the border. There, carefully, they'd refresh, drink, bathe, and fill their waterskins, before moving inland toward the Woods—toward his family.

Nearer the lake, the morning light twinkled upon the water, and Darion knew that if there were any watch towers or guards patrolling, they would be sighted immediately. This was not a safe place for them. He walked carefully, trying to keep his thoughts from Nala.

"What's that? Do you hear that rushing sound?"

It had begun a while back. He could smell the great pooling liquid ahead. Lake Thread. The water rippled peculiarly, unaided by wind in one area, and there was a rushing sound, like a boat cutting through the water. Darion gripped his sword, as did Edmond. He reached out with his senses, trying to focus on the sounds. The smells. The... the life around him.

"What the..." he trailed off, as Triumph leapt forward galloping toward the beach.

Darion detected creatures in the water. The merfolk! And there was something else. Darion had no idea how it could be possible, but his link with Triumph told him that the impossible had happened.

Zola.

He sped after Triumph, followed by Soren and Edmond. Their intent of being circumspect long forgotten.

Darion's boots reached the beach in time to see Triumph splashing into the water toward two unicorn heads bobbing near the edge. Darion watched in wonder as Triumph bounded into the water and waited anxiously for the unicorns to near the shallow edge where they could stand unaided. As the dawn's spectacular light shone upon the Lake, it illuminated the scene like a brilliant spotlight. Darion could see a majestic female unicorn emerging from the water. He knew without a doubt what she was, with or without a horn. What stole Darion's breath, however, was the tiny fleck of life glued to her side. On shaky legs, a small black unicorn parted from the water.

Triumph shook with elation and anticipation. He moved forward to nuzzle the unicorn. Zola seemed standoffish, unsure of how to react at this sudden meeting, but soon she, too, looked excited and returned his affection. Turning, she nodded to the infant at her side.

Darion knew he would remember this moment for the rest of his life. He also knew that he was going to have a hell of a lot of fun teasing Triumph… *a grandpa!*

Zola's body language shifted as Darion approached, turning to protect her son with her body.

"It is alright, Zola… my daughter," Triumph spoke in a voice Darion had never heard from him. Triumph was changed. Joy embellished his paternal tone.

"This is Prince Darion, the Marked Heir, and my bonded companion."

Zola looked between Triumph and Darion, and then to the merman who was sitting upright in the shallow water, observing the reunion. The merman nodded to her, and his approval seemed to be enough for her.

Fully leaving the water, Zola and her son stepped out onto the beach and bowed to Darion. Her son tried to emulate her regal posture.

"Hi," Darion said.

Idiot. Well, he'd never been good at opening lines, so no use faking it now.

Triumph's booming laugh rang out. He nuzzled Darion and then stood, still quaking with energy, near his daughter.

"I am Zola, and this is my son, Trigger," Zola told him, her voice flooded with maternal pride.

Darion smiled.

Shannic was introduced, too, and they stood gathered on the beach for long moments, sharing what had taken place and what had brought them all here. Darion couldn't believe he was standing with unicorns and a merman. It was in these moments of surprise and splendor that he really loved Nav'Aria.

Nav'Aria! They had crossed the border. They were back in Nav'Aria. A castle boasting a stone façade and solid ramparts appeared across the water. Up until now, he'd paid little attention to it, so caught up in the reunion with Zola. *So that's Castle Dintarran.*

He knew his father longed to return to his home, and though it looked amazing, it held no sentiment for Darion. Not yet, anyway.

Darion had come to learn that it wasn't shared blood or a home that made you a family, but instead the people—*or creatures*— who you loved, he thought, smiling at Triumph. Those that chose to love you no matter what and were always there for you. They were what made a family.

So, as he looked at the Castle, though it was remarkable, it wasn't where he was meant to be. His family—Rick, Vikaris, Lyrianna, Ansel, Tony—were waiting for him. It was time to return to the Woods of the Willow to share their Shazla findings and get to know Lyrianna. She deserved a chance. He knew it was what Carol would have wanted. As he looked back at his friends, declaring it was time to be on the move, a green light flashed in his mind.

Soren, Triumph, and Zola all shook their heads, as if dazed by an eclipse.

"It has begun," Soren said solemnly, their heads turning in the direction of the Nav'Arian Plains. "We must make haste."

Goosebumps raised on Darion's arms. He gave a final farewell wave to the grave merfolk left behind. Though Shannic and the rest had helped rescue Zola and Trigger, no rescue would be coming for them… at least not yet.

Darion vowed he would be back, and the dam would be broken.

Shannic had clasped his arm in a firm grip at his words.

The battle has begun, Triumph echoed Soren. Darion could only pray that his loved ones were safe, and that their mission had been worth it.

As they traveled, he allowed Zola and Triumph their time to catch up while he thought about the puzzle pieces of the Shazla… and how Narco fit into it all.

Who the hell is Tarsin?

***

"The battle has begun. Creator, be with us all," Elsra whispered as she moved to nuzzle both Trinidad and Lyrianna. They stood united, looking at one another in the Shovlan Tree.

Their two families had been intertwined since the beginning with Vondulus and Tribute. The Meridia and First Horn families would stand together—the key to defeating Narco.

Elsra clung to this belief as she pictured her Drigidor and her grandson Trixon in the fight.

***

Though lacking any military discipline, the soldiers still came.

The fight had been going on now for much of the morning, and Vikaris's sword arm throbbed from the exertion. He knew they could not keep this up, and though his forces were enclosing Narco's, the crazed unicorns slashed and terrorized his front lines. Vikaris guessed they would have to kill each and every last one of them. They did not look the sort to surrender.

And still Narco sat watching the battle from afar. A demented coward, comfortable with seeing his men—his monsters—used as fodder.

The Rav'Arians heavily attacked Kragar's right section. Cries rang out—some in anger, many in agony. Vikaris called for the center formation's back lines to go and aid them. He hated to spread his force too thin. They had to maintain a strong wall of opposition and surround the enemy, attacking them at their vulnerable points, such as the sides and rear formation.

Weak points.

As Vikaris swung his blade again, connecting with a large, hideous, red-eyed troll, he realized what he had to do.

Trixon didn't hesitate. Spinning on the spot, he tore after the troops. Some of his soldiers hesitated.

Was the King retreating?

"Steady the lines," Vikaris called.

And as Trixon moved, he called to the other unicorns, relaying their intent. He found an area where the dead had been piled up so high that the fighting had been forced to move on. Bloodied corpses and pikes lay strewn around. Trixon clamored onto the pile, his hooves perilously teetering on the dead.

Vikaris, confident in his mount, had eyes only for Narco. "UNCLE!" Vikaris roared. His arm glowing and blood slicking his blade.

Gore dripped from Trixon's razor-sharp horn as he stood upon the piled bodies.

The fighting around them stopped at the King's potent words. "I challenge you to single-combat."

When Vikaris raised his bloodied sword, his Marked Arm and Ruby-adorned throat commanded attention. None there could deny that he was the Marked King.

Yet the enemy soldiers looked back and forth, torn. The Rav'Arians ran at the humans who looked near retreat, snapping at them with their maws. The Kingdom humans knew that if they retreated, they would end up in a Rav'Arian's belly or a troll's cookpot. They remained.

Vikaris and Trixon tore across the field, aiming straight for Narco and bellowing "AZALT!"

Narco swallowed. Silver Seeker neighed and reared at the sight of Trixon's fury.

"So be it, nephew," Narco whispered, but before drawing his blade, he grasped the vial that hung at his throat, jerkily ripping it from its cord. He swallowed the contents in one gulp before throwing it aside. He could feel the strength from the Reoul's ancient blood pulsing through his veins instantly. He laughed wickedly, all his insecurities and fears put aside.

"Yes, nephew. Come fight me!" Narco laughed and drew his gleaming blade with the embossed hilt. He dug his heels into Silver Seeker, who practically flew down the slope to meet Vikaris and his steed.

"Azalt," Narco yelled, sword raised, pointing straight for Vikaris's heart. "Let us see today who is the true ruler of Nav'Aria!"

EPILOGUE

And so, I killed it.

I cut open its chest... and ate its still-warm heart. For so it had taken my heart from me, I tore its heart from its body and consumed it for my own. I burned it afterwards and left the Pyre burning for all to see... there beside my sweet L'Asha's grave. To let it serve as a warning to any other beast who would wish to come between me and mine ever again!

Morta sat thinking about that fateful day from long ago, his hooded face deep-set and hidden from Trigger as he ran a soft, pale hand over the velvety coat.

He had not understood then the changes that had taken place. The shadow that had reigned in the creature's heart took hold of his own. A maniacal laugh escaped his lips, echoing off the wooden building. Oh, but he would not trade any of it, for that day had given him new meaning. New purpose. New power.

His laughs rebounded off the walls as he pictured the insolent Narco riding into battle. He cared not what happened to Narco, for this was all part of his plan. His grip on Nav'Aria—his evil taint—was spreading across the land, just as that evil agent had spread through his bloodstream years ago.

It had been so long since he'd heard his given name, he hardly knew why he even thought of it now. He paused his musings, looking at the young unicorn. "Would you like to know my name, pet? My real name?" The unicorn trembled slightly as he pulled his hood back to reveal his face.

"Tarsin." He whispered wickedly. "I was called Tarsin back then. Many years ago." He pictured the naive youth he had been and considered the god he'd become. The one in power of this entire Realm.

"Morta, is my name now," he breathed. "Morta is the name they will all grow to fear."

Acknowledgments:

To my Readers: Thank YOU for reading *Nav'Aria: The Pyre of Tarsin*!

I have been blown away by the response this series is receiving—that is all you. THANK YOU! Please keep SHARING on social media and REVIEWING *Nav'Aria* on Amazon so more readers can discover Darion's story! I appreciate every single download, purchase, retweet, blog interview, and review.

You are always at the forefront of my mind as I work. I want Nav'Aria to be an EPIC, stirring experience for you. I can't wait to share book three, *Nav'Aria: The Winged Crescent*, with YOU! Stay tuned for details!

Connect with me on Twitter, Instagram, Facebook, and Goodreads. For the latest book updates and events, sign up for my newsletter at: kjbacker.com.

***

To Keil Backer (Husband and Book Formatter): You were the FIRST person to read (and love!) this book. Your support, PATIENCE, and help has been paramount to getting this book published. I couldn't have done any of this without you. Your formatting skills are incredible, and you made this book look perfect. Thank you for taking on this new role as book formatter. And of course, thank you for lugging allllll of the books, tables, chairs, and tent at this year's festivals. You—and your big biceps—are SO appreciated!

You knew going into our relationship nearly a decade ago that I was a bit of a dreamer/go-getter, but you had no idea where that would lead us. Thank you for being by my side, and even more than that, for encouraging me to chase my dreams. You've shown me—and our daughter—that my dreams and goals have value. Sharing in this journey with you is a true privilege. You are my partner. You are my friend. You are my love.

To Heather Peers (Editor and Proofreader): Thank you SO much for your dedication to this series. Your support, love for the characters, and passion for this project inspires me. You made this book sound polished and EPIC! I am excited to dive into the third book—I know you'll push me to get it done quickly. That's why you're the BEST person for this job! Thank you for your guidance, support, and help with both *The Marked Heir*, and now, *The Pyre of Tarsin*. You are a literary magician!

To Jessica Robbins and Hunter Jones (Beta Readers): Thank you for believing in this series and being Darion's biggest fans! Your input and time examining the world of Nav'Aria has been a wonderful help.

To Jarica Backer (Daughter and "Book Manager"): You, my darling girl, are the greatest gift of all. You have blessed our family greatly in just our two years together. Being your mom is my greatest joy and accomplishment. Never forget that.

Sharing this book journey with you has been a blast! I love having you with me "closing book deals", setting up festival booths, taking countless pictures, and remembering the quarters for our downtown parking meters. I couldn't do this without you, kid. Thanks for being the best "book manager" around!

To my family (Hunter, Diana, David, Danny, and relatives): Thank you for your unceasing support. You have taught me the value of love, loyalty, and commitment. You inspired this book series, and the family/adoption themes within it. Thank you for that fantastic gift, and for your cherished support.

To my Twitter "Writing Group" (Shanna Swenson, C.R. Pugh, M.B. Davis, Patricia Adams, Joseph Kaiser, and Jennifer Soucy): You guys are the BEST! I know that I can come to you—anytime—with questions, or writing struggles, and that you'll always be there to help. Thank you for reading, sharing, reviewing, and blogging about Nav'Aria! You are a gift! Thank you for everything.

To Kelsea Schreiner and Josh Wirth (Marketing): Thank you so much for your help and attention with my website, author photos, promotional ideas, and documenting the fun we've had at this year's book signings and festivals.

To Terry Emilia: This cover is FIRE! It is exactly what I envisioned and fits the tone of the book perfectly. Thank you.

AUTHOR'S NOTE✦

I started writing *Nav'Aria: The Marked Heir* while working as a substitute teacher in 2011. It evolved into a little hobby—my secret summer project when I wasn't teaching—until 2017, when we adopted our daughter. That's when I got the inspiration needed to write the entire second half of the book in a two-week span. I PUMPED IT OUT. That's what had been missing—my why!

Why did I want to finish the book? Did I really want to go after my goal of becoming an author, or stay complacent with half a manuscript?

Adoption has always had a huge place in my heart—and my writing! After years of working with struggling teens and then adopting my daughter, I realized that I wanted to finish the book for her, 'for the "Darions" of the world.' In honor of those who feel lost or alone as they navigate foster care, adoption, and adulthood. I dedicated the first book (*The Marked Heir*) to them.

Darion's story is not unique. Okay, let me back up... yes, having a glowing arm, a bonded unicorn, and living in a parallel universe is crazy EPIC, but the idea of longing for a family, searching for his identity, desiring to belong, and questioning his worth is unfortunately something many young people face today. There are millions of orphans globally and thousands of kids in the U.S. who cannot go home today due to tragic or dangerous circumstances. On top of it all, the rising suicide rate is staggering.

Call-to-action!

How can you help?

Become a foster-parent or CASA volunteer; Sponsor a child in a third-world orphanage; Begin the adoption process if you feel so led; Give to your local CPS; Donate to a reputable organization that helps women with micro-loans or children with school fees; Volunteer with a mentor program; Coach or sponsor an activity; Support a foster family from your church or school. Check in on the people in your life.

Whatever it is, help! Together, WE can support these people in their quest to belong, and to feel loved.

And for the "Darions" reading this!

The teens or adults struggling with self-doubt, loss, and or lack of family stability: I want to speak to you for a moment. <u>YOU ARE IMPORTANT.</u> YOU have a purpose. YOU have overcome much, and you can do so much in your life. Seek positive role-models and influences. If you're in a dangerous situation, please seek help. If you're struggling with suicidal thoughts, call the National Suicide Prevention Lifeline 1-800-273-8255.

Keep working. Keep trying. Keep believing. And more than anything, remember **YOU matter. I believe in you.**

Made in the
USA
Monee, IL